CAMP
DAZE
I0712528

ALSO BY KATY L. WOOD

NOVELS

The Pits
Poison in the Blood

ARTBOOKS

Into the Background

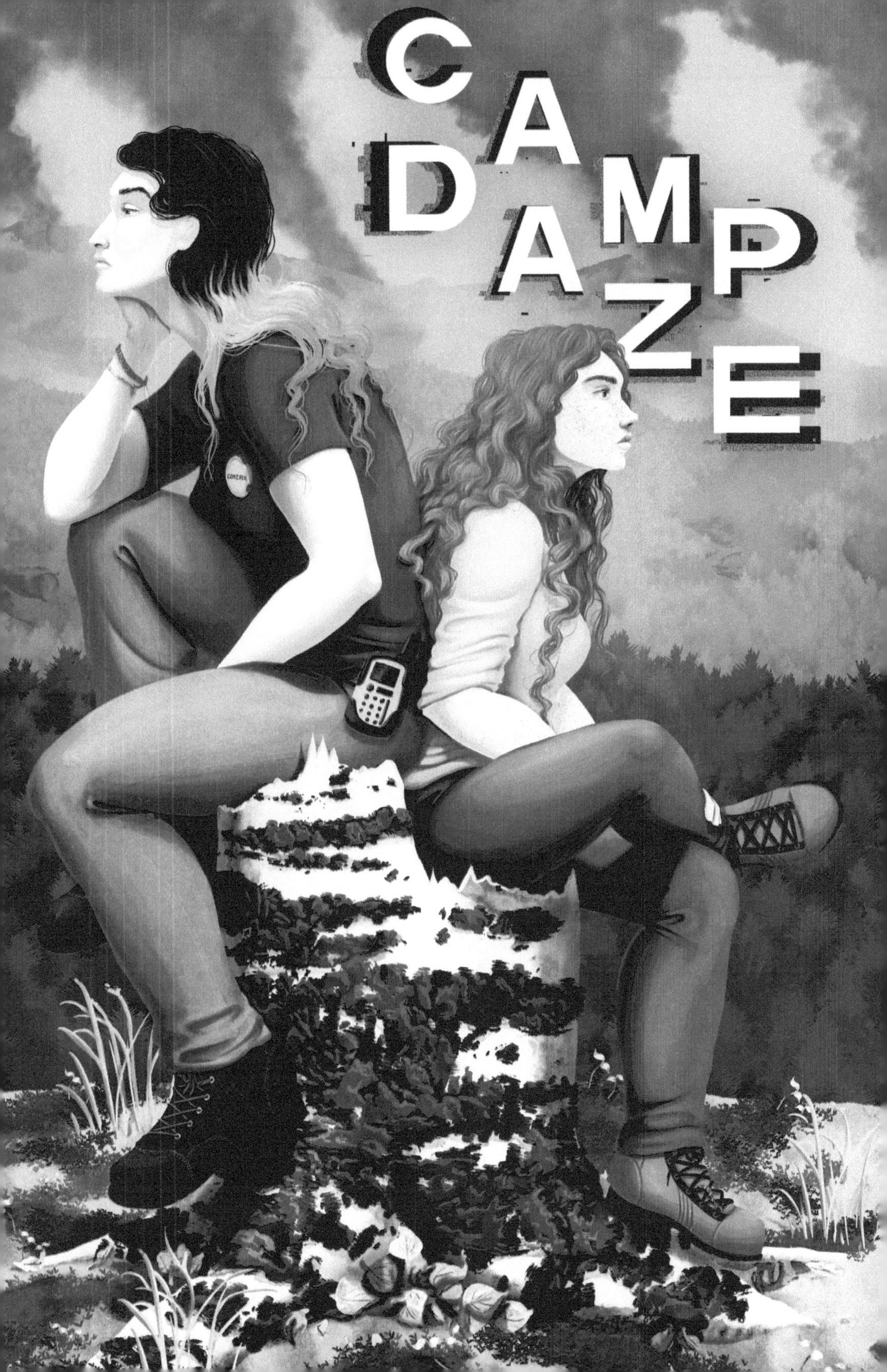

CAMP DAZE

Text © 2024 by Katy L. Wood
Cover Illustration © 2024 by Katy L. Wood
Cover Layout © 2024 by Katy L. Wood
Interior Illustrations © 2024 by Katy L. Wood
Book Design and Layout © 2024 by Katy L. Wood

All rights reserved. Published in the United States by Aspen & Copper Publishing. Special hardback edition published 2024.

www.AspenAndCopper.com

Hello@AspenAndCopper.com

Educators, librarians, and others interested in arranging an appearance by Katy L. Wood at their event should contact her at the above provided e-mail.

Summary: A sudden nuclear apocalypse leaves a rural girl's camp to fend for themselves with only a few dozen mostly young counselors attempting to help keep over a-hundred-fifty children alive through the coming winter.

Kickstarter Special Edition Hardback ISBN: N/A

Hardback ISBN: 9798986113777
Paperback ISBN: 9798986113791
EBook ISBN: 9798986113784

"What one has to do usually can be done."

-Elanor Roosevelt

West Branch Trail
West Trail
West Trail
The Boat Trail
Boat House
Crater Lake
Old Mining Camp
Hill Trail
Lake Trail
Upper Campground
Miner's Trail
Hill Creek
Lake Trail
Crater Creek
Hideaway Cave
Pond Creek
Cave Trail
Marguerite de la Rocque Unit
Tin Hinan Unit
Rope Course
Shower
The Loop Trail
Chiyome Mochizuki Unit
Rope Trail
Sybil Ludington Unit
Crossover Trail
Rock Garden
Nana Asma'u Unit
Shower
Josefina Guerrero Unit
Osh-Tisch Unit
Archery Range
Lodge Trail
Main Lodge
Emmeline Pankhurst Unit
Art Trail
Med Lodge
Art Shed
Barn Trail
Barn
Storage Shed
Greenhouses
Main Road
Counselor Lot
Flag Ring
Pasture Pond
Pasture

PART 1

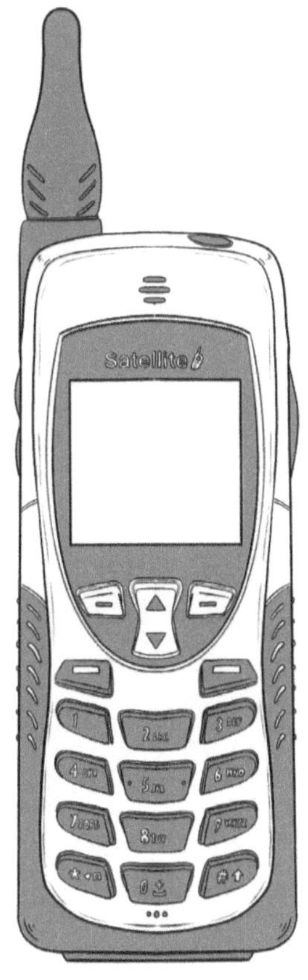

CHAPTER 1
DROP OFF

"Try hitting it again, I'm sure it'll work this time," Marauder said. She was in the passenger seat of the stationary Bronco, facing backwards with her legs thrown over the back of the bench seat and shoulders against the dash.

Conifer gave her fellow camp counselor a withering stare. "Maybe if you weren't draped across my dashboard, I could get the radio to work *without* hitting it."

Marauder shrugged, giving a smile that was clearly meant to be cute. Most of what Marauder did came off as cute, though. It was hard not to when the girl didn't even crack five-feet tall and had the underlayer of her shoulder length white-blond hair dyed bubblegum pink. Conifer had spent the whole summer so far trying to pin down if she actually did find Marauder cute, or if it was just an objective observance. In general she hadn't figured it out, but as for right now, Marauder was just in the way.

"Shoo." Conifer poked at Marauder's shoulder.

Marauder sighed and made a great show of shuffling around to sit with her back against the door, throwing her legs out across Conifer's lap instead.

Hands hovering in the air, Conifer stared down at the tanned legs now sprawled across her lap. There was a lot of exposed skin between Marauder's pink hiking boots and tan cargo shorts. Was this better? Conifer didn't think this was better.

"I don't see why you even need the radio to work. All you pick up on that thing is the rare trucker that detours through the valley. And Jim, that weird dude from town."

Conifer gave up on figuring out her feelings on Marauder's legs and went back to messing with her radio. "I want it to work because it is supposed to work."

"It" was a bulky thing, not at all meant to be where it was. CBs this size were meant for bigrigs, not fifty-year-old Ford Broncos with rusted out rims and almost bald tires. So she'd had to go at the dashboard with a hacksaw to get it in there at all, so she'd cut some stuff she shouldn't have in the process, so the radio was now cased in in a way that sort of resembled Frankenstein. The truck was the closest thing she had to a permanent home since she'd moved out four years ago to work odd jobs instead of going to college, and sometimes it was fun to listen to the truckers chat, plus anyone else who had a CB in range. Even Jim, who was usually trying to get in touch with aliens, could be interesting to listen to. Besides, you never knew when you might really need a radio like this.

Conifer had made it a habit to come out to her truck in the staff parking lot every day on her breaks and flip on the radio for a few minutes just to know the rest of the world was still there outside their isolated summer camp. No one's cellphones worked at the camp and there was no internet. Even regular radios struggled, if not failed, to pick things up most of the time due to the terrain. Aside from the satellite phones carried by the backpacking groups, which were only to be used in emergencies, and the janky old ham radio, they were cut off.

Which was fine.

Conifer had grown up learning all about how to survive being cut off. But just because she knew what to do if the world ended didn't mean she wanted it to, despite what a lot of people tended to assume about survivalist families like hers.

She just wanted her radio back and, after two days of

nothing but static from it, she was starting to get ticked off.

"I'm so glad you let me dye your hair," Marauder said. "The flame colors suit you."

Conifer glanced down, examining the hair that splayed across her chest in messy waves. It was now an ombre of her natural deep brown fading into yellow, then orange, then red. It had indeed been Marauder's idea. Conifer was mostly apathetic to it, and to her looks in general, but a bunch of the counselors had been doing it during the break between camp sessions, so she'd gone along with the group.

"They are fun colors," Conifer replied, jamming the little screwdriver she'd been using back into the guts of her radio.

Marauder huffed. "Buy the poor thing dinner first!"

"It doesn't get dinner until it works," Conifer told her. "It just needs to work."

"Uh uh. What was it you said when you were complaining about this yesterday? You 'like to know the rest of the world is out there'? Would it perhaps, actually, be because you are slightly paranoid?"

Conifer scoffed. "I am not."

"Mmmmmmhm. I'm sure you would be reacting exactly the same way to the death of your radio if the paper Silver brought back from her day off in town last week hadn't had that little blurb about escalating tensions with whatever country it is this month."

Conifer glanced over to see Marauder watching her with a quirked eyebrow, but she didn't bother to disagree. There was a lot more in that paper that had her hackles up, aside from the one blurb. And in the paper before that. And the one before that.

"Well," Marauder said, straightening up and slapping the dash, "if you want proof the world is still out there, here it comes. Time for a new batch of kids."

Conifer twisted around and watched as the head counselor, Jackalope, aka Jack, threw open the gate and started waving the line of waiting parents in. With them would be over 150 new campers ready to spend the next two weeks camping and hiking and learning archery and doing crafts and a dozen other activities.

The knot in Conifer's shoulders loosened a little. If things really were bad, the parents would have kept their kids home, but there were just as many cars as always. Everything was fine.

Everything was fine.

Slamming the door behind her—it was the only way to get the driver's side to latch—Conifer headed towards the check-in table for her unit, Marauder skipping along next to her. Skipping almost, almost, brought Marauder to the height of Conifer's shoulder. This was, however, because Marauder wasn't really trying. Conifer had seen her friend make a four-foot vertical leap onto a boulder when she wanted to show off. It wasn't until you looked closer at Marauder's slim build that you realized it was stacked with muscle. The girl had earned every one of her three MMA featherweight belts.

"Hello!" Marauder said, bounding up to a haggard looking mom with a twelveish-year-old daughter and two squabbling twin babies—almost toddlers—in a side-by-side stroller. Conifer couldn't imagine making the long drive out here with that many children packed in the car. Denver was, at best, six hours away. There were plenty of other little towns scattered through the mountains, but even then the drive up to Aspen Heart was long and slow.

While Marauder dazzled the twins into giggling and clapping with her, Conifer went over to the clipboards on their table and started going through them. They had eleven campers in their group this time, half what most of the units had, but that was intentional. They were a specialized, survival themed session that wasn't as popular as some of the others.

"What's your name?" Conifer asked the older girl with a smile.

"Tabatha!"

Conifer pulled out the proper clipboard and scanned down the sheet. Tabatha Lilley. First time at camp. Just turned twelve. Allergy to strawberries, but it was minor.

"Well, welcome to Camp Aspen Heart, Tabatha! I'm Conifer, and this is Marauder." Marauder gave a wave from over by the stroller. "We'll be your unit counselors for the next two weeks, which means you'll be spending most of your days, and every night, with us. Our unit is called Marguerite de la Rocque, and we're all the way at the back of the camp. Go ahead and put your suitcase in the trailer and hang out while we wait for the rest of our group to get here."

Tabatha nodded and hauled her suitcase into the empty trailer for their unit, refusing her mother's help. Horseshoe, the barn director, would use the camp truck to bring all the trailers up to the units later.

Over the next hour more and more campers trickled in, some with parents who lingered and others with parents who dashed off after quick goodbyes. Usually, the ones who left quickly were parents of campers who had been to camp before. Not always, though, and Conifer felt bad for the two first timers whose parents left quickly, making a mental note to keep an eye on them.

"Conifer," a voice said from behind her.

She turned and saw Jack striding over, a mother and young girl following behind. It only took a second to clock the mother as military with the way she walked, the perfectly, tightly pulled back bun, and the hard, quick handshake she offered. The girl, her daughter presumably, looked a little embarrassed, trailing in her mother's wake, suitcase dragging behind. Unlike her mother, her hair was wild and long, reddish-brown curls trailing down to her waist.

"What can I do for you?" Conifer asked.

"Miranda was hoping you'd be alright with having

Cheyenne switched into your unit?" Jack asked.

"She signed up for the horsemanship unit, but we were talking on the way over, and I think she'd really enjoy your survivalism unit even more," Miranda said.

Conifer glanced at Cheyenne, trying to gage if this was actually her idea or just her mother's. There was something familiar about the girl, but beyond that Conifer couldn't really get a read on her.

Cheyenne shrugged. "It's fine. I already did the horse backpacking unit at the start of summer. This one sounds fun too."

Ah, that was it, Conifer realized. Cheyenne had been here before. It wasn't too uncommon for kids to come multiple times in a summer. Conifer herself had been coming here since she was seven, and there were a few summers she'd come three separate times. Once she'd turned eighteen she'd spent that summer as a junior counselor, and in the summers since she'd been a full counselor. This camp was almost literally her second home.

"Well, as long as you're sure," Conifer said. "We want you to have a good time."

"She's sure," Miranda said.

Cheyenne rolled her eyes. "My mom's all determined to get me into the military just like her. Wants me to get a head start."

Miranda gave a tight lipped smile that seemed like it was holding a longer explanation back. Conifer glanced at Jack who shrugged. The knot between Conifer's shoulders tightened back up slightly.

"Well, alright then, as long as it's okay with Jackalope," Conifer said, not sure what else to do.

Of all the moms to try and drag their daughter into a survival themed unit, why a military mom? Why now? Marauder and Conifer had been running this session all summer, in both one week and two week versions. Unlike the other counselors, they didn't move around. Conifer was the whole reason the session existed, having pitched it to Jack at the end of the previous summer. She'd grown up a survivalist and knew just about everything there was to know about how to survive in the woods; how to hunt, how to fish, how to set up and break down any sort of camp, how to track, and plenty of other skills. She even had a wilderness EMT certification. Marauder had a wilderness EMT certification as well, plus a bachelor's degree in botany under her belt, and she was starting a Master's Degree to become a Field Naturalist soon. Survival, first aid, and foraging. Between the two of them, they had it covered better than anyone else.

Conifer knew she was reading too much into it. Plenty of parents tried to drag their kids into their own careers. If it was up to Conifer's own mother she would be going to school to be a vet. For all she knew Miranda had tried to get Cheyenne to do the survival session earlier, but hadn't talked her into it until now. This was nothing.

"I'm fine with it, and you've got the empty slot, so," Jack replied with another shrug.

"Well, welcome to Marguerite then, Cheyenne. I'm Conifer, and the bouncy pink one over there is Marauder."

"Nice to meet you," Cheyenne said, glancing over at Marauder who was teaching everyone else a clapping game. "She seems...bubbly."

Conifer chuckled. "She grows on you. Here, I'll take your suitcase while you say goodbye to your mom."

Cheyenne handed the large, dark green rolling case over and Conifer dragged it through the gravel to the trailer, sliding it in with the others. When she turned around she saw Miranda standing a foot away from Cheyenne, hands on her upper arms.

"Promise you'll be good?" Miranda said.

"No, mom, I'm going to stage a rebellion with all the other campers and we'll take over the camp and lock the counselors in the basement of the lodge."

Miranda sighed, squatting and sliding her hands down

to hold Cheyenne's. "Come on. Serious face. I need to know you'll be good. I'm...going to be in the mountain pretty much 24/7 while you're here, so I won't be able to send you postcards like normal, or get yours."

Cheyenne squeezed her mom's hands. "Yeah, I'll be good, Mom, promise."

Miranda smiled and pulled her daughter into a hug. Conifer tried not to read too much into the expression on Miranda's face. Scared was the best word she could think to put to it, but that had to just be Conifer being paranoid again. Plenty of parents got a little worked up about leaving their daughters at camp for two weeks.

Miranda stood up, kissed the top of her daughter's head, and shooed Cheyenne off in the direction of the rest of the group before turning around to face Conifer again.

"Thanks for agreeing to take her," Miranda asked. "She loves this camp so much, and I know she'll enjoy this unit once she actually gets into it. If you don't mind my asking, Jackalope said you're a survivalist yourself?"

Jack beamed like a proud parent which, Conifer had to admit, she sort of was given how much time Conifer spent at Aspen Heart growing up. "Oh yes, Conifer knows everything you'd ever want to know about living off the grid. Her whole family does."

Conifer resisted the urge to wince at Jack's way of putting it. Once people started making assumptions about her lifestyle it was hard to bring them back around to not thinking she was a gun toting nut. She'd had to make the attempt so often, though, that she already had her response ready to go: "We're survivalists, not some weird libertarian preppers," Conifer tried to clarify. "No militia mindset, no hoarding, just learning how to survive when things go a little sideways. No one expects the world to end or anything, but that doesn't mean our skills aren't important. You never know when you're going to lose power for a week because of an ice storm, or get caught in a flash flood, or just get lost on a hike."

Miranda nodded. "Good. That's exactly what I want her learning. Well, it was nice to meet you. Thanks for taking care of my daughter."

With that she made a sharp turn more suited to a military drill and strode back to the emptying temporary parking lot set up for parents. Conifer watched her climb into a black Jeep, the knot in her back tightening once again at the sight of a NORAD crest bumpersticker on the back window.

"Conifer, you look like you're clenching every muscle in your body," Jack observed.

"What's your judgment on all of that, Jack? Because I don't think I trust mine."

Jack glanced at the Jeep as it pulled out and joined the line of departing parents and shrugged. "Just seemed like a bit of an overbearing mom to me. Not like we don't get those all the time."

"An overbearing mom who works for NORAD in Cheyenne Mountain," Conifer muttered, chewing her lip. The pieces weren't hard to put together. Miranda had said she'd be "in the mountain" for the next two weeks. What else could that be but the hollow mountain NORAD base in Colorado Springs?

Jack knocked her shoulder into Conifer's, jarring her out of her thoughts. "Hey. I know you. I trust your judgment. If something feels funny, tell me."

Conifer sighed, pinching the bridge of her nose. "I don't know. Everything feels funny these days. I think it's just the news in general getting to me."

Jack nodded. "Yeah. Every summer I hope the digital detox of being up here will help, but it's almost worse not knowing, isn't it?"

Conifer's shoulders dropped in relief that Jack got it. "Yes, exactly."

"I'll let you sneak in and use one of the satellite phones if you want to make some calls," she offered. "Ask your parents what they think. We'll consider the cost of the calls a bonus for all the extra stuff you've been helping me with this summer."

Conifer contemplated. The "extra stuff" was mostly just being an extra set of hands when Jack was busy, and she didn't think it really added up to the cost of a handful of satellite calls. "Nah. It's fine. I'm sure I'm reading too much into it."

Just knowing Jack trusted her helped enough that, by the time she went over to help Marauder lead the campers up to Marguerite, Conifer was able to put the paranoia away. Mostly.

Cheyenne had melded into the group effortlessly and it was pretty clear she was the most experienced camper among them. She walked with confidence, seeming familiar enough with the camp to not feel the need to follow Marauder as closely. Her wrists were stacked with camp bracelets of all sorts, some made with creatively knotted embroidery thread, some with hemp and beads, others made of lengths of flat shiny plastic woven together. Not all of them were new either. Some looked like they had at least a year of age on them, maybe more.

"We're in the Marguerite de la Rocque unit aaaaallll the way at the back of the camp, so let's get walking!" Marauder said. She gave a quick double clap and led the way up the stairs built into the slope that the lodge sat on, giving the campers a rundown of the building as they walked. "The lodge was initially built in the late 1800s to serve as the base for a mining camp that used to be here, and it has been added onto over the years. It is the central hub of Aspen Heart. We'll eat most meals here, and there's a little post office for you to send letters home."

It was a good, sturdy heart, Conifer thought. The original building made up the bulk of it: worn logs stacked two stories high, offices and the post office room making up the first level while the second level consisted of Jack's office and the counselor lounge, along with some storage and a large activity room. There was an expansive attic area, which was technically finished with a few different rooms, but the area served mostly as more storage. A long, squat dining room and kitchen area clung onto the west side of the building, added in the nineteen-forties to accommodate the change from mining camp to girls camp, and there was a small walkout basement mostly used for more storage under that. A large porch that went around the entire front and west side of the building wrapped it all up. Conifer gave the weathered wooden walls an affectionate pat as they went around the back of the building, heading towards the Loop Trail that provided access to all the units.

There was no quick way to Marguerite, only the curving trail road. It took about twenty to thirty minutes to walk from the lodge back to the unit, depending on how fast the campers walked. Aspen Heart was more spread out than a lot of camps tended to be, meaning their group would generally only be in the actual unit at night, and thus only have to make the long walk twice a day—once in the morning and once in the evening—but the distance still meant it remained reserved for the older groups like this one, though they weren't the oldest overall. The youngest in their unit this time was eleven, the oldest thirteen. Other units had campers as young as seven and as old as sixteen.

Marauder walked backwards up the trail road, pointing out features of the camp from trails to other units to activity areas. "And see the cliffs that surround three sides of the camp? That's because we're in an old volcanic crater! This place erupted thousands of years ago a lot like Mt. Saint Helens, with a whole side of the mountain sliding off. But don't worry, she hasn't been active since then. Now her cliffs just keep us safe from the wind."

And cut the place off from the world, but Conifer didn't say that out loud. The closest town—an hour away down the mountain—had only about a thousand permanent residents, and the next town after that was another hour away on a good day, two on a bad one. That was going south, though. Any other direction and there wasn't even a way to get to a town by vehicle. There was nothing but wilderness on all three sides. If you walked straight north you'd hit Wyoming before you hit another town in Colorado, and it would be another few days of walking before you found somewhere in Wyoming that had people.

"How is she not falling over?" Cheyenne asked, forcing Conifer to stop mulling over their isolation.

Marauder was still walking backward, talking animatedly and not glancing over her shoulder once.

"You have no idea how many times we've walked this trail," Conifer said.

Cheyenne hummed, still watching Marauder somewhat suspiciously.

"So, you sure you want to join this unit?" Conifer asked. She was just looking out for Cheyenne, she told herself. Not fishing for information on her mother.

"Yeah, it sounds cool. I thought about signing up for it when we got the catalog for the summer, but it was the same time as the horsemanship one and Mom said I could only do two this year. But it's fine. I'll do horsemanship next year."

"And the military?"

Cheyenne groaned. "I don't know. She started bringing that up, like, a week ago all of a sudden. I think it's because I skipped a grade, so I start High School this fall."

"Ah, so you're *smart* then," Conifer said with a grin. Cheyenne was growing on her, which helped chase away some of the paranoia induced by her mother.

"I'm *bored*," Cheyenne clarified. "I hate school. I just want to be done with it."

"That's fair. I never liked it much either."

They lapsed into silence, boots crunching on the gravel as they trailed behind everyone else up the slope. The afternoon was still warm, and there was plenty of daylight left, but the shadows of the cliffs were starting to creep across the camp. As they hiked higher and started the turn west the trees began to thin, offering a view of the rest of the camp spread out below them. A lot of it was still hidden, but there were glimpses of the white tarp roofs of the platform tents in other units, the green corrugated roof of the lodge, and the red walls of the barn. Beyond it all layers and layers of mountains stretched in all directions, fading away into atmospheric haze.

Everyone reached the unit a moment later, gathering in the center. The trailer of the girl's bags was already there, parked off to the side. A ring of six tents stood around the edges of the clearing, each consisting of a sturdy wooden platform, raised a foot or two off the ground with two or three steps for access. On top of the platforms were house-shaped frames, over top of which were stretched faded green canvases topped with thick, waterproof white tarps. To the east and about ten yards behind the tents was a small building containing two toilets, two trough sinks, and a storage closet. About twenty yards from that was a covered cement slab with a couple grills, tables, and benches; their outdoor kitchen space for the couple of meals they'd have in-unit. Pine trees ringed the whole setup, along with a few scattered aspens. Conifer loved it. Marguerite had always been her favorite unit at the camp. Quiet. The best view. A little more distance between the tents. It was comfortable.

Conifer took over for Marauder, stepping up to the front. "Alright y'all, since there's only twelve of you we're doing three to a tent rather than the full four. Marauder and I are in that tent—" Conifer pointed to tent four opposite the entrance to the unit — "and we've already assigned you to yours. Once I call your name and give you your tent number head over to the trailer with Marauder and she'll help you get your bag out. Go ahead and get settled, and we'll head down for dinner at 4:30. Bring your winter coats out to us; we'll put them in the storage closet between the bathrooms so they're out of the way unless they're needed."

They all nodded and Conifer took the list out of her pocket, reading off names and pointing at tents. She put Cheyenne in the one tent that had had only two kids, Aadila and Giselle. There was a flurry of movement and then all the campers vanished into their tents. Laughter floated out and snatches of conversation joined it, mostly debates about who got what cot.

"I feel good about this group," Marauder said as she and Conifer waited to collect coats. All the campers were required to bring one—and a good set of gloves—in case Colorado decided to get extra creative about the order of the seasons, which it was fond of doing. The campers had lighter jackets and hoodies that should suffice as long as the weather behaved, though.

"Oh yeah?" Conifer asked.

"Yeah. It feels like a good bunch. Not one of them seems like they might try to burn down the forest after we teach them to make fire!"

Conifer groaned. "Don't remind me."

At an earlier session a girl, thankfully not in their unit, did exactly that. Bluebird had had to use a fire extinguisher to put it out and there was still a char mark up the side of the main storage shed near the lodge. The girl got sent home early because she'd been so shaken up and the rest of the camp got a lecture on fire safety. Going through that again was not something Conifer wanted to deal with. They only had a couple more sessions left before the end of summer, not including this one, and the smoother they went the better. Conifer's paranoia was already causing her enough problems. No need to add fire on top of that.

Chapter 2
The Art Shed

"Blech…these eggs are overeasy," Marauder said, sticking her tongue out as she poked at the serving plate.

Their first night had passed uneventfully and now they, along with the forty or so other counselors and staff, and hundred-and-sixty or so total campers, were crammed into the dining room of the lodge shoveling down breakfast. Legally, the main room of the lodge could hold around three-hundred people. Practically, with all the square tables and benches, it could not hold nearly that many. Meals were cozy affairs full of knocking elbows and noisy chatter, all the windows thrown open to counter the heat of so many bodies and piles of food.

"Sucks for you," Conifer said, taking the serving plate and Marauder's egg, plopping it on top of her own egg.

"Can I have your apple then?" She asked.

Conifer nodded and Marauder's hand darted out, snagging the shiny green fruit and pulling it under the table, likely to deposit in a pocket of her cargo shorts. She always had food in there. Food on the left, first aid supplies on the right, walkie-talkie clipped to the waistband. Conifer teased her about being a cartoon character for having five pairs of the same shorts, though they were at least in different colors. She, in turn, teased Conifer for owning eighteen different flannels, which Conifer had to admit felt fair.

Sitting here among the chatter and excitement, Conifer

was finding it hard to justify the paranoia she'd been feeling the day before. Kids were far more observant than adults usually gave them credit for, so if there was something going on out in the world there was no way this many kids would be this relaxed and happy, right? Right.

"Don't they usually switch which counselors are together every session?" One of the campers at their table asked. She wasn't in Conifer and Marauder's unit this time, but she had been during a previous session.

"Conifer is a feral forest child," Marauder said. "So Jackalope decided she just has to do this all the time, and I'm the only one who knows how to find her when she wanders off, so I have to be with her all the time."

Conifer nodded sagely as she buttered her roll. Always had to be a little dramatic for the kids. It was part of the mystique of being a camp counselor. Not quite a teacher, not quite a parent, not quite a sibling, not quite a friend, but a little bit of all of them.

"You look like a cat," one of the other campers piped up, looking directly at Conifer. She didn't look any more than seven or eight-years-old.

Conifer knew the girl was referring to the fact that her left iris was split slightly from a childhood incident involving tripping over a chicken and smacking into a fencepost face first. The old injury made the pupil of that eye appear to have a sort of diamond shape if it was dilated right, and the green tones that came out of the hazel in the sunlight only increased the effect of it sort of looking like a cat's eye.

"Maybe I am," Conifer said, winking with the split eye.

The girl giggled and stuffed some ketchup smothered hashbrowns in her mouth.

Once everyone finished eating a clamor of activity rose from the unit of campers on lodge duty for the day. They got the gray plastic basins to collect dishes, filling them up before taking them to the counter to be washed. Jack stood up, dismissing tables using random attributes to pick who went first so there wasn't a crush at the door. Tables where someone was wearing a red shirt, tables with someone who had a braid, tables with someone whose birthday was in April. Marauder and Conifer's table was released by the call for tables that had someone with unnaturally colored hair.

They found most of their unit clustered together under the large pine tree about twenty feet from the lodge steps, Cheyenne again at the center. She was trying to explain to the other kids how to make one of the more complicated bracelets on her right wrist. Once the rest of their campers joined them, Marauder made a sweeping motion out to the east.

"To the art shed!" She announced, skipping off in that direction.

Some of the campers grinned and started skipping with her towards the steps that led down the steep hill while the rest followed at a normal walk.

The art shed was a colorful red and white building, ran this summer by a woman called Robin. She was in her forties and had come over from Hong Kong to work at the camp for the summer to improve her English, and her skills with crafts were unmatched.

"Morning, campers! I'm Robin," she said, smiling brightly from the top of the steps.

"Morning, Robin!" They chorused, spreading out at the beat up and paint splattered picnic tables in front of the shed.

"Making journals today," she said.

"You'll use them to record what you learn in the session," Conifer added.

Robin nodded. "We're doing the covers from scratch too. Extra fun."

Scratchish. Really, they were just tearing up and blending old paper and reforming it into new paper, then sewing it together with regular sheets of printer paper. Conifer's suggestion that they start all the way from wood pulp had been shot down as "too involved," which was probably fair.

They weren't a craft session, after all.

"Choose colors," Robin instructed, pointing to the boxes of scrap paper she'd already set out on each table.

"How big are the journals going to be?" Cheyenne asked.

"Eight and a half by eleven, folded in half," Conifer told her. "Pretty thick, too, for covers."

She nodded and began carefully gathering pieces, going between all the boxes to get what she wanted. It seemed obvious she had a specific plan and Conifer was curious to see what it was. So far Conifer was having a hard time figuring her out beyond the fact she was quiet, smart, and her mother was interested in survival tactics for a possibly concerning reason.

Marauder helped negotiate between the kids for some of the rarer colors until everyone had a good enough pile. As they worked Robin and Conifer brought out a collection of beat-up old blenders, plugging them in to various extension cords, along with lots of empty bowls and jugs of water.

Without instruction Cheyenne began tearing up her sheets into small bits and distributing them between three bowls, filling each with water as well. Robin nodded and told the other campers to do the same.

"Okay, while that's soaking, I think we should all get to know one another a little!" Marauder said.

"And we'll work on the inner sheets while we do," Conifer added. "Ten pages, folded in half, and I want you to draw one plant from the *Colorado Foraging* books on the table in the bottom corner of each page. Just a little drawing, no bigger than two-by-two inches, and write the name of the plant underneath."

Paper was passed out and folded, books perused, and doodling begun.

"So, let's start simple. Tell us your name, where you're from, and a fact about yourself. I'm Marauder. I'm from Texas but I've lived in Colorado since I was eight, and my favorite flowers are fairy slippers."

"Conifer, from Montana but lived in Colorado since I was two, and I've been to all fifty states," Conifer told them. The answer was instinctual now, having done these introductions so many times over the summer. She had better fun facts, but according to Jack they were the sort of things that might give kids bad ideas about what activities qualified as safe.

"How come you don't use your real names at camp?" One of the kids asked.

"It's more fun," Marauder told her. "We don't want anyone to worry about what the proper thing to call is, like Ms. or Miss or Mx. or anything. We just want to be your counselors, so we use nicknames."

The campers went next, answering one by one around each table, and Conifer did her best to pair their names with something noticeable about them to help her remember, because otherwise their names would go in one ear and out the other. Conifer had never been good with names and mostly she just tried not to have to use them at all, though that was a lot harder as a camp counselor than it was in general life.

"Lorelai, I live in West Virginia, and my mom is a senator." Blond, shaggy hair that had probably been a buzz-cut several months prior.

"Aadila, my family just moved to Colorado from southern Iraq, and I'm looking forward to seeing snow for the first time this winter!" The tallest girl in the unit, a few inches taller than even Marauder. Not that it was difficult.

"Sierra, from Colorado, and I grew up on a farm." A little scar on her chin that looked like a hoofprint.

"Farrah, from Kansas, and I play piano." A very slight frame.

"Orlaith, from Oklahoma, I go by Orla. I have a cat named Corncob." She had a streak of frizzy purple hair that looked like it had been fried somewhat when she bleached it from its natural dark brown.

"Giselle, from New York, and I came to camp so I didn't

have to sit around a hotel room while my mom is on a big business trip in Denver." Light brunette hair with such a perfect edge to the bottom—which just brushed her shoulders—that it had to have been cut only a day or two before she came to camp. Conifer couldn't help but notice she looked bored out of her mind and remembered that she was one of the newbie campers whose mother had left immediately. She also vaguely remembered that Giselle's mother had been wearing a pants suit and heels, hardly a good outfit for up here, even if you were just dropping your kid off and leaving.

"Tai, and I was born in South Korea but my parents are military, so I've lived all over. Fact about me is...ah...I learned to shoot when I was seven." She always seemed to be moving, tapping her fingers or bobbing her legs.

"Amy-Leigh, from Colorado, and I was born two months premature." One of her eyebrows was half white, a patch of skin surrounding it just a bit paler and pinker than the rest of her face.

"Premie fist-bump!" Marauder said, bumping fists with Giselle.

Maybe that was why Marauder was so small.

"Tabatha, from California, and I have three metal pins and a plate in my left leg because I fell out of a tree last year. I'm getting them removed after camp, though." A lot of little scars on her light brown skin. Conifer doubted a tree was the only thing she'd ever fallen out of. They'd have to keep an eye on her.

"Sammy-Jo, from Alabama, and I have six toes on each foot."

This resulted in a scramble to see as Sammy-Jo took a shoe off to prove it, propping her foot on the table and wiggling her toes. The kids ooed and awed, delighted by this bit of weirdness until Sammy-Jo put her shoe back on. Looking for something that could be seen with her shoes on, Conifer noted her slightly chipped right canine tooth.

"Paloma, I'm from Nevada but I was born in the Bahamas

because my parents got stuck there after a bad hurricane and my mom went into labor early. I like to go rock-hounding on the weekends with my big sister." A silver ring with a cross on it on her right ring finger, and stunningly blue eyes.

Cheyenne took a moment to answer, distracted by her drawing of a wild onion. "Oh, sorry. I'm Cheyenne. Born and raised in Colorado, and I play soccer."

Conifer had already memorized who Cheyenne was. The rest of them, though, were already starting to fuzz out in her mind. It was looking like another session of surreptitiously elbowing Marauder to get reminders about names.

"Cool group," Robin nodded.

"Where are you from?" Sammy-Jo asked her.

"Hong Kong."

The kids continued chattering happily, some asking Robin more questions as they worked on their doodles. Marauder, Robin, and Conifer moved between them to help with the plant drawings. The point wasn't to get them perfect, not yet, just to get the kids paying attention to the details of the plants. The amount of points on a leaf was frequently the difference between a well-seasoned meal and a trip to the ER. Conifer had multiple cousins that had nearly killed themselves due to a bad identification of a mushroom.

"Conifer?" Cheyenne asked, waving a hand to get her attention. "Do we have any wildflower seeds? I wanna make my cover seed paper."

"In back, little...uh...sky color? drawers," Robin said. Her face was screwed up in a way that Conifer recognized as meaning she knew the word she was looking for, her brain was just refusing to actually provide it. It was a face Robin frequently sported this time of day, as she was very much not a morning person.

"Blue," Conifer supplied, going to find the seeds.

"Blue! Blue, blue," Robin said as Conifer passed her, working to commit the word to her memory.

It took a little wiggling to get the heavy wooden drawers

to come out as they had no actual tracks, just slotted into the frame. Conifer found some packets of seeds in the third one and gathered them up. It was safe to assume that if Cheyenne wanted to make seed paper some of the other kids would decide they wanted to as well.

Conifer came back out to find Marauder setting up the screens for the paper pulp while Robin talked the kids through how to blend the paper to the right consistency and thickness. There were only eight blenders, so they'd have to take turns. Once the paper was pulped, it would be spread out on the screens and dried with hair-driers since they didn't have time to wait for it to dry on its own.

Cheyenne had already poured one of her bowls into a blender and, once Robin was done talking, she started it up, pulsing it until she was happy, then pouring it back into her bowl. She did this with all three of her bowls, then passed the blender on.

"She's very methodical," Marauder said, coming to stand at Conifer's elbow and nodding towards Cheyenne who was now carefully pouring the first bowl out onto a screen and pushing it around to form some sort of shape along the top edge. Marauder stood close enough for their elbows to touch and Conifer was reminded of the way Marauder had thrown her legs over Conifer's own the day before. She still had no idea what to do with that, though, so she ignored it.

"Mmmhm," Conifer hummed, watching Cheyenne.

Cheyenne dug her fingers into the pulp of the second bowl and started adding it to the rough shape she'd already formed, wiggling her fingers along the edges to make sure the layers stuck together well. It was hard to tell what she was doing just yet, but the first bowl was a light blue, the second a lavender color, and the third a darker purple. She seemed to be layering the colors to create uneven stripes on the cover. As she added the third layer, Conifer realized she was shaping the purple layers like mountains, creating an atmospheric mountain range against the sky. Conifer had to admit she was rather impressed. It was a neat design, and Cheyenne had executed it well. Once all the colors were down, Cheyenne tore open a packet of seeds and pressed them into the damp pulp, then patted it all down so it was even and the right thickness.

She was quiet the whole time, unaware of or ignoring it as the other campers snuck glances at her paper. A few even negotiated to share their colors so they could do similar patterns. By the end most of the drying sheets of paper were swirls and swatches and stripes of multiple colors, all with seeds pressed in.

"Where'd you learn how to do that, Cheyenne?" Lorelai asked as the, also limited, hairdryers were passed out.

Cheyenne shrugged. "It was just an idea I got. Wasn't sure if it would work or not."

For the next few minutes it was noisy as the campers ran the hairdryers over their pulp covered screens, Marauder and Conifer stepping back a bit to talk.

"Cheyenne reminds me of you," Marauder said. "Contemplative and methodical and a little lost in her own head."

"Aww, thanks."

"Not a bad thing!" Marauder said. "But my record for 'amount of times I have to call your name before you noticed' is eight."

"You keep track?"

"It amuses me. Usually I try to leave you be when you're that focused but, ya know, responsibilities."

Once the drying was done, the kids peeled the paper off the screens and sat down to cut it to the right size, trimming off the uneven edges. Marauder and Conifer came back up and Conifer perched on the empty end of one of the tables.

"Alright y'all, in this unit we are going to cover shelter building, fire building, foraging, basic hunting, wild game preparation, first aid, knot tying, archery, and self rescue. With that we've got room for some other survival stuff if any of you have things you'd like to learn," Conifer said.

"Okay, we're learning survival stuff, but, like, surviving *what*?" Farrah asked.

"Anything," Conifer told them. "There is such thing as specific survival knowledge for different scenarios, of course, but the basics are the same no matter what situation you're in, and that's what we'll be covering here."

"What about Yellowstone erupting?" Amy-Leigh asked.

"Or a meteor?" Tai said.

"Or a bigfoot attack?" Tabatha asked, which sent nearly all the kids into fits of giggles.

"No, no! Godzilla!" Paloma gasped through her laughs.

"I promise you will be able to survive all the things that do not exist," Conifer chuckled. "As for Yellowstone and meteors, again, the basics will apply no matter what. Besides, Yellowstone isn't a threat either. That's a myth."

"Does that mean we'll only cover basic first aid, or will we cover bigger injuries?" Cheyenne asked. "Like, will we cover treating gunshots and stuff?"

The other campers went still, all looking to Conifer and Marauder.

Conifer swallowed, forcibly keeping her tone even. The fact that so many kids these days just expected to get shot at some point in their lives always made her livid. She'd finished her time at school right as the rate of shootings started to really pick up, so she'd missed a lot of that trauma, but she'd seen plenty of it now as a counselor here. "Yeah, we'll cover bigger stuff as well."

Cheyenne nodded and went back to carefully folding her cover around the inner pages, dampening the bend so it wouldn't tear or break.

"What about animal tracking?" Tai asked after a moment of awkward silence.

"Yeah, we'll do a little work on animal tracking as part of the hunting stuff," Marauder agreed, voice somewhat tight. Conifer knew Marauder, especially, hated questions like what

Cheyenne had asked. She'd only missed being at a shooting at her own High School because she'd ditched the last period of the day to take her then girlfriend to a job interview. Three people had been killed. Marauder said she hadn't known any of them the one time she'd talked to Conifer about it, but that didn't really make much of a difference.

Hammers were handed out, along with thick nails, and the kids used them to punch holes along the spines of their journals and the pages, winding embroidery thread through to hold the journals together. Cheyenne asked for extra thread for bracelets and showed the other campers how to tie it around the lowest loop of their boot laces, then tuck it all inside. Having it secured like that made the bracelets easier to make, and then you always had them with you, cutting them loose when finished.

The journals done, everyone cleaned up, waved goodbye to Robin, and went back up to the lodge for lunch.

Their afternoon was spent examining plants in the rock garden that was inside the confines of the Loop Trail. None of them were picked or consumed, just analyzed. Dinner was a hearty stew, green beans, and corn-on-the-cob. Stomachs full and the first hints of tiredness starting to prick at the campers, they all headed down to the flag ring to close out the day. The ring—a large, flat field below the lodge—was where every day at camp started and ended. It also served as the parking lot when parents were dropping off and picking up their daughters. The lodge may have been the heart of the camp, but the flag ring was the hands welcoming you in and eventually bidding you goodbye.

Marauder, never out of energy, led their group in a mimic game while they waited for everyone to arrive. She'd do a fast, complicated, series of claps mixed with crossing her arms and clapping her hands against different parts of her body.

The campers would then attempt to replicate the pattern and whoever messed up was out. Sammy-Jo was the last one left standing and Marauder gave her a fist-bump as the group spread out to stand in single file with everyone else until everyone, campers and counselors alike, surrounded the flag ring in a large U.

At the center of the bend in the U stood a flagpole made of a lodgepole pine. It was topped with the camp flag, placed there during the morning version of the ceremony before breakfast. The flag fluttered in a soft breeze, a blur of blue with a white and yellow aspen tree, branches in the shape of a heart, at the center.

"I like this flag better than the old design," Cheyenne whispered.

"Me too," Conifer replied. The flag had been redesigned last summer. All the campers had been invited to submit designs and then they'd been voted on by the last session. The previous flag had been a hideous orange color with a plain white heart in the center.

"Well! How was everyone's first day?" Jack asked, standing in the center of the ring.

There was a chorus of "good" and "awesome" and "fun" from every camper, and many of the counselors as well.

"I'm glad!" Jack said. "The Chiyome Mochizuki Unit will be handling the closing flag ceremony tonight, but first let's give the camp promise!"

She held out her right hand palm up with her thumb folded across it, the gesture that was made when reciting the motto of the camp. The four fingers pointed outward represented the tenants of what everyone offered to others: friendship, safety, compassion, and patience. The thumb, pointing back at your own body, represented never giving away so much of those things to others that you forgot you were important as well. One by one everyone else around the ring did the same.

"Repeat after me," Jack said. "I promise to always do my best to be friendly and compassionate; I will show patience and provide safety to all those I meet; and I will do the same in my actions towards myself."

The camp repeated each line after her, finishing at different times before dropping their hands. Jack smiled and thanked everyone, stepping back to an empty spot in the line. Silver, one of the counselors in Chiyome, stepped forward, followed by a group of five campers. Silver led the whole camp in a camp song about a restful night as one of her campers lowered the flag while four more caught it and folded it down into a triangle. The campers presented it to Jack and then returned to the U and the rest of their unit.

"Goodnight, then!" Jack said. "See you all bright and early tomorrow!"

"Should we report the comment?" Marauder asked as they got ready for bed that night. They'd been discussing what Cheyenne said at the art shed about gunshot wounds ever since they'd sent the campers to bed.

"I mean, it's not like she said she's planning on shooting anyone," Conifer reasoned, flinging her bra under her bed before slipping on a ratty long-sleeved t-shirt. "What kid isn't worried about that sort of stuff these days?"

As Marauder and Conifer were the only two counselors in the unit, they'd taken the extra two cots and doubled up their beds at the back of the tent to give them both more sleeping room. This left the front open to be used as a living area where they'd stuck a couple folding chairs and a rickety card table they'd found in the attic of the lodge.

"I guess that's true," Marauder said. She'd stolen one of Conifer's shirts a month ago, using it as pajamas, and the thing looked like a circus tent on her. Conifer was average sized leaning towards lithe, but that still made her half a giant compared to Marauder. "But still, we're mandated reporters."

Conifer sighed, putting her hands on her hips and thinking

it over. "She asked about *treating* wounds, though, and in the context of us telling her that we were going to learn to do just that in a more general sense. If anything, she wants to be the one to make sure someone who *does* get shot lives, and that's a good thing."

"Yeah, you're probably right," Marauder said, flopping back on her bed.

"We'll keep an eye on her," Conifer replied. "I really don't think it's an issue. She's just a curious kid."

A curious kid with a suspicious mom. A suspicious military mom who wanted her to learn how to survive. A curious kid who was now asking about treating bullet wounds.

Conifer sucked in a frustrated breath through her teeth. Every new thing she learned about Cheyenne made it harder and harder to tamp down her paranoia. Maybe she *would* go use one of the satellite phones tomorrow, just to get her mind to shut up. Or ask Jack for an extra couple hours off so she could drive to somewhere with a cell signal.

"Okay," Marauder agreed, seemingly missing Conifer's tension as she burrowed under her sleeping bags. She had three of them and kept them all unzipped to act as regular blankets. Conifer had asked her why she had three—the cliffs sheltering the camp kept the whole area relatively warm in the summer as the warm air couldn't really get blown out— and she'd claimed she just appreciated being cozy, which was hardly something Conifer could argue with.

"I'm gonna read for a bit," Conifer told her.

"Mmmkay. Night," she yawned, throwing one of the sleeping bag blankets up over her head.

Conifer pulled out her current read on the psychology of natural disaster response and settled in at the card table with her booklight, but it was apparent within minutes that reading wasn't going to happen. Not with so much on her mind. Sleep likely wasn't going to be any easier. Turning off the light and setting the book aside, she went and sat on the steps of the tent instead, gazing out over the camp and out at the stars. There was no moon, but the starlight was enough to make everything visible anyway.

Leaning back against the center support pole, she tried to regulate her breathing in a way that would help her relax. Tried to just focus on what was around her. The crisp summer night air that smelled like pines. The distant thunderstorm, probably all the way out over Grand Junction almost a hundred miles away. She couldn't hear it from so far, but could see as lightning illuminated the clouds every few seconds. Everything was fine. She'd call her parents in the morning during her break, get the low down on the outside world, and then go back to work.

Everything was fine.

CHAPTER 3
SHELTER BUILDING

The day dawned cool and slightly foggy as everyone had a rushed breakfast in the unit's outdoor kitchen with food delivered from the lodge. Conifer was supposed to have gotten a break over breakfast, but the counselor who was supposed to relieve her for a couple hours had woken up with a migraine. Given their schedule for the day, there wasn't time to get a replacement in place without throwing everything out of whack. Marauder and Conifer were taking their campers to the upper campground for an overnight and practice building shelters, something they needed to leave for soon. Trying to figure out a replacement and Conifer going back and forth to the lodge would delay their hike, preventing them from having enough time for everything they intended to do at the campground. The phonecall home would have to wait.

The kids were only carrying their daypacks with mostly just a change of clothes, water bottles, and food, along with their sleeping bags and mats strapped to the bottoms of their packs. Meanwhile Marauder and Conifer had full-sized framed backpacks. They carried much the same as their campers, plus a pump water filter, a bunch of tarps, lots of rope, and first aid supplies.

There were plenty of yawns as everyone set out up the Lake Trail, a few kids shivering a bit as the sun, while up, hadn't crested the cliffs yet to burn away the morning chill. From the unit the hike to the campground was only a bit less than a mile as the crow flew, but it switched back several times, stretching it out to almost two miles. It also got a touch steep in some areas, which served to wake everyone up better than the sun. Marauder was leading and Conifer took the rear, as usual. They'd established a good system over the summer. Marauder navigated and called out warnings for roots and rocks in the trail while Conifer hung back and watched for trouble. There was always the risk of a kid wandering off or tripping.

"Can we go all the way to the lake?" Cheyenne asked.

At the top of the slope was a small lake—more of a pond, really—in the old crater of the volcano. Scientists had studied the body of water and never found the bottom of it, something that inspired many camp legends.

"We're going there tomorrow before we go back to camp," Conifer told her.

She seemed excited, telling the other campers about how the lake was a really pretty, deep teal blue with emerald green along the edges.

The group was slow, Marauder frequently stopping to show the campers something about an interesting plant. Conifer always listened just as intently as the kids during these stops. Her foraging knowledge was passable, but she knew she had nothing on an actual botanist like Marauder. It wasn't until nearly ten-o'clock that they took a right turn down the short path to the campground. The area was a relatively flat clearing about a hundred yards long and twenty yards wide, the ground covered in spongy clover. There were three stone firepits set in a row down the middle, each with about fifteen yards between them. Conifer was glad it had been a wet enough summer to be able to safely use the pits. Camping just wasn't as fun without a little fire.

"Packs off, and sit in a half circle in the middle!" Marauder instructed.

The kids complied, sprawling out on the ground, some munching on granola bars, as Marauder and Conifer unloaded the tarps and rope.

"Alright, we're practicing tarp shelters today," Conifer told them, standing between the ends of the half circle. "You're going to split into teams of two and each team will get a tarp and five lengths of rope. Your challenge is to come up with a unique shelter. You can also use the trees, rocks—but not from the firepits, and the pre-cut sticks over on the east edge of the clearing. Also, we've got stakes for you to use. You've got one hour, and when you're done, we'll all go around and look at each shelter to discuss them. Oh, and you'll be sleeping in the shelter you make. Go!"

They scrambled into teams, each team grabbing their tarp and ropes before breaking off to find an area to work. Cheyenne paired up with Giselle who still just looked bored. She hadn't even tried to find a partner, just accepted when Cheyenne came up to her. Conifer elbowed Marauder and nodded towards Giselle, who was standing with her arms folded and merely watching as Cheyenne laid out their supplies. Marauder looked at the two kids as well and nodded, giving Conifer a knowing look. They'd both have to keep an eye on that. Clearly Giselle didn't want to be here, which was fine, but they'd still have to try to make it at least somewhat enjoyable for her, and prevent her from bringing down the rest of the group.

Cheyenne didn't seem to mind Giselle's aloof nature and Conifer suspected Cheyenne might have an advantage in this activity as she'd been to camp so many times already. Most of the kids started out with a standard a-frame formed by throwing a tarp over a rope between two trees and tying the corners to stakes, but when they saw this wasn't unique, they started again. Cheyenne and Giselle—whose help started and ended with holding the end of a rope to keep tension while Cheyenne tied knots—started with what looked like an A-frame, but slightly lopsided, leaving the shorter edge flapping in the wind and not quite touching the ground. Weighting the back edge down with rocks, they used another two pieces of rope to pull the short edge taut, staking the ropes into the ground. They grabbed their packs and set them under the tent on top of the small section of tarp they'd folded under, watching the other campers work. Conifer went and sat in the space between them, which was quite wide.

"I think you've done this before," Conifer said with a grin.

Cheyenne grinned back. "Maybe."

"What about you, Giselle? Have you ever been camping before?" Conifer asked.

Giselle snorted and rolled her eyes. "Why would I have gone camping before?"

Conifer caught Cheyenne shaking her head slightly in what seemed like exasperation, but she had a little smile as well, like it was really no big deal.

"Usually, for stuff like that," Conifer said, waving her hand out in an arc to indicate the view through the trees. It wasn't quite as good as from the unit—the trees up here grew closer together, blocking a lot of the view—but it was still pretty.

"Ooo. Rocks," Giselle said, tone flat.

"Well, what do you like to do?" Conifer tried. She wasn't going to press the girl too hard, she knew exactly how annoying that could be, but she had to try just a little.

Giselle shrugged.

"Oh, come on, you've gotta like something," Conifer said, keeping her tone playful. She tried to think of an activity she liked that didn't involve the outdoors and came up rather short. "I...uh...I love to read."

"Reading's fun, I guess," Giselle admitted. "I like mysteries."

Cheyenne perked up. "Oh, me too! Have you read *The Quiet Green Garden*?"

Conifer smiled and left them to discuss books, hoping this would get Giselle to open up a little. Soon enough the other campers finished, each with a unique shelter, and Conifer indicated for everyone to cluster around the first tent—the only team to have kept an A-frame.

"A good old classic," Marauder said. "Quick, simple, ample room. You need to worry about water flow if it rains, though. A trench around the high-ground side can help, depending on the amount of water, or you can use another tarp for ground cover, with the high-ground side lifted slightly so the water will flow underneath."

The next one was a modified version of an A-frame, but lower to the ground with both edges folded under to cover the ground as well.

"Okay, I know it's a terrible name, but this style is actually called a 'body bag,'" Conifer told them. "A great way to modify an A-frame for adverse weather. You have to be careful how you layer the bottom edges, though, to make sure any rain water flows under the tent and not inside of it, and depending on the size of your tarp it won't always have the most room, hence the name." This one would be fine for two young campers, though, so Conifer didn't bother to have them redo it.

"This one is a lean-to," Marauder said about the next setup. It was a tarp strung flat with the upper edge suspended between the trees and the bottom edge staked into the ground at an angle from the top edge creating a triangle of space under it. "It doesn't provide a ton of shelter from rain or snow, but it can be a good windbreak."

"This is a windshed wedge," Conifer said, indicating Cheyenne and Farrah's design. "Good for light rain, depending on the angle it is coming down from, and a windbreak. The folded under bottom edge can also help protect from water flowing on the ground. Just remember, with this and any other tarp tent, the angle you set it up at is the most important part. Take time to really study your environment so you know where the high ground is, which way the wind is going, and how the water will flow."

They went over the last one which was done in a manner Conifer didn't know a name for. It had one corner as high up a tree as the team could reach, then they'd staked the opposite corner into the ground. The two remaining corners had been stretched taut with rope and staked into the ground as well. Almost like an A-frame strung on the side of a tree rather than between two trees. Maybe not the most functional thing, but it would do.

As they broke out lunch—peanut butter and jelly sandwiches with apples and chips—Marauder and Conifer told the campers about other ways to build shelters. Cutting pine boughs and layering them together on a frame of sticks, using pine-boughs for ground insulation, digging snow holes, warming rocks in the fire for all-night heat (and reminding them to never do it with river rocks, as they could explode due to trapped water). The others listened well, taking notes in their journals, but Cheyenne was the most attentive, asking detailed questions about everything. Maybe she really was just interested in survival. Maybe all Conifer's paranoia was for nothing.

"Okay, all food into the bear bag since we've got everything out," Marauder said as the meal finished, passing around a large canvass sack. "We'll put it in the trees after dinner."

Once the food was gathered, Conifer passed out two-foot lengths of paracord to all the campers. The rest of the afternoon was spent practicing better knots and fixing the knots on their tents before taking a break to play a game of human knot. Marauder and Conifer gathered the campers together in a cluster, instructing them to grab random hands, then try to untangle themselves into a circle without anyone letting go. It was twisty and hilarious, everyone laughing as they clambered about, threading in and out of the tangle of limbs while Marauder and Conifer watched. Even Giselle seemed to be enjoying herself.

The sun vanished quickly in the crater but darkness came slow, the sky lingering in twilight as a dinner of baked potatoes and corn on the cob roasted over the fire. Conifer had a surprise for them after dinner as well: her favorite campfire dessert. Smores were just too predictable, and this was a recipe she'd learned during her own time at Aspen Heart as a kid.

The kids watched in confusion as Conifer handed each of them an orange cut into halves, telling them not to peel the halves but instead carve out and eat the oranges using spoons. Marauder, knowing things were about to get sticky, passed out papertowels as well. Once everyone had cleaned out their peels, forming little cups, Conifer mixed up a batch of chocolate cake batter that only needed water, dolloping a scoop into each cup. Wrapping them in foil, Marauder and Conifer set them on the coals around the edge of the fire. As they cooked the remaining orange flavor would leach into the batter, creating orange flavored chocolate cakes.

The whole clearing began to fill with the scent of baking oranges and chocolate, and the kids kept scooting closer to the fire, eying the shiny packages. After enough time had passed, and with a careful use of forks and sticks, Marauder and Conifer extracted them, passing one to each girl. Everyone eagerly peeled back the foil and plunged their forks in.

"These taste like those chocolate oranges you get on Christmas, the ones you have to smack on the table to break open," Tabatha said. "Love those things."

"Very messy though," Aadila replied, trying to contain any crumbs on her foil and being very careful to keep anything from dripping onto her hijab. Conifer got the sense that she was the sort of person who did not like to be dirty. Not the best trait for camp.

Aside from Aadila's aversion to the mess, everyone loved the treat, and even Aadila seemed to enjoy the actual food. Conifer felt nice being able to share this fun little thing with them. Not everything about a survival session had to be bleak. She had always been raised to believe that the best way to survive was to make sure you kept your humanity, that you made sure to take time for a little bit of regular life among whatever chaos you found yourself in. Even if the world was burning, the ritual of a messy, fun dessert with friends could be the difference between pushing forward for another day and giving up.

🌲

After a quick washup in the creek the last of the food was secured and the bear-bag hung in the trees away from the camp. As far as anyone knew there hadn't been a bear down in the crater in years—mostly they stuck to the area at the top of the cliffs and away from all the noise produced by two-hundred or so people, most of them children—but it was important to teach the campers proper behavior. Besides, there were plenty of other critters that could come dig through the food.

There was still about an hour before bed, though, and the campers asked if they could tell ghost stories. Marauder and Conifer agreed, but both watched all the campers to make sure no one was getting too scared. Each girl took a turn, however Orla was the most natural storyteller, telling the longest and most engaging one. She paced and inflected her words just right to get the best reactions to her story about a house full of living shadows.

Cheyenne was the only one who didn't tell a story, sitting a bit to the side, chin resting on her knee and using the firelight to work on one of the bracelets tied to her boots. She didn't seem scared, just uninterested, so Conifer scooted over next to her.

"Not going to tell a story?" Conifer asked.

She shrugged. "I don't think the things that are scary are out here in the forest, or in old houses and mines or whatever."

Conifer contemplated this a moment, putting it together with Cheyenne's comment about treating gunshots and her mother's behavior during drop-off. Maybe Conifer was paranoid about the wrong thing here, her upbringing blinding her to other options. "...Everything okay at home?"

Cheyenne shrugged again. "It's just me and mom, and we're getting by."

"Sometimes just getting by kind of sucks," Conifer said gently.

Marauder was watching them out of the corner of her eye but left it to Conifer to handle. Conifer was pretty sure Marauder couldn't actually hear them, but Conifer felt the general mood of the conversation was rather clear even without words.

"Mom used to call me her prophet baby," Cheyenne said eventually, still working on her bracelets. "Six months after I was born she got an unexpected transfer to work in Cheyenne Mountain. I don't really know what she does exactly."

So Conifer had been right about where Miranda worked. Knowing the details of what her mother did or not, Cheyenne must have been getting a close up look on everything that was happening in that mountain. She would see how tired her mother was when she got home, see if her mother seemed unsettled or scared. Just like Conifer, she'd be getting a partial picture that was easy to distort into something it wasn't.

"You ever get to go inside?" Conifer asked. She knew she was walking a tightrope between just being a diligent counselor checking on one of her kids and digging too deep, but she kept going, hoping she didn't tip to the wrong side. She just wanted her own blurry picture to clear up, even a little.

Cheyenne shook her head. "Nah. And I don't want to. I don't like being underground."

"Understandable," Conifer said, lapsing into silence.

Cheyenne finished up the bracelet and used her pocketknife to cut it loose, then looped it around her wrist. With her teeth and free hand she tied the ends together, then immediately pulled out a barely started bracelet from her other boot and set to work on that.

"What do you want to do when you grow up?" Conifer asked, trying to keep the conversation going.

"I dunno," she admitted. "I used to want to work in a museum somewhere, but now I kinda want to do something bigger. Maybe be an EMT."

"You seem like you'd be a good one," Conifer told her. It wasn't just a general platitude either. It hadn't taken long to see how level-headed Cheyenne was, how smart and quick. Wanting to be an EMT made the bullet-wound comment even less concerning than Conifer had already found it. It had also dulled the paranoia she'd been stewing in even more. Cheyenne was just a smart girl who wanted to help people, and she just happened to have a military mom.

Cheyenne smiled at the praise and they hit another lull in the conversation, half listening to the stories the others were telling as Cheyenne continued to work on her bracelet.

"Conifer...you're a survivalist, right? Like, a real one, not just someone who knows a few things about hunting and gardening or whatever?" Cheyenne seemed to be staring at her bracelet much more intently now, and she wiggled one of her shoulders to rearrange her hair to form a curtain between her and Conifer.

A little paranoia crept back in.

"Yes, I am. Most of my family is, though my parents and I probably know the most out of everyone. Why?"

"Mom thinks things aren't going to get better," Cheyenne mumbled. "With the government and stuff. I think that's why she wanted me to do this session. So I'll know what to do if people start rioting or a war breaks out or whatever." Her voice was so quiet Conifer almost didn't hear her over the crackle of the fire.

Ah. There was the rest of the paranoia. And more. Awesome.

"...oh?" Conifer said, forcing herself to let Cheyenne continue to lead the conversation. "Did she tell you that?"

Cheyenne gave a little shake of her head without picking her chin up off her knee. "I heard her say it on the phone last week when she thought I was still at soccer practice, but it had ended early. I think she was talking to her boss."

"She say anything else?"

Cheyenne shook her head again. "I only caught that part."

Conifer took a long, slow breath, trying to find the right angle to approach this from despite her own instincts screaming in the back of her head. She knew Cheyenne would see through any generic platitudes she tried to offer. "Well, from what I've seen, I think it depends on your definition of better. Things are certainly going to change, and I doubt they'll change in a way that is familiar, or comfortable at first, but that doesn't mean we won't be okay."

"You think so?"

"I do," Conifer said, voice firm. "People are resilient. We always find a way forward and, despite what the news likes to focus on when things go wrong, people are generally good and will generally help one another."

They were interrupted by Marauder calling out that it was time for bed. Conifer winced, wishing the interruption hadn't come. Cheyenne tucked her bracelet back in her boot, pausing to glance at Conifer as she moved to stand up. Without warning she dove in for a quick hug, catching Conifer off guard. She didn't mind hugs, she just didn't get them quite often enough to be prepared for spontaneous ones. Marauder had given her enough that she was getting better at it, though, which kept her from hesitating too long before hugging Cheyenne back. Cheyenne pulled away and smiled at her, though it didn't quite reach her eyes, and got up to go with the rest of the campers towards their tents.

Marauder and Conifer poured water over the remnants of the fire while the campers got settled, stirring it up thoroughly to make sure it was out completely. As important as it was, Conifer had never felt less focused on a task. She *had* to call her parents now, no matter the cost of the calls. First thing when they got back to the lodge. Hell, maybe she'd even try to convince Jack to let her go into town. She could go to the little town library and use their sole computer to dig into things herself. At some point on her trip down the mountain she'd be bound to get some sort of cell signal too, even if the data speeds would be limited.

Marauder and Conifer set up their own A-frame using sticks rather than trees so they could be centered among the campers, though Conifer was so distracted Marauder did most of the work. Once done they crawled inside, sprawling out on their mats.

"You good?" Marauder asked, rolling to face Conifer in the dark. "Sorry for interrupting you and Cheyenne, but we were already fifteen minutes past curfew."

It took Conifer all of five seconds to decide to unload everything on her friend. It was specifically because Marauder *wasn't* a survivalist that Conifer did it. She hoped Marauder would be able to find some other, calmer, explanation.

Once Conifer finished talking Marauder rolled onto her back, folding her hands over her stomach and staring up at the tarp above them. "Well that's…"

"Unsettling?" Conifer replied, shoving her face into the hoodie she'd folded up to use as a pillow.

"Little bit, yeah. But…she's just a kid, maybe she misunderstood?"

Conifer huffed into her hoodie. There was nothing she wanted more than for it to be that simple.

Marauder sighed and lightly knocked her head against Conifer's shoulder. "I know I always tell you not to be pessimistic about things, but…."

"But you're starting to realize it's more accuracy than pessimism?"

Conifer felt a nod against her shoulder.

"We'll make it through," Conifer offered after awhile. That much she was sure of. "If something is wrong, and we're not just making too much out of it. It might get messy, but we'll make it out the other side."

"What makes you so sure?" She whispered.

"I'm not actually a pessimist."

CHAPTER 4
DUST

Conifer slept fitfully, woken several times by distant thunder. There'd been no storms in the forecast for the area, but that didn't mean much. Storms happened when and where they pleased this high in the mountains. Several times Conifer dredged herself into enough of a wakeful state to ascertain that the thunder was still far off before falling back into sleep. It never did get any closer, so she figured a storm was just stalled out somewhere to the east. Though, at one point, it did sound like it was coming from the west instead. Probably she'd just been disoriented by sleep, though.

Marauder woke first, which wasn't unusual as she liked to workout in the mornings, but before Conifer could settle back into another half-hour of sleep Marauder poked her head back into the tent.

"Conifer, come look at this," she said, a note of confusion in her voice.

Conifer crawled out of the tent with a yawn, rubbing the sleep out of her eyes. Once Conifer stood up fully she looked around with a frown, then rubbed her eyes again. The sky seemed...off. The color wasn't quite right. Her heart tripped for a moment, mind instantly turning towards a wildfire. But... no. She had seen plenty of wildfires burn away the blue of the sky, and this wasn't that. It was more of a gray brown than a red or yellow brown, and there was no scent of woodsmoke on the wind. There was a scent of *something*, but Conifer couldn't place it.

"Dust?" Marauder said from next to her. Conifer turned to see her frowning up at the off-color sky, hands on her hips.

"Yeah, probably. Must've blown in on the wind," Conifer guessed, trying to remember if she'd heard any wind when she'd been awake. She didn't think she had. Not enough to be remarkable, anyway. It could've been higher altitude winds, though, she supposed.

Marauder frowned and glanced around, taking in the whole clearing, before glancing back up at the sky. Dust storms weren't unheard of in Colorado, and Conifer seen a few true haboobs in her life, but this seemed...different. If she weren't responsible for a bunch of kids right now, she'd run back to the lodge to call her parents and see what they thought about everything.

"I'm sure someone down in camp will tell us what happened when we get back," Marauder said after a minute. "They'll have checked the weather, and if something *was* really wrong they would have radioed us on the walkies."

Conifer knew Marauder was right. Their walkie had been silent all morning, so things must be fine. They set about quietly getting breakfast going, letting the campers sleep in. By the time they woke them up an hour later the brown of the sky had dissipated in the full light of the sun. Tai's asthma seemed to be acting up slightly, though, and Conifer wondered what might still be in the air that they just couldn't see.

When Conifer called in their morning check-in on the walkie she asked about the strange sky. Jack said she'd noticed, but wasn't worried about it since whatever it was seemed to have blown out.

▲▲▲

Their adventure at the lake went by quickly, just a bit of time exploring along the south shore and letting the campers take pictures before they headed back down the trail, stopping for lunch along the way. As they walked, the kids compared their little credit-card sized photos from their instant cameras. Only four of the campers had the cameras, but they'd nicely offered to take one photo of each of their fellow campers so everyone could have a photo to send home. This meant a stop at the post office was required, so Marauder led the group to the lodge after dropping everyone's sleeping bags and mats off in the unit.

The post office was a room on the main floor of the lodge, just off the porch. It was crammed full of random stationary, envelopes, and writing supplies mostly sourced from thrift stores. Once kids wrote a letter they'd deposit it in a post box and Jack would add postage, then send the box to town with the driver who brought the delivery of fresh fruit and vegetables that came from the local grocery store every other day.

"Aren't you gonna write home, Conifer?" Aadila asked.

"Not this time," Conifer told her. What she wanted to do was dash upstairs and use one of the satellite. She couldn't leave Marauder alone with the kids, though, and there was no one around to take her place.

"But letters are the only way to talk to home...?" Paloma said. "There's no cell signal here, and no internet, and I heard there isn't even a landline."

"No, the landline stopped working a few years ago," Conifer said distractedly. "There's a couple satellite phones for emergencies, and the old HAM radio. I wrote my parents last week."

"Come oooonnnn," the campers wheedled.

"Yeah, come oooooonnnnn," Marauder joined in, already halfway through filling a postcard.

Conifer sighed dramatically, miming being dragged over to the pile of blank cards. "Fiiiinnnee."

The campers whooped and hollered as Conifer selected a large postcard with a cartoon bear on one side. The bear was wearing little hummingbird wings and sipping from a hummingbird feeder with a silly straw while holding a sign with the words, "I am hummingbird," scrawled in a messy script. Across the top of the blank side Conifer quickly wrote, "Hi, my campers are insisting I write home, so here they all are:" then passed it around for all the campers, and Marauder, to sign. It ended up a cute little card crammed full of fun messages and Conifer resolved to smuggle it out when the kids weren't looking, rather than mail it, so she could hang it in her tent.

As Conifer gathered everyone's mail in a postal box Jack came in, seemingly surprised to see everyone there. Conifer had known Jack since Conifer had first come to Aspen Heart at seven years old and though she was in her fifties now, brown hair gone mostly silver, she still had an air of youth about her. Usually. It seemed to be lacking today. Her hair was lank and unwashed, chestnut eyes tired.

"Oh, hello girls. I'm sorry, but the post is going to be going out a bit...ah...late today, just so you know," she said, smile tight.

Conifer glanced over at Marauder who gave a nearly imperceptible shrug.

"Delivery late?" Marauder asked.

"Yes, they're having trouble with their truck. Bad carburetor, I think," Jack said.

Marauder and Conifer shared another look. Paloma was right, they had very little outside communication, and the satellite phones were too expensive to be used for calling about deliveries. The HAM radio worked, technically, but it had never been well maintained, making it staticky at best. Besides, the only person in town who might answer was Jim, and he'd just start talking your ear off about The Grays. So how did Jack know they were having trouble with the truck?

Conifer noticed Cheyenne seemed to be studying Jack as intently as she and Marauder, though the other campers seem unconcerned.

"Well, we've got to get to archery y'all," Conifer said, handing their box of post to Jack. "I'm sure Jack will make sure your letters get sent out whenever the delivery people make it here."

Jack nodded and stepped to the side to make room for everyone to exit. Conifer lingered behind the others, knowing she didn't have long.

"Jack?" Conifer asked, keeping her voice low and one eye on the kids as they walked off with Marauder.

Jack shook her head. "I don't know. I'm working on it. Just take the kids to archery for right now, please."

Conifer wanted to stay, to demand answers from Jack, but the others were getting too far away and she was out of time. Reluctantly, she left Jack standing alone in the post office.

The archery range was on the west side of camp in a clearing about the size of the upper campground. Six hay-filled targets were arranged in a line along the back, against the cliff wall, and there was a storage shed on the northeast side.

They were greeted by Polar Bear, a stout, muscled woman in her mid-twenties with a short faux hawk. Conifer had heard she'd won several strong-woman competitions in college. As Polar Bear started talking the campers through safe archery practices and how to use all the equipment Marauder pulled Conifer back from the group, grip a little tighter than Conifer expected.

"Conifer, the mail," she said, voice pitched low. "What did Jackalope say when you hung back?"

"Nothing," Conifer muttered, feeling frustrated. "Just that she's working on it."

"The carburetor," Marauder pressed. "Jackalope couldn't know that."

Conifer was silent, staring at their campers, trying to come up with a plausible answer. The deliveries of fresh produce from town came every other day. One of the three oldest kids of the local supermarket owners would make the two-hour drive up the mountain to the camp with a load of fruit and veggies grown by the locals. The rest of the camp food supplies were delivered once a month by some big company the camp was contracted with. There were also greenhouses on camp that could have a good yield if the gardening units did well, but they were hit or miss and, this summer, had mostly been misses.

Conifer thought hard about their meals the last couple days. They'd had apples a couple times, there'd been the oranges Conifer brought to the campout, and there'd been fresh broccoli, potatoes, carrots, corn, and a handful of other things. Nothing about any of it seemed less than the usual amount the camp kept around, but the point of fresh produce was that it was fresh. They didn't keep a stock of it, so if the deliveries got off schedule they'd run out quick.

The last big delivery of other food had showed up just fine a week earlier, as had the Monday delivery of produce. Today was Wednesday, and the truck usually made its appearance around one in the afternoon. It was nearing three-thirty now. It was well past the time that it might have just been a random minor delay like getting started late packing the truck, or getting distracted talking to someone in town. Besides, Conifer was pretty sure the supermarket owners and their kids had multiple trucks. If one had gone out they would've just used another, knowing the camp needed the food. Maybe there had been some sort of accident?

Except it wasn't just a missing delivery. If it was Conifer would've felt a lot more comfortable writing it off as a fluke. Marauder was right, there was no way Jack could have known about a bad carburetor, not without having called down. Which, sure, maybe she had done that despite the cost, but it just didn't feel right to Conifer. It still felt like Jack was hiding something. Added to that was the strange dust storm they had yet to get an answer about, plus Cheyenne's comments the night before. It felt like all the little strange things were building upon one another, even though they were most likely completely unrelated.

Conifer glanced down at Marauder to see real worry behind her light blue eyes, teeth nibbling at her lower lip.

"It's fine," Conifer told her. "I think we just caught Jack off guard and she talked without thinking. I'm sure the delivery will show up later, or maybe tomorrow. Maybe they even told her last time that the truck was having problems."

Marauder contemplated this a bit before dropping her shoulders, smiling slightly. "Yeah, that makes sense. I say random stuff all the time when people surprise me."

Conifer nodded, glad she'd believed her. Now she just had to convince herself.

As the campers wound down their last turns shooting Conifer slipped into the shed and pulled out the key to her trunk that was stored in there. Jack allowed her to have her bows at camp under the condition she only use them at the range, and that they stayed locked up in the archery shed when not in use. Conifer was fine with that.

"Hello, darling," Conifer said, pulling out her recurve bow and gently stroking her hands along the polished wood. It had been a high school graduation gift from her parents and while she favored her compound bow for hunting, the recurve was fun for just playing around and shooting targets. She grabbed both for demonstration purposes, along with a quiver of practice arrows.

The campers who weren't currently shooting noticed Conifer exiting the shed and perked up, interest clear in their faces at the sight of her bows. The camp bows were smaller, green fiberglass recurves sized for kids. Most of them had a draw of only twenty pounds at most. On their own they looked decent. Next to Conifer's well cared for, professionally made equipment, their age and use showed.

"Showing off for us today?" Polar Bear asked.

"Gotta teach my campers about the real thing, no offense to Aspen Heart's equipment," Conifer replied, sitting down with the bows in her lap.

Everyone finished shooting and gathered around Conifer in a half-circle, journals out and pencils ready.

"So this is a recurve," Conifer said, holding it up. "Every archer you talk to is going to tell you something different about the types of bows and arrows and other equipment and what they're good for. If you're interested in archery, the best thing you can do is go to a range with a variety of rentals available, and try a little bit of everything. For me, recurves are great for target shooting and small game, but for bigger game I prefer my compound." Conifer held it up next. It was black carbon fiber and had several accessories mounted on it. "I feel more in control with it, which is important when you're hunting things large enough to cause you harm."

Conifer talked them through each of the accessories on her compound bow as well as its other attributes: the weights for balance, the built in quiver, the adjustable sights, the adjustable draw strength, how it locked into the draw to reduce the weight the archer felt. She explained what her caliper release was as well; a little gadget she strapped to her wrist and clipped onto a special loop on the bowstring to pull it back so her arm would take the weight of the draw, rather than her fingertips. Plus it gave her the ability to shoot with a trigger, rather than rolling the string off her fingers, which helped with accuracy. She went through the same explanation with the recurve, though it was a much shorter conversation due to the simpler nature of the weapon. She explained the basic attributes of arrows next, showing a sheet with example pictures of different types of arrowheads.

The campers were starting to look a little overwhelmed

by all the information so Conifer stood up, dusting off her pants. "*Now* I am going to show off," she said, grinning at Polar Bear who chuckled back.

Marauder got up as well, dashing to the shed and coming back with a handful of tennis balls from Conifer's trunk. Together, they stood at the lineup for the targets, the campers watching from behind as Conifer nocked an arrow into her compound and nodded at Marauder. She lobbed the first tennis ball up and forward and Conifer easily sunk an arrow through it. The same thing repeated with the other four balls, each of Marauder's throws different. She'd been trying to get Conifer to miss all summer and had yet to succeed.

The campers cheered for each hit and clustered forward to examine the skewered balls once they were retrieved. Most of them still had the arrows slotted through their middles, the arrows not having enough power to get all the way through with their blunt tips and the low draw-weight her bow was currently set to. If she set it too high and the arrow went off target, she'd never find it again and arrows were expensive.

"Time to clean up and head down for dinner," Conifer called to everyone after locking her bows and all the arrows back up in the shed. They all scrambled to bring their own bows, quivers, and arrows back, handing them to Polar Bear and Conifer to hang up as there was not enough room in the shed for everyone.

"I know what I want for Christmas," Cheyenne said as Conifer stepped back out, eyes bright with excitement. "Your compound bow is amazing."

"Remind me and I'll give you the name of my favorite shop in Denver when your mom comes to pick you up," Conifer told her. Cheyenne's eyes lit up even more and she nodded.

"Do you do archery often, Cheyenne? That was not your first time shooting." Polar Bear asked Cheyenne as they walked, Polar Bear accompanying them down to dinner.

Conifer had noticed the same thing as Polar Bear. Cheyenne had clearly shot a bow before, and she'd done it a lot. She'd gotten more arrow clusters than anyone else and never missed the target once.

"Camp. I've been coming since I was eight," Cheyenne said. "And then my mom got me a bow for my birthday when I turned ten. I shoot it in our backyard all the time. Usually at old homework." This last bit was accompanied by a mischievous grin.

Polar Bear and Conifer both laughed.

"I always burned my old homework," Polar Bear said. "Safely in a stove, mind you, but it was very cathartic."

"I'm sure it was," Conifer said. She was also sure it hadn't been safely in a stove.

Most of the other campers were already at the lodge, milling around in front of the wide stone steps up to the porch. Conifer couldn't help scanning the crowd for Jack, though she didn't find her. Conifer needed some direct answers from someone and she was tired of not getting them. If she didn't find Jack soon, she was going up and using a phone with or without permission.

As more people arrived campers clustered in front of the steps, laughing and chatting with counselors ringing the outside of the group. Silver, her unit on meal duty today, started leading everyone through camp songs. They'd sing until the tables were set by the campers and other counselors in Silver's unit, then everyone would be let inside in groups to find a seat. Conifer was hardly paying attention, still looking for any sign of Jack, but the loud, off-key singing of over a hundred kids was hard to ignore.

The camp had a whole thirty page booklet of songs. Some were old classics like *Taps* while others were strange creations you'd only hear at camp, like songs about black socks being the best because you could never see them getting dirty, or a song about smashing up and eating baby bumble bees, or an Irish Murder Ballad. The first song Silver chose was in the weird category, which she was very fond of. This, though, topped the list of the weird as it focused on ghost chickens rising up and killing the founder of KFC, sung to the tune of Johnny Cash's *Ghost Riders in the Sky*. The rendition was an equal mix of laughter and singing before Silver moved them into a song about Mary and her little lamb. Except in this version Mary stuck her head out the window every morning to say hello to her lamb until one day the window crashed down and chopped off her head, sending it rolling across the yard. Probably it was a good thing no parents had a copy of the camp song book, at least when Silver was in charge.

After a few more songs it was time to head in, and there was still no sign of Jack. Campers wearing bandannas went in first, then campers in yellow shirts, campers with braids, and on and on it went until everyone was inside. Conifer took a seat by the door at a table full of campers she didn't know, waving hello to them but still distracted. Jack had five minutes to show up or Conifer was taking this into her own hands.

There was a short, non-denominational thanks given for the meal, and then the noise swelled as platters got passed around. They were having chili and cornbread, but something seemed off about the meal. It took Conifer a moment before she realized there weren't any other side dishes. Making as if to cool down her bowl of chili, Conifer swirled her spoon through it. A few onions floated around, but not many. Everything else was ground-beef, beans, and broth.

The truck hadn't come.

Conifer looked up and caught Marauder's eye a couple tables over. The pinched look was back on her face as she looked pointedly at the pot of chili on her table, then back at Conifer.

"I'm going to find Jack," Conifer mouthed.

Marauder nodded, looking worried.

CHAPTER 5
NIGHT SWIM

Jack was in her office, pacing back and forth as she talked on a satellite phone. The office was a cluttered space with a large south facing window and stacks of file boxes perched everywhere they fit. A fan hummed away in a corner of the room and the walls were completely covered in a collage of pinned pictures of the camp. Some of them were old and faded, a large one from the opening of the camp in the thirties taking pride of place in the center of the north wall, behind Jack's desk. The desk itself was a large wooden one with decades of counselor initials carved into the sides and around the edges of the top.

The curly charging cord of the phone trailed after her as she paced, twisting up on itself over and over before being pulled apart again. She wasn't talking, though, just pacing. When Conifer stepped in through the open office door, Jack glanced at her and hung up the phone.

"No one is answering at the store," Jack said without preamble. "They haven't been all day."

"I'm going into town," Conifer responded, already turning to leave. It was her and Marauder's night off anyway. Jack could find someone to help Marauder with their kids for the few extra hours she was now going to take by leaving early, at least until their actual coverage for the night was available.

"Not this late you're not," Jack said, stepping out from behind her desk to cut Conifer off. "No one goes on that road in the dark."

"Jack, I have been on much worse roads in much worse conditions than just 'dark,'" Conifer shot back.

Jack shook her head. "No. I'm not denying that something is going on, but I am in charge of this camp—and you are my employee—and you need to let me handle it for now. If we still don't have answers by morning, I'll send you down."

Conifer eyed her warily, not feeling all that comforted. "I'm calling my parents."

Jack stepped aside and waved her hand out towards the phone. "Please."

Conifer went over and picked up the phone, dialing her mother's number first. Wednesdays were the nights her dad usually went out for dinner with his brothers, so he was less likely to answer. The phone rang several times, eventually switching over to voicemail. Conifer hesitated, caught off guard by the lack of answer, before she left a short message. "Hey Mom, it's me. Guess you're busy. Things are getting a little wonky up here at camp, and I've got a weird feeling. Call me back and catch me up on the news, please? Or just call back and do the same for Jack, since she'll probably be the one to answer. Love you."

Conifer hung up and tried her father's number next, only to get the same lack of answer. Those were the only two numbers she had memorized. If she wanted to call anyone else, she'd have to go dig her cellphone out of the Bronco and charge it to look through her contacts.

"I'm sure it's fine," Jack said when Conifer hung up for the second time. "I'm sure it's fine. If something were really wrong, someone in town would have come up to tell us. Everyone in town loves this camp, and they know how cut off we are."

Conifer was getting sick of the excuses. They were starting to feel a lot like bystander syndrome, everyone assuming someone else was doing something while, in reality, no one was. She debated how mad Jack might get if she just got in the Bronco and left anyway. If anyone could pull that off without getting fired, it was Conifer. Jack liked her enough that it would likely just result in a reprimand.

Jack had gone to slump into the chair behind her desk, scrubbing her hands over her face. Conifer felt for the older woman, she really did. But something had to be done. Conifer opened her mouth to say so, only for Jack to interrupt.

"If all these little pieces fit together better, I would send you into town right now, Conifer, but they just don't." Jack looked up at her, looking exhausted.

Conifer swallowed and looked at her shoes, knowing she'd been thinking the same thing earlier. It was just a bunch of little things that didn't add up, even if she couldn't shake the feeling of a pattern forming.

"Just give me until morning. Go take your night off. You were planning on going camping up at the lake, right?" Jack said.

Conifer nodded.

"Good. Go do that. Enjoy yourself, then come see me in the morning and if I need to send you into town I will, deal?"

Conifer sighed. "Fair enough."

🌲

"I love our children but freedom is sweet," Marauder said as they hiked the lake trail several hours later. This time it was just the two of them, plus Silver and another unit counselor who went by Trout. The four of them all had the night off together, and had decided over a week ago to do a lake camp out of their own. It was more fun without kids to watch, and the stars up there were extraordinary.

Marauder had jumped on Conifer the second she came back to dinner, demanding to know what had happened with Jack. She'd been calmed by Jack's lack of worry, even if no one answered the phones. Or at least she was pretending to be calm. Conifer thought it seemed somewhat forced.

But she was putting on an act too, not wanting to worry Silver and Trout, so she couldn't exactly call Marauder on it.

"Can we trade girls?" Silver asked, long legs carrying her faster than the rest of the group so she had to shout to be understood. The neon green stripes on her runner's shirt flashed in the fading light. "One of my girls has a habit of sleepwalking. I nearly died when I was on my way back from the bathroom the other night. Just standing in the mouth of her tent and staring at me like the grudge."

"She doesn't leave the tent, does she?" Trout asked worriedly, shoving her glasses back up her bugspray slick nose. She bathed in the stuff, which made Conifer's skin crawl just thinking about. Bugspray was such a horrid texture. There was only one brand she willingly used, and if the bugs weren't too bad she preferred natural solutions like citronella or rosemary.

"Not so far," Silver said, pausing to let everyone catch up a bit. "Her mom warned us ahead of time, so we hung jingle bells on all the edges, and there's a motion activated baby monitor thing in her tent and ours. Buzzes real loud if she gets up."

"When I was ten a girl sleep walked out of her tent in my unit," Conifer said. "Wandered about a quarter mile. Freaked everyone right out. They found her sleeping on a rock in the rock garden. She thought it was a prank and someone had carried her out there."

"At least she went to the center of camp, not down the hill or something," Marauder replied.

Conversation tapered off as they reached the steepest part of the trail, loose rocks and gravel shifting under their feet and forcing them to pay attention to their steps. After another twenty minutes they crested the top of the trail and saw the lake spread out in front of them. The water sparkled in the falling light, now pitch black in the center, fading out to a dark jade around the edges. Conifer had seen a lot of alpine lakes, in Colorado and otherwise, but none were the colors of this one. She never got tired of seeing it.

The gray cliffs soared up on three sides while the side they were on consisted of a tumble of boulders, the thin and winding trail, and a couple bare patches just big enough for a single tent. The trail branched off to the left and right, winding through the boulders. The left path went up a small hill and came down at the boat house where a bunch of kayaks were stored, then continued up the west side of the cliffs. It was a deceptive trail. The first half was easy, coming to a large flat area covered in scrub about halfway up the cliff. Once there you'd come around a switchback and see the second half going straight up an almost impossibly steep grade. But if you took the right fork from where they now stood, the trail turned into a whole series of switchbacks to make the grade more manageable as you worked your way up the eastern cliffs.

"Always takes my breath away," Silver said, dropping her bag on a rock and stretching. Conifer had no doubt that they'd wake up to find her running laps around the lake tomorrow, likely with Marauder.

"Doesn't it?" Marauder agreed, dropping her bag as well.

Marauder and Conifer claimed the lower patch of clear dirt while Trout and Silver took one ten yards or so farther up the trail. It was going to be a clear night so they'd decided not to bother with tents, bringing only their sleeping pads and bags. It being a warm evening, and having already eaten dinner, they didn't really need a campfire, but they built a little one anyway, just as the sun set behind the cliffs.

"So, the fruit and veggies," Silver said unprompted, sprawling in the dirt on the other side of the fire, her braided red hair trailing out behind her. "Where they be?"

Part of Conifer wanted to tell Silver to drop it. It would just be more of the same excuses, the same useless wonderings without enough data to make any progress on the situation. But she just couldn't not talk about it, the festering annoyance forcing the conversation on her part.

"Well, when we tried to send letters yesterday Jack said the carburetor in the delivery truck was having problems—" Conifer started.

"She couldn't know that," Silver interrupted.

"Exactly," Marauder said. "We figured she made something up without thinking because we caught her off guard. But then it still never showed up later either. I know the shop owners have other trucks."

"We haven't had any storms that would wash out the road," Trout said, voice slow as she worked through the thought.

"There were far off storms the other night, though," Conifer said. "I heard them."

"Me too," Silver said. "They sounded kinda different, though. Echoed off the cliffs weirdly or something."

"There was that dust storm that blew in at the same time," Trout mused. "Maybe it was worse in town? Like...they needed to do a lot of clean-up or something?"

Everyone lapsed into silence, staring at the stars as they thought about it. The whole Milky Way was spread out above them, coming into focus as the last of the daylight faded, a couple planets sparkling a brighter in its midst. A light sped across the sky and Conifer wasn't sure if it was a satellite or the space station. The only sounds were the crackle of the fire and soft knocking of old, weathered logs that had fallen into the lake and now floated along the edges, clattering together as the water lapped softly underneath them.

"There's still our own farm and greenhouses," Silver said after a bit. "Yeah, we grow that stuff for the food bank so the girls can learn gardening and charity, but if we've got to take a little then we've got to take a little."

"Most of it has already been harvested and taken to the bank," Conifer pointed out. "And, not to disparage our campers, but the whole point is that they're *learning* gardening, not that they're good at it. Even if we kept that food back it wouldn't be much."

"Well, I'm sure Jackalope will figure it out. It probably was just car trouble, or maybe the grocers had some family thing they needed to deal with immediately, or the dust storm," Trout said, her tone making it clear that she was done with this conversation. Conifer didn't feel done with it, but she let it drop anyway.

They lapsed back into silence for awhile and Conifer, at least, was enjoying the quiet. She loved kids, loved working with them, but a night without noise was very welcome, especially with so many thoughts buzzing in her head.

"How long has it been since this thing erupted?" Marauder asked after a bit, chin on her knees as she stared at the lake over the fire. It glittered under the starlight, the reflected pinpricks of light coming and going as the water rippled under a soft breeze.

"No idea," Conifer admitted. "A long damn time, though. The place isn't even geothermally active anymore, that's why the lake is so cold and there's no sulfur smell around here."

Marauder's eyes continued to scan the lake, then glanced up at the stars. "Hmmm…. And they've really never found the bottom of it?"

"Guess not," Conifer said. "That's what I've heard, anyways. There's been a handful of studies done over the years. I know the School of Mines did a couple, and the Denver Museum of Nature and Science was involved in one with some other college."

Marauder nodded and stood up, shucking off her shirt before slipping out of her pants as well. Another few seconds passed and she was standing there fully nude as the rest of the group watched in confusion.

"Whatchya doin', Love?" Silver asked, a bemused expression on her face.

"No good witch would say no to taking a swim in something so ancient under the starlight," Marauder replied, picking her way down to the shore.

"Uh, you'll freeze!" Conifer said, scrambling after her.

"Cold water shock is a thing and you are well aware of that, I know you are!"

"That's what the campfire is for!" Marauder laughed, walking out along a large, secure log and balancing on the end, holding the roots to stay in position. Firelight and starlight carved her muscles into sharp relief, bringing attention to what was usually somewhat hidden. She took a deep breath and a little leap, one hand still on the root, sliding down with her as she disappeared into the water.

Silver and Trout were standing next to Conifer now, watching as Marauder reappeared and paddled out a few yards before flipping over to float on her back. Her small breasts stuck out slightly, along with her face and hands, but the rest of her was obscured beneath the star-flecked water.

"Does witchcraft require nudity?" Silver shouted, a laugh in her voice.

"No! Well, sometimes. But I only brought one bra and one pair of underwear," Marauder replied.

"Get back here before you get hypothermia, please!" Conifer said. She could respect Marauder's beliefs on witchcraft just fine, but she was not going to accept her just floating there in an alpine lake in the dark forever. Especially with no connection to the world outside the camp currently working.

Marauder giggled and flipped over, paddling back to shore and clambering over the rocks and trees to get back to the group. She was already shivering but had a huge grin on her face.

"Ridiculous," Conifer muttered, handing Marauder her spare sweatshirt to use as a towel.

"Committed to my craft," she returned. "I just couldn't say no to the opportunity to experience something so ancient and pure."

Back at the fire Marauder redressed while Conifer unzipped a sleeping bag and to drape over her shoulders, muttering about how it had been a ridiculous idea in the first place.

"Was it all you hoped for?" Silver asked.

Marauder contemplated a moment, staring back out at the lake. "It felt...cleansing. Like I could get out and start fresh."

"Get out and get hypothermia," Conifer muttered, mostly teasing at this point.

Marauder stuck her tongue out. Conifer returned the gesture.

"So, back to the delivery," Silver said.

Trout groaned and threw a handful of dry pine-needles at her. "Must we?"

"We must, because no clear answers have been found," Silver replied.

"And you think we're going to find them up here? If anything the best course of action is to wait until we get back tomorrow so we can see what Jackalope may have found out since we left," Trout said. "Otherwise it's just pointless guesswork."

Silver made an affronted noise, dramatically clutching her chest. "Pointless guesswork! And to think I shared my old Scooby-Doo DVDs with you on our last day off! The Mystery Gang would be so disappointed."

Trout rolled her eyes and threw another fistful of pine needles.

"I noticed something else, aside from the delivery," Marauder said, voice soft. Her quiet, serious tone caught Conifer off guard and she glanced over to see Marauder chewing on her lip and staring at the dirt.

"What else?" Conifer asked.

"Well...it's...maybe I'm wrong, maybe I'm just not paying enough attention, but...I haven't heard any planes all day," she said.

The whole group went quiet and Conifer could see that Trout and even Silver now looked worried. Conifer was replaying the whole day in her mind and she was sure they were as well. It was difficult to remember the absence of something that usually wasn't worth noting, but no matter how hard Conifer thought about it she couldn't remember any planes either. The camp sat under a relatively major thoroughfare for planes going to and from Denver International Airport, as well as several regional airports, so there was always something. There was always *supposed* to be something.

Trout was the oldest of them at twenty-six, Silver was twenty-four, and Marauder and Conifer were both twenty-two. But their ages didn't matter here. Even though they hadn't all been alive, or had been too young to understand it, they all knew about 9/11, about how it haunted everyone just a little bit older than them. Relatives dead or stranded in other countries, icons shattered, safety disillusioned. Conifer's mother always called it "one of the first disasters of the internet age," saying she felt that was why it had stuck in everyone's memories so much more than previous disasters. People saw so much more of it, not just carefully curated news segments.

The overzealous patriotism born of the incident had become a meme more than anything these days, but the core event, the immediate pain and trauma, had haunted their childhoods in strange ways. They'd all heard the same stories from their parents and teachers about the horrific deaths that day, about the fear. They'd all had moments of silence during school when the anniversaries were still fresh enough to sting. Sure, the national worries had shifted since then, but they still knew about how quickly the skies had emptied, how unsettling the silence had been. Even people who hadn't been impacted directly experienced that silence focused in on it. Built their memories around it. Felt it settle in their bones as they stared up at a sky now so different than the one they'd known their whole lives. Conifer could feel a bit of that ache settling into her own bones now and suddenly the silence she'd been enjoying all evening wasn't so comforting.

"Should...should we go back to camp?" Trout asked eventually.

Conifer couldn't blame her. Even if they stayed, Conifer doubted she'd be sleeping. Too busy straining her ears for any sign of an engine. Even a little Cessna would've made her feel better. It didn't matter if the pieces didn't fit anymore. Silent skies, dust, some half-heard words from the child of someone who worked for NORAD, and a missing delivery. That was too many unsettling things for such a short span of time, and Conifer was done sitting around.

"Let's go," Conifer said. "But this trail can get dangerous in the dark. We need to be careful."

"I'm willing to risk it," Silver said. "I want to talk to Jackalope. If she's not willing to start giving some solid answers, I'm stealing someone's car and going into town myself."

Conifer nodded. "Pack up then. I'll take care of the fire. And if it comes to it, we can take my truck."

Everyone agreed and Conifer used a spare water bottle to douse the fire with water from the lake, stirring it until there was no trace of heat or smoke even though she wanted to rush. Marauder packed up for her and they all donned their headlamps, setting them to red so they could see without straining their eyes, and headed out back down the trail.

CHAPTER 6
MEETING WITH JACK

They made it down the worst part of the lake trail without incident and started around the Loop Trail, heading for the lodge. Not one word was uttered as they walked and Conifer knew that, for her at least, it was because there was a hope of hearing a plane. There was nothing, though. Just silence pressing in on all sides. Even the bugs seemed quieter, the volume of their buzzing turned down, like they were listening too. This didn't help as all it did was make Conifer think about how animals were prone to knowing something was wrong before humans did.

Conifer had told Marauder the truth when she said she wasn't a pessimist, but that was an easy thing to say when things seemed mostly alright. A few comments from Cheyenne and a weird experience with her mother during dropoff weren't, retrospectively, anything to get up in arms about. But there were now so many little things that seemed strange and they were starting to form an equation Conifer didn't like, pessimist or not. What if something really was wrong? What were we supposed to do?

Stop it, she told herself. She still didn't have enough information to warrant panic, only curiosity. It was just a bunch of random events with no real connection that she could parse out. Even if she did have enough information panic wasn't helpful. But, really, it was the lack of information itself that was the problem. If Conifer knew what was happening she could deal with it, she could make a plan. But all she had right now were a few vague suspicions.

As they stepped around the side of the lodge, having made rather incredible time for doing the journey in the dark, they could see that the light was on in Jack's office. A glance traveled around the group. Jack was a stickler for keeping to her sleep schedule. She never went to bed later than eleven if she could help it, and it was nearing in on two in the morning now. Without a word, the group headed inside and up the stairs.

"Jack?" Conifer called out as they stepped inside the first floor, not wanting to startle her. She appeared at the top of the stairs and even in the dark hallway Conifer could see her eyes wide with worry. She stared down at them for a moment before she turned and went back to her office, gesturing for them to follow.

Glancing at the others, Conifer led the way up and into the cozy room. Jack was at her desk, head in her hands and the satellite phone sitting in front of her.

"Thought I told you to go take your night off at the lake," she said, a slight tremble in her voice.

Silver, Trout, and Marauder looked to Conifer, knowing she knew Jack the best from growing up going to the camp.

"We were," Conifer said. "But...we got to talking about the delivery not showing up, and then Marauder pointed out that she hadn't heard any planes all day, and there was that strange dust storm, plus a few things Cheyenne has said involving her mom. It kept adding up in a bad way, so we decided to come back and see if you had heard anything."

Jack let out a single dry laugh. "Marauder is right. There haven't been any planes. They're all grounded. After you left I tried calling a ton of other people and didn't get a single answer, if the calls went through at all and most didn't. I decided to just drive down to that turnoff where we sometimes get signal. And, well. I got it." She pulled her phone out of the chest pocket of her green flannel shit, swiped in her code, pulled up the browser, and handed it to Conifer with a multitude of pre-loaded news articles opened in different tabs.

Conifer felt her pulse speeding up as she reached out and took the device, knowing from Jack's voice that something was very wrong. Marauder's gasp as she looked over Conifer's arm was enough to finally get Conifer to look at the headlines listed at the top of each tab.

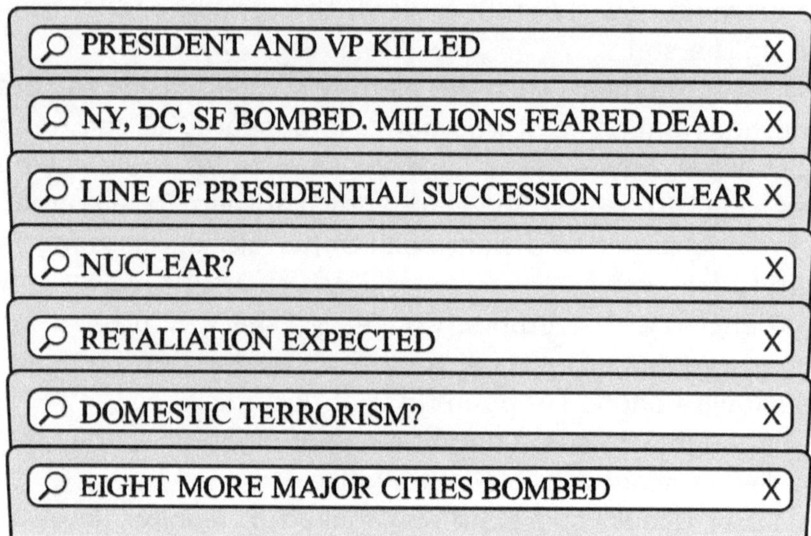

Marauder was clinging so tightly to Conifer's arm she could feel her fingers going numb. Trout stumbled over to Jack's two-seater patchwork couch and sat down with a whump that sent dust into the air. Silver shakily made her way over to the front window and threw it open, leaning heavily on the sill as she sucked in the fresh air. Slowly Conifer turned the phone over and set it facedown on the desk, her fingers lingering and pressing it into the wood as she tried to gather her thoughts.

It hadn't been thunder.

It hadn't been a dust storm.

"Denver?" Conifer asked Jack.

"I don't know. Maybe. But...Colorado Springs...yes,"

she said.

Conifer sucked in a breath, mind instantly jumping to Cheyenne. Maybe her mother had been at work, safe inside the mountain as she worked with the military to figure out what was going on. Maybe Cheyenne wasn't an orphan.

"I tried to make calls on my phone after I read the articles," Jack said. "But nothing went through. After about half-an-hour the signal went away entirely."

"Who'd you try?" Conifer asked, mind already spinning out different scenarios, different plans for how to handle the impossible situation they were now facing.

"911, plus the direct line to the local fire department and police. I even tried a few friends as well, but nothing would get through."

"Why didn't you go to town?" Conifer pressed.

She looked defeated. "I was closer to here when I got signal, and I knew the satellite phone works, so I thought I should come back and use it to get help. When I was trying to call before, I only tried the store because I thought whatever was wrong, it must just be them."

"It did work, right?" Marauder said, voice cracking with fear. "It had to work. It's a satellite."

"It did," Jack admitted, voice heavy, "but nearly every emergency service I tried I got a busy signal and a message about emergency services being over capacity, and to try calling back later."

Conifer tilted her head back, willing my tears of frustration not to fall. This couldn't be happening. Not now. Not with so many kids under their care. What the hell was she supposed to do with this? Growing up, it had been a common game in her household to come up with outlandish, impossible scenarios and then everyone else had to try to come up with ways to survive them. Not one of those scenarios had ever involved anything close to the real life situation she found herself in now. Over a hundred-and-fifty kids alone and isolated in the woods, nuclear war crumbling the world around them. What the fuck was she supposed to do with that? It couldn't be happening.

No.

It was happening. There was nothing they could do to change that except push forward. Conifer had facts now, so she needed to use them. She'd grown up knowing nuclear war was always a possibility. Now, it was time to put what she'd learned to the test, even if there were factors she hadn't prepared for. Letting a deep breath out between her lips, Conifer tilted her head back down, leveling her gaze on Jack.

"Did anyone at all answer?" Conifer asked.

"A few," Jack replied. "The Gunnison Fire Department, the Grand Junction Air Rescue, and the Hot Sulphur Springs Police Department. I was trying every emergency number I have at that point, no matter how far away they are. As soon as I told them none of us were in immediate danger they advised that we shelter in place and not use the satellite phone unless an immediate danger or emergency arose so the lines could remain open for them."

Trout and Marauder were crying now while Silver just looked out the window in silence. Conifer ignored them for the moment.

"The kids?" Conifer asked. "Their parents, I'd think they would be showing up to get their children."

"I think the lady at the air rescue said something about the highways being shut down, but she was talking so fast I'm not sure," Jack said. She looked like she'd aged ten years since Conifer had seen her during dinner.

"We have to have a procedure for this," Silver said, speaking for the first time.

"We have procedures for wildfires, for sickness, for broken bones, for floods, for snow, for windstorms," Jack rattled off, "but a massive war?"

"What's the wildfire procedure?" Trout asked. "It has to involve an evacuation for the entire camp, right?"

"It does," Jack agreed. "But it operates under the

assumption that we have somewhere safe to go, to take the kids and wait for their parents to come get them."

"And right now we don't," Conifer filled in. Jack nodded.

"So what do we *do*?" Marauder asked, still tucked into Conifer's side with hands clasped around her arm.

Jack opened and closed her mouth a few times, hands held out in supplication before she just shook her head and dropped it back into her hands.

"What about the HAM radio?" Conifer asked.

"Tried it. It isn't getting signal," Jack mumbled.

"I have a newer CB radio in my Bronco," Conifer said. "It's been broken, but I finally got a crappy signal yesterday for a few minutes. Let's go try that. It doesn't get the best signal in general up here either, but maybe it'll do better than the HAM."

Having a plan, even a tiny one, seemed to lighten the room a fraction. Leaving their backpacks behind, the five of them left the lodge, headlamps on, and headed for the counselor parking lot. It wasn't very full as a lot of people got rides to the camp from friends and family, but there were still about a dozen or so cars. Conifer's Bronco was parked towards the far end, chipped dark blue paint appearing almost black in the darkness.

The keys were back in Conifer's tent up at the unit, but it was hardly the first time she'd had to break into her own truck due to a bad habit of leaving the keys inside. Standing on the running board she got a firm grip on the driver-side handle and used her weight to bounce the whole truck, yanking the door up slightly as she did and pulling the handle out at the same time. There was a satisfying click as the door popped open and Conifer moved to the side to swing it all the way out before sliding down onto the worn, woven fabric of the front seat.

The others clustered around the open door, watching Conifer flip the radio on, glad she'd had the foresight to give it its own battery when she'd installed it years prior. Turning the truck on would've woken half the camp, and would have required hot wiring without the keys.

Conifer fiddled with the dials, trying to tune it in to something other than static. There had been a loose wire causing its earlier problems, but Conifer was sure it was fine now and she hadn't driven the Bronco since so it wasn't like the wire could've rattled loose once more. Eventually they caught a few snatches of unintelligible words, but the radio refused to stay on anything let alone clear up. Finally Conifer picked up the mic and started to try calling out on different channels, remaining vague about who they were and where they were. Better safe than sorry.

"Hello hello, can anyone hear me? Looking for an update. Over," Conifer repeated again and again, pausing between each in hopes of an answer. None came, at least none that they could hear.

"We should drive your truck down the mountain to a place with a better signal," Silver said. "Out of the cliffs."

"Not tonight," Jack responded, holding a hand up as Silver started to protest. "The road is too dangerous at night, especially going on no sleep, and it may just be that no one in range is awake to answer."

Conifer hated to admit it, but she agreed. It had been one thing to take the road as the sun set when she was just a little annoyed. To take it now in the dark when she was fully worked up, Conifer knew that was a bad idea. Some sleep needed to happen, even if it was only a few hours. "In the morning then?"

Jack nodded. "Come down and try again at first light. If you don't get anything while still here, come get me and we'll go down together."

"What about the kids?" Marauder asked. She was hanging onto the edge of the still open door now, just like she'd been hanging onto Conifer's arm back in Jack's office. "What are we going to tell them?"

Jack was silent for several minutes this time.

"Nothing yet," she said eventually. "There's ten days left in the session. Maybe by then we'll have figured out an evacuation plan so they won't be as panicked when we tell them."

"Jack, this isn't something that is going to go away in ten days," Conifer said. She left out any mention of how groups panicking during disasters was actually mostly a myth because she wasn't sure if it *was* a myth when it came to kids.

"Then give me a better option, Conifer. Please. Because I can't think of one," she returned, voice rough. Even in the poor light from the worn-out overhead cab light Conifer could see how strained she looked.

"I'll get back to you on that," Conifer said eventually.

"Well, until then, we keep the kids out of the loop. No reason to scare them if we don't have to. Agreed?" Jack stated, looking at each of them in turn. "I'll pull the other counselors aside one by one tomorrow and tell them what's going on. Then we'll go from there based on what happens tomorrow."

Everyone nodded, though Conifer at least wasn't sure if it was the best plan. Kids were smart. If all the counselors knew, the kids would figure it out. Maybe not the specifics, but they would know something was up. And if they weren't given specifics they'd start making things up.

Jack deflated a little, wrapping her arms around herself as she looked around at the silhouettes of trees and cliffs surrounding the camp on all sides. "I always felt so safe here."

"We still are," Conifer said. That much she was sure of. How they were going to keep everyone alive she didn't know, but this camp was safe. Safer than most places, at this point. They just needed a plan.

CHAPTER 7
MORNING CALLOUT

Marauder, Silver, Trout, and Conifer crawled into the spare bunks in a small room off the side of the counselor lounge down the hall from Jack's office. Conifer doubted anyone was actually sleeping, though, and she could hear at least one of them crying. Jack had gone back to her office, saying she was going to dig through every emergency procedure binder the camp had. Conifer offered to help, but Jack told her to go sleep.

Conifer laid in the dark on a bottom bunk, staring up at the mattress above her. Impossible options up to and including using buses to get the campers to an airport and then commandeering a plane floated through her mind. That was how the game she'd played growing up worked: if the situation was wild and outlandish, the solution probably had to be as well. But the thing all the plans came back to was having nowhere solid to go, let alone a way to get so many kids there. The wildfire evacuation procedure called for the use of school buses deployed by the local fire department, so where the hell were they? If things were really this bad how had no one in town thought to come check on the camp? Was it a bad case of bystander syndrome, everyone thinking someone else had gone? Or had something happened in town as well? It wasn't like the little town would warrant any sort of attention during a situation like this. They'd be as on their own as the camp. Conifer could understand if a lot of them had chosen to hole up and not go out, but she knew there were at least a handful of people in town who would've risked coming up to at least check on the camp. Yet no one had.

Eventually Conifer started to fade in and out of sleep, wild plans merging with wilder dreams until the sun started to rise, pulling her back to full consciousness. Swinging her legs out of bed, she looked across the room and saw Marauder staring at her from under the covers. Glancing at the other beds she saw that Trout and Silver at least looked like they were still sleeping.

"Coffee?" Conifer mouthed at Marauder. The blankets moved slightly as she shrugged. Conifer made the executive decision that she definitely needed coffee. As much as she knew they needed to go try the radio again, she didn't want to go down and do it. It was just going to be a disappointment. If they hadn't gotten a solid signal at night, they weren't going to get one during the day. No, they'd be driving down into town. It was the only way at this point, and it was fair to want some strong coffee before making that trip.

There was a coffeemaker in the counselor lounge, one of those little single serving ones with different flavors in small cups. Knowing Marauder liked things sweet, Conifer selected a hazelnut pod and put it in. Once it was finished Conifer popped the plastic container out and snorted a laugh at the "please recycle me!" embossed on the inside of the bottom. That hardly mattered now. Conifer tossed it in the regular trash before putting her own cup of dark roast in.

Marauder padded up behind Conifer and accepted her cup, pouring three creamers and four sugars in before taking it to one of the couches where she curled up. Conifer joined her a moment later, sitting so that there was a few inches of space between them.

"I have friends in Colorado Springs," Marauder whispered.

"I do too," Conifer said. She'd spent half a summer there helping repair trails damaged by wildfires when she was sixteen.

"And Cheyenne..." Marauder said. "I don't know how I'm going to be able to look her in the eye. Look any of them in the eye."

Conifer took a shaky breath and nodded. There had to be plenty of other campers in camp from the Springs as well, and there was just no way at least some, if not many, of them weren't orphans now. Orphans who were going to wake up thinking this was just another day at camp. That they were going to make bracelets and ride horses and maybe even write letters to homes that were no longer standing, believing that in less than ten days they'd be sitting at home telling their parents all about it. Even if Jack did manage to evacuate the camp, who would come to get the orphaned kids from the evacuation centers? Who would care about them? Look through their records to check their allergies? Make sure they each had a bed? Tuck them in after bad dreams?

"We'll do it because we have to," Conifer said, forcing strength into her voice. "Because they need us to."

Marauder sniffled and didn't respond.

They continued to sip their coffees as the sun rose higher and eventually they could hear campers approaching outside. Their laughter was dulled through the walls, but it was still laughter. Conifer waited until she heard them be let into the dining room before going to wake Trout and Silver.

"I'm going to my truck," Conifer told them. She hadn't seen Jack yet, but she'd find her on the way. "You three should go down to breakfast. Try to seem normal. The kids will be expecting you back." Conifer looked to Marauder. "Just tell them I'm helping Jack with something if they ask you, and grab one of the activity counselors to help you out if I'm not back by the time breakfast is over. I don't think there's an archery lesson this morning for any of the units, so Polar Bear is probably free."

They all nodded and Marauder dove in for a quick hug before disappearing down the stairs. Conifer downed the last of her coffee before checking Jack's office. It was empty so she headed downstairs, stepping out onto the porch only to find Cheyenne and Farrah coming up the steps. Conifer froze.

"What are you two doing out here?" Conifer asked after far too long of a moment.

"Had to pee," Farrah said.

"Bathroom buddy," Cheyenne said. "Obviously, there is a huge danger of getting lost in the twenty yards between the lodge and the outhouse."

When Conifer didn't laugh Cheyenne looked confused. Conifer tried and failed to rally a smile.

"You never know when that rule could come in handy," Conifer said. "You two should get back inside before all the good food is gone."

"What about you, Conifer?" Farrah asked, Cheyenne still staring at her quizzically.

"I'll eat later," Conifer told them. "I'm helping Jack with a few things."

"Like the delivery that still hasn't shown up?" Cheyenne asked shrewdly. Of course she'd noticed too. Conifer wasn't surprised.

"Yeah," Conifer said, glad it wasn't really a lie. It just wasn't all of the truth either.

Silence hung between them for a moment before Farrah shrugged and pulled Cheyenne inside, the door thunking closed behind them.

Before she could get caught by anyone else Conifer jogged down to her truck and slid back into the driver's seat. Knowing it was pointless without darkness to carry the signals farther, Conifer flicked the radio on anyway and went through the same routine as before, but more methodically.

At one point she thought she caught the word "bomb," but she sort of suspected she was hearing words where they weren't because she'd been trying to hear them for so long. Either way, nothing was solid and none of her callouts were answered. After half-an-hour she gave up and flicked the radio off, intending to go find Jack. Before she could even get out of the truck Jack appeared at her window. Conifer rolled it down with the hand crank to speak with her.

"Anything?" Jack asked, fingers curled around the frame, desperation in her eyes.

"Nothing," Conifer told her. "Silver was right. The best chance of getting a signal is going to be driving down the mountain."

Jack nodded slowly, looking around the interior of the truck. "How much gas do you have?"

"Three quarters of a tank. I topped up last time I went to town, and it didn't take much to get up the mountain." It wasn't a long drive into town in terms of distance, just a slow one due to the condition of the road.

"Let's go then," Jack said, moving to go around the truck to the passenger side.

"No," Conifer said with a shake of her head that made Jack stop. "The whole camp is awake now. You need to stay here. I'll be fine on my own."

"I don't like the idea of you going alone, Conifer. Not all the way to town. We don't know what the…state of it might be." Her words hung somewhat heavy in the air.

Conifer sighed. "Jack, look, I'm tired of debating this and hemming and hawing over it. Someone needs to go, and I'm going. You're staying here and taking care of this camp. I'll be back by lunch at the latest, and if I'm not you can send someone after me, deal?"

"Okay, okay," Jack said, running a hand back through her hair that was in a messy, slept-in braid. "But first, just go down to the turnoff where I got phone signal, the one for Hunter's Gulch, then park and try there for a bit. If you can pick something up there, or get a call out, you might not have to go all the way into town to get the information we need." Jack said. "Who's your phone provider?"

"Verizon," Conifer told her, skirting around Jack's request. She was going to wherever got her answers.

"Here." Jack pulled Conifer's keys out of her pocket and

tossed them to Conifer through the window.

"Ransacking my tent, Jack?" Conifer said, lifting out the key to her Bronco.

"Figured I'd let you sleep in," Jack replied. That explained where she'd been this morning.

"Back in a bit then," Conifer told her, unsure what else to say.

Conifer turned over the engine as Jack stepped back. The old truck spluttered a few times from sitting idle for so long, but eventually it roared to life. Conifer wanted to wave to Jack as she backed out of her spot, but a wave felt too lighthearted for the situation. Instead she just nodded once before shifting into first and heading off down the mountain.

Most of the road wasn't *bad*, it was just windy, full of switchbacks, and only wide enough for two cars if both drivers were feeling daring and didn't value their side view mirrors. Jack had been negotiating with the county to have a new road cut, or at least this one improved, for over a decade, but the terrain was so tricky there weren't many options, and all of the ones that could've worked involved a hell of a lot of money getting thrown around.

A large boulder marked the turnoff for Hunter's Gulch, a road that went to a popular parking spot for hunters at the base of the western cliffs where they tapered off back into the regular slope of the mountain. As Conifer passed the boulder she kept an eye on her phone in its holder clipped to a vent, waiting for it to light up with a notification that would tell her if she was in range of a worthwhile signal. After a couple more minutes it did, dozens of notifications filling up the screen at a rapid pace. Conifer drove a bit farther until she was clear of the trees and found a small pullout to park in.

Grabbing her phone she scrolled through the messages.

It was a mix of emergency alerts from social media—the only thing she used social media for—and official alerts from local agencies, plus lots of text messages and calls from friends and family. As she scrolled, mostly just glancing at everything, she noticed that the messages seemed to have tapered off overnight based on their timestamps. Getting a sinking feeling, Conifer opened her phone and tried to pull up Facebook. It took a long time and a few refreshes to get it to load. Even then only the top couple posts ended up coming through. One was from a high school friend and just said "internet is starting to go out too." The second was from an ecologist Conifer followed and said, "War's gone global last I heard. Fuck everything."

Taking a shaky breath Conifer went through the same reloading process until she got Aspen Heart's page to come up. It was rather neglected with them not having any way to post from camp, but it was clear a lot of parents had come to post frantic messages on the page, desperate for news of their daughters. Unsure if it would go through, and figuring a shorter message had a better chance, Conifer typed out a quick few words: "I'm a counselor. Aspen Heart is safe. Working on evac. Will update if we can."

Her thumb hovered over the "post" button as she re-read the words. Even if the internet *was* going out anyone could see this post. See the word "safe" and want a piece of that safety for themselves. With so many young kids under their care, Conifer wasn't working to risk it.

Conifer deleted the message and typed out a new one: "I'm a counselor. Working on evac. Stay strong."

Conifer stared at the new message for just as long, still unsure. Even though she had no kids of her own she could still imagine at least some of the pain and terror their parents must be feeling. It felt wrong to leave them with nothing. But at the same time, their fear wasn't Conifer's main responsibility, their children were. Conifer deleted the second message and navigated away from the page before she could change her mind.

Her own page struggled to load just as the others had, pieces of it failing to come through at all, replaced instead with grayed out boxes with little red Xes in the corners. At the very top was the last post she'd made, months ago, thanking everyone for wishing her happy birthday, though it had actually only been a few people. But the comments on that post were no longer filled with further well wishes. Instead they were frantic messages from friends, family, and people she barely knew. Neither of her parents had left a response, at least not one that would load. Conifer started to read through the other messages, curiosity getting the better of her.

One message, from a guy Conifer hadn't talked to since elementary school and barely remembered, said, "I'm sorry for pushing you at recess and breaking your wrist when we were eight. I'm sorry. I'm sorry."

"What do I do? You always talked about this. Help me." A former co-worker at a ski-resort.

"What did Uncle Ralph say about when the air would be safe again? My nuclear binder got lost in that flood last year." A cousin.

"You told me where to go if we got bombed but I don't remember! Please answer, my whole family is stranded." Another old coworker.

"I thought you were joking. God, I wish you had been joking." A high school acquaintance.

"Fuck," Conifer muttered, dropping the phone to her lap. "Fuck, fuck, fuck."

This was real. This was so real.

How many people were dead? How many were going to be dead in the coming days, weeks, months, years? Conifer sucked in gasps of air, resting her head in her hands and elbows on the steering-wheel. Conifer hated herself for it, but their messages all put a bitter taste in the back of her throat. She'd been trying to connect with some of those people for years, always texting first or offering to help move or bringing over icecream after a breakup. No one ever did those things for her. She couldn't even remember the last time someone had texted her first, or offered to help her out with something. No one reached out to her instead of waiting for her to reach out to them. Yet here they were now, expecting help once again. None of them even asked if she was safe herself. Not even her cousin.

Shoving the bitterness down, Conifer typed out a quick, bulleted list of advice and pushed 'post.' The chances of it going through were minimal, but it was all she could do. No point being mad at people she'd likely never see or hear from again.

Looking through the calls and texts, Conifer noted none were from her parents, an uneasy feeling in her gut about why. There were no voicemails as her voicemail had been full for ages and she never bothered to empty it, something she regretted now.

Putting the phone back in its holder, Conifer turned to the radio to give that a try. One by one she twirled the dial through the frequencies. When a voice actually came through, it made her jump. It was still staticky, dropping in and out at times, and Conifer had to strain to hear it, occasionally moving the dial a hair in either direction to clear the signal up slightly, but she could get snippets which was more than they'd had so far. It sounded like a regular station, rather than individual communication.

"—unknown number of cities bombed. Confirmed bombings include DC, New York—Colorado Springs——Salt Lake———Seattle—Denver—"

Conifer inhaled sharply as Denver was named, but forced herself to stay tuned in. She could grieve her parents later.

"—speculation about nuclear, but not all have been confirmed as su—"

Noting the frequency Conifer spun the dial away, searching for anything else. They weren't saying anything she didn't already know, except about Denver, and she was hoping for something discussing what to do next. What resources had been deployed, where evacuation centers were, anything like that. A few frequencies away Conifer found the clearest signal yet, though there was still an edge of static. It sounded like a repeated emergency message in a computerized voice.

"Shelter in place. Local emergency services will assist you as soon as possible. Lock all doors, conserve food and water, review emergency procedures with family and neighbors. This is a declared nationwide emergency. Shelter in place. Local emerg—"

Conifer spun the dial again, picking up the handset to try and call out. She needed a *person*.

"Looking for an update, can anyone read me? Please respond. Over. Looking for an update, can anyone read me? Please respond. Over."

She sent the message out across every frequency she could, not getting a single response on any of them. Finally she had to admit defeat, hanging up the mic. She tried to go back to the first station she had found to see if it was talking about anything else yet, but she couldn't find it again.

Sitting back in the seat, she stared out at the surrounding trees, debating what to do next. A big part of her still wanted to go down into town, but a new plan was starting to form in her mind. If Denver and Colorado Springs were indeed both gone, going east out of camp would not be safe at all. There'd be too much fallout there if the bombs had indeed been nuclear. Same with going west due to the loss of Salt Lake. The mountains wouldn't shelter them from everything, Conifer knew that, but that didn't mean they needed to waltz out through major fallout zones either. So if they left, they'd have to go north or south, which would only lead to small towns that likely couldn't handle the arrival of two-hundred new people during a time like this.

Which left.... "Staying put," Conifer groaned. "Fuck."

Conifer found Jack waiting in the staff lot, sitting on the tailgate of her own truck, a much newer F-350. Conifer pulled up next to her and got out, not bothering to sugarcoat what had happened, but holding back on her new plan for now. She had to approach the idea carefully so that Jack would actually go for it.

"I got tuned in to one radio broadcast, sort of," Conifer started, "and Denver has been bombed too, plus Salt Lake. There's also a repeating emergency signal on another channel saying to shelter in place and wait for help from local emergency services. Calling out didn't work. I did manage to get online, sort of, and it sounds like the internet is starting to go in and out as well. There were a lot of messages from parents on the Aspen Heart page, but I didn't respond. We can't run the risk of other people seeing it and realizing the camp is a safe place to be." Conifer didn't tell her about the messages she'd seen on her own page, not wanting to think about them.

"So it is all true then," Jack said. She no longer seemed as panicked, just resigned.

"Did you find anything in the old manuals?" Conifer asked.

"Well, I found the one from during World War II, and it does have evacuation procedures in the event of open warfare," Jack said, and Conifer felt a spark of hope. Jack smothered it out with a sad look. "It has the same problem as everything else, Conifer. We have nowhere to *go*. Not with this many kids under our care and so little information. Back when that manual was written no one could imagine the level of warfare we're capable of today in anything but fiction. Pearl Harbor, sure. Hiroshima, sure. They were bad, but they were one city at a time. Entire swaths of the US, the *world*, getting wiped out like this? It's...beyond what they could account for."

"What do you want to do now, then?" Conifer asked, trying to get a better read on Jack's mood.

Jack sighed, pinching the bridge of her nose. "I need to think. Marauder and Polar Bear took your girls to the ropes course. You should go meet them."

Conifer wanted to object, to say she'd stay and help her figure it out, but her tone made it clear she wanted some space. Knowing how delicate she needed to be about this, Conifer watched Jack for a moment before turning and heading up the hill towards the ropes course. She'd give Jack the requested space, if only to give herself more time to flesh out her plan.

The rope course was on the west side of camp, farther up than the archery range, and Conifer was so lost in her own thoughts she nearly missed the turnoff. A few steps down the trail to the course, Conifer started to hear the campers' laughter floating out of the trees and she schooled my expression into something that hopefully wouldn't cause panic.

Conifer came into the clearing to see Cheyenne hanging upside down from a net strung perpendicular to the ground between two trees, about fifteen feet up. She was supposed to be working her way across it standing up, but was instead clinging onto the bottom like a monkey and laughing maniacally. The rope's course instructor, a woman called Moose, was plaintively asking her to climb back up the net and go across it standing up like Moose had shown them. Not that Cheyenne could fall; she was well secured, but Moose still seemed off put by her antics.

As soon as Marauder saw Conifer she perked up, eyes hopeful. Conifer just shook her head at her and went to help Giselle into a harness. Giselle looked deeply annoyed at the whole affair, but begrudgingly did it anyway. Every girl got a turn going through the rope course; scuttling up the spinning wood ladder, clambering across the high net strung between two trees that Cheyenne had hung from, wobbling their way across the balance log, hopping between the wooden lily-pads, dashing over the shaker bridge, then ziplining down to the ground. They were all breathless with adrenaline and excitement as they completed the course, discussing all the different things they'd each done. Even Giselle looked a little more animated by the time she was done. As the last girl, Lorelai, finished everyone clapped.

"Now that we've had a little fun, I'm turning things over to Marauder so she can teach you about rescue rope work!" Moose said. She seemed chipper enough that Conifer doubted anyone had yet had the chance to tell her what was going on.

To her credit Marauder managed to put on a smile as she stepped up in front of the campers and started showing them how to tie a harness with a single rope. Watching her, Conifer was struck with the unsettling realization that the things she and Marauder had been teaching them, the things they had planned to teach them but hadn't gotten to yet, were now a thousand more times important.

They had to tell them.

The kids had to know how crucial listening to Conifer and Marauder had suddenly become. These weren't just interesting exercises at camp anymore, they were real. Conifer could only hope their other campers earlier in the summer had listened.

Half-an-hour later they were heading down the trail for lunch, the campers still talking about their adventurous morning. By now Moose and Polar Bear both seemed to have picked up that something was going on from the way Marauder and Conifer were acting, but the campers seemed oblivious. Even Cheyenne was too wrapped up in the fun she'd had to pay them any mind. Conifer was thankful as she didn't think she could lie to a direct question from her like she had this morning.

As they reached the lodge Jack appeared.

"Hi girls. Gotta steal Conifer for a minute. Why don't the rest of you go join the others at the porch?" Jack said.

Most of the campers went without comment, but Cheyenne lingered until Polar Bear ushered her along. Marauder stayed, though, standing with her arms crossed right next to Conifer.

Jack waited until the campers were out of sight but kept her voice low as she said, "We have a problem. The satellite phone has stopped working as well."

Conifer's face twisted up in confusion. "What?"

"I decided to try to call some parents, and I couldn't get through to any. The phone was giving a warning message that said 'service has been lost.' I found the manuals, and there was nothing about that message in there," Jack explained. "I tried resetting it and the message was still there. It was the same with all three phones."

"But it's a satellite," Marauder said, eyes wide with worry. "It's...it's a satellite?"

Conifer bit her lip, turning the problem over and over in her mind. She highly doubted whatever random little satellite their camp phones connected to would've been a target in a nuclear war, but maybe it had been collateral damage somehow? Or, "Maybe the issue isn't the satellite, but the connection to it. There's obviously a middleman company between the actual phone and actual satellite. If that company went down, maybe it brought the phones down too." She was bullshitting at this point, but she didn't really care. "It doesn't matter, though. The point is, the phones don't work. We have to get answers, and we can't get them by staying here."

Jack stared Conifer down, face tight. Conifer held the eye contact much longer than she otherwise would've been willing to. She wasn't going to be the one to break here.

Finally, Jack nodded. "We're going to town. Me and you, right now."

Conifer gave a short, sharp nod in return. "Let's go."

"I'm coming too," Marauder declared.

"I think you should stay with the kids," Conifer told her. This was partially true, but mostly she wanted to be alone with Jack. It would make things easier to only have one person to convince at a time, and she needed to convince Jack first. "Cheyenne at least is already starting to suspect something is up, and if she starts talking to the others about it they could start to panic."

Marauder made a frustrated sound but nodded.

"I'll get someone to help you with them, Marauder," Jack said. "Conifer, meet me at your truck in ten minutes. I need to grab a few things."

Conifer nodded. "Ten minutes."

Chapter 8
To Town

Conifer was already sitting in her truck, fingers tapping on the wheel, when Jack arrived with a backpack in tow, the satellite phone in one pocket. She climbed in and shoved the bag down by her feet as Conifer started the engine. They set out with the radio on, but did not say a word to one another. Jack fiddled with the dials of the radio as Conifer drove. Conifer couldn't help but wonder what was in the bag. She knew the camp had a gun for protection against animals, but that was a rifle and obviously not in the bag. She couldn't think of what else Jack might have deemed necessary to bring. Maybe just general supplies?

Nearing the turnoff for Hunter's Gulch, Conifer kept an eye on her phone was still in its holder on the dashboard. The screen stayed dark.

"Jack…how much food do we have left at camp?" Conifer asked, dancing around the edges of the plan that had been forming all day. The camp tended to keep a lot, due to how remote they were, but Conifer wasn't sure of the actual numbers.

Jack was still fiddling with the dials and didn't seem to be paying Conifer much mind. "Uh, probably enough for a few weeks, maybe a bit more. Why?"

"Just thinking," Conifer told her.

Three weeks of three meals a day, meals that included

main courses, sides, and sometimes dessert. That could easily be spread out if needed. And the camp was off the grid, all power coming from wind, solar, and hydro. Their ability to preserve food via freezing wasn't going away. Then there were their animals: forty-two horses, twelve sheep, six dairy cows, eight pigs, sixteen goats, twenty-four chickens, two donkeys, three dogs, two barn cats. They'd be easy enough to feed for now off of mostly grazing and a little hunting. They'd give the camp some milk and eggs, even meat if it came to that. There was plenty of water, and multiple systems for filtering it. Plus the hunting on top of the cliffs was good, huge herds of elk and plenty of deer and small game, and there were wild edible plants all around. Conifer knew it wouldn't be that easy, that underestimating food needs tripped up even the most skilled survivalists, but they weren't starting from nothing.

Conifer had been turning it over and over in her mind all morning and the more she thought about it the more she realized the camp was the ideal place to be. There were some flaws in it, of course, sturdy shelter being the biggest one, but not unsolvable flaws. She still didn't know how Jack would feel about the idea, though, so Conifer resolved not to bring it up until they saw what was happening in town.

Really, though, calling it a town was giving the place a bit too much credit. It had been a booming miner's town in the 1800s but had now dwindled down to a population of around a thousand. Most of the place was a ghost town, derelict buildings all gone the same shade of gray-brown as they were left for nature to reclaim. A lot of the residents didn't even live in the town proper, instead spread out across little ranches and cabins covering the south side of the mountain. Main Street generally still buzzed with life, though. There was always some little festival or event going on that brought everyone together.

Conifer stopped the truck as they neared the first houses, turning to see Jack eying her in confusion.

"Here's the deal," Conifer said. "Shit has hit the fan. We do not know what we are driving into. I think it is safe to assume that the townspeople will have armed up, and will be distrustful of outsiders. Not all that different from how isolated mountain towns like this normally are, if we're being honest, but still. If they don't recognize either of us, we do not say where we are from. We do not say what we are after. We do not give our real names, or our camp names. We do not leave the truck unattended and functional." Conifer trusted people, she really did. She knew disaster panic was not what it was portrayed to be. But she wasn't going to be stupid about this either. Caution first.

Jack swallowed heavily before she nodded. Conifer eased the truck back into motion, turning them down a sideroad that would loop them around town. That way, when they came into the town proper, it would look like they had come from down the mountain and not up at the camp. The entire time they did not see a single soul, and Main Street wasn't any different. There were hardly even any cars parked along it. Jack glanced at Conifer, worry in her eyes, as Conifer rolled the Bronco slowly down the road, looking in the windows of the shops. No one looked back out at them.

"People could be inside," Jack offered.

"Maybe," Conifer admitted, confusion and fear warring for attention in her mind. "But where are their cars?"

"Go to the store," Jack said.

The owners were the people they knew best in town, so it felt like the right answer and Conifer headed for it willingly.

The store was one of the newest buildings in town, at the very end of Main Street with a parking lot on the side. There was only one vehicle there, parked at the back of the lot. Jack's expression was growing more and more tight and Conifer could feel hers doing the same. When Jack moved to get out, Conifer held up a hand to make her wait. Conifer scanned her eyes over the area around them as she gathered up her hair, tucking it under a beanie she fished out from between the seats. The less memorable she was the better, and flame dyed hair was far too memorable. When nothing moved in the surrounding trees Conifer tentatively opened the door and waited again, Jack watching her the whole time. After a long minute Conifer stepped all the way out, pulling the lever to pop the hood as she did.

"Watch my back," she told Jack.

Throwing the hood up, Conifer popped open the fusebox and plucked out the fuses for the fuel pump relay and the ignition, sliding them into her pocket before dropping the hood back down. It wouldn't be enough to stop someone really wanting to take the truck, but it would slow them down. She didn't want to do anything more, in case she and Jack needed to get out of there quickly themselves.

Truck secured, she and Jack walked together up to the front doors of the store, coming at them from an angle. Pausing to the side to listen, and hearing nothing, Jack reached out for the doors, pulling on one of the handles. Conifer was surprised when they swung open for her. With the town so empty she expected them to be locked.

"Hello?" Jack called out as they stepped inside.

Conifer cringed, wishing she hadn't done it. There was no one in sight, thankfully, the registers standing empty. The store's lights were still on, but they were flickering and dim, likely running on a dying generator. Conifer had expected the store to have already been picked over, people panic buying at the first sign of bad news, but it looked mostly untouched save for a few bare spots on the shelves that were standard in such a remote store. It seemed like everyone in the town had just vanished without ever having the chance to prepare, a thought that brought back the war of confusion and dread in her mind. They couldn't have been evacuated, not without someone coming up to the camp, right?

Just when Conifer thought no one was coming, a woman in a long white medical coat popped out from behind a shelf, her eyes wide. The nametag on her jacket read "Sandra:

Pharmacy Technician." She was on the short side, a little stocky with mousy brown hair in a chin-length cut, but looked friendly enough. Conifer wished she didn't have the baggy coat on, though. It made it hard to tell if she was armed.

"Oh, thank god, we were starting to think the town was abandoned," Jack said. The clear relief in her voice seemed to cause Sandra to relax as well.

"Most everyone left the morning after the first bombs for a county meeting in the next town over," she told us. "They were supposed to be deciding what to do, but no one has come back. Me and the others who stayed, there's only about five of us, think the military or police or someone must have come in and evacuated everyone without giving them a choice."

"The military was *that close*?" Jack said incredulously.

Conifer couldn't blame her. If they'd been only one town away, if they'd evacuated everyone from the county, how had no one mentioned the camp full of kids that also needed help?

"Well, ah, we're not sure," Sandra said, looking confused. "That's just our theory. We're planning to leave today to try and meet up with them. I came to get some supplies from work, just in case. Why...?"

"We're stranded near here," Conifer told her, picking her words carefully. "There's kids, and we don't really know the full extent of what's going on."

Sandra paled. "Oh my god, we...oh my god! I forgot about the camp! I live in Grand Junction, I was just here on rotation to deliver meds!"

Clearly Conifer hadn't picked her words carefully enough.

Jack dropped into a chair that was part of a display of cheap molded plastic patio furniture, head in her hands.

"Yeah. The camp. What do you know about what's happening?" Conifer pressed on. "We've only gotten snippets of information. We know Denver and Colorado Springs were bombed, as well as Salt Lake, and that there's been a lot of deaths in the government, and other bombings, and I found some speculation that things have gone global."

"Ye-yeah," Sandra said, voice shaky. "They were saying most of the attacked cities have been completely wiped out. With the bombings in Denver and Colorado Springs they're saying there's no good way out of Colorado going east, and with Salt Lake gone west isn't much better either." Exactly as Conifer had expected. "Besides, all major highways and interstates have been shut down for military and emergency traffic only. They said on the news yesterday that anyone in a civilian vehicle on the highways will be jailed."

"Is the news still going?" Conifer asked.

Sandra shook her head. "I don't think so? The cable at my motel went out overnight, anyway."

Jack groaned. "Where are we going to take the kids?"

"Nowhere," Conifer said, finally voicing her idea.

Jack balked, looking up at Conifer like she'd sprouted a second head. Sandra looked about the same.

Conifer held up a placating hand. "Hear me out. We've got some food, we've got an uncontaminated volcanic spring for water, we've got a ton of supplies, we've got some shelter, we've got animals. We've even got electricity since we're off grid. Where else are we going to find enough of any of that for the amount of kids we have with us? Right now we are a tiny, protected speck in the middle of the Rocky Mountains. But out on the roads? We're a huge, moving target that will draw a ton of attention. We have to stay."

Silence hung as Jack stared at Conifer. She could see the woman who, at times, felt like a second mother to her thinking, running everything through in her mind. Jack knew the camp even better than Conifer did and she hoped that would be enough for Jack to realize she was right.

"Okay," she said, nodding slowly. "I...okay."

"There's nothing else you can do?" Sandra asked, looking unconvinced.

"We have over two-hundred people in the camp, mostly

kids, no way to transport them, and nowhere to go even if we did," Conifer said. "And a lot of them are probably orphans now anyway. They'd have nowhere to go and no one to protect them but us. It was our responsibility as soon as their parents dropped them off, even if we never imagined it would turn into this."

Jack made a small, distressed sound, closing her eyes tightly.

Sandra contemplated before taking a deep, shaky breath and giving a small nod. "Well, in that case, you need the meds more than we do. How much room do you have in your vehicle? I don't have much, but I'll give you what I've got."

"Plenty of room," Conifer told her, already planning to load up on a lot more than a few meds.

Together, the three of them went to the back to grab some empty boxes, carrying them to the pharmacy, which was more of a large closet. Jack looked a bit lost the whole time, following without comment.

"Could we convince you to come back to camp with us, Sandra?" Jack asked as they worked to get everything packed up. "We have a nurse, and a handful of people with various medical certifications, but still."

Conifer was relieved when Sandra shook her head no. Medical knowledge or not, they were going to have a hard enough time feeding everyone already at the camp. They couldn't afford more mouths if they could help it.

"I have family in Grand Junction," Sandra said. "A sister and a baby nephew. I need to get to them. But I'll try and send help back for the camp."

"Thank you," Conifer told her. "But...be careful when you tell people, and about what kind of people you tell. We can't risk the camp being overrun."

She nodded and started handing Jack and Conifer bottles of pills before letting out a startled laugh as she looked at her arms. "I put on my lab coat! I didn't even realize it. Habits, I guess...."

A long moment passed as they all stared at the coat. It was such a simple thing, to go into work and put on your lab coat. But it was probably the last time Sandra would ever do it, Conifer realized.

They went back to loading boxes until they'd taken all the medicine before turning to the shelves. There was only one ten-foot long, shoulder high ones with medical supplies. Band-aids, aspirin, Neosporin, slings and braces. Just the basics. All told the supplies didn't even fill ten apple-crate sized boxes. Using a stockers U-cart they brought everything out to the Bronco and stacked it in the back.

"I need to go," Sandra said. "I promise I'll try to send help, carefully."

Conifer and Jack thanked her again and watched her climb into the driver's seat of the other car and drive away.

"So," Conifer said, side-eying Jack. "Law and order seems to be off the table, and we're going to need a lot more than a few boxes of medical supplies."

"I don't know, Conifer...the meds, Sandra gave us those, but to start taking other things...."

"Jack," Conifer said, voice firm, "we have two choices right now. We can sit and hope for some miracle that isn't going to come, using up valuable time in the process, or we can just accept what's happening and start dealing with it now while we have time."

"Conifer—"

"*This isn't going to get better*, Jack!" Conifer hated how hard her voice sounded but she needed Jack to get it. Jack was in charge. She had to get it, more than anyone else did. "The generator for that store is going to fail any minute now, and all the cold food will go to waste anyway. Animals will get in and get at the rest soon enough."

Jack took a deep breath, a war raging on her face. "Fine. But we're leaving cash to pay for what we take."

Conifer felt her face screw up. "What cash?"

Jack shrugged off her bag and gave it a little shake.

Conifer looked between the bag and Jack's face. "How much cash is in that bag, Jack?"

"Few thousand."

Conifer opened and closed her mouth a few times, trying to formulate a response. "*Why?*"

"Aren't you the one saying to always carry cash in case of shit hitting the fan? I think the first time you told me that you were, like, eight," Jack replied.

"Not a backpack full!" Conifer spluttered, struggling not to laugh.

Jack shrugged. "Well, I tried."

Conifer shook her head. "Okay. Sure. Whatever. Pay for it if it makes you feel better, but we're cleaning this store out."

Jack looked dubious. "What's your towing capacity?"

"It'll be a slow pull, but she can take a lot. And, well, if we're stealing supplies and a trailer we may as well just go all in and steal another truck and bigger trailer as well. Might exceed the contents of your backpack, though."

Jack rolled her eyes. "Well it's something, at least. You go back inside and start boxing things up. I'll take your Bronco and find a trailer for it, bring it back, then find a truck and trailer for myself."

Conifer agreed, reluctantly. Splitting up didn't seem wise, but Sandra had said the town was emptied out and they were running out of daylight. Jack swore to be careful so Conifer gave in, handed over the fuses and keys, and went back inside, taking the U-cart with her. She started with dry, shelf stable food, wanting to save the cold stuff for last. Pastas, sauces, rice, canned goods, it all got stacked in boxes she found in the back and put on the cart. Conifer had three carts loaded by the time Jack showed up with the Bronco pulling an extended two-horse trailer. Jack parked it right in front of the doors and tossed Conifer the keys, saying she'd spotted an already hitched truck and huge horse trailer a few streets over.

"You know how to hotwire?" Conifer asked, ready to

switch places with Jack if she didn't.

"Yes, actually," Jack said. "I broke the key off in the ignition of my first car two days after I got it, and I was so terrified to tell my parents I just asked a friend to teach me how to hotwire it. My parents never found out."

Conifer couldn't help but laugh. "Nice."

She smiled and walked away, going to get the truck as Conifer started transferring boxes to the trailer. Staying at the camp was still an unsettling proposition, and telling the kids was a constant thought in the back of Conifer's mind, but at this moment it felt like progress. They had a plan now, the start of one anyway, and they were actively working towards it by gathering supplies. The forward motion felt good after so much stalling out.

Jack returned shortly in a big Chevy with a huge fifth wheel horse trailer and together they had the store mostly cleared of food and other useful supplies by around six o'clock. They'd packed the frozen food last so that it would all be together, wrapping it all in horse blankets that had been in the front storage area of the fifth wheel. They weren't sure how much would actually fit in the camp freezers, but Conifer reasoned that even if the freezers didn't have much room left it was better to take everything and cram in what they could. The rest they would use over the next few days.

The store was small and they were efficient packers, so they ended up with about half of Jack's tailer left empty.

"Ranch store next," Conifer said, already forming a mental list of what she wanted to find.

Jack agreed and they left the Bronco in the lot, fuses removed once again, taking Jack's truck to the next street over and parking in front of the ranch store. Conifer had been in the store a few times over the years, sent on errands for the camp. There were a lot of things in there that could be useful, especially in the lumber yard out back, but right now she was most interested in a few specific items, going straight to them at the back of the store. There stood a display of ten cast-iron wood-burning stoves in varying sizes, all free-standing and elevated on iron pedestals. In front of each was a little rack of cards for you to take up to the cashier to order your own version of whatever stove you'd picked.

"We're taking these," Conifer said. "And all the stovepipe they have. The nights are going to get cold soon. We're getting a log splitter as well, and as much gas as we can bring up. The gas is only good for awhile anyway, so we should split as much wood with it as we can while we've got it."

"What do you mean it's only good for awhile?" Jack asked.

Conifer had grown up so entrenched in survival culture, sometimes she forgot that the things that felt like basic knowledge to her weren't actually basic knowledge. "This isn't a Mad Max movie, Jack. Gas expires."

Jack's eyes widened. "It does?"

"Yeah. In, like, three to six months. Depends what the quality is and what kind of tank you've got it in. I'm sure the altitude has an effect too."

Jack groaned, pressing the heels of her hands to her eyes. "You know, I've known you since you were a kid, Conifer, and I always thought your parents were a little weird. They always talked about the survival trips you three went on, and I honestly thought it was a bit much. But I'm feeling real grateful to them at the moment."

"Me too," Conifer admitted, trying not to think about them too much, feeling a little guilty at how easy it had been. They just weren't the current problem, and she had to focus on the current problem. Maybe her parents were dead, maybe they weren't. There was nothing Conifer could do for them either way.

Jack watched her, looking sad. She knew exactly where Conifer's parents lived. What had likely happened to them.

"We need to get moving," Conifer said.

Jack stared for a moment longer, then grabbed a handcart. Conifer grabbed some straps and one by one they wheeled the heavy cast-iron stoves out and slid them into the trailer, wrapping each in a moving blanket to keep them from getting scuffed before securing them with rope. The unwieldy pipe took more effort but eventually they got all of it as well. The three log splitters were next and Conifer grabbed several chainsaws to go with. They had two chainsaws at the camp already, but now wasn't the time to be stingy. Jugs of oil were gathered as well, along with spare chains, and Conifer sent Jack across the street with a cart and every gas can in the store. It turned out the power to the station was off entirely, though, and Conifer had to go over and help Jack get the tanks open which ended up being quite the arduous task.

Leaving Jack to use a manual pump on the tanks, Conifer went back to the store and looked around, already aware they'd need to be making more trips if they really wanted to get everything useful. For now she stuck with food for the animals, as it was easy to pack the flexible bags into the areas around the stoves. After that she shoved in every cooler in the store, plus the bait fridge and the fridge from the break room. There was still room in the cab of the truck, so Conifer stuffed it full of more horse blankets, leaving the bed for the gas cans and helping Jack load them in the areas clear of the fifth-wheel mount once they were all filled.

It was nearing sunset now and they needed to get going if they were going to make it up the mountain before full dark.

"Here," Conifer said, handing Jack one of a set of walkie-talkies she'd taken off a shelf. "I'll go second to watch your back tires on the sharp turns."

Jack took it, staring at the little black and yellow device. "Conifer...I think you should be in charge."

Conifer had been busy grabbing the last gas can, intending to top off the Bronco with it, and it took her a moment to process what Jack said.

"In charge of what?"

She lifted her face to look at Conifer. "The camp. You understand what's going on in a way I don't, and—"

Conifer cut her off with a wave of her hand. "You're being ridiculous, Jack. This is your camp."

Jack looked like she was about to say more, but Conifer didn't give her the chance, setting off down the street in the direction of the Bronco. Jack's words nagged at Conifer as she walked. Just because she knew how to survive on her own didn't mean she should be in charge of any of this. She'd help, no problem, but she couldn't be the one calling every single shot. She was too blunt, too no-nonsense for the subtle work of navigating the control of a whole camp during the end of the world. No. Jack was being ridiculous.

The drive up was as slow as Conifer had expected, dragging out past dark as they inched along. Any other time, Conifer would have been worried about blowing the engine as it strained under the weight of the trailer. But, like Conifer had told Jack, cars were going to be useless soon anyway. May as well use them for all they were worth while they had them.

They parked the trailers in the flag circle, the only place big enough. The only lights were coming from the porch of the lodge. Everyone would be back in their units by now, many already asleep, and Conifer wondered how Marauder had pulled off the afternoon.

"When are we going to tell the kids?" Conifer asked Jack as they met in front of their trucks. "There's no way we can put it off anymore. It has gotten too serious and they need to know—"

Jack held out a hand to stop her. "I know. We'll tell them after breakfast," she said, sounding solemn. The forward motion seemed to have helped her as much as it had Conifer back in town, but now that they'd returned to camp the reality of what they were doing was settling in. They stood in silence for several minutes, just staring up at the lodge.

Eventually they had to turn away, getting to work on unloading the frozen food through a side-door in Jack's trailer, hand-carrying it up into the kitchen at the back of the lodge. They found Polar Bear sitting on the porch looking worried. Without a word she joined them in carrying the boxes, seeming to realize what they and the trailers meant. Several of the cooks had still been in the kitchen as well, looking much the same, and joined the group.

It took a few hours even with help, due to having to walk up and down the hill, but somehow all of the frozen food fit into the two walk-in freezers. There was room to walk in, but the shelves were stacked so tightly you could hardly get at anything. That would have to be dealt with later, probably by taking more fridges and freezers from town. Having the food was the important part for the moment.

There was nothing else to be done until morning so, with a nod to Jack and the others, Conifer headed up the trail to Marguerite, not bothering with a flashlight as she knew the Loop Trail so well. Her arms and legs ached, but she kept a good pace anyway.

Conifer found Marauder sitting up in the center of her bed talking to Moose who was perched on the edge of Conifer's.

Taking a deep breath, Conifer told them everything. That there was no safe way out of the mountains, that the town had been abandoned for reasons they weren't sure of, and that Jack and Conifer had made the decision to keep everyone at the camp, bringing back as many supplies as they could with just the two of them.

By the end of it both Marauder and Moose were in tears. They hugged onto one another tightly while Conifer watched from her seat at the card table, feeling slightly cut off from the display. She'd already had time to digest the information and it didn't sting her as much as it clearly did them.

"I...I need to go back to my own tent in the counselor unit," Moose said eventually, voice raw.

"Are you sure?" Conifer asked. "Marauder has extra

sleeping bags, you can stay here for the night."

Moose shook her head, standing and grabbing her jacket and flashlight. "I...my phone is there. And I...I want to watch my videos. My family."

Conifer nodded in understanding. "Stay safe on the walk back."

The activity counselors not directly in charge of any groups of campers bunked in an unnamed unit of tents, nearly all the way back to the lodge. Part of Conifer wanted to insist Moose stay until morning, rather than make the walk in the dark while she was upset, but Conifer could hardly tell her to wait for the comfort of her family, even if they were just in videos.

"Conifer..." Marauder said once Moose was gone. "Can I... would you be okay with it if...maybe we...shared a bed? I just...I really don't want to be alone."

"Yes," Conifer said. She usually hated sharing a bed with other people while they slept, but it wasn't really a request that could be denied. Not everyone was as put off by such things as she was, and she could deal with it for one night.

Conifer quickly changed into sweats and crawled in under Marauder's mound of sleeping bags, settling in to one side. Marauder was still sniffling as she curled up with her forehead resting against Conifer's shoulder. Now that they'd turned the lights off Conifer felt a few tears of her own fall for the first time. She had to believe they could do this, had to keep acting like she believed it, but deep down she was terrified.

CHAPTER 9
TELLING THE KIDS

"Ready?" Conifer asked Marauder as they prepared to step out of their tent and wake the campers. The two of them had been up for about an hour, unable to feign sleep any longer. Marauder had spent most of that time looking at all the pictures she'd pinned to the wooden pole supporting the back center of the tent. At her friends, her family, her home. Conifer spent hers looking at the postcard all the campers had signed just the other day, marveling at how happy they'd been. She'd been. The mild unease she'd felt at the time, which had seemed all-consuming, felt like nothing now.

A call had gone out on the counselor walkie-talkies fifteen minutes earlier from Jack, telling all the counselors to go straight into the lodge with their kids. No morning flag ceremony. No morning singing. Jack had shut down any attempts at questions and the walkies had been silent since.

"Nope. But here we go," Marauder said, marching out of the tent with the large alarm bell in her hand. Conifer followed a bit slower, dreading what was coming next. How was she supposed to do this?

Marauder stepped to the center of the unit and gave the bell a few good shakes. There were groans and calls for five more minutes of sleep from the tents, but slowly and with a few more shakes of the bell the campers started to zombie-shuffle outside. Most wandered in the direction of the bathrooms, not yet awake enough to pay Marauder and Conifer any mind.

"I keep thinking about something really stupid," Marauder whispered so only Conifer could hear.

"Your brain wants something else to focus on," Conifer replied. "It's normal."

"I was going to ask you out when camp was over for the summer," Marauder admitted.

Conifer let out a slow breath, resisting the urge to shimmy away from the words. As much as she liked Marauder, and as objectively pretty as she found the other woman, Conifer just couldn't see herself ever saying yes to that. "I'm aromantic, and asexual. Sorry."

Marauder let out a sad laugh. "Yeah, I was starting to pick up on that. It's okay. I just...I don't know. I wanted to put it out there, so you knew, because I also want you to know that's not why I asked you to sleep next to me last night. You don't date or anything, and that's fine. I just really couldn't stand the idea of being alone."

"Thanks," Conifer said. "As for last night, I actually didn't mind as much as I normally would have. I think I needed it too." She had woken up so many times last night she wasn't sure she'd actually slept at all. Marauder curled up next to her was the only thing that had kept Conifer from getting up and going to pace through the woods until dawn.

The campers began to circle up around them, their daypacks slung over their shoulders and many of them still yawning, all of them expecting just another normal day at camp. The group was supposed to practice wilderness medicine today, acting out various scenarios so they'd know what to do in the event of the real thing. Conifer wished they'd already had a chance to cover that, because now she wasn't sure when they'd find the time, if ever.

"When did you get back, Conifer?" Cheyenne asked. She was wearing a pink flannel that was knotted in the front over a gray t-shirt, and sporting two French braids that she'd twisted up into a bun at the nape of her neck. Conifer suspected they must have been done after the campers had taken showers the day before during the unit's allotted shower time. Conifer could see suspicion in Cheyenne's eyes. Imagined images of Colorado Springs burning were flickering behind Conifer's, and she wondered if Cheyenne could see them. It hit Conifer all of a sudden that she was staring at orphans. Orphans who didn't know they were orphans.

"Last night, late," Conifer said, deciding there was no way to keep the campers totally out of the loop at this point. "I had to go into town with Jack to find out where the delivery was. We're going to talk about it more at the lodge, so everyone can hear it together."

This sent a wave of worried mutters through the campers, all of them glancing between one another as well as at Marauder and Conifer. Marauder attempted to put on a smile, but it didn't reach her eyes.

"Let's get walking, girls," she said, taking her place at the head of the group.

It was a quiet walk, the group staying bunched up tighter than they usually did. Cheyenne kept glancing at Conifer out of the corner of her eye.

"Is it bad?" She whispered so that only Conifer could hear.

Conifer swallowed heavily, afraid that if she spoke the first thing out of her mouth would be that Cheyenne was probably an orphan. Cheyenne gave a slow nod and took a deep breath, keeping her head held high.

"What about flag ceremony?" Paloma asked as the group went straight to the lodge, rather than to the flag ring.

"Not today," Marauder said.

Another wary glance went around the group. As everyone rounded the side of the lodge, headed for the front, the campers caught sight of Jack and Conifer's trucks and trailers parked in the ring. A few of them stopped to stare in confusion, including Cheyenne. There was no way to see the contents of the trailers from here, but it was high enough above the ring to see into the bed of Jack's stolen truck, to see all the gas cans there.

"Conifer—" Cheyenne started.

"Soon, I promise," Conifer told her.

Cheyenne looked at her with wide eyes tinged with fear but nodded once, turning to the other campers, all of whom had stopped now. "Come on, breakfast is getting cold."

The campers hesitated but then followed her and Marauder. There was another round of confused murmurs as they were taken straight inside, rather than singing out front first. Inside, a few other units had already arrived, looking just as confused, and had clustered together in their individual groups rather than spreading out at random tables. Several of the counselors were trying to lead the kids in a few songs, but it was clear everyone was too unsettled to really get into it.

Marauder took their campers to a couple tables next to the fireplace on the west wall while Conifer stepped away to talk to Jack who was leaning against the serving counter, eyes roving over those who had arrived. Behind her the counter was stacked with platters of breakfast burritos. Only breakfast burritos.

"Are you really planning to make them wait until after breakfast?" Conifer asked quietly.

"They need to eat, and they certainly won't do that if we tell them before," she replied. Heavy bags hung under her eyes and Conifer realized she'd been wearing the same clothes for two days. "I'm telling the counselors as they come in, so they'll be ready."

She was right about the food, Conifer had to admit, so she grabbed a couple platters of burritos and brought them to the tables where her group had sat down. There was already a pitcher of water and one of orange juice on each table, but that was all aside from the place settings. The other tables started to get their platters while the rest of the camp trickled in, all looking equally confused. It was the quietest breakfast

Conifer could ever remember experiencing during her time at Aspen Heart.

Once the noise of forks and knives scraping across plates, and whispered speculation, subsided, Jack stood up from the counter and walked across the room to the fireplace. Every step she took turned down the volume a little more, quiet voices dying off as everyone turned to watch her. Her face was stoic as she climbed up onto the stone ledge in front of the fireplace, giving herself an extra foot of height so everyone could see her clearly as she faced the room.

Every single camper and counselor was silent, staring up at her. No one said a word as Jack seemed to gather herself. The only sounds in the silence were the soft wind outside, and the sniffles of a few campers who had already begun to cry.

Jack took a deep breath and began what Conifer suspected was one of the hardest conversations in her life. "As many of you know, our country has been having a hard time lately. A lot of scary stuff has happened, and your parents may have told you about some of it. Over the last few days something scarier happened, and I believe you deserve to know what is going on. What appears to be a global war has begun, including within this country and this state. We are doing everything we can to find the best path forward. After a lot of tough thinking it has been decided that, for the time being, there will be no evacuation from the camp, at least not until we have more solid information about what is going on. We are safer here than we would be anywhere else. I want you all to know that, no matter what happens, you are safe in this camp and you will be safe here for as long as needed until we can get you back to your parents."

Still it was silent. Conifer could see several campers crying, their eyes wide, but not one was making a sound. Finally Cheyenne stood up from her place at Marauder's table, hands in fists at her sides, and a few tears running down her freckled cheeks. The sound of her heavy wooden bench scraping against the floor as she stood echoed through the room, making several people jump.

"You're not telling us everything," she said, anger in her voice. "I know you're trying to make it less scary, but we grew up with this. There are buckets of rocks in every classroom in my school to throw at shooters. I've marched for climate action with my mom. I ran a lemonade stand to help raise money for kids in without access to clean water in our own country. Don't fucking hide things from us because you think we can't handle it. We can."

Conifer felt like someone had shot her in the gut, and a few other counselors failed to suppress sobs, including Jack. When it seemed clear that Jack was too thrown by the statement to know what to say next, Conifer got up from her table and went to Cheyenne, putting her hands on the young girl's shoulders and looking her in the eye.

"You're right, Cheyenne," Conifer said, speaking loud enough for the whole room to hear. "You did grow up with this. I did too, maybe not as much, but more than enough. We never should have, but we did. Jack and the rest of us are going to do everything we can to find out more about what's going on, and keep you safe, but right now we're in the dark on a lot of it too. All we know for sure is that there's been multiple attacks across the country, maybe the world, including in Colorado, and there's been multiple deaths, including the president and vice president, that have thrown the government into chaos. Before we could learn more the internet and our cellphones stopped working, and they haven't come back. The radios work, but only intermittently and we have to go down the mountain to get even a little bit of signal. We managed to contact some emergency services with the satellite phone and they told us to stay put and leave the lines open. Since then the satellite phones have stopped working, and we don't know why. There's speculations that at least some of the bombs have been nuclear, but we don't know how many or where. That is all we know right now."

Cheyenne's eyes searched Conifer's and she said two more words that almost doubled Conifer over. "Colorado Springs?"

"Bombed," Conifer managed to say. The sobbing around them increased.

Cheyenne closed her eyes for a moment, then said two more words. "My mom?"

Conifer choked back a sob, forcing herself to stay together. "I don't know, sweetheart. I don't know."

Cheyenne fell forward into Conifer's arms and Conifer pulled her close, tucking Cheyenne in under her chin. She wished she could transport the two of them back to drop off, could tell Cheyenne's mother to take her home so at least they'd be together. Or maybe find some excuse for Cheyenne's mother to stay. Cheyenne sniffled against Conifer's chest and Conifer looked around to see much of the rest of the room crying and clinging to one another. The littlest campers just looked confused, upset because everyone else was rather than because of the news, and Conifer knew someone would have to break things down more for them, explain it to them in a way they could understand.

"You are safe here, all of you," Conifer said, voice firm. "You will *not* be abandoned. You will *not* be left behind. You will *not* be hurt by us. Jack, myself, and the other counselors are working on the best way to move forward, and we will let you know what it is. We will not lie to you." Conifer knew that was promising a lot, but she was bound and determined to follow through on every single promise.

Jack, still standing in front of the fireplace, nodded, tears streaking her face. "I know this is a lot, that this is hard, but we will get through it. I know most of you would feel safer all together, rather than out at your units, so we're going to move everyone into the lodge for now. It'll be cramped, but we'll make it work. Please go with your unit counselors to retrieve your sleeping bags. We're going to work on bringing all the mattresses in as well, but it might take until tomorrow to get all of them as we can't use any vehicles due to lack of gas."

The campers nodded and rubbed tears out of their eyes, sounds other than crying finally breaking out as they murmured and jostled back into their groups, seeking out their counselors. Cheyenne pulled away from Conifer and wiped her tears too, looking resolute.

"I'll help carry mattresses," she said, voice firm.

Conifer cupped her face and wiped away a tear she'd missed. Marauder had been right when she'd said Cheyenne was like her, and Conifer understood her need to be doing something no matter how terrible the last five minutes of her life had been. To have momentum.

"Remember the knots I taught y'all at the campout? And what Marauder taught you at the ropes course?" Conifer asked. She nodded. "Good girl. We can make harnesses to make them easier to carry."

Cheyenne nodded again and went to stand with the rest of the unit, the campers clustering together in one big hug, many still crying. Marauder was tucked in with the group as well, rubbing their backs and pushing away tears of her own.

"What now?" Jack asked, coming to stand at Conifer's elbow.

"Now you go get some sleep. You need it, and we need you to get it," Conifer said.

She didn't even argue, just sighed and nodded. "And then?"

"Then we prepare for the worst. Maybe, hopefully, this will be over before then, or at least over enough for us to leave, but it's better to prepare anyway."

Jack turned to face Conifer, face pinched with new worry. "This *isn't* the worst?"

"No," Conifer said quietly. "Winter is."

CHAPTER 10
COUNSELOR ROUND TABLE

It took all day, but the camp ended up getting enough mattress for all the kids down to the lodge before dark. They weren't heavy, just cumbersome. The barn operator, Horseshoe, had suggested using the horses which greatly sped things up. By securing the mattresses sideways across the horses' backs, with a girl walking on one side to keep them stable while another girl led the horse, they'd been able to bring the mattresses down in sets of four per pair of campers rather than one at a time. The horses, having spent years being ridden by excitable children, were bombproof enough that they didn't mind the strange new task.

All the tables had been folded up and put out on the wrap-around porch to make room on the floor of the dining room, the mattresses set up in long rows with only a few inches between the head of each row and the foot of the next. They didn't quite all fit, but with the mattresses all together in the rows it would still work, all the kids having a place to sleep.

Sleep didn't seem to be something they were keen on, however. They were wrapped up in their sleeping bags, but most were sitting up in little clusters on the mattresses, talking softly among themselves. Conifer had been working with the other counselors to try and get them to sleep, stopping to sooth those who were crying again, except all this had really accomplished was to get them to lie down while talking rather than sitting up. A few campers were combative, insisting the counselors had to be wrong about what was happening, and Marauder had been taking them outside to talk alone rather than upset the other kids. She'd been showing them what proof Jack had pre-loaded on her phone from her trip to the turnoff, and so far each one had come back in looking dejected, curling up in their bags without a word. The littlest ones kept asking questions about their friends, their pets, their homes, and Conifer choked on her answers to them.

After a bit Silver disappeared only to come back with her guitar. She sat on the fireplace ledge and started softly strumming, singing slow, comforting songs from the camp songbook. Things about the beauty of nature, the sisterhood of camp, the strength of friendship. Little by little the conversation died off. Silver gave one last strum of her guitar before picking her way over to Conifer where she was standing at the door, Marauder standing close by.

"I think I feel little pieces of my soul breaking off every time I look at them," Silver muttered. "They're so scared."

Conifer nodded, knowing exactly how she felt.

Jack poked her head in the door then, glancing around. None of the counselors were sleeping. There wasn't room for them on the floor. Jack waved to everyone to come outside and, after picking their way over to the door, everyone congregated on the porch. Conifer left the door cracked as the last counselor came out so they could hear if, when, any of the campers called out.

The night outside was crisp, just a tinge of the oncoming weather changes to it, but enough to make Conifer worry. Before everything went wrong the meteorologists had already been predicting a bad winter, as had the farmer's almanac. With the altitude the camp sat at, Conifer knew they were staring down the barrel of a gun.

Everyone clustered together, looking lost. Some sat on the stone steps, some in the dirt at the base of them, others stood or leaned against the porch railings. Conifer was struck by how young most of them were. There were a few older counselors, but the majority were under twenty-five, people here for a little bit of money and a place to live between the spring and fall semesters of college. Most of them weren't even that outdoorsy, just enough to be willing to take the job. And, hell, the oldest campers were only a few years younger than the youngest counselors. But, no matter their ages, there were only forty something of them, plus ten odd other adult staff members. Fifty something adults, one-hundred-sixty something kids. Nothing Conifer's parents had taught her prepared her for those sort of odds.

"Well," Jack said, looking out at everyone from the top of the steps. "This has been...a day."

The bags were mostly gone from under her eyes, and she'd changed into a new pair of jeans and a new baggy flannel, but she still looked exhausted.

"That's putting it mildly," Marauder muttered so only Conifer could hear.

"I don't understand why we can't leave," someone said.

"We have nowhere to go with this many children," Jack told her, explaining what they'd learned about the bombings on either side of the mountains, the state of the roads, the ban on using them, the direction from emergency services to shelter in place.

"What about the kids' parents?" Another spoke up.

"If any of them can get here we will of course release their children to them," Jack said. "But, at this point, there's very little way to get to the camp."

"I hate to say it," Conifer added, "but I would guess most of them used a GPS app to find their way here in the first place and with the internet down they may not even know how to get here on their own."

"Can...can *we* leave?" A tiny voice said from the back. "On our own?"

Conifer felt her shoulders tense. They couldn't afford to lose any of the adults here.

Jack took a deep breath and gave a slow nod. "Yes, any of you can. You're all over eighteen and can do what you feel you need to. But please understand that I truly think you will be safer here. If you do decide to go, please tell me before you do so I can keep an accurate count of the people in this camp."

The woman with the tiny voice spoke again and Conifer realized it was Juniper, a twenty-year-old from Mexico. "I just...I'm not saying I will, but if I did I'd send back help."

Jack nodded. "I understand, though I will say that when Conifer and I went to town yesterday we spoke with someone who was leaving, and she said she would do her best to send back help as well. Which brings us to the next point; the town has been abandoned. According to the person we spoke to, Sandra, there was a county meeting in the next town over that near everyone went to, but no one came back. She wasn't sure why, but she and the remaining few residents left to try and find out, and to send help back to us. Before she left she helped us pack up some medicine and other supplies, and after she left Conifer and I gathered as many other supplies as we could."

"Just how long do you think we're going to be here?" Polar Bear asked.

"I honestly don't know," Jack said. "But we need to prepare like it will be awhile, because if we don't..." she glanced at Conifer, "if we don't then winter is going to kill us."

This sobering statement stilled the whole group, everyone glancing around nervously.

"I'm from Georgia," Moose said warily. "I've only seen pictures of the Rockies in winter."

"They don't kid around, not up here at over nine-thousand feet," Marauder replied.

"And the cliffs that protect the camp will also protect the snow," Conifer added. "Keep it from melting due to lack of direct sun. We're basically in a bowl and if the winter gets bad there could be times when the snow is fifteen, twenty, even thirty feet deep, or more, because it just keeps building up."

"And you want to *stay*?" Moose said incredulously. "Why not at least move down into town?"

"They're on the grid," Conifer said simply. "They will lose electricity and running water, and the electricity at least already seemed to be failing when we were there yesterday. Plus, there's a much higher chance of looters down there. At least up here anyone dangerous can only feasibly come from one direction. Everything behind us is wilderness for miles."

"But there's houses there," another counselor pressed. "We can't keep all the girls and ourselves in the lodge for the whole winter! The kids will eat one another alive being crammed in like that for months."

"Yeah!" Several voices echoed.

Conifer rolled her shoulders, frustrated that they weren't getting it. "Look, I don't like the idea either. It's not the decision I would make if we were in this situation with a camp full of only older teens or adults. But the fact is we are in a camp full of kids that outnumber us four to one. There aren't easy decisions or good answers anymore. Our best chance of keeping this many kids alive through whatever comes next is with resources like clean running water, electricity, and a defensible position. Town does not have those things so right now, it isn't an option."

"Who put you in charge?" Someone spat back.

Conifer threw up her hands. "Fine. Head to town. I give it a week before everyone starts shitting themselves to death from contaminated water."

"Enough," Jack said, directing it more at the other counselors but still giving Conifer a quick, pointed glance. "We are staying here, and that is final. If you want to leave, you are allowed, as I said. Anyone who wishes to discuss things further can see me privately, or in small groups if you prefer. Winter isn't here yet, and we do still have a little time to solidify our plans."

"Fine, we stay," Moose said. "I still don't think we can keep all the kids in the lodge, and if the snow gets as bad as you say then the tents aren't an option, so where are we going to put them?"

"I've been thinking about it all day," Marauder piped up. "The platform tents are only secured into the ground with four cement blocks, one at each corner. We could dig them out and move the platforms into one spot, forming the floor for one big cabin, then building the rest with supplies from town and any leftover platforms."

Conifer straightened up, already running over the logistics, thinking of what sort of supplies she'd seen at the ranch store. "We wouldn't even have to make more than a few. A lot of campers *can* stay in the lodge. We'll have to use the space carefully, so it isn't overcrowded—"

"Who cares about overcrowded if it's safer?" Someone interrupted.

"It wouldn't be safer, though," Jack said, voice firm. "The mental safety of the girls is just as important as the physical safety. They deserve to have their own spaces, as much as we can provide."

"What about heat?" Moose asked.

"Jack and I took a bunch of cast-iron stoves from town," Conifer said. "One will be enough for each of those cabins, and we can install the rest around the lodge."

"Could work," Polar Bear said, looking contemplative. "I built houses for Habitat for Humanity last summer, up in northern Canada. We insulated them with sawdust and built hills around the sides and back for more insulation. Could do that for the cabins."

"This is good," Jack said. "There's plenty of lumber in town that we can use, and we've got the Bobcat Skidsteer in camp. We could even take the forklift from the ranch store."

"This is bullshit is what it is," someone snapped. Conifer searched the group until she saw who had spoken: Blizzard, a woman in her twenties from Oklahoma. She was standing at the base of the stairs, a few feet below Marauder, Jack, and Conifer, arms crossed tightly across her chest and glaring up at Jack and Conifer. Conifer had never talked to Blizzard much, but she knew the woman had a husband fighting in the Middle East. She'd tried to enlist as well, but due to medical issues she'd been rejected. Conifer tried to remember what those medical issues were, but she couldn't recall.

"Blizzard—" Jack started, only to be interrupted.

"Fuck that. My name is Elizabeth. This isn't some cutesy summer camp anymore, it's a deathtrap. We. Need. To. Leave," she snapped. "If Colorado, the center of the country, has been bombed, if cities have been wiped off the map, then that means this *is* a nuclear war. No maybes involved."

An unsettled rustle went through the others at this proclamation.

She wasn't wrong, but Conifer had hoped to stave off the nuclear discussion for when everyone was less panicked, after the immediate shock had faded.

"How much do you know about nuclear radiation?" Conifer asked her.

"More than you fucking do, I bet," she snapped.

"Maybe," Conifer admitted. "But I do know that if we'd had a serious exposure we'd already be showing symptoms, or at least the kids would. Nausea, vomiting, headaches, maybe even burns and blisters. Have you seen any of that?" When her only answer was a glare, Conifer continued. "I haven't. We're far enough away, and sheltered enough by the mountains, that the immediate effects of the bombs weren't a threat, at least not here. But out on the road? Who knows what we'd be exposed to."

"And what about the long-term effects?" Elizabeth growled. "Contaminated rain, contaminated dust, contaminated animals?"

Conifer shrugged, not bothering to be nice about it to someone who was being so antagonistic. "If this is really as bad as we think there's nowhere that won't have long-term effects. Cancer is the big one, obviously, and birth defects. People with prior conditions could have other problems as well. But, again, leaving won't fix that. I don't know about any of you, but I'd rather survive in relative safety and comfort here for a potentially long time rather than go out and die of radiation poisoning or cholera or whatever else tomorrow."

Elizabeth didn't answer, but she didn't look convinced either.

"There's people to worry about too," Polar Bear pointed out. "Hate to say it ladies, but enough men were dicks before this started and I doubt there'll be any less so now. Not to mention people who are just straight up desperate and willing to do anything to steal what you have."

This quieted everyone. Even Elizabeth finally looked a bit more worried than pissed.

Polar Bear continued, "I agree with Conifer and Jackalope. We need to stay here. We have resources and a defensible position. There's a shit ton of work to do, and maybe all of us won't survive, but more of us will make it here than we would anywhere else."

"Polar Bear is right," Conifer said. "People behave a lot better during disasters than Hollywood has always liked to make it seem, but at the end of the day it all comes back to the amount of kids we have with us. What would work, what would be the best answer in any other situation, won't work here. So we just have to hang tight and do the best we can."

"Anyone else want to comment?" Jack asked the now silent group. "Or can we get back to planning?"

No one said anything else, but Conifer doubted Elizabeth was really done.

"Combining the tents is a good idea," Jack said, directing the words at Marauder. "What else?"

"Food?" Robin asked.

"After emptying the store yesterday, plus with what we have here, we're at about two-and-a-half months' worth," Jack told the group.

"Oh good, so we die in November instead then," Silver replied, still cradling her guitar.

"No," Conifer said, tone firm. "That's what we have *so far*. Most people in town don't get to go to the store often, so they will hopefully have more supplies in their homes than the average person. Probably still only two or three weeks of food for their whole family, but that's still a fair amount. If we cut down to two meals a day we can extend things even more. The town has a population of around 1,000, so if we assume at least half of them are stocked for three meals a day for two weeks, that's 21,000 meals for them. For us, with about two-hundred people and two meals a day, that's an additional threeish months of food. It'll get us to spring."

"Wait, are you saying we're going to rob people?" Someone said.

"Rob or die," Silver said. "Would you like to explain to those kids that you put your morals about kicking in a door over their ability to survive? I sure wouldn't."

This quieted everyone.

"Silver is right. We aren't going in to steal personal mementos or cash or anything, we're going to retrieve food and supplies that would otherwise go to waste," Marauder said.

"We can hunt too," Conifer added. "We'll only be able to get so much, but everything will help at this point, even if only a little. Ready-made supplies should be our focus, but if we see a deer or something while we're out shooting it can't hurt."

"And there's more wild food up here than you'd think," Marauder added. "The prime season for raspberries starts any day now, plus strawberries and rosehips, and there are always mushrooms."

"We've also got eggs and milk from the animals," Horseshoe pointed out. "But, in that vein, we need to talk about the animals. There's just no way we can keep all of them fed through winter. Especially the horses."

The silence that settled over the group this time was somber.

"We can't eat them," one woman said. "We can't do that to the kids. It's like asking them to eat their pets."

A murmur of agreement went around the group. Conifer almost pointed out that not eating the horses was an easy decision to make when the freezers were still full, but she doubted anyone would care at the moment. They'd have to get to that point on their own.

"How many do you think you *can* keep alive, Horseshoe?" Conifer asked.

"Hard to say," she admitted. "I think that's a decision to be made after we raid the town a few times, see what we can get down there."

"We'll come back to it in a couple weeks or so, then," Jack said.

"Conifer, Jackalope, you said that everyone from town left intending to come back?" Trout asked. When Conifer and Jack nodded she continued, "Well, if that's the case, I'm guessing they left all their own animals behind. We could get even more food producers or, er...immediate food by taking them in. The kids don't know those animals, and I'm not saying we need to lie to them about where their food is coming from, but it might be easier that way."

Jack let out a little huff of relief, nodding. "*This* is why we crowd-source solutions."

It was clear the mood of most of the group was starting to lift a little, despite Conifer's somewhat dire math and Elizabeth's outburst. Rather than curling in on themselves as they had been when the discussion started, most everyone was sitting or standing a little straighter, leaning in towards the conversation. Conifer felt her mood lifting along with the rest of them, though in the back of her mind she knew her calculations had been on the optimistic side.

"Okay, that's food and shelter planned for. Water is easy, all our filters were replaced at the beginning of the summer and they're good for five years. The water is gravity fed out of the old volcanic spring, so it won't be contaminated by what's happened. We'll probably need to insulate a lot of pipe to keep it from freezing and breaking once the cold hits, but otherwise water is taken care of. What else?" Jack asked.

"Winter clothes," someone said.

This one was harder and everyone went quiet as they puzzled it out. Conifer was beyond grateful for the camp's policy of always having the kids bring winter coats and gloves, so they weren't starting from nothing, but still. There wasn't a clothing store in town, not for several towns, in fact. Maybe a thrift store or two, but those would be small and unpredictable in their offerings.

Marauder hmmed for a moment before turning and going through the door to the post office, coming back out with a three foot tall pad of paper, an easel, and a large marker. She wrote down "shelter" in big letters, underlined it, then made bullet points of the plans for shelter. She did the same for food and water, making a fourth list for clothing.

"Gotta keep organized," she said, wiggling the marker between her fingers.

Jack nodded.

Finally, Horseshoe spoke, looking directly at Conifer. "You know how to hunt, but do you know how to tan pelts?"

"Well, yes," Conifer said. "I'm more familiar with modern methods, but those involve chemicals that will be tricky to get. I know some other methods, like brain tanning, but I haven't practiced them as much."

"We'll take it," Marauder said, writing the word "pelts" under the clothing heading.

"I think we should use any pelts for shoes," Conifer said. "We can find clothes, but shoes in the right sizes are a lot harder, and none of the campers have snow boots. We can cut up old tires for the soles of them."

Jack agreed and Marauder put a dash next to "pelts," adding the words "shoes/tire soles."

"If we're stealing other stuff from houses, may as well take people's winter clothing as well," Silver pointed out. "We can avoid anything that looks too worn in, like it might have specific value to someone."

Marauder wrote "B&E" under "pelts."

"Wool spinning," Robin offered. "Knitting, crochet. I have lots of spindles, needles."

"Oh yeah, I gave her the wool from the sheering this spring!" Horseshoe said. "Plenty left I think. There's more sheep in town as well, and we can sheer them before using them for meat."

Marauder wrote "wool."

"Anything else?" Marauder asked. "I'm assuming B&E covers cloth and sewing supplies as well."

"Not clothing, exactly," Trout said, "but we're going to need a *lot* of sanitary pads too, and in that same vein, toilet paper."

"Sew reusable pads and toilet paper with scrap cloth from the other projects?" Someone suggested.

It was agreed this was the best plan and Marauder added it to the list under clothing. Fuel for the stoves was the next thing brought up, and Conifer explained about the log splitters and chainsaws.

"Well, I think that's a pretty damn good start," Jack said, eying Marauder's list. "It's a lot, though...."

"The kids will help," Marauder said assuredly. "They need to. Both to get it done and so they feel like they're going to be okay, like they're in control of their own fate."

"How?" Jack asked.

Marauder looked at the list, contemplating for a few moments. "Well, the youngest girls can help with carding and spinning the wool for now, and maybe with cleaning out the lodge to make room for beds. I know we've got some cloth in the craft shed, so maybe the middle girls can start sewing sanitary pads since what we have will run out quick, and the oldest girls can help start prepping the units to convert the tents into cabins. The kids can't operate the chainsaws, or splitters, but they can all help transport the wood and gather kindling from deadfall around camp."

"Nothing says camp activities like apocalypse prep," Silver said with a grin. The statement was met with a mix of nervous laughter and glares.

"It's a good plan, Marauder," Jack said. "Once we do a few more town runs we can split the girls into even more groups based on the supplies we can get."

"Who's going into town, then?" Horseshoe asked.

"You are," Conifer said. "At least for the run to get any animals."

Horseshoe was one of the other older women at the camp, somewhere in her forties, and she'd run the barn for the last eight years. All the animals the camp had, save for the horses, were bought as babies or yearlings at the beginning of the season, then sold off at the end. The horses were rented from a local ranch every spring. Horseshoe came from a family of ranchers and knew how to handle any farm animal sent her way.

"It'll be a balancing act," Horseshoe said. "We need to be able to feed anything we bring. A lot of them will have to be slaughtered."

"In that case, you should try and get some chest freezers in town as well," Jack said. "Ours are full up."

"We can preserve the meat other ways," Conifer pointed out. "Smoking, for one, we just need to be careful about when and how we do the smoking so it doesn't give away our position."

Marauder added this to the list under food.

"Alright then," Conifer said. "First run focuses on animals, freezers, lumber, and other building supplies. There's a forklift at the ranch store we should take, to help move the platforms. Jack and I stole that big truck and trailer and that can take a lot. We should probably use Jack's actual truck, rather than my Bronco, for the run, though. Something with more power that can pick up another big trailer. Maybe even steal another truck or two."

"What about gas?" Polar Bear asked. "Guessing the town station isn't expecting another delivery."

"We got a lot for the chainsaws and splitter since those are of top importance right now," Conifer said. "But the tanks at the station are huge to allow for less frequent deliveries. I'd guess some of the ranches around here have their own private tanks as well. Top off the trucks whenever you go down, and take any gas cans you find to fill up and bring back here."

"We'll need gas for the Bobcat and forklift as well," someone pointed out.

"Yes, but we'll do our best to run those as little as possible," Jack replied.

In the end the activity counselors and the cooks were selected for the first run into town the next day, allowing the unit counselors to stay with their kids for support during the first day of the new routine. This made for a group of nine, and they decided they'd stay tomorrow night in town since unloading the trailers of their current contents would take a good chunk of the morning. It was also decided that Conifer's Bronco would go, but it would be parked near the turnoff for Hunter's Gulch, concealed somehow, and the fuses to start it removed. That way every time anyone on a run passed by they could stop and try the radio to check for updates. By the time the rest of the group had organized an activity schedule for the kids the next day, it was nearing in on midnight.

"There's one other thing we need to discuss," Conifer said before the group could break up. "Defense, and safety procedures. We are a camp full of women and girls, as Polar Bear pointed out, and a place that is already well prepared to survive. Those two things, well, if anyone with bad intentions found out, it wouldn't be good." A nervous ripple went around the group as Conifer spoke. "Never mention who or where we are on any radios, even the walkies. If you manage to get on the internet do the same. We need to consider blocking off the road as well, probably even fully disabling it for vehicle traffic once our gas runs out. It *is* possible to get up here on foot and horseback, but I'll take people coming that way over people in vehicles full of who knows what. We also need to institute a blackout policy after dark, and block off any south facing windows in the lodge as an extra precaution. People can't know we are here."

"Again, who put you in charge anyway?" Elizabeth muttered.

Conifer rolled her eyes. "No one. If you don't like my advice offer a productive alternative instead of just bitching about it."

She glared but didn't say anything else.

Jack, looking more exhausted than when the conversation started, said, "*I'm* in charge. Conifer grew up with survivalist parents, so I trust what she's saying. And, as she said, alternatives are welcome. None of us know everything, but together we know a hell of a lot. We've made a good start, but it's getting late. We can discuss security, and anything else, more tomorrow."

There was a lot of worried muttering, and some sniffling and crying, but the group dispersed without further comment. A few counselors went back into the dining room, saying they'd sleep on the serving counter as it was the only room left. Others wandered into other areas of the lodge while most decided to just sleep outside in gathered tents and sleeping bags. They'd have to figure out better arrangements eventually, but for tonight this would work.

Marauder and Conifer lingered on the porch, standing shoulder to shoulder as they leaned against the railing, staring out at the stars. It looked so deceptively peaceful out there.

"It feels weird to be hopeful," Marauder said.

"A bit, yeah," Conifer agreed.

"This also almost feels too easy," she continued. "I never

pictured the apocalypse going so smoothly."

Conifer chuckled, the sound heavy in her throat. It seemed easy now, but she knew it wouldn't stay that way. Planning was one thing. Executing plans was another.

"Camps like this are designed to be self-sufficient and to teach kids how to do survival things," Conifer said eventually. "Yeah, it's usually wrapped up in a pretty package of fun activities and merit badges, but we were always prepared for this in some form, even if it was mostly for teaching."

"I suppose that's true," she agreed. After a pause she continued, "Do you really think we can make it through winter, if it comes to that?"

Conifer glanced back at Marauder's list, which had been left out. "I think we've got a solid plan, and that believing in it is just as important as having it."

"Would you tell me if you didn't believe it?" She asked, voice so soft Conifer almost missed the words.

Conifer didn't answer.

Marauder sighed and nodded. "And Bliz—Elizabeth? Juniper?"

Conifer shrugged. "They're upset, grieving, and they have every right to be. Everyone is going to take this differently. Elizabeth went straight to the anger stage. Hopefully she won't stay there."

"What about you?"

"What about me?"

"What stage are you at?"

Conifer thought about it for awhile. She sucked at analyzing her own feelings. That was something she'd known about herself for a long time. She didn't think she was angry, and she didn't have any gods to be bargaining with. She certainly wasn't in denial about what was happening.

"A little overwhelmed," Conifer decided, "I guess. There's a lot happening at once. The way I grew up...I was raised to survive on my own, or in a more balanced group. I know how to do that. But this? With so many kids relying on me, on us?

It feels like everything I was ever taught has flown out the window."

Marauder sighed, bending over to rest her chin on her folded arms. "Yeah. It's...scary. I love being a camp counselor, I really do. And I know I signed up to protect them and keep them safe through anything, but I'm pretty sure 'nuclear world war' was not in the brochure."

"We just have to keep moving," Conifer said eventually. "We'll have time to grieve later."

Marauder heaved a long, slow sigh, still focusing on the stars. They stayed there in silence for awhile, Marauder stepping aside for a moment to move the list of plans inside before coming back out to the railing.

"Sorry to interrupt," Jack said from behind them.

They both jumped, turning to find Jack standing in the doorway to the second floor.

"Could I have a moment alone with Conifer, please?" Jack asked.

"Of course," Marauder said with a yawn. She gave a little wave and wandered off to, presumably, find some sort of flat surface to sleep on.

Jack watched her go before waving Conifer inside. She didn't go far, turning to face Conifer in the dimly lit alcove on the other side of the door. She contemplated Conifer a moment, then sighed, sitting down on the stairs.

"That was quite the day," she said.

Conifer nodded in agreement, leaning against the door with her arms crossed.

"Conifer, you can't bite people's heads off for asking basic questions," Jack said.

Conifer shrugged. She didn't have time for being nice right now.

"No. I know you turned me down when we were in town, but I truly believe the future of this camp involves you being in charge, so you need to be willing to be a little more patient with people."

Conifer let out a long, slow breath. "What today proved is that, like you said, we need to be working together. Which we are. So why change things up?"

"Conifer—"

"I said no, Jack. Like you said, I'm impatient and I bite people's heads off. I'm not a leader. I can help, I can point in the right direction, but I am not, nor will I ever be, in charge."

Without waiting for her to speak again, Conifer turned and left.

CHAPTER 11
PREP WORK BEGINS

"Hrrgg. I vote we steal memory foam mattresses next," Marauder groaned, extracting herself from her sleeping bag that she'd spread out next to Conifer's on the porch.

"I doubt there's many of those in town," Conifer replied, stretching and yawning before wiggling out of her bag as well. "Also, have you ever tried to sleep on memory foam in the cold? It turns into a brick."

"Let me dream."

Around them everyone else was waking too, many with the same complaints as Marauder. The cots back in the tents were hardly top of the line, but they were better than wooden planks or the hard packed walkway dirt in front of the porch. Conifer watched as Marauder did a series of stretches, working the kinks out of her back with a couple loud cracks that had her sighing in contentment. No sounds came from the diningroom where the kids were sleeping, but it was only a matter of time. Jack had said they'd be doing breakfast burritos again, since they were easy to eat without plates so they wouldn't need to worry about bringing the tables back in.

After that it would be time to jump headfirst into, as Silver was calling it, their first day of the apocalypse. When she'd started calling it that Conifer realized she didn't even know when the real first day was. The not-thunder had obviously been the bombings in Colorado, but when had the *first* bombs dropped, and where? Somehow Conifer had never bothered to check during the short times the opportunity had arisen to do so. Had it all happened the night of the not-thunder, or had some of them been dropped earlier? It had to have been after dropoff, at the earliest. Maybe that night? Maybe the next morning?

Conifer wandered into the diningroom, finding some of the campers beginning to stir. Cheyenne was snuggled in between Farrah and Aadila, her hair still in braids but the bun undone, leaving the braids to snake out across her pillow. There was a crust of tears on her eyelashes and Conifer sighed as she bent down to wake her, gently stroking her hair.

"Time to get up, Cheyenne, Farrah, Aadila."

Cheyenne pried her eyes open, rubbing away the crust around her eyes and sniffing as she looked up at Conifer. "Any chance yesterday was a bad dream?"

"Sorry, hun," Conifer told her.

"I miss my parents," Aadila sniffled, eyes widening as soon as the words were out of her mouth, glancing at Cheyenne.

"It's alright, Aadila," Cheyenne said quietly, giving a little shrug. "I hope yours are okay."

Conifer pulled her and the other two into a tight hug, then moved on to help wake everyone else. No one really moved from their beds. Most didn't even get out of their sleeping bags, just sat up and clustered together in little knots that quietly watched the counselors picking their way around the room. Foil wrapped burritos were passed out, with instructions to save the foil, along with bottles of water.

"So," Jack said, taking her spot at the fireplace again, her voice loud enough to be heard across the room. "I'm sure there's a lot of questions, and I think now is a good time for us counselors to do our best to answer them. First, though, let me tell you what our plan is."

She went into most everything the counselors and other staff had all discussed last night: the preparations, the supplies, the runs to town, the new activities everyone would be doing. She left out any mention of nuclear radiation or possible invasion from hostile people, though. Conifer watched from next to the fireplace, leaning against the wall as she ate her burrito. All the kids looked scared but the youngest looked the worst, eyes wide and faces still splotchy from crying. Conifer made a mental note to ask Horseshoe and the others going on the run today to look for stuffed animals, some little piece of personal comfort for the kids. Board games too. Survival wasn't just food and shelter, it was mental. If they were going to be locked up in close quarters all winter they'd need things to keep them distracted.

"Questions?" Jack asked.

"What happens when this is over?" A girl no more than ten asked.

Jack glanced at Conifer and she could read the debate in the older woman's eyes. Should they give them hope that was likely false, or should they be honest with them?

"I don't know right now," Jack said after a beat. "I wish I could answer that for you, but I just don't know. None of us do. A lot will change, but I can't guess at how."

"What cities have been bombed?" An older girl, maybe fourteen or fifteen, asked. Fifteen was the oldest age among the kids in this session, and there were no junior counselors around this time either.

Jack listed off the cities they knew of, adding that there were more but she didn't know which ones.

"I want to go home," one of the littlest campers sniffled. "Why won't you let us go home?"

"Your home is gone, stupid," a girl a few years older snapped.

"Hey, hey," Marauder said, stepping up to the girl who snapped as she was closest. Silver had gone to the girl who'd spoken originally, who was now sobbing, to scoop her up and comfort her. Marauder knelt down in front of the girl who snapped and who was now sending furtive glances at the crying girl. "What's your name?" Marauder asked.

"Wanda," the girl muttered. Conifer guessed she was around ten or eleven.

"Wanda, that wasn't a nice thing to do," Marauder said.

"But I'm *right*," Wanda said.

Marauder sighed, glancing around at everyone, all of them watching the exchange in silence. "It doesn't matter if you're right or not, the way you said it wasn't okay. Everyone is scared, and we need to help one another, not make them feel worse."

"But I'm *right*," Wanda repeated, tears gathering in her own eyes. "It's gone. It's all gone. Her home is gone. My home is gone. It's all gone."

"I know," Marauder said softly. "But that doesn't give you the right to be mean, and that was mean. Can you please try not to be mean from now on?"

Wanda sniffled and, after a pause, she nodded. Marauder gave her a gentle hug before standing back up.

"You said only some of us can stay in the lodge," another girl asked after a moment of silence. "Who gets to stay?"

"Priority will be given to the youngest campers first," Jack said. "But before we make any decisions on that we need to figure out exactly how many people can fit comfortably, which is what I'll be doing today. I'll get you a more solid plan for where everyone will be staying in the next few days."

No more questions were forthcoming, so Jack dismissed everyone. No one moved, though, until Cheyenne stood up, looking around at her fellow campers.

"Well, let's get started then," she said.

The room shuffled into motion at her words and Conifer felt a flare of pride tinged with sorrow. Having a camper willing to step up and lead the way just as much as the counselors would help close the divide between the kids and the adults, help the campers see that everyone was working together. See that the counselors weren't just some ridiculous adults with strange schemes. But Cheyenne shouldn't have had to do it. None of them should have.

"Marguerite, meet out front under the tree!" Marauder called out over the noise.

Conifer saw Jack trying to get her attention but pretended she hadn't seen her, moving outside with the crowd. She found Marauder already explaining to their campers that they'd be spending the day cleaning out the storage shed and inventorying what was in there, leaving it empty so that it could be converted into another barn. They followed Marauder and Conifer quietly to the shed, just off the north side of the flag ring, and all gathered around the east doors. It was an old log structure, turned gray-brown with age and only about seven-feet tall with a flat, sloping tin roof. The char mark up the west side had been rained on enough that it no longer looked fresh. Looking at it now, Conifer couldn't believe it had happened only a few weeks ago. It had seemed so important at the time, like it was the worst thing that could have ever happened. Conifer wondered where the girl who lit the fire was now.

"When exactly was the last time this was cleaned out?" Cheyenne asked as Conifer wrestled the double doors open, fighting the rust on the hinges.

"Probably never," Conifer grunted, using her foot to slide a rock in front of each door.

"Let's just start by pulling things out onto the grass out front, and sorting them into piles based on what they are," Marauder suggested. She'd wrestled the doors at the west end of the fifty foot long building open as well.

The kids nodded and split up into two teams, one working from each end. A couple of them, Lorelai and Tai, just went and sat in front of the shed, whispering quietly to one another as tears leaked out of their eyes. Conifer guessed they were talking about their parents, Lorelai's mother the senator and Tai's military parents, and left them to it for now. Counselors barging into every conversation would just make things worse. They still deserved some privacy to work out their feelings.

The rest of the kids were silent as they worked, speaking only to get one another's attention or ask for a moment of help. Conifer left them to their thoughts as well while she and Marauder helped with the heavier stuff because, really, what could she say?

On Conifer's end of the shed the first thing they came across was a pile of the camp's backpacking backpacks. Some campers who came for the backpacking sessions brought their own, but most borrowed one of these. There were all sorts, sizes, and ages. Faded army green ones, roughed up and patched red ones, mud splattered blue ones. They set up a line and passed them out one by one, stacking them in the grass.

As a green one went down the line it stopped midway when Cheyenne failed to pass it on to Orla. Cheyenne gave it an experimental shake, then flipped open the top and stuck an arm in, pulling it back out to reveal a monster potato covered in white and green sprouts clutched in her hand. She and the other kids all stared at it in confusion. Conifer did too, trying to figure out how a potato had gotten in there. The bag had been towards the front of the pile, so it had likely been used somewhat recently, but they were sticklers for making sure all food got removed from the bags after they were used to prevent issues with animals.

"Well," Cheyenne said, still holding the spud aloft, tentacle-like sprouts dangling down. The kids on the other end of the shed, including Marauder, stopped to stare in confusion too. "If this is what it looks like before radiation, I can't imagine what it's going to look like later."

There was a moment of silence after Cheyenne's deadpan delivery, then laughter slowly bubbled up out of everyone. Morbid or not, the comment had clearly broken the tension. Cheyenne looked pleased, smiling as she handed the thing off to Conifer. Conifer chuckled as well, turning the sprawling tuber over a few times to examine it.

"Maybe we can plant it and see if it'll grow," Marauder said.

"Can't hurt to try," Conifer agreed. "Throw it in a big pot and keep it inside out of the cold."

"We'll have to give it a name," Marauder declared, poking at one of the white sprouts.

"It's a potato?" Cheyenne said, eyebrows pulled down in confusion.

"I vote for 'The Magnificent Spud!'" Tabatha said, voice giddy.

It was decided by the others that this was agreeable and they set The Magnificent Spud on a rock safely out of the way before diving back into the shed. This time there was a lot more conversation, the kids marveling over the treasures being uncovering and speculating about ways to adapt them for survival. Even Lorelai and Tai joined in, though their eyes were rimmed with red.

"Why are there so many license plates stacked over here?"

"Are the backsides still shiny? Maybe we can use them as reflectors for heat?"

"Ohhh, look, a spinning wheel! It's kind of broken, though."

"I bet we can fix it. We'll bring it to the art shed."

"Is this a wheel from a stagecoach?"

"I don't know what we could use that for, but it is neat."

"Maybe we could make another spinning wheel with it!"

"Oooo, metal prospecting pans!"

"We can cook in those."

"Look at these cool walking sticks!"

After a quick break for lunch in front of the lodge—peanut butter and jelly sandwiches—they were back at it, finishing clearing out the last of the shed.

"Woah, look at this," Sammy-Jo said, bending down and brushing her hands across a patch of the dirt floor that had been exposed.

Conifer could just make out some large letters appearing under her fingers. Quickly everyone came over, helping to uncover the old metal sign that had been buried. It took about twenty minutes, but eventually they had the eight foot by two foot sign pried out of the dirt and hauled outside, leaning it up against the front of the shed. It was still clogged with dirt hanging onto the raised metal letters, rust flaking off where the dirt had fallen away, but the words were clear enough.

Aspen Heart
Where Girls Become Strong
This sign was made and dedicated by the girls of the summer of 1946.

"We're cleaning this up," Marauder said. "Cleaning it, and hanging it under the current sign down at the gate."

"No, at the lodge," Conifer said. "From the porch. So everyone can see it."

There was something extremely comforting in the fact that the sign had been made in 1946. Those campers had gone through war too, if in a different way. They'd survived. Maybe some of that luck would rub off on the people here now.

Everything from the shed was cataloged in a notebook, then brought up to be re-stored in the cellar of the lodge. The Sybil Ludington unit had spent the day cataloging and organizing down there. Silver's unit, made up of the oldest campers, had spent the morning helping unload the rest of Jack and Conifer's trailers and cataloging the contents of them as well as the frozen food that had already been unloaded. All the records were turned in to Jack's office as everyone headed to dinner.

Unpacking the trailers had taken longer than expected due to having to haul everything up the steep hill to the lodge one box at a time, rather than hauling things in batches on carts. Finding room for all of it had been tricky as well. This had delayed the run into town until tomorrow, which Conifer was grateful for as it gave her a chance to clean out her Bronco before it was taken down the hill. Conifer intended to do so while the kids were having dinner, but as she turned to leave them at the lodge Cheyenne came up and asked where she was going.

"Need to clean out my truck," Conifer told her.

"Can I come?" She asked. "It's just…I kinda want to be somewhere…quiet for awhile."

Conifer searched her eyes, seeing the tiredness there. She'd cheered up the rest of the group, but Conifer doubted she'd managed to make herself feel much better.

"Yeah, run inside and tell Marauder you're coming with me, and grab yourself a plate of whatever's for dinner, then meet me by the cellar."

She nodded and disappeared inside. Conifer retrieved the largest backpacking pack she could find, then turned to wait for Cheyenne. She appeared a moment later, holding two things wrapped in foil along with a couple forks. There was just a hint of a grin on her face as she offered Conifer one of the foil wrapped packages.

"We're having baked potatoes."

Conifer snorted and took one, enjoying the warmth of it pressed against her palm and thanking Cheyenne as they headed down to the Bronco. They sat on the ground, leaning against the front bumper, to eat. The potatoes were cut into slices and drenched in butter, seasoned with pepper and a blend of other spices, dripping messily onto their hands. Cheyenne didn't say anything and neither did Conifer, content to enjoy the silence together. When Conifer finished she shook out the foil, smoothed it out, and folded it up, setting it aside with her fork to bring back to the lodge.

Absently, she wiped her buttery hands on her pants, bringing to mind that laundry had gotten a lot more complicated now. They had three washers and three driers at camp, but they were meant for just the counselors and emergency washing for the kids. They were not enough to handle all the laundry they'd now have. Just another thing they hadn't considered and would have to figure out a solution for. Conifer was sure there would be a lot more in that category as time wore on.

There wasn't much in Conifer's Bronco that hadn't already made its way into her tent back at the unit, but Conifer still wanted to get every last thing out just in case she never saw it again. The photos tucked into the visor, the odd socks that seemed to be everywhere, the water bottles that had rolled under the seats. Her get-home bag was in there too; a supply of just the things she would have needed to get somewhere safe if she'd been alone when shit hit the fan. It contained a few days worth of freeze-dried meals, a basic medical kit, a compass, a water filter, and some other important bits and bobs. Conifer was already somewhere safe, though, so the kit didn't really matter aside from being something else to catalog and add to the group supplies. There *were* a few things of more importance in the Bronco as well, however. Her winter boots, six sets of gloves, a wool balaclava, two of her own winter jackets, two pairs of fleece lined pants, and....

Conifer glanced up at Cheyenne through the windshield, making sure she was still occupied with watching the horses in their pasture on the east side of the ring, before Conifer popped open her glove compartment halfway. She reached into the hollow space above it and felt her hand close on the grip of her pistol, held up there by a magnetic holster where the airbag was supposed to be. The airbag had been sacrificed to make room for the radio, but there had still been space left. It made for a good hidey-hole. Conifer pulled the gun out and wrapped it in the balaclava before Cheyenne could see, stuffing it deep into the pack she'd brought. The two boxes of bullets came next, each quickly stuffed out of sight as well.

Conifer had always been drawn towards archery more than guns, but she kept the pistol anyway as a backup. Arrows could kill just as quickly if not quicker than a bullet, but bows were better for hunting than being hunted, and if there was ever a mountain lion or a bear after her, she wanted the easiest option at her side. Jack didn't know Conifer had it, and if she did Conifer would've been fired without question, but what else was Conifer supposed to do with it? It was a huge pain in the ass to try and mail a gun, not to mention she'd have no address for them to eventually send it back to her at. She'd come directly to camp from her last job on a dude ranch, and her original plan had been to go straight on to whatever job she ended up working next. Keeping the gun and hiding it away had just been the most convenient solution. If war hadn't broken out no one would've ever known.

Conifer slammed the glove compartment shut and gave it a little wiggle so it would latch, then cast her eyes around the now empty vehicle. Taking a step back and pulling the stuffed pack with her, she slammed the door shut.

"You better not start if anyone brings their own parts and tries to steal you," Conifer said, patting the closed door fondly.

"Done?" Cheyenne asked, standing up and brushing off her pants.

Conifer nodded and heaved the pack up to perch it on the running boards, squatting down to wiggle her arms into the straps.

"Conifer...can I ask you something?" Cheyenne asked as Conifer stood and secured the waist buckle.

"Anything."

She took a deep breath before plunging on, her voice

quick. "My mom is probably dead, and we have no other family. Not even some distant cousin or anything. So…if this does end…what's going to happen to me?"

Conifer searched her expression, saw the building tears in the corners of her eyes, noted her use of the word "if" in relation to things ending. Conifer stepped forward and put her hands on Cheyenne's shoulders. "If we get to the point where we leave this camp, whenever that may be, you are staying with me. As far as I'm concerned, from this point forward, you are my little sister."

It was the easiest thing in the world to say, and Conifer meant it.

Cheyenne sniffed and nodded, leaning in for a hug made slightly difficult by the huge pack Conifer had on.

"Thanks, Conifer," she said, the words mumbled into Conifer's shirt.

⁂

"Jack, I need to talk to you for a second," Conifer said, looking up at her from the bottom of the porch steps. She couldn't help but notice that Jack looked completely exhausted again, more than anyone else.

The campers had all been put to bed, still in the diningroom, and most of the counselors were sleeping in tents out front, now on more mattresses that had been brought down. Conifer had kept the borrowed pack full of her stuff with her and well away from the kids, and other counselors, all evening until everyone else was asleep or busy elsewhere.

Jack came down off the porch and watched as Conifer dug into the pack, inhaling sharply when Conifer pulled out the pistol and handed it to her.

"You're fired," she muttered.

"I appreciate that you seem to believe you'll still be able to pay me at some point," Conifer returned, earning just the smallest quirk of Jack's lips.

"It's a 9mm," Conifer told her. "Currently unloaded, and I've got a hundred rounds in my bag."

"We should send it with the people doing runs into town," Jack said after a moment. "I was going to send the camp rifle with them, but this will be less cumbersome."

It was probably a lot more accurate than the old, neglected camp rifle as well. That gun was kept around for much the same reason as Conifer's pistol—uppity animals with large teeth—but Conifer doubted it got as much maintenance as her pistol.

"Your camp, your rules," Conifer said, handing her the two boxes of ammo as well. "But with that said, we should be taking more guns from town too. For defense, for hunting, and just so one else can get them."

Jack nodded, staring at the items in her hands and swallowing heavily. "We'll add gun safety and shooting lessons to the activity schedule as well."

"As long as we're careful about the sound carrying. I was thinking we could use the auditorium," Conifer suggested. The auditorium was a large cavern at the base of the western cliffs, a little more than halfway up to the crater. It would dampen the sound nicely, given the small entrance. As long as they had ear protection for everyone inside, it would be fine.

"Do you think we could store stuff in there as well?" Jack asked. "That cave network is huge, and it'll stay a good temperature."

"I mean, yeah, but we'd have to hand-carry everything up there and we won't be able to get at any of it all winter," Conifer pointed out. "And, as big as it is, the auditorium is the only large area we can access without spelunking." Conifer thought about it a bit more. "The caves could make a good seed vault, though, and that wouldn't be a bad thing to have."

Jack nodded again, eyes focused on the gun as she ran her thumb back and forth above the trigger.

"One other thing," Conifer said. "The cabins we're

planning, the ranch store likely won't have enough supplies to build all of them. We'll need to strip material from houses and check farms for more lumber and hardware."

Jack surveyed Conifer. "Would you continue to ignore me if I asked you to officially be in charge again?"

Conifer answered honestly. "Yes."

"I need you to tell me why, Conifer," Jack said, looking so intently into Conifer's eyes it made her skin itch and she had to look away.

"I just can't, Jack. This is—I know a lot, I'm not denying that, I just—I can't," Conifer fumbled.

Jack continued to stare at Conifer before sighing, letting the gun drop to her side. "I wish you'd reconsider.

"I won't."

"Just think about it, please," she said, not giving Conifer a chance to answer before she turned to go into the lodge.

Conifer watched the closed door she'd gone through, listening to her ascend the stairs, before dragging her pack over to the tent Marauder had set up for them. Marauder was already asleep inside and Conifer crawled into her sleeping bag that Marauder had spread out on the mattress next to her. Exhaustion had been creeping up on Conifer all afternoon, the stress of the last few days weighing heavier and heavier on her shoulders, and she was out within moments.

CHAPTER 12
HUNTING

Three days had passed since what they'd deemed Day 1, and the mood of the camp seemed to have lifted slightly. There was still an air of worry, of fear, over campers and counselors alike, but it was hard to stay worried when the sky was still blue, the trees still green, and things were getting done. It didn't feel like the world had ended here, and Conifer was of two minds on that. On the one hand, it was an enormous relief because every day that passed without signs of radiation sickness meant they were a little bit safer. Never entirely safe, of course, but she'd take whatever she could get. On the other hand, it made it harder to keep up the urgency she knew they needed to survive.

Two counselors had left, feeling things couldn't actually be that bad, and that they'd do fine out on the road. Juniper, the young woman from Mexico, and another woman who went by the name Trapper. Elizabeth, surprisingly, had stayed, though her attitude hadn't improved much. Jack gave Juniper and Trapper a pack with two days of food and a pump water filter each, but beyond that had only allowed them to take their own belongings. Conifer gave them a basic rundown of where to try to go, how to try to stay alive, how to recognize signs of radiation sickness and what to do about it. Juniper seemed to waver as Conifer told her about the level of contamination that was possible outside the shelter of the mountains, but she'd still gone.

Jack had done the math and determined that, if they built bunkbeds, they could fit around one-hundred-thirty-seven people in the lodge, leaving a couple areas open to serve as communal spaces. That left about ninety people needing shelter, and how those ninety would be divided was still being worked out. The youngest campers were given priority in the lodge, along with their counselors, as were any other kids and other counselors with medical issues that made the cold more dangerous. The units of the oldest campers, including Marauder and Conifer's, would be building cabins in the manner Marauder had suggested, but it had been decided to build them closer to the lodge rather than where the units currently sat. Conifer's group had moved all their belongings to the new area already, living in regular tents and beginning prep work for combining most of the platform tents into one cabin.

Marauder and Conifer weren't with them this morning, though, leaving them with Moose and Robin. Conifer had wanted to get started hunting as soon as possible, mostly for the sake of pelts so they'd have time to tan as many as possible before winter hit, and Marauder had asked to come with so she could start learning how to hunt as well. They were in the barn now, saddling up a couple horses, an hour before dawn. Marauder had to stand on an apple crate to swing her saddle up onto the back of the appaloosa she'd selected. Conifer picked an older bay mare named Knight. She gently prodded Knight in the side with her knee as she tightened the girth, knowing Knight had a tendency to suck in air and bloat herself up, preventing the saddle from being tight enough. Knight let out a huff, exhaling the extra air, and Conifer tightened the girth a few more notches.

"Logically, I understand the benefits of hunting," Marauder said, hopping up into her saddle. "But why do all the tasty critters have to be so cute?"

"You're going to have to get over that if you're going to

keep hunting with me," Conifer pointed out, swinging into her own saddle.

Conifer had rigged up a hanger for her compound bow on the side of the saddle using some stiff wire and leather cording, hanging a quiver of extra arrows on the other side. She had eighteen hunting arrows, sixteen of them standard points and two of them with special tips for bird hunting. It wasn't much. Even if she was careful, arrows were easy to lose. To break. There'd been two runs into town now, and Conifer had asked that on the next one someone try to find more arrows, maybe even another good bow or two so she could teach more people to hunt. Lots of the other counselors knew how to shoot a bow, but they'd never hunted with one. One of the fifteen-year-old campers in Silver's unit was a bow hunter, though, and she'd offered to go with Conifer. Conifer was planning on taking her out to the range sometime in the next week so she could get a real idea of her skills. Guns were an option for hunting as well, but for now Conifer wanted to stick to the quieter option as much as possible.

"They're just so fuzzyyyyy," Marauder said.

"Fuzzy is exactly why we're shooting them," Conifer replied. "Fuzzy critters make warm shoes."

Marauder groaned as they left the barn, leaning over to close the door behind them before they set off down the road. The sky to the east showed the faintest hint of blue crawling into the black, but dawn was still a way off. They were sticking to the south side of camp today, rather than heading up the cliffs to the better hunting grounds, so that they could also check the road for signs of other people. Conifer wanted to survey the road for ways to disable it when they were done with it as well, but that wasn't an immediate concern. They still had a lot of supplies to bring up from town.

It wasn't that there weren't deer and elk on the south side, there were just less, and they tended to be more skittish of humans from being exposed to them more often. However, Conifer was hopeful that she could get at least a few down here as it would be quicker than a trip up the cliffs. Any hunting attempts up there would have to be at least three days: one to go up and get settled, at least one to hunt, and one to get back down. They'd probably need to involve multiple people as well, to make them worth it.

"So, how's this work?" Marauder whispered. They were still on the road and, for now, Conifer was content to stick to it, sliding her eyes back and forth through the trees.

"Well, honestly, today I'm looking for sign more than anything," Conifer whispered back. "If I can find a few good deer trails I'll come back and put up some tree stands. But other than that it's sort of just wandering and seeing if we see anything. If we do I'll probably get off Knight and give you her reins, then try to follow it on foot to get a better shot."

"How far can you make a deer or an elk go, supply wise?" Marauder asked.

"Not very," Conifer admitted. "Not for two-hundred people. But everything counts."

"Didn't they used to chase whole herds of animals off cliffs to get a lot at once?" Marauder said. "We have cliffs."

Conifer chuckled. "Yeah, some cultures did that. I guess if we got desperate we could try, but it would probably ruin most of the animals. Our cliffs are too high. Things that die scared don't taste good, and neither do ones that die from blunt trauma. It would probably tear up the pelts too."

Marauder nodded and they lapsed back into silence. There were some tracks in the soft dirt on the side of the road in a few places, but most looked like they were at least a few days old and from smaller yearling deer. Conifer let her mind dance between hunting and disabling the road. There were several places where one of the creeks passed under the road through culverts, and those could easily be blocked to divert the water over the road and wash it out, but the creeks were running shallow this late in the season and likely wouldn't do enough to matter. Explosives weren't a good option either, as they risked exposing the camp's location. Downing trees was a possibility, but trees could be moved. When the snow came it would prevent even the hardiest of four-wheel drives from making it up the mountain, but it would do nothing to stop snowmobiles if they still had any good gas. Maybe wreaking cars across the road would work. They might be harder to move than trees, if positioned properly, but with enough snowfall even they wouldn't provide an obstacle during the height of winter.

"What are you thinking about?" Marauder whispered.

"Destruction," Conifer admitted, clarifying that she meant the road when Marauder looked confused. Conifer laid out her ideas and Marauder hmmed softly, glancing all around.

"Hate to say it," Marauder said, "but short of learning earthbending to make a fourth cliff on this side there's just no way to prevent all access."

"Nerd," Conifer chuckled, pleased to understand the reference even though she didn't watch all that much TV and never really had. "You're right, though. We'll just have to do what we can. Road spikes and downed trees for now, wreaking cars on the road, and wash out the road with the spring melt."

"Soooo," Marauder said a few minutes later, her voice still quiet. "Jackalope came to talk to me this morning."

Conifer glanced over at her for a long moment before answering. "Oh?"

"Mmmmhm."

"And was your topic of conversation something along the lines of me taking control of the camp?"

"Sure was."

Conifer groaned. "I'm not doing it."

"Why?" Marauder asked, her tone genuinely curious.

Conifer squirmed under her gaze, trying to come up with a reasonable excuse. She'd come up with many that seemed reasonable at first over the last few days, but if she looked too closely at them they all tended to start falling apart.

So she'd just stopped looking closely.

"Well," Marauder said after an extended silence, "I think you'd be good at it, if you did. But it's up to you."

"Think you can convince Jack that it's up to me?" Conifer muttered.

"Nope, because I think she's right, remember?" Marauder replied. "I'm just not going to push it. If you don't want her to push it too, take it up with her."

Conifer sighed and clucked her tongue to get Knight moving a bit faster. With dawn getting closer Conifer turned them off the road and into the trees. There was some deadfall they had to negotiate, but mostly the floor of the forest here was clear, though rocky and steep in areas.

Conifer was urging Knight over a downed tree the mare had deemed suspicious when she felt something thunk softly against her arm. Conifer turned back to see Marauder gesturing through the trees down towards the road. Following the line of her arm it took Conifer a moment to pick out what she'd seen; a large human figure striding along the road below them. Whoever they were they had on an external frame backpacking pack, sleeping pad strapped to the bottom, and a sunflower yellow hoodie, the hood pulled up against the chill of the morning and obscuring their face. Maybe it was a trick of perspective, but the person looked huge. And they weren't someone from the camp. Everyone but Juniper and Trapper were *in* camp, and neither Juniper nor Trapper were the size of this person.

Gesturing to Marauder to do the same, Conifer dismounted, tying Knight's reins loosely to a low branch before lifting her bow off its mount and nocking an arrow.

"Behind me," Conifer mouthed to Marauder, keeping the arrow aimed down.

She did as requested, stepping where Conifer stepped as she worked her way through the trees, keeping an eye on the bright yellow hoodie wearer working their way up the road. Maybe the person was friendly, just a backpacker who was looking for a place to hide out. Maybe they didn't even know they were heading towards Aspen Heart. But maybe the apocalypse was about to get a little more apocalyptic, and this person wasn't here for any good reason. Conifer wasn't willing to take the chance.

Getting closer, Conifer realized that it hadn't been a trick of perspective; Hoodie really was huge. Easily over six feet tall, broad shouldered, black pants tight around thighs that, if Hoodie's speed up the incline was any indication, were solid muscle. Approaching from behind, though, Conifer still couldn't see their face.

Conifer turned back to whisper to Marauder that they needed to change direction so they could come out ahead of the person at the switchback they were all heading towards, only to find that Marauder wasn't there. Before Conifer had a chance to register any real worry a twig snapped along the road. Conifer turned back just in time to see Marauder pop out behind the person at a run, leap, jam her foot into the space between the sleeping pad and the bottom of the backpack, push herself up, and wrap her hands around the top bar of the frame. Hoodie gave a surprised shout, arms pinwheeling, but before they could do anything Marauder used her weight and location to fling the person sideways and land on top of them. Hoodie landed facedown in a sprawling heap on the dirt road with Marauder on their back, Marauder reaching around to grab one of their arms and twist it backwards in a painful manner.

Conifer scrambled out, not entirely sure what just happened, but realizing now was not the time for hesitation. Conifer drew her bow and pointed the arrow at Hoodie's head, their hood still up, as they spluttered and wiggled in the dirt. Between the awkward weight of their backpack, Marauder's weight, Marauder's hold, and the doubtless pain of being slammed into the dirt, Hoodie didn't seem to be going anywhere.

"I'm armed. Who are you?" Conifer snapped, finger

hovering above the trigger on her caliper release.

"Firefighter! I'm a firefighter!" The person, a woman Conifer now realized from her voice, gasped. "I went to Aspen Heart as a kid and I met a woman on the road who said the camp needed help!"

Conifer eyed her for a minute, glancing up at Marauder. Marauder shrugged, the woman's hand still held in her own. After debating for a moment longer Conifer nodded for Marauder to move and told the woman to sit up, slowly, but not stand. Marauder scurried to stand behind Conifer as the woman got to her hands and knees before wiggling and wincing her way into a sitting position. She had messy brown hair in a ponytail hanging out the side of her hood, bright blue eyes, and a fresh scrape oozing blood on her square chin. Her hoodie was emblazoned with the logo of the Grand Lake Volunteer Fire Department.

"What's your name?" Conifer asked, keeping her aim steady. Even with the draw locked in she was starting to feel her muscles burn with the strain of holding it.

"Valora," she said, glancing between the two of them. "Wait...if *you're* armed, that means *you* flipped me?"

"Yep," Marauder said. Conifer couldn't see her, but she could hear how pleased she was.

"But you're *tiny*," Valora said. "Like, really, really tiny."

"Also an MMA featherweight champion for the last three years," Marauder said proudly.

"Well...ah...good for you I guess?" Valora said from the ground. "I'm twenty-three and was going to college to be an arson investigator."

Conifer raised her eyebrows. "Thanks for the info?"

"Just trying to humanize myself to the lady with an arrow pointed at my face," Valora replied.

Conifer sighed and lowered it, slowly releasing the draw without firing, but she kept the arrow noced. "You said you went to Aspen Heart. When?"

"Only a couple times," Valora said. "Once when I was ten

and once again when I was twelve."

Conifer stared at her, studying her features as a twinge of recognition crept into her mind. "I think...I remember you. You were the tallest kid at camp. Six feet at twelve-years-old. Taller than anyone else there, including the counselors."

Valora looked relieved. "Yep. Six-six now. Everyone in my family is over six feet."

Marauder let out a soft whistle behind her and Conifer realized this meant that, standing, Valora would be an impressive eighteen inches taller than Marauder and eight inches taller than Conifer.

Valora grinned, looking at Marauder. "Do I win for biggest takedown you've ever had?"

"By far."

"What's the name of the woman who sent you?" Conifer interrupted, trying to get the conversation back on track.

"Sandra, she's a pharmacy technician. We met walking along a frontage road. She said she'd met a couple of counselors from Aspen Heart who told her no one had come to evacuate the camp, and who asked her to send back help," Valora said.

Conifer wanted to point out that they hadn't asked that. Sandra had offered and Conifer had demanded caution more than accepting the offer.

"So...is help coming?" Marauder asked. "I mean, more Grand Lake firefighters or something?"

Valora shuffled uncomfortably. "No. I mean, no more Grand Lake firefighters, anyways. I told Sandra to keep asking for help as she went, but I'm alone."

"Why come, then?" Conifer asked. "I don't mean that in a harsh way, it's just that you said you had family."

"In Sweden," Valora replied. "No way I'm getting all the way there. And, yeah, I only came to Aspen Heart a couple times, but I loved it here. It's a big part of why I moved to Colorado from Sweden when I turned eighteen."

"What was your plan, then?" Marauder asked.

Valora shrugged. "Extra set of hands? I know the ratio of kids to adults can't be very favorable in this situation. I don't know, I just wanted to come check on the place and I figured if there was a way for me to help you'd tell me. I mean, I've been assuming you two *are* from the camp, but feel free to correct me if I'm wrong."

"We are," Marauder said. "I'm Marauder, and this is Conifer."

"No real names?"

"Camp names are kind of habit by now," Marauder said. "I'm not all that attached to my real name anyways."

"Neither am I," Conifer admitted. It also felt like it would be strange to go back to using it right now. Like she'd be making a futile attempt at reclaiming her life before any of this had happened. It felt easier to just be Conifer.

"Fair enough," Valora said.

The three of them went silent for a long stretch, Marauder and Conifer watching Valora as she watched them.

"You *are* with the Grand Lake fire department, though?" Conifer said after a minute, gesturing at her hoodie with the arrow.

"Yep."

"What's the name of the other lake next to the town?" Conifer asked.

"Testing me?" Valora replied.

"The world ended. Of course I'm testing you."

"Shadow Mountain Lake, which is way bigger so I don't know why it's the smaller one that's called 'grand.'"

"Name some restaurants in town."

"Well, I am a firefighter. The 'eating out' budget is thin. But I go to the Fat Cat Cafe a lot, and Cy's deli."

"What famous cartoon character is hanging from the ceiling near the sign for the restrooms in Fat Cat?"

"Specific much, Conifer?" Marauder muttered.

Conifer shrugged. Anyone could drive through a town and remember a couple restaurants. Only locals would go often enough to remember the decor.

Valora's face screwed up as she thought about it. "Uhhhhh...the...buxom red-haired one? J—Je...umm...Jessica Rabbit?"

Conifer sighed and lowered her bow completely. She'd answered everything correctly, and she seemed nice enough. The more Conifer looked at her, the more she was sure she had gone to camp with her once. She hadn't been in Conifer's unit, but Conifer had a distinct memory of her standing in the middle of everyone as they stood singing outside the lodge before meals, head and shoulders and even elbows above the rest of the campers.

"Well, she's clearly got some muscles on her," Marauder reasoned after another long, silent moment. "And muscles like that will make cabin building go a lot faster."

"I can bench 200 and squat lift 280," Valora offered. "Just putting that out there." The statement earned another impressed whistle from Marauder.

Conifer huffed, giving in to the inevitable. "Alright, Valora, guess you're coming back to camp with us."

"We've only got two horses, but we can put your pack on mine so you don't have to carry it as you walk," Marauder offered. "Least I can do after beating you up."

Valora chuckled. "I'll take you up on that, but I can hardly blame you for the flip. You didn't know who I was and I know I can cut a pretty intimidating figure."

"At least your hoodie wasn't brown. Might've thought you were bigfoot," Conifer muttered, still a bit unsure about inviting Valora to come back with them. What if other people started showing up? Would this set a dangerous, resource draining precedent by letting her come with? Conifer wasn't one to hoard resources, she'd been taught better than that, but it was just another thing that didn't seem to apply now that there were so many kids involved.

"That's my go-to Halloween costume," Valora grinned, undoing the straps of her bag and shimmying out of it.

"How'd you even get up this far?" Conifer asked as Marauder went to retrieve the horses. She couldn't have walked all this way from Grand Lake, it would've taken more time than there had been since all of this had started.

"Dirtbike. It died yesterday, though. Not sure why. It had gas."

Marauder returned a couple minutes later. Valora was still sitting on the ground, dabbing her no longer bleeding chin with a clean rag she'd pulled from her backpack and wetted with her water bottle. Within a few more minutes they had Valora's bag strapped to the back of Marauder's horse and were working their way back up the road, Valora keeping pace with the horses.

Conifer had a thousand questions for Valora about everything that was going on, but she also felt it was only right to wait for Jack to be there when she ask them, so the ride back was silent.

CHAPTER 13
VALORA MEETS JACK

Their return to camp did not go unnoticed. A group of the older campers were hard at work building a fence around the old storage shed so it could function as a sheep barn, and they immediately noticed Valora walking with Conifer and Marauder. Conifer could see their eyes roving over the logo on Valora's hoodie as they got close enough for them to read it, and Conifer wished that she'd thought to ask Valora to take it off or turn it inside out. Conifer could see in their faces that they didn't just see it as some random hoodie that, for all they knew, might not even belong to Valora at all. It had ignited a spark of hope in them, and as much as Conifer wanted them to remain hopeful in general, she didn't want it to be false hope.

Conifer trotted Knight ahead, stopping by the fence. "She's alone," Conifer told them. There just wasn't a good way to soften the blow.

Shoulders sagged and one girl angrily chucked her shovel off to the side.

"Does she know anything?" One of their counselors, Wildfire, asked.

"Probably. We're taking her to Jack to talk things out. Have you seen her?"

"At the lodge, working with the cooks on the rationing schedules," Wildfire replied.

Conifer nodded and clucked her tongue at Knight, pulling her back over to Marauder and Valora, who had stopped to wait a few yards back. Valora gave the campers a wave as the three of them turned to go up the hill to the lodge. None of the campers waved back.

"Cross your arms over your hoodie," Conifer told Valora as they approached the lodge. "Or take it off."

"Why?" Marauder asked.

"She's getting people's hopes up."

Valora had the good sense to look a little ashamed and quickly removed the hoodie, tying it around her waist with the logo hidden.

Securing their reins to the porch they went inside, finding Jack and the cooks standing around the serving counter. It was covered in papers that were in turn covered in scribbled and scratched figures and calculations. None of them noticed Conifer and the others picking their way across the rows of mattresses until they were right next to the counter. Jack glanced up first, her gray-streaked brown hair wild around her face from what Conifer suspected was the amount of times her hands had run through it. She gave Valora an appraising once-over as the cooks watched.

"I know you," Jack said.

"I'm a former camper," Valora explained. "My name's Valora Karlsson. I was part of a group of people evacuating the mountains when I heard the camp was in trouble from a woman named Sandra, so I came to see if there was anything I could do."

Jack glanced from Valora to Conifer, who shrugged. "We haven't talked much yet. Figured it was best to wait for you, but I do believe she is who she says she is."

Jack nodded and turned to the cooks. "Keep working on this. I'll be back to check in later. You three," she addressed

Marauder, Valora, and Conifer, "come with me."

Conifer waited for Marauder and Valora to go, then followed all of them through the kitchen, down a hallway, up a back set of stairs, down another hallway, and into Jack's office. Once the door was closed Jack took her spot behind her desk and indicated for Valora to take one of the chairs in front of it. Marauder took the other, and Conifer remained by the door, watching Valora's profile.

"Is there any more help coming?" Jack asked.

"For the camp? I don't know," Valora admitted, repeating what she'd told Marauder and Conifer about her encounter with Sandra.

"You said you were evacuating. Where to? Who was leading it?" Jack asked, leaning forward.

Valora glanced between everyone in the room. "You really don't know much, do you?"

"No," Conifer admitted. "Maybe it's best you give us a rundown of everything, and then we'll ask questions."

Jack and Marauder nodded in agreement.

"Okay, okay," Valora said, tilting her head back and forth a few times as if she were trying to jostle her thoughts into position. "So, before this all started, I'd gone to Glenwood for a training thing. I was staying in the Hotel Colorado, but my insomnia was kicking my ass so I got up to walk around a little at about two in the morning. When I went down to the lobby I found the front desk attendant and a few other employees clustered around a computer screen and crying. I thought, well, I thought it must be another mass shooting or something like that, you know? Something bad, but not the end of the *world* or anything.

"I went over and asked what was going on, and the clerk just turned the monitor towards me. They were watching a live news broadcast, I think out of Grand Junction, and it...it was this same video over and over. A view of Colorado Springs from some camera up in the mountains so that you could see the whole town sparkling below. Perfect clear night. Then, suddenly, this streak of light falls out of the sky and for barely a second you could see this mushroom cloud ballooning up before the camera went dead. The crawling banner along the bottom of the screen said 'Nuclear bomb dropped on Colorado Springs: five confirmed nuclear bombs dropped on US soil in the last hour, eighteen suspected worldwide. Millions dead.' The reporter was talking about other strikes and locations and potential sources for the bombs and retaliation, but I couldn't really *hear* her. I just kept watching that video as they played it over and over again. That banner is…it's going to be burned into my memory for the rest of my life, I think." Valora swallowed heavily, looking down at her shoes.

A chill settled in Conifer's bones as every video of vintage nuclear tests she'd ever seen was merged with the places she knew. Pine trees along the trails she'd helped cut bursting into flame, then crumbling into nothing. The rocks she'd climbed in the Garden of the Gods toppling and charring. Houses she'd stayed in splintering into millions of pieces. Friends burning away into shadows.

Valora continued, "None of us really knew what to do. I think we just sat there watching it in silence until the sun started to rise. As other guests woke up and saw the news on their phones everyone started to congregate in the lobby and it got a little chaotic. People were desperate to leave, to get back to their homes and their families. But so many people in that hotel had arrived by train that they didn't have a way to leave on their own, myself included. I helped coordinate things most of that day, getting people onto buses and carpools, then went to my room and got my important stuff. By the time I got back downstairs most people had left, and those who were still around were calmer. The workers that were still there told us they'd been called by the police and instructed to stay put for now, but if people still wanted to leave they should go to the train station. Trains were going to take people to Grand Junction to be evacuated from there. Everyone else went to the trains. The footbridge across the

Colorado River was packed, and people were even walking across the highway overpass, which was jammed with so many cars none of them were moving. But the weirdest thing was how calm everyone was. You always see people panic in the movies, but no one really did aside from a handful. Mostly, there was a lot of crying, a lot of begging, and a lot of praying."

Conifer could picture exactly what that scene must have looked like. The fear and desperation that would've hung so heavy in the air you could taste it. A train, even packed, could only carry so many people. It would have taken dozens of train cars to evacuate every tourist from Glenwood, let alone the surrounding areas and all the other towns along the line. With everything to the east gone, or at least dangerously radioactive at that point, all trains would have had to come in from Grand Junction, get people, and then turn around to evacuate them, and there were only so many trains to be had anyway. It would not have been an efficient system, but it would've been all they had with the highways jammed.

"You didn't get on a train?" Marauder asked softly.

Valora shook her head. "It didn't seem right. There were so many kids, so many families. I just…I couldn't take up space that should go to them. By the time I got out there, most of the locals had already made their runs on the stores and were just milling around, so I found a little cafe on a quieter street and went in until I could figure something out. Drank a lot of coffee and watched the news broadcasts. The workers were gone, but it didn't matter, except for the owner who just kept quietly working. There were other people there, and no one was talking. Stayed there until dark before I wandered back to the hotel, which was pretty much empty by then. The next morning I went to the lobby and found a group of people preparing to walk to Grand Junction. They said they didn't want to wait for the trains, and asked if I wanted to come. I figured, what the hell? I'm not accomplishing anything sitting around here. So we went. Met up with Sandra a couple days after that, found an abandoned truck with a dirtbike on a trailer, and rode it up here. Well, almost up here. It died, like I told Conifer."

Jack's office was silent as Valora finished her story. Jack dropped her head into her hands and Marauder curled her knees up to her chest, wrapping her arms around them. Conifer had a strong urge to slide down the wall and curl up on herself as well, but she knew it wouldn't do any good. Not that Conifer could think of anything else that *would* do any good. She'd been trying to ignore the nuclear problem, knowing they couldn't do anything about it now. But hearing Valora describe that news video had forced her to look it straight in the face. Worldwide nuclear strikes. They seemed to have avoided the initial effects, the primary exposures, like she'd pointed out several nights earlier when talking with the other counselors. But what about the long-term effects? Radioactive rain, radioactive snow, radiation in the air, radiation in migrating animals? And Conifer's mind just kept jumping back to Colorado Springs, to Denver. How many kilotons had those bombs been? How far had the destruction spread? The power some countries had was mortifying to consider.

Had people even known it was coming, felt their houses shake for just a moment before the worst of the impact killed them?

"So...what do we do?" Marauder asked.

"Do you think it is worth it for us to try and evacuate the camp, Valora?" Jack asked.

Valora seemed to think about it for several minutes before slowly shaking her head. "Who knows what would happen to all these kids out there, with people who don't actually know or care about them? They'd get split up, shipped off who knows where, probably never see anyone they know ever again. There's just too much chaos. If you think you can all survive here, then you should stay. You actually care about them."

"But we can't treat radiation sickness, or anything related to it," Conifer murmured, leaning her head back against the wall. Baking soda and potassium iodide didn't exactly grow on trees, and even then those could only do so much.

"Conifer, you said we were okay...?" Marauder asked, turning her wide blue eyes up to Conifer. They were lighter than Valora's. More of a sky blue.

Conifer didn't bother to be gentle in her answer. "Not exactly. I said we didn't seem to be suffering from primary exposure. But secondary exposure...with that many bombs, there's no way we'll avoid it. Not forever."

What about those who hadn't been killed immediately? Those on the fringes who must've felt their skin burn away, peeling back from their bodies?

"And those secondary effects, obviously there's cancer, but what else? How long do we have?" Jack asked.

"I don't know," Conifer admitted, hearing the hollowness in her own voice. "It depends on the weather, what direction the radiation from the blasts gets carried, how strong it is by the time it gets here, how it gets into our food supply. Animal migration patterns will change wildly, and we'll get animals coming in from all over, including blast zones. And it'll effect everyone differently depending on their age, their general health. We might not see effects for thirty years, or we might see some in a week."

"Please don't use the word 'years,'" Marauder muttered. "I do not want to think about years at the moment, especially thirty of them."

The bomb that hit Colorado Springs had dropped at night, but what time? How many people had been awake? How many were lucky enough to die in their sleep without ever knowing?

"So, what you're saying, and I just want to be completely clear on this, Conifer, is that there is nothing we can do about radiation?" Jack said, voice heavy.

Conifer closed her eyes. "At this point, no, not that I

know of."

"I don't know that anyone else can do anything about it either," Valora said quietly. "This is so widespread, the whole world is under some sort of risk, and there aren't going to be enough doctors, let alone enough medicine to go around."

"Fuck," Marauder said, smearing tears out of her eyes with the heel of her hand.

The room descended into silence once again, a heavier one this time which just made Conifer's thoughts louder.

"Well," Valora said, voice tentative, "I guess that means you just have to keep doing what you were already going to do, doesn't it? It's not like any of us can sit down and die because we might start to develop cancer tomorrow. We're here now, alive now, so we keep moving forward."

She made it sound so simple. Like radiation was just a stray breeze that could be noticed but easily ignored. Like they didn't have nearly two-hundred people in camp, mostly children, who were staring at a slow, agonizing death.

How many people had vanished into nothingness, no trace they had ever existed, not even a shadow?

Conifer turned and walked out of the office, forcing herself not to slam the door on her way. She heard Marauder scramble after her, calling out her name, but Conifer ignored her as she strode up to the third level of the lodge. The rooms up there were mostly storage they hadn't gotten to inventorying yet; old bedframes packed into the odd angles under the sloping roof, tattered old canvass from the tents, old camping equipment, and who knew what else. Without knowing she was doing it Conifer kicked out at a door that was slightly ajar, sending it slamming into the wall and puffing out a cloud of dust into the air. Her boot took the impact and the only feeling she got from it was a sense of relief. It bled away as the sound of the impact faded, though, and Conifer found herself wanting to find something else to kick.

"Conifer," Marauder said from behind her. Conifer turned to find her standing at the end of the hallway, arms crossed and one hand on her shoulder.

"We're fucked." Conifer hadn't meant to say it, let alone so harshly.

She shrugged. "Maybe. Probably. But Valora was right. We're here now, alive now, so we have to keep trying. We don't know what's going to happen, but how is that any different from before? No one has ever known the future, just guessed at it."

"I've seen you use tarot cards practically every morning," Conifer pointed out, voice still harsh in a way she couldn't control.

Marauder shrugged again, a sad little smile on her face as she scuffed her shoe across the worn and faded carpet. "And I believe in them, and other types of divination, but there's not exactly a card for 'your thyroid is going to swell to the size of a grapefruit and you're going to die of stomach cancer from eating contaminated deer meat.' I guess it explains why I've been drawing 'The Tower' all summer, though."

"And what does that one mean?"

"Sudden upheaval, disaster, that sort of thing."

"Any happier cards popping up?"

"Depends on the questions I ask."

"Have you asked them if we survive?" Conifer asked, not sure if she cared about the answer. They were just pieces of paper and yet...she wanted to know.

"No."

"Why not?"

"I'm afraid to."

Conifer huffed and went back to pacing, still struggling to resist the urge to kick things.

Marauder watched her pace, the feeling of the other girl's eyes making Conifer's skin crawl more than it already was.

"I'm not asking this to be rude, I swear, but with everything going on, I gotta ask, as a friend who wants to be able to help you if I can, are you on meds that ran out?" Marauder asked.

Conifer sighed, running her thumbs over the curled

knuckles of her fingers. She knew Marauder meant well. "It's fine, and no, I'm not. I'm...my parents have pretty much always thought I might be autistic, but they never got me tested or diagnosed. They helped in other ways, and they were great about it, they were just really worried what an on paper diagnosis might do down the line. Do you know how many countries ban autistic people from immigrating there?"

"Ah...no, no I do not."

"A lot," Conifer told her. "Canada, New Zealand, plenty of others. And our own country has never exactly treated autistic people well either, let alone autistic girls. They wanted to protect me from that until I was old enough to decide for myself if I wanted a diagnosis, and I didn't."

Marauder didn't say anything for over a minute. "Well... anything I can do to help?" She finally asked.

Conifer shook her head. "I just...need a minute. Too much going on right now. Too many thoughts. Too much noise."

Marauder nodded. "Alright. We'll figure it out when you're feeling better then."

With that, Marauder turned and went back down the stairs. Conifer felt her shoulders unknot and let her fingers relax slightly, but she kept pacing, trying to work out the overstimulation through movement. Objectively, she knew Valora was right. She'd been saying exactly the same thing this whole time: they just needed to keep pushing forward. But she was tired of being objective. She was tired of being the one everyone was looking too and leaning on. It was too much weight on her shoulders, and she felt like she was going to snap.

CHAPTER 14
UNIT CONVERSION

Jack agreed to let Valora stay and set her up on the oversized couch in the counselor's lounge, as none of the beds around camp were long enough for her. The campers, especially the younger ones, seemed utterly delighted by how large and strong Valora was, welcoming the distraction an interesting new person provided. They'd made a game of seeing how many of them could hang off her biceps while she flexed. Two days in the record was six, though this seemed to be the limit purely because of the length of Valora's arms rather than her strength.

"I want to climb her," Marauder said. They were watching Valora—in a well-fitting tank-top that was riding up a bit to reveal a peek at abs that matched her biceps—help Jack fight with the forklift that had been taken from the ranch store. It seemed to have very interesting ideas about what each of its buttons and levers did, no matter what they were labeled as.

Conifer huffed out a laugh, secretly glad Marauder's attentions seemed to have shifted off of herself. They were better as friends, especially right now.

"Are you two going to help us with all this sawing or not?" Cheyenne asked, waving her marking pencil in Conifer and Marauder's general direction from where she was crouched next to the pile of supplies with everyone else from their unit.

Today was the first day of real work on cabin building.

Horseshoe had already been by to smooth out an area for it that morning with the camp's little tractor, and the kids had helped to measure out and dig holes for the posts. Next came moving the actual platforms down the hill from the Emmeline Pankhurst unit to the area behind the lodge they'd selected for the cabin, hence the need for the forklift.

"Coming, sorry," Conifer said.

"If I kick it I'm either going to break my foot or I'm going to break *it*," Valora said from over by the forklift.

"You're a witch, Marauder, can you perform exorcisms on machines?" Sammy-Jo asked.

"That's called being a mechanic," Marauder replied, sitting down in the dirt and retrieving the clipboard of plans. They'd been drawn up by Wildfire, who was getting a degree in architectural design.

"Everything has been measured twice?" Conifer asked.

"Three times, since Marauder was so busy crushing on Valora," Cheyenne said, a mischievous glint in her eyes.

"Whoopsie," Marauder said. Conifer could see the tops of her cheeks reddening.

"Sorry girls, I didn't mean for you to overhear any of that," Marauder said.

"Well, to be fair, we saw it, and then we kind of intentionally overheard it," Lorelai said, looking just as amused as Cheyenne.

"It was very easy to see," Paloma added.

"You would give cartoon heart eyes a run for their money," Tabatha said.

"Also, you crushing on Conifer was equally obvious, you know that, right?" Farrah chimed in. "Though, we all kinda get the vibe that's no longer a thing? We have a betting pool."

"Alright, topic change!" Conifer declared. She spared a glance over at Valora, but she was now hanging halfway into the cab of the forklift and did not seem to have overheard anything. The campers all giggled but obligingly dropped the topic.

Marauder, hair pulled back with a bandanna as it was too short for a ponytail but long enough to be in the way, set to work sawing the boards with battery-powered saw, cheeks still a little red.

Several minutes later the forklift finally roared to life and Conifer went to help with the platforms. This was the first cabin being built, so there was a bit of winging it going on, and thus they weren't entirely sure how moving the platforms was going to go. The theory was that they could use the forklift to do the actual lifting, securing the platforms with towing straps. They only needed to lift them out of their current spots—about two feet up in the air—and then move them to the lodge, line them up properly with their new spots, and drop them down. It was just that they weren't sure if things were going to stay balanced nicely once the platforms were lifted.

Nothing to do but give it a shot, though.

Jack drove the forklift from the build site, with Valora and Conifer following, up to Emmeline Pankhurst and slid the forks under the closest platform. The canvas and frame had already been removed, and the dirt around the cement plugs dug out. Jack waited as Valora and Conifer secured the tow straps. Conifer couldn't hear it over the roar of the engine, but she saw Jack take a deep breath before pulling back the lever that lifted the forks—though it was labeled as the one that extended them. The wood groaned and creaked, but lifted without incident, the old cement plugs shedding dirt as they went.

"Alright, step one: successful!" Valora shouted.

Conifer nodded and they both moved to carefully test the balance of the platform. Conifer could feel it wanting to tip and guessed that the tips of the forks were sitting right under the balance point, but the tow straps seemed to be holding. Valora shook her head, though, glancing from the platform to the forklift to the grade of the hill. Conifer could see what she was thinking: the whole thing might tip forward. The forklift had plenty of weight on the back to help mitigate the problem, but that was on flat ground. The forks would have to stay lifted about five or six feet as well, to keep the platform from dragging, which wouldn't help.

"Counterbalance!" Conifer shouted, waving Valora to the back of the forklift and clambering up. It took some effort, and they had to hook their arms together, but eventually they were both up there and secure, providing a three-hundred-and-seventy-five or so pounds of extra weight to balance out the platform. It would reduce fuel efficiency, carrying that extra weight, but it was better than wreaking the valuable platforms.

Jack looked back to make sure they were steady before she started crawling back down the hill. It took about twenty minutes of careful driving to get down to the right spot, and then another three minutes to get everything aligned properly with the pre-dug holes. As soon as they dropped it four of the kids, including Cheyenne, raced over with car-jacks and a couple levels. Conifer watched as they worked together to level the platform, feeling a flare of pride at how well they were working together. Most of them, anyway. A few weren't pitching in quite as much—especially Giselle—but they were at least helping a little by sorting screws and nails or other little projects, so Conifer wasn't going to press it for now. Construction wasn't everyone's forte, and that was fair. They'd find other ways for those kids to contribute at some point.

"We are committing so many OSHA violations right now!" Marauder shouted, though she didn't sound angry about it.

The rest of the morning passed in much the same manner. By the time Polar Bear showed up on horseback to deliver lunch they had all the platforms in place. They now formed one large rectangle with four platforms forming the long sides, one-and-a-half forming the short sides, and the remaining halves set aside to be broken down and used elsewhere. The cabins would be exactly as big as they needed to be, no bigger, to help with heating. Everything had been leveled, and the post-holes had been filled with Quikrete that would be fully set by mid-afternoon. That gave them plenty of time to finish cutting down boards and beams to size, and they could spend the rest of the afternoon and evening getting to work framing the walls.

"Mind if I join you ladies?" Polar Bear asked as she handed out sandwiches and chips to everyone. "You're my last stop."

"Of course not," Marauder said.

Everyone found a patch of dirt or stack of boards to sit on, digging into their food. The kids were chattering happily, thrilled at what they'd been able to help create in just one morning. Sometimes, though, the conversation drifted to other things. Things everyone missed, mostly.

"I miss TikTok," Tabatha said. She was sprawled out in the dirt and sawdust, looking up at the murky sky.

"What's TikTok?" Conifer asked.

Everyone slowly turned to look at her, looking flabbergasted. Even Tabatha raised her head off the ground in what seemed like an uncomfortable position just to be able to see Conifer.

"What?" Conifer said, glancing around. "I'm guessing it's some social media site? I've just never heard of it."

"You know…" Marauder said, head tilted, "usually, when people are chronically online, they're told to go outside and touch grass. You, however, need to go inside and watch a movie or something. A recent movie."

"Not much of a movie person," Conifer said.

Marauder waved a hand over her blank expression. "This is my shocked face."

Conifer rolled her eyes.

"Back to the cabins," Cheyenne redirected. "We're keeping it simple with four walls and a sloped roof, but what are we doing with the inside?"

"Well, Wildfire said not to add interior walls so that we can keep the heat even," Jack told her.

"Would canvass walls be okay? Like, out of the old tents?" Orlaith suggested. "Maybe turn each end into a bedroom that way, then have a communal area in the middle?"

Jack gave a little tilted nod, a contemplative expression on her face. "I think that would be alright. The canvass would be easy enough to move when needed and it wouldn't completely stop the flow of heat."

Conifer tuned out the conversation, letting it fade into gibberish as her thoughts drifted. They'd had another meeting with the whole camp after Valora told them what she had, but somehow it didn't seem to have really changed anything. Part of Conifer suspected that it had all become too big of a thing for everyone to wrap their heads around, so they didn't. They'd accepted it was bad, but the level of bad no longer really mattered.

Conifer wished she could ignore it that easily. It felt like bugs were crawling under her skin every time she thought about the state of things outside their sheltered enclave, which was nearly all the time at this point, despite Marauder's attempts to distract her. She was too exhausted for nightmares, but any still moment during the day left her mind free to play nuclear explosions on a loop. Looking at the kids usually made it worse. They were so much more susceptible to radiation and the health issues it could cause. Conifer found herself looking each of them up and down, studying every aspect of their features. Was Amy-Leigh pale because she was still upset about her mom and dad, or was she anemic from radiation exposure? Were Giselle's eyes red from crying, or had radiation begun to leach into them? Was Tabatha picking at her sandwich because she didn't like turkey, or had radiation begun to poison her stomach?

Conifer felt something nudge at her boot and looked up to see Polar Bear sitting across from her on a stack of two-by-fours. She hadn't been there before, and Conifer hadn't noticed her sit down. Jack had come with her, sitting to her right.

"What's up?" Conifer asked, wondering if Polar Bear was Jack's next recruit in attempting to get her to take control of the camp.

Jack shrugged and looked to Polar Bear.

"I'm leaving," Polar Bear said. "Kind of."

Jack and Conifer exchanged a glance. Polar Bear was a big part of converting the tents into cabins. Her work with Habitat for Humanity in Canada had proved invaluable. They couldn't afford to lose her.

"Quantify 'kinda,'" Conifer said.

"I'm going up on the cliffs, to the rim of the crater, and I'm going to build myself a cabin up there as a lookout station. The view goes to, damn, it goes to the edge of the earth in every direction. We need someone up there to keep an eye on things. From up there I can see any groups trying to come into the camp, planes way off in the distance, explosions. Hell, even just oncoming storms so that we have some warning for them."

Jack and Conifer glanced at one another again. She wasn't wrong.

"The weather up there is going to be brutal, though," Conifer said. "The winds alone, there's nothing in their way. They could reach hurricane force."

She nodded. "I've thought about that. I can survive the snow fine. As for the wind, I won't build my cabin right on the edge, I'll find a place where it's sheltered a bit. Back in the trees, probably, in one of the boulder fields, and I'll brace the walls."

"You likely won't be able to come back down the cliffs until spring, though," Jack said, face drawn in a frown. "And we won't be able to go up them to you, not easily and certainly not quickly. You'll be completely cut off. You'd have to bring and store at *least* three or four months of food right off the bat. And if you got hurt you'd be on your own."

"It won't be any harder on me than the Northern Territories were," Polar Bear replied. "And what it gains the camp as a whole is worth the risk on my part."

"How do you intend to get supplies for building a cabin up there?" Conifer asked. The trails were thin and windy, even covered in loose and slippery gravel in parts. It was one thing to load up horses with softer supplies that fit in saddlebags, like food, but the idea of getting horses to carry lumber up there seemed sketchy.

"Drive," Polar Bear said simply. "I'll have to go around quite a ways, and the hunter's roads are shit, but I'll manage."

Jack sighed, rubbing her temples. "I get the logic, I do, but I still don't like the idea of sending you up there alone."

"You aren't sending me, I'm going," Polar Bear said simply. "I wasn't asking for permission."

Jack huffed but didn't argue. "You'll take a walkie to communicate with us, I assume?"

"Probably a couple, in case one dies," Polar Bear said. "Also thinking about building a flagpole and making different colored flags for signaling purposes, but that'll only be if I have time after building the shelter. Have to find a safe way to do it that doesn't give away our position, too. Still thinking on it."

"More wind means more potential radiation exposure too," Conifer pointed out. She didn't really know if it did, at least not in any way that would be different from down in the crater, but it felt like it had to be said none the less.

Polar Bear shrugged and gave a sad smile. "Already had cancer once. Figure I'm screwed no matter what. May as well be helpful while I can."

"I didn't know that," Jack said, eyes wide.

Conifer hadn't known it either, but she was more caught on Jack's reaction to it. Something in Jack's face had shifted at Polar Bear's statement, but Conifer couldn't pin down what it was.

Polar Bear shrugged again. "It was ten years ago, when I was in High School. Did the chemo, kicked its ass, but there was always a risk of remission even without radiation."

Jack pulled her into a hug that Polar Bear didn't quite seem to know what to do with before letting go with a nod. "Alright, but you keep me up to date on whatever you're doing. Take whatever truck you need, and find another person to go with you to get the building done faster. They can come back down the trail before the snow hits."

"Wait, she's *leaving*?" Cheyenne asked.

They were sitting on one of the logs around the firepit, daylight fading around them. Work had tapered off about an hour earlier, once they'd finished framing three walls of the cabin. Some of the kids had already gone into their tents, either to sleep or just relax, and others were milling around in small groups. Cheyenne and Conifer were the only ones sitting around the little fire.

"Only kind of," Conifer told her.

Cheyenne sighed and kicked some dirt into the flames. Conifer knew she should comfort her, but she didn't have the faintest idea how. Things were terrible and, realistically, they were only going to get worse. How was she supposed to convince her to feel better, to have hope, when everything she knew was gone?

"We planted the potato when you were out hunting yesterday," Cheyenne said after awhile.

"Don't you mean 'The Magnificent Spud'?" Conifer replied, managing a little grin.

"I still don't understand why we had to name it. It is a *potato*."

"A *magnificent* potato."

This time she kicked the dirt at Conifer's boots and a laugh escaped Conifer as she shook the dirt off. It was short, but it was real, and it felt nice.

"Where'd you plant it?" Conifer asked.

"It's in a big pot on the porch of the lodge. Sammy-Jo

even made a label for it with that ridiculous name."

Conifer smiled and lightly knocked her shoulder against Cheyenne's. "It's just for fun. We need a little fun right now."

"It is a *potato*." She didn't seem annoyed or anything, just flabbergasted that anyone would consider a potato fun.

"Alright, potatoes aren't your tiny fun thing, then. Any ideas what might be? I'll steal you whatever you want."

This time she was the one who laughed. "I always wanted a big sister, but the criminal part is unexpected."

"Gotta keep you on your toes. But seriously. Puzzles? A favorite book? A musical instrument? We have a small window to grab onto things from before, and it would be a shame to waste it."

Cheyenne shrugged without answering, and Conifer tried to put herself in the younger girl's place. Conifer had a home, but she hadn't lived there since she'd been eighteen. Hadn't even lived there much before that, either, with how much she traveled—with and without her parents. She had things there, but nothing she couldn't easily live without. She had parents, and loved them immensely, but she was old enough that they weren't her whole world anymore. Had they ever been her whole world? She was sure they must have been, when she was very little, but for as long as she could remember she'd always been independent, always ready to climb out the window and go on an adventure.

"I keep thinking about when I was packing," Cheyenne whispered. Her eyes were unfocused, gazing off at the trees around them. "My mom was reading off that list the camp sends, and I was ignoring her because I thought she was being ridiculous. I've gone to camp so many times, we'd both memorized that list."

Conifer let the silence linger as Cheyenne worked through her next thought, opening and closing her mouth a few times.

"I wish I'd brought something of hers," Cheyenne said finally. "Accidentally grabbed one of her shirts or...something. I don't even have a picture of her with me."

A few tears trickled down her face and Conifer held out her arm, offering a hug if Cheyenne wanted it. She hesitated for a moment, then leaned into Conifer's side. Conifer squeezed lightly, resting her cheek on Cheyenne's head, the bumps of her braids pressing into Conifer's skin.

As they sat there curled together on the log, the last bits of sunlight faded away, leaving the world around them painted in soft blues and greens and gray-browns. Their incomplete new home stood stark in front of them, harsh straight lines against the softer, organic forms of the trees behind it. Turning it into a house would be easy, but Conifer knew it would never be a home. Not for Cheyenne and the other campers. They had lost too much.

CHAPTER 15
LEAVING DAY

"I don't want to do this," Marauder muttered, tears already sparkling in her eyes in the early morning light.

Conifer reached over and gently took the alarm bell from her hand. She didn't want to do it either, but someone had to.

It had been about a week since they'd started building the cabins, and today was pick up day. Today was *supposed to be* pick up day. Marauder and Conifer should've been telling the campers to check under their beds for forgotten items, stacking their suitcases in the trailer to be taken to the flag ring, handing out shirts with the camp logo for all of them to wear and sign so they'd have a memento of their time at camp. Their parents should've been winding their way up the road, parking in the flag ring, and walking up the hill to the lodge to sign out their children.

Now, none of that was going to happen. Ever.

There had been a counselor meeting the night before to plan how to handle the day. Handle the fact that it was going to be the exact same as every other day so far, yet feel so different. There was no reason for their parents to show up; if they could've gotten here already, they would have, and if they were trying to get here it could be any day. But that didn't matter. It still *felt* like they should be here today. It still felt like today should be the day everyone went home. That feeling was what mattered, not the actuality of the situation, and that was what Conifer and the other adults had to care about.

Taking a deep breath, Conifer gave the bell a good shake. Marauder quickly wiped her tears, sniffing and tilting her head back in an attempt to keep more from gathering. At first there was no sound from the tents, then, slowly, flaps began to unzip and one by one everyone crawled out. They looked like cornered animals. Scared in a way Conifer hadn't seen yet. Cheyenne lingered at the back of the group, arms wrapped tightly around herself and eyes focused on the dirt at her feet.

"Hey," Conifer said softly, holding up her arms to any of them that needed it. Paloma, Orlaith, and Tai came over and curled up against her, and a few others went to Marauder. Cheyenne stayed where she was. "We're going to go to the lodge, and we're going to have breakfast. Then we're going to wait in the front yard of the lodge, with some activities we can do there. If you don't want to wait, we have other groups you can go help out for the day. Jack sent a few counselors down to town to watch for anyone coming. We'll also have counselors in the lodge that you can talk to one on one all day."

It felt so clinical, laying it all out like this. Clinical, and yet agonizing. Looking at them Conifer could see a clear divide in the group: campers whose parents weren't from a city that was known to have been had been bombed, and campers who had already started to realize no one was coming for them. The second group, like Cheyenne and Amy-Leigh, just looked hollow. The first group had enough hope left to cry.

"We're here for you," Marauder said. "We'll do whatever we can."

Still, none of the campers said anything.

"Let's go have breakfast," Conifer said softly.

They all shuffled into motion, heading around to enter the lodge through the front. Cheyenne lingered until she and Conifer were the only ones still standing there.

"Can I stay at the cabin and work on painting?" She whispered.

Their cabin was nearly finished now, with just aesthetic details left on the interior and burying the back and sides with dirt for insulation on the outside. During one of the recent town runs Trout had figured out how to work the paint mixer at the ranch store, a process that had apparently been rather messy, and brought back multiple gallons in tons of colors. She had been hoping that letting the campers paint the cabins fun colors would be another little thing that would make all of this even a tiny bit better.

"Sure," Conifer said. "But you need to come have breakfast, okay?"

She nodded and followed Conifer into the lodge, keeping her arms wrapped around herself. Once inside she joined the line to pick up her meal at the serving counter and Conifer stepped aside to join Marauder and Silver by the fireplace. Most of the mattresses had been stacked along the walls, making room for everyone to sit on the floor to eat. It wasn't the best solution, just a transitional one. The whole dining room was just as quiet as Marauder and Conifer's unit had been that morning.

"I wish I'd been sent to town," Silver muttered. "Woulda been less heartbreaking."

"I don't know if it would be better or worse for parents to show up now," Marauder said quietly. "Can you imagine being the other girls? Seeing one of your friends get to leave, get to be with someone they love, while you have to stay behind with people who are basically strangers?"

Conifer didn't respond, though she knew Marauder was right. No outcome was a completely good one at this point. If a parent showed up they'd either want to take their child, putting that child in potential danger out on the road, or they'd want to stay here, giving the camp more mouths to feed and likely making the other campers jealous of the one kid whose parents had made it, or they just wouldn't show up at all.

"But it's go home day!" A little shout sounded, making everyone all jump at the unexpectedness of a loud voice. Conifer scanned the line until she saw Elizabeth kneeling in front of a little girl with caramel eyes and fuzzy curls. Conifer felt a jolt of recognition: she was the one who'd said Conifer looked like a cat on the first day of the session.

"Lia, remember what we talked about last night?" Elizabeth said.

By now the entire room was frozen, everyone watching.

"But it's go home day!" Lia said, stomping her foot. "That means we go home! My daddy told me he'd be here today, and that we'd get ice cream on the way home! He told me!"

Conifer saw Elizabeth's shoulders tensing and walked up behind her, ready to help if she needed it.

"Lia—" Elizabeth started.

"My daddy doesn't lie!" Lia said, tears building in her eyes.

Elizabeth glanced around and caught sight of Conifer standing behind her. Conifer saw anger flash in her eyes which could've just as easily been directed at her as it could've been directed at the situation in general.

"I know your daddy doesn't lie, honey," Elizabeth said, attention back on Lia. "But, sometimes, things happen that no one expected to happen, and things...things have to change."

"But it's go home day!" Lia said.

Elizabeth opened and closed her mouth a few times, so Conifer finally knelt down next to her. "You remember me, Lia? We met on the first day."

Lia sniffed and nodded.

"Why don't you and I go sit outside and talk about your daddy? How's that sound?" Conifer asked.

"Can Lizzy come?" Lia asked, still sniffling.

"Of course."

Lia nodded so Conifer stood up, reaching out to take her hand. Together, with Elizabeth, they went out and sat on the top step of the porch. Lia sat between them and Elizabeth draped an arm around her shoulders.

"Where does your daddy work?" Conifer asked.

"He fights big fires," Lia said.

"He's a wildland firefighter out of Colorado Springs," Elizabeth clarified. "I met him at drop off."

Elizabeth she gave Conifer a look that clearly showed she didn't think he was alive.

"Is it just the two of them?" Conifer mouthed at Elizabeth.

"Mom died last year," Elizabeth mouthed back.

Conifer winced, unable to imagine what Lia was going through right now.

"Your daddy sounds like a really good guy," Conifer told Lia. "I bet he loves you so, so much."

"More than all the stars," Lia hiccupped, and Conifer could hear the way she was quoting her father in her voice.

Conifer moved so that she was kneeling in front of Lia on a lower step, gently taking the little girl's hands in hers. "Lia, I want you to remember that, okay? I want you to remember it every night when you look at the stars, because even if your daddy doesn't come to pick you up today, he still loves you more than all the stars and he always, always will. Can you remember that for me?"

She hiccupped and nodded as Elizabeth pulled her in a little tighter. Conifer looked up and saw Cheyenne standing just outside the doors to the diningroom. Conifer had no idea how long she'd been there. Cheyenne watched for another moment before coming over and sitting down in Conifer's previous place next to Lia. Without a word she pulled a sharpie out of her pocket and gently took one of Lia's hands. Conifer's mind latched onto the marker, heart tripping at the sight of it. Cheyenne had been here so many times. She knew how pick up days went. She knew that, right now, she should've been getting a t-shirt with the camp logo and year, should've been using that sharpie to sign her name and maybe even phone number on the shirts of her friends so they could remember one another.

Uncapping the sharpie, Cheyenne leaned over and very carefully drew a star on the back of Lia's hand.

Cheyenne and Amy-Leigh both left to paint the cabin after breakfast finished. Conifer was fine with letting them go alone as they were just behind the lodge and easy enough to check on. There was only so much that could go wrong with taping, after all, and they knew to come get Conifer or another counselor before they started applying primer.

About fifty other campers had decided they didn't want to wait at the lodge either, and they'd been split into groups to work on the other two cabins and collecting firewood with the help of various counselors. Everyone else was in the yard in front of the lodge. There were a few activity stations set up for those who needed to be busy; creating hardware kits for the bunk-bed frames that were being built, carding and spinning wool, hand-sewing menstrual pads from scrap cloth.

It was still quiet, and even the campers working on projects couldn't stop glancing at the road, couldn't stop straining their ears for the sound of an engine.

Valora had stepped in as just another counselor and was mostly helping with the hardware kits. Conifer was starting to like Valora now. She'd integrated into the camp well, and was always ready and willing to jump in and help with everything from hard projects to upset kids.

"What's Horseshoe got?" Marauder said, looking over at towards the barn.

Conifer followed her gaze to see Horseshoe ascending the steps up the hill to the lodge and carrying a very large box, which seemed to be moving. "No idea."

Horseshoe made it up the last step and walked to the middle of the yard before gently setting the box on the ground. By now she, and the box, had everyone's attention. There were scuffling sounds coming from inside, along with little yips. Conifer was starting to guess what Horseshoe was up to, only to be proven right when Horseshoe leaned down and flipped open the flaps of the box to reveal a bunch of wiggling Border Collie puppies.

Many of the kids gasped and rushed the box, carefully pulling out puppies to cuddle, passing them between one another. There were eight of them, and they looked like they were even more excited to see the campers than the campers were to see them.

Looking quite pleased with herself Horseshoe came over to stand with Marauder and Conifer. "Found 'em at a ranch on the first run I went on, but they were still a bit young so I didn't say anything. Almost ten weeks old now, though, and they all seem strong. Figured today was a good day to share."

"A damn good day to share," Conifer agreed, feeling herself smile. She didn't like how unfamiliar it felt.

"What are you going to do with them?" Marauder asked.

"Well, their mama is down in the barn. Damn fine dog. Figure I'll keep her to help with the sheep; she's well trained. The pups should stay with the girls, I think. Keep them company. One per cabin, and the rest in the lodge. I'm gonna keep one to train, though. And I want to try and find some other dogs in town so we can breed them eventually. We'll need good working dogs."

"I like that idea," Marauder said, leaving to join the group playing with the puppies.

"What are you planning to feed them?" Conifer asked. "Don't get me wrong, I think the dogs will do the kids a lot of good, but still."

"Start with dog food from town, then transition them to a raw diet of scrap meat and bones."

Conifer nodded slowly. "Okay. And...the radiation? These ones were born before it hit, but they've got a lot of growing left to do, and if you're planning on breeding them...."

Horseshoe sighed, looking out over the campers and puppies. "Can't do anything for it but hope."

Conifer sat on the top step of the porch, watching everyone in the front yard of the lodge. Things were becoming more and more subdued as the day wore on, not that they'd been all that active before. The growing stillness made her skin itch. A heavy sigh pulled her from her thoughts and Conifer looked up to see Jack standing next to her. She didn't say anything, looking out over all the clusters of children before giving another sigh and sitting down a few inches away. The motion was slow, as if her joints were stiff, and she looked exhausted. Conifer had been so studiously avoiding her that this was the closest they'd been in days.

"I needed a break from talking to the kids," Jack said after a moment.

"Can't blame you," Conifer replied. She knew Jack had been talking to many of them one on one all morning. It was a strain every counselor knew the weight of at this point.

"How are you?" Jack asked.

Conifer shrugged.

She knocked her shoulder into Conifers and shot her a look that made it clear a shrug was not enough of an answer.

"They've all lost everything..." Conifer said after a minute, trailing off as she tried to put her feelings into words in a way she usually didn't.

"So did you," Jack replied.

Conifer shook her head. "Not like them. I love my parents, but...their loss...it isn't earth-shattering for me. I don't even have a real home, Jack. Everything I care about was in my truck. I was never going to have a—a pick up day. I wasn't even going to go back and visit my parents for the weekend after this summer. I was just going to go find another job, probably as a ranch hand or trail guide or something until ski season started, then go work ski patrol."

Jack was silent, sweeping her eyes over the solemn children in front of them. A few were crying silently, others were curled up with their faces hidden in their arms and propped on their knees, but most just looked more and more hollow as the minutes ticked by.

"Maybe you didn't lose the sort of concrete things everyone else did, but you still lost things, Conifer," Jack said eventually. "Your sense of safety. The level of independence that let you just jump from job to job across the country. Bookstores, movie theaters, aspirin—"

"We can make aspirin out of the willows along the creeks," Conifer offered.

Jack shot her a withering, though still fond, look. "My point is, you still lost things. It's okay to feel that, even if they may not be the same things everyone else is mourning."

"Maybe," Conifer admitted after a moment. "But not today."

No one came. As the sun began to sink tears began to fall, no longer silent. The other campers who had gone to do other things, including Cheyenne and Amy-Leigh, came back to the yard, clustering together with their friends. Conifer couldn't see a single person not crying, including the counselors who were all trying to hide it but mostly failing.

Jack, who had gone back inside to continue talking to campers one on one, came out onto the porch. She looked out over everyone, then turned and went through the door to the post office. Conifer wasn't sure what she was doing until she came back out several minutes later wheeling the large tank of helium they used for when campers had birthdays at camp. In her other hand was a grocery bag of balloons and ribbon, along with a second bag that looked to be full of stationary and pens.

"Everyone come here, please," Jack said, setting everything down next to her on the top step.

The whole camp shuffled towards the porch, eight of

them still holding the puppies that had hardly touched the ground since Horseshoe brought them up hours before, and clustered around the base of the steps like they used to do before meals. They hadn't come together in front of the lodge like that since before everything went wrong, though.

"Today was an important day," Jack said, voice heavy, "and a hard one. I know that, for many of you, it has made what is happening real in a way that it wasn't before. It was a...goodbye, to the way things were before. That means tomorrow is a new start. Your families, no matter where they are, they want you to be safe. To be alive. And you *are*, so remember that. Remember how much you love them, and how much they love you, and push through. Survive. For yourself and for them."

She paused, letting her words sink through the group. Conifer thought she'd picked exactly the right ones. Honest, but not in a way that drew attention to how bad things were. Just the right amount of hope.

"We're going to write messages to your families and send them out on balloons," Jack continued. "But we have to be careful. You can't say where we are. Everyone is going to get a card, and you can write whatever else you want on it. When you're done, your counselors will check your notes to be sure they don't say where we are, and then we'll give you a balloon and help you tie your note to it. When everyone is done, and it is completely dark, we'll let them go. You don't have to do it if you don't want to, but there are only enough balloons for everyone to get one."

A few of the older campers were the first to step up and get stationary, taking the bag and helping to pass things out to everyone else. Conifer went up the steps to stand with Jack.

"Good idea," Conifer said.

"We did it when my grandfather died suddenly of bone cancer. I know it's not exactly a good thing ecologically, but I felt like it was the best way for the girls to say—to say goodbye," Jack said, voice tripping on the last few words.

"Nothing's a good thing ecologically anymore," Conifer muttered, pulling out a ball of red ribbon.

Jack huffed. "There is that."

Jack started blowing up balloons, handing them to Conifer so she could attach ribbons. Conifer let them float in the rafters of the porch, behind the sign from 1946 that had finally been hung at the top of the steps the day before, collecting them there until there was one for everyone. One by one the campers, their cards checked by their counselors, came up and got a balloon, taping it to their cards before going back to stand in the yard, ribbons clutched in their hands.

"Jack," Conifer said between campers. "This is why I can't take charge. I never would have thought of this, but it is what they needed."

Jack glanced over at Conifer. "I think you underestimate yourself, Conifer."

Conifer shrugged and Jack didn't press it further.

Once everyone who wanted a balloon had one, there were still a handful left floating in the rafters. Jack gently pushed a blank card and a pen into Conifer's hands. Conifer took them reluctantly, staring at the slightly bent card with a simple daisy drawn on the front. She didn't see the point in doing this herself. It didn't feel like what she needed, though she didn't know that anything else would either. In the end, she scrawled a quick message more so that everyone else, especially the kids, could see her doing it.

> I love you, Mom. I love you, Dad. I miss you. I wish I could see you both one last time. Thank you for everything you ever did for me.

Once it was attached to a bright green balloon, Conifer stepped out into the yard with it. No one seemed to want to be the first one to release their balloon, all glancing between one another. Then, amidst the silence, a little voice said, "I love you as much as the stars, Daddy," and a blue balloon drifted up above the rest.

Conifer searched the crowd until she saw Lia, standing with one hand in Cheyenne's. As soon as Lia's balloon was let loose everyone else began to let theirs go. Over a hundred of them rose into the freshly fallen darkness, drifting up towards the stars until the breeze caught them, pulling them out of view.

PART 2
2 MONTHS LATER

CHAPTER 16
FIRST SNOW

A blast of icy wind burned the back of Conifer's ears, curling up under the flaps of her hat and yanking at her leaf-patterned camo jacket. Conifer ducked into the gust, keeping a grip on her bow with one hand and using the other to hang onto a little outcropping of rock, glad she'd had the foresight to tuck all her hair up under the cap. After a long moment the wind faded away, though it took the trees awhile longer to settle. It was the third big gust in fifteen minutes, a clear signal that it was time to call this clifftop hunting trip over before the storm the wind heralded arrived. Polar Bear and Conifer had spotted it coming in earlier that morning, but it seemed to be arriving sooner than expected.

Conifer glanced back at the draft horse she'd taken up the cliffs with her so that she could hunt in the alpine fields covering the slope on the other side and huffed out a little laugh. Rockheart was standing there chewing on some clover looking unbothered.

"You didn't even feel that wind, did you? Practically a hurricane and you couldn't care less."

He just continued to chew.

Shaking her head, Conifer secured her bow next to the two gutted deer she'd draped over his back and grabbed his reins, heading towards Polar Bear's cabin. She'd been hoping for more than two deer on this trip up the cliffs, but the storm meant she was going to have to call it now. She'd managed to bag a couple turkeys as well, at least. Better than nothing, and she wasn't the only one hunting now which helped a lot. They'd set up a count at the lodge, to keep track of what everyone was getting, by spray-painting small silhouettes of each animal type on the outside of the east wall of the dining room. So far they'd gotten nineteen deer—including these two, eight elk, twelve turkeys, and sixty something grouse. They'd backed off the grouse a little, not wanting to dent their population too much, but everything else was still fair game.

It was hard to tell how much the migration patterns of the animals had changed, as Conifer had never hunted in the area before, but it did seem a more chaotic than she was used to seeing. They seemed to be going in all sorts of directions and the sizes of the herds and flocks varied wildly. It made hunting a bit difficult, given that tracking didn't amount to much under those conditions, but she'd still had decent luck calling things in.

"Thought that wind might chase you back here," Polar Bear called as Conifer approached her cabin.

The building was small, maybe a hundred square feet, and sandwiched between two boulders to protect from the wind. It was about three hundred yards down the slope on the back of the cliffs. She'd built a stone fireplace on one end, put a bed against the opposite wall, and placed a little table with a single chair in the remaining space. The attic area was filled with her supplies, and a hefty woodpile was stacked under the overhang of another boulder just outside the front door.

Having her up there had already proven valuable. She'd spotted two big storms—rainstorms—coming with plenty of time to spare. Neither ended up hitting the camp directly, but it had proven what she said when she left: her being up here would give them time to prepare that they wouldn't otherwise get. That left them torn between the relief of not being hit by potentially radioactive rain, and the worry about how dry things were, which raised the risk of fires. Something would hit them eventually though and, given the chill in the wind, Conifer was pretty sure this storm heralded snow, not rain, at their altitude.

"Can't hunt if I can't stand up," Conifer said, looping Rockheart's reins onto a low branch of a nearby pine tree. "This wind'll have everything taking cover anyway."

She nodded. "How's things down below?"

Conifer sighed, giving a little shrug. It had been about two months since pick up day and still no parents had shown up. The subject was now taboo. A couple fights had even broken out when something got brought up that someone else found upsetting.

"The cabins are done," Conifer said eventually. "And nearly all the bunk-beds are as well. We've officially divided everyone up for who's staying in the lodge and who's staying in the cabins."

"How many you got in your cabin?" Polar Bear asked, offering her a canteen of tea. Conifer waved it off, not wanting to take any of her limited supplies. She was about to be even more cut off than the rest of them.

"Fifteen campers," Conifer told her. "Me, Marauder, Valora, and nine of our original campers, plus a few other older campers. Tai went to the lodge because of her asthma, Amy-Leigh went because she has a history of bronchitis, and Giselle..." Conifer sighed again. "Giselle went because she kept picking fights with the others, telling them they were stupid for missing their parents, dumb for wanting things to go back to normal, that sort of thing."

"Putting her in the lodge ain't gonna help any of that," Polar Bear said.

"No, but right now it's just a handful of campers reacting that way. About fifteen. We've got them all together in one room in the attic of the lodge, with a couple counselors who have backgrounds working with troubled kids. It's not the best, but we couldn't figure out a better solution. It's not like they're locked in there. It just gives them a separate space, and the other campers a separate space from them, when needed."

Polar Bear gave a grim nod and changed the subject. "How'd the firefighter end up with you?"

Conifer shrugged. "We had room."

At first she'd been a little annoyed at having Valora around—she'd gotten so used to it just being her and Marauder—but she'd gotten used to it after a few days. She was great with the campers, and had the sort of slow, even reading voice that had you ready to fall asleep in moments. It had become tradition for her to read to the whole cabin before bed every night. The current book, taken from the library in town, was *The Pits*, some fantasy western adventure.

"Anyone sick?" Polar Bear asked, voice deceptively light.

"Some sniffles, some headaches," Conifer admitted. "Aloe is hoping it's just the stress and allergies."

"This was her first job as a nurse, wasn't it? Just graduated?"

Conifer could tell what she was asking. Was Aloe right? Did she know enough to *be* right?

"She could've been an eighty-year-old doctor, it wouldn't make a difference," Conifer said. "There's only so much she can do with what we have and how little we know."

Polar Bear sighed and nodded. "Didn't mean anything by it. I know she's doing her best."

The conversation broke off as another gust of wind attempted to knock them sideways. They clasped hands to hold one another up against it, eyes screwed shut. It felt different from the others, though, pinpricks of it driving into her skin. She cracked open her eyes to see frost dancing around them. As the wind died it remained suspended in the air, glittering in the weak sunlight.

Polar Bear glanced around, then looked at Conifer with worry in her eyes. "Are we ready?"

"I guess we're about to find out."

Conifer led Rockheart down the cliffs and back towards camp, a slow and steady journey that took about an hour-and-a-half. As soon as they crested the lip of the crater and started the journey down no more wind reached them, though Conifer could still hear it howling up above. She hoped Polar Bear was ready, trying not to think about the potential that this could be the last time she saw her for months, if not forever. They'd be lucky to even hear her on the walkies if the weather was bad enough, and if both of hers—or their solar charger—broke she'd be cut off from the camp completely.

The path down switched back and forth along the grade created by some ancient collapse of the cliffs, and while the switchbacks kept the trail manageable, they did not eliminate the steep drop-offs on the western side. Conifer kept a close eye on Rockheart as he plodded along behind her, making sure to watch his footing on the thinner parts of the trail. It happened before she'd ever started coming to Aspen Heart, but she knew at one point a group of campers in a backpacking session had been leading a few pack-horses down when one spooked and fell off the trail. None of the campers were hurt, but the horse had been killed immediately as she'd tumbled down, stopping just short of the lake. Rockheart didn't seem likely to spook, though. They'd taken him from one of the ranches and so far he seemed to be the calmest horse they'd ever had at the camp. This, along with his size and strength, meant he was one of the handful of horses they'd kept. Sometimes the horses were spotted on runs into town and, so far, they seemed to be doing alright, but the real test would come once the snow started.

Once they made it down to the lake Conifer stopped

Rockheart next to flat boulder and used it to climb onto his back. She'd have to ride him bareback, as she hadn't put a saddle on him, wanting him to be able to carry as many kills as possible. It didn't matter now, though. There was plenty of room since she'd only gotten the two deer and two turkeys, and she wanted to get back to the lodge quickly.

The air down in the crater was clear of frost, but when she looked back she saw that the clouds had already sunk to swallow the tops of the cliffs. Knocking her feet against Rockheart's sides, Conifer turned them down the lake trail at a trot. When they eventually passed Marguerite Conifer glanced over, surveying what was left of the place she and Marauder had lived all summer. Only the outdoor kitchen and bathrooms still stood, everything else having been deconstructed to provide materials for the cabins. It twisted her gut a little, seeing the reminder of better times stripped bare like that. It had been such a lovely, simple summer, lazing with Marauder in their tent and listening to their various groups of campers chattering in theirs. Conifer wondered, not for the first time, what happened to the rest of them, those who had been at camp earlier in the summer and left before everything went wrong. Cutting off the thought before it could sink into her mind, Conifer kicked her heels against Rockheart again to urge him a little faster.

Conifer's new cabin came into view a short time later, farthest to the east in the line of three cabins standing behind the much larger lodge. Marauder had taken to calling them hobbit holes once they'd finished burying the backs, sides, and parts of the tops in dirt.

A group of six campers, led by Cheyenne, dashed out to meet her. They all had on their coats to ward off the chill, and several of them had on buckskin and tire boots. They had only managed to make about dozen pairs so far, making the boots communal property for whoever needed them for the day.

"What did you get?" Cheyenne asked, already inspecting

what Rockheart had on his back as she rolled up her two braids and shoved a couple thin sticks through to hold the bundle in place.

"Two does, two toms," Conifer told her. "You good to take charge of skinning and plucking? I need to talk to Marauder."

"Yep, and she's in the cabin with Valora," Cheyenne said, sizing up the two does.

Conifer had taught Cheyenne how to prep game shortly after pick up day, and she'd taken to it with gusto. Nothing about the gore of the task seemed to bother her. The other campers were fine with plucking birds, and helping prep meat once it was off the bone, but Cheyenne was the only one in their group willing to do the skinning and deboning.

Before Conifer could even slide off Rockheart Cheyenne wrangled Paloma and Farrah into helping her pull down the first doe and carry it over to a skinning pole shaped like an upside-down L. Cheyenne tied off the doe's back legs to a sturdy stick that spread them apart and, with the help of the other two, hauled the carcass into the air, tying off the rope to the pole. She'd have to drag over a stump to reach the upper parts of the deer, but that hadn't stopped her yet. Conifer watched with a small smile as Cheyenne softly patted the deer's shoulder, whispering a soft thanks before pulling her skinning knife out of the sheath on her own hip and setting to work. Conifer had given her the knife a few weeks earlier and it had been permanently attached to her ever since. She'd poured over the knife care manual they had at camp, learning how to properly clean, sharpen, and care for it.

Finally swinging off Rockheart, Conifer tied his reins to the hitching post in front of their cabin. Tai waved from where she was helping Tabatha and Sammy-Jo stack firewood under a lean-to they'd built on the front of the cabin. Conifer waved back, kicking mud off her boots as she ascended the steps up to their front door, which was propped open with a rock.

"This was your idea," Valora said. She was sprawled halfway under their cast-iron stove—which had been installed on the back wall a little to the right of the center and just across from the front door—and struggling with a drill. Marauder, who was laughing, was standing awkwardly over top of her, draped across the top of the stove, and was attempting to support a large metal plate against the wall. The plate, about five feet wide and four feet tall, but not very thick, was a dark, glossy black with a scene of mountains cut out along the top edge.

"What are you doing?" Conifer asked, stepping over Valora's legs to lean down and peer under the fireplace so she could get a better look at the project.

"Oh thank god, someone taller than a tree stump, please hold that plate up since you can actually reach it without practically standing on me," Valora said.

"Taller than a tree stump?" Conifer laughed, standing back up to take Marauder's place.

"'Hobbit' seemed too on the nose," Valora said, going back to attempting to secure the plate in place.

"Where'd you get this thing?" Conifer asked.

"In town, at the ranch store, during the run yesterday," Marauder said brightly. She was bouncing a bit as she spoke, sending her faded pink hair fluttering about her face. "It was hidden behind some shelves. Must've been forgotten about. I thought it looked nice, and that it would be good to have a heat reflector behind the stove, so we brought it back."

"It weighs more than she does," Valora muttered, wiggling around to reposition herself so she could screw in the other side.

"What did you get up on the cliffs?" Marauder asked. "I thought you weren't coming back until tomorrow?"

"Two does and two toms," Conifer told her. "But I had to come back early. The storm we radioed about this morning, it's snow."

The cabin went silent and Valora slid out from under the stove, sitting up to look at Marauder and Conifer, drill hanging from one hand. There was grease smudged on her face and on the light gray turtle neck she had on, sleeves rolled up. Her ponytailed hair was mussed on one side where it had rubbed along the bottom of the stove as she'd pulled out from under it.

"What sort of storm?" Valora asked.

"Something from the north west," Conifer told them.

"So, maybe less chance of it picking up as much radiation based on the bombings we know about, but more chance of it dumping snow on us?" Marauder surmised.

"Yeah, that about sums it up," Conifer said.

They went silent again, all three of them surveying the little cabin. Three walls were a soft blue-green color while the back wall was an in-progress mural the kids worked on at night before bed. A few support poles went down the center and the west end was walled off with canvass from the tents, behind which stood the bunk beds. They'd walled off the east end with an actual wall to create a small bathroom in one corner, installing a composting toilet from a campervan there. They'd even laid some new pipe to add a sink, trenching it in to prevent it from freezing. The other corner had been turned into a pantry. The rest of the cabin was left open with a few scrap-wood tables, a couple armchairs, and some bookshelves, along with lanterns for light. Two windows, just big enough for a person to get out through if needed, let in more light, and the entry door faced the lodge, about twenty yards from its back door.

It honestly did look homey and already had an air of being lived in; dog-eared books sat on a couple of the tables, some knitting had been left out on top of the stack of firewood they'd brought inside, paint brushes and paints were still scattered along the back wall. But was it enough to get them through winter?

"Can I use your walkie, Marauder?" Conifer asked. "Mine's almost dead."

She unclipped it from her belt and handed it over.

"No one is still on a run, right?" Conifer asked.

She and Valora shook their heads.

"We all came back yesterday. The next one was supposed to leave tomorrow, though," Marauder told her.

Conifer nodded and pressed the button on the side of the little black and yellow device. They tried not to call out like she was about to often, but the range on the little camp walkies was short enough she wasn't too worried about being overheard. She'd just have to make it quick. "This is Cabin One, I need all groups to copy me for an announcement, over."

"Woodcutters copy."

"Barn copies."

"Lower hunters copy."

"Cabin three copies."

"Crafters copy."

"Cabin two copies."

"Lodge one copies."

"Cooks copy."

"Lodge two copies."

"Smokers copy."

"Office copies."

Conifer hesitated a moment at the sound of Jack's voice over the last response. In the last two months Jack hadn't brought up her taking control once, but Conifer knew Jack still wanted her to. There was something in the way Jack was always giving her detailed rundowns of how and why she was doing things, the way she kept finding excuses to put Conifer in charge over little random things. Being the one to make this announcement, rather than going to Jack and having Jack make it, felt like a thorn under Conifer's nail, proof that Jack's tactics were working without Conifer having realized until too late. There was no going back now, though, so Conifer clicked the button again. "Just got back from visiting our friend. The first snow is here." Even though they were spread out over the whole camp Conifer felt the tension ramp up, felt how thick it made the air feel. "We've likely got an hour or two before it really hits us. Wrap up your projects, bring wood inside, cabins string your ropes out to the lodge, collect as much jugged water as possible in case something goes wrong with the pipes. Use walkies to communicate with other groups. Do not leave your buildings unless you have no other choice. Cover all skin and check in if you do have to leave."

An echoed chorus of "okay" came across the radio one by one.

Conifer clicked the button one last time once everyone had spoken. "And remember; do not eat the snow. We have to minimize exposure any way we can."

Chapter 17
Up the cliffs

Sleep did not come easy for anyone in their cabin. Valora tried to read to everyone as usual, but it was clear no one was paying attention so she'd given up after half a chapter. Eventually everyone wandered off on their own, some hanging in the common area and others going to their beds. Conifer curled up in an armchair that gave a good view of one of their two windows. The puppy their cabin had claimed and named Arrow settled in at Conifer's feet. Conifer didn't remember falling asleep, but she woke with a jolt sometime shortly after dawn, still in the chair. No one else seemed to be awake, but Marauder was asleep in the other armchair. A glance at the clock they'd hung on the wall near the door told Conifer it was just past dawn.

Extracting herself from the chair, Conifer shuffled over to the window, Arrow getting up to follow. The knot of fear in Conifer's chest loosened when she pulled back the curtain and found it was light out. She shielded her eyes against the light of dawn bouncing off the snow until they adjusted. Her shoulders dropped as the rest of the tension bled out of them the clearer her vision became. There wasn't more than a couple inches of snow, with some small drifts up against the buildings.

"Not quite winter just yet, then," Valora whispered from behind her. Conifer was surprised she hadn't heard the floor creak as she'd walked up.

"Not quite," she agreed off-handedly, mind already calculating their next move. "But close enough."

"What are you thinking?" Valora asked, glancing at Conifer.

"The cliff trail will still be passable if we're careful, but more storms could come any time," Conifer told her.

"You want to do another hunting trip," she surmised.

She nodded. "Me, you, five or six horses, maybe a week up there...."

"*Me*?" Valora said, eyes wide. "I've never hunted in my life, and I've only practiced with the guns we have twice."

"Yeah, but you've got the dexterity and training to be safe on the cliff trail even if it is somewhat icy, and the strength to help move kills quickly," Conifer explained. She was already moving to grab her pack from the day before. "I don't need you to hunt. You don't even have to carry a weapon if you're not comfortable, I just need you to assist. Let's go."

"Now?" Valora said, scrambling to fill the spare pack hanging by the door with supplies.

"Now."

Conifer tip-toed into the bedroom and over to Marauder's bunk, changing into clean pants and a new shirt. Valora was right behind her, pulling some clothes off the shelf she shared with Marauder and Conifer, stuffing them into her pack. Coming back out into the main room, Conifer crouched next the armchair where Marauder was still sleeping and lightly nudged her shoulder.

"Hey, wake up," Conifer whispered.

She stirred and blinked up at Conifer, eyes still somewhat hazy with sleep. "How bad is it?"

"Hardly anything," Conifer assured. Marauder let out a deep sigh of relief. "I'm going back up the cliffs, and Valora's coming with. We'll be gone a week. I'm going to get every damn thing I can before the trails become impassable."

She nodded and yawned. "Stay safe."

"I will," Conifer told her. "Remember to keep everyone out of the snow."

"Does it even make a difference?" Marauder muttered, rubbing at one of her eyes. "There's no escaping exposure now."

Conifer shrugged, not really sure how to answer. "Just do what you can."

She nodded, waving goodbye as Conifer and Valora stepped out the front door.

They went to the barn first and found Horseshoe there putting out the morning feed. She'd brought all the animals in and things were a little tighter than was probably wise, but she seemed to be managing. Horseshoe was sleeping in the tack room of the barn, along with two of the camp maintenance workers who had turned into barn helpers.

"Ladies," Horseshoe said, inclining her head in their direction as she hauled a hay bale towards a stall. In the end they had only kept ten horses, turning the rest out to roam. The hope was that they'd fend for themselves well enough to make it through winter, and establish themselves as a wild herd they could pull from if needed. Personally, Conifer doubted this line of reasoning and figured many of them would likely die, but it made the rest of the camp feel better so she kept her mouth shut. She also kept her mouth shut about the fact that, if things did start to go downhill, she had no qualms about shooting any of the horses and butchering them before coming back to camp so no one would ever know the origin of the meat.

"Morning, Horseshoe," Conifer said. "We're gonna need six horses for a long hunting trip up the cliffs. Who do you want us to take?"

Horseshoe dropped the bale into a wheelbarrow and glanced up and down the stalls, hands on her hips. "Take Rockheart again. Knight, Alamosa, Appleseed, Newt, and Iroh. They get along well, and they're good walking a roped line. Should make for a calm group."

Conifer nodded, noting each horse as Horseshoe pointed them out.

"Conifer..." Valora said as they worked to gather all six horses. "Can we bring your radio up?"

Conifer frowned, trying to figure out a reason for it. They'd brought her Bronco back to camp a month earlier, deciding it was just too noticeable where it was, and ever since then it had been sitting idle in the counselor lot. They'd brought the radio into the lodge so it was easier to access, but it had yet to pick up a signal.

"You want to test the signal up there?" Conifer guessed. She nodded.

"No one is going to answer," Conifer said.

"We can't know that unless we try," Valora returned. Conifer had learned over the last two months that the only time Valora had an accent was when she was being stubborn about something, and that was fully in evidence now.

"Alright, sure." Conifer shrugged. It wasn't worth the argument. As far as she was concerned that radio was nothing more than an interesting antique now. If Valora wanted to haul it around that was up to her. "Take Iroh and go get it packed up. I'll meet you at the lodge."

She nodded again and took the reins of the large dappled gray and white horse, leading him out of the barn. After packing up supplies for the horses, Conifer secured the other five in a long line with breakaway knots, putting Knight in the lead and swinging up into her saddle. The group plodded easily up to the lodge where Valora was busy securing the radio and its battery, all wrapped in a blanket, to the back of Iroh's saddle. Iroh, unconcerned with her actions, shook a low-hanging branch of the pine tree in the middle of the yard, nudging it up and down with his nose. It made snow cascade down over him, Valora taking care to try and duck out of the way.

Jack was watching from the porch of the lodge. She looked worried, and a bit pale. Conifer suspected that she hadn't been sleeping much, feeling a twinge of guilt that she might be part of the cause.

"We'll be back soon," Conifer called.

Jack nodded. "Stay safe."

Polar Bear was waiting for them when they trotted up to her cabin. There was even less snow up there, all of it blown away by the wind.

"What's the plan?" Polar Bear asked.

"Leave four of the horses with you, hunt, bring back any game we get to you, you start prepping it while we go back out to hunt more. We're going to stay as long as we can, up to a week," Conifer said.

"And I brought Conifer's radio," Valora added. "I want to try it up here to see if we get anything."

Polar Bear and Conifer shared a glance that Valora didn't see, one that made it clear she thought the radio plan was just as pointless as Conifer did. She didn't say it though, instead waving Valora inside with the bundle of radio equipment. Conifer stayed outside, using rope to create a temporary paddock in a copse of trees, turning the horses out into it. Valora still hadn't come back out by the time she was done so she headed inside, starting to get annoyed that they were wasting time better spent hunting. Polar Bear had placed the radio on top of the little bookshelf, the battery propped next to it. Valora was already sat in front of it and fiddling with the dials. Conifer sighed and leaned against the door frame, hoping she'd finish soon.

"This isn't a bad idea, Conifer," Valora muttered.

"I never said it was a bad idea. I just think it's pointless to keep trying."

Valora turned to glare at her. "You know, Conifer, sometimes you're kind of a bitch."

"I think that's a bit much," Polar Bear muttered, gaze

dancing back and forth between them.

"No, it isn't," Valora said, still kneeling and glaring.

"Why? Because I'm telling you a hard truth?" Conifer returned.

"No, you're telling me *your* truth and insisting it's the only one," She snapped. "I get that you know the most survival crap of anyone in this camp, and I am grateful for that, but you don't know what's going on outside our little bubble. *None of us do*. Maybe there won't be any signal today, but what about tomorrow? You think we're the only ones in the world who survived? Because we aren't. There's still other people out there and I, for one, would like to take every opportunity to check in with the rest of humanity."

"And what if the people on the other end aren't good people, Valora?" Conifer snapped back. "You can track radio signals. What if whoever's listening decides to come for us? To take what we have? To hurt the campers?"

"And what if they fucking don't, Conifer?" Valora shouted, standing up and nearly slamming her head into one of the beams supporting the roof. "What do you get out of being so fucking negative?"

"*Our lives*. The lives of every child in this camp! If we were all adults that would be one thing, but we're not! The camp is full of a fucking bunch of little fucking kids! They can't protect themselves if something happens! They can't survive on their own! And I'm not being negative, I'm being fucking realistic!"

"Ladies—" Polar Bear tried.

Valora bowled over her. "No, you're being scared!"

"Yes, I fucking am! We're in the middle of a fucking nuclear war! If you aren't terrified you aren't fucking paying attention!"

Silence hung heavy, both of them breathing hard as they glared across the few feet between them.

Valora was the one to break it. "We can't be alone here forever. That will kill us as surely as anything else. No one needs to know what we have here. All they'll hear is a single voice. We won't give them a reason to track us down."

Conifer stared at her, taking in the tears sparkling in the corners of her eyes, her chest heaving with heavy breaths. She was bound and determined to do this, no matter what Conifer said. Conifer could see that. And she could see what Valora meant about not giving away anything that would jeopardize the camp. It wouldn't be worth it to try and track down what seemed to be nothing more than a lone person. Probably.

"Be careful," Conifer muttered.

She gave a curt nod and turned back to the radio, sitting down and fiddling with the knobs again.

Conifer sighed and went over to her. "You're doing it too quickly. Let me show you."

"Thank you," she said, voice still stiff.

Conifer demonstrated how to carefully scan each frequency, taking the time to listen, repeating the same callout each time. "Hello hello, can anyone hear me? This is someone reaching out."

They found the emergency broadcast that Conifer found when she'd first gone down the mountain in search of a signal, but nothing else. The broadcast hadn't changed, still repeating the directive to shelter in place. Conifer wondered where it was coming from, what was powering it.

Valora sat back, looking crestfallen.

"You two ever heard of Buckskin Radio?" Polar Bear asked from where she'd sat on the edge of her bed.

"No," Valora said, sniffing.

"It rings a bell," Conifer admitted. She felt like maybe she'd heard an uncle mention it during some drunken holiday storytelling session.

"It was a big thing back before satellite phones and cell phones, but it dwindled when they got popular. Every night during hunting season, at the top of the hour, local stations would send out messages from the families of hunters.

Hunters could listen in and get important information from home that they'd otherwise be cut off from. 'Aunt Becky had an accident, please come home.' 'Anne's had her baby, a healthy boy.' That sort of thing," Polar Bear said.

"So?" Valora said.

Conifer eyed Polar Bear, thinking through what she was saying. "She thinks we should stop listening for signals, and start sending some out," Conifer guessed. "Something regular that people could know to look for."

Polar Bear nodded. "Ain't no way anyone'll try to track the signal over winter, if they even know enough to track it. And Valora's right. Why would anyone even bother for only one or two people?"

"Even up here the range won't be great," Conifer pointed out. "This radio isn't meant for long distance transmission, just back and forth on the highway. That's probably a big part of why we aren't getting much of anything now."

Valora gave Conifer a withering look.

Conifer held up her hands, giving a little wide-eyed shrug. "Sorry. Just saying."

"How do I call out?" Valora asked.

"Pick a frequency, pick up the mic, hit the button on the side," Conifer instructed.

She did it, hesitating a moment before speaking. "Hello. This is—this is someone reaching out. I've been listening, hoping, to hear someone else since this all started, but nothing yet. I figure, maybe that's what the rest of you are doing too. Waiting for someone else to be the first to speak. So I'm taking the plunge. I'm speaking. Is anyone listening?"

She clicked off the mic and all three of them stared at the radio, waiting to see if anyone answered back. It seemed like she was trying to hide it, but the longer the silence stretched on the sadder Valora's face became.

After a minute of silence Valora started again. "That's okay. I'd be wary too. I don't really know what else to say, but I hope just hearing another voice helps—"

Valora broke off, looking out at Conifer's hand that she'd held out. Conifer wiggled her fingers towards her until she slowly handed over the mic. Maybe no one was on the other side. Maybe someone *was* on the other side, and they were a horrible person who was already trying to track them down. But they'd taken the plunge, so they may as well make it worth something.

"I'm with the woman you just heard," Conifer said into the mic. "It's just the two of us, but we're doing pretty good so far. I get that might not be true for the rest of you, though, so here's what you can do:"

Valora looked elated as Conifer started running over basic survival tips. How to keep warm, how to clean water—though it wouldn't do much for radiation, what to do for radiation exposure, how to field dress a deer, types of shelters that could be built, and other bits and bobs that popped into her head. She kept having to switch the mic back and forth between her hands as they got tired from holding down the button. The system wasn't really designed for long broadcasts like this.

By the time Conifer lost steam the sun was hanging low in the sky. It had been at least a couple hours since they'd started broadcasting. More than long enough for someone to track the signal if they'd really wanted to.

"Well, that's all I've got for now," Conifer said. "My partner and I will only be in a place with signal for a short time, but we'll come back on each night we're here with more tips. Nine p.m. mountain time, same frequency."

Valora took the mic back with a smile. "Goodnight, everyone. This...this has been Buckskin Radio."

Conifer nodded once, still unsure about what they'd done, shaking out her sore hand.

"You probably just saved some lives, Conifer," Valora said. Polar Bear nodded in agreement.

Conifer shrugged, hoping they were right but not wanting to dwell on it. It was easier just worrying about keeping their own people alive. If a bit of advice could help others that was a nice bonus, but focusing on their individuality was a little too much for Conifer.

"I'm going to go get our bedrolls," Conifer said, standing up and stretching.

She was relieved when Valora didn't follow immediately, staying behind to talk to Polar Bear about leaving the radio on. It couldn't stay on forever, with only the one battery, but Polar Bear agreed to turn it on for ten minutes at the top of every hour. Shutting the door behind her, Conifer strode over to where she'd stacked their supplies under a tarp and pulled their bedrolls out of the pile, but she didn't go back to the house.

Valora found her several minutes later, sitting with the bedrolls on her lap. She came and sat next to Conifer, arms looped around her knees.

"Sorry for calling you a bitch," she said eventually.

"It was deserved," Conifer replied. She wasn't an idiot. She knew she could come off as cold and cruel without meaning to, especially when she was frustrated. "It's...before all this, I knew, I *knew* that the idea of people acting like animals during an apocalyptic scenario was bullshit. That has been proven over and over through studies of various natural and man-made disasters. But then all of a sudden I was confronted with having to protect so many kids and I just...I don't know how, Valora. You're right, I'm fucking scared. And I'm sorry."

She nodded. "I get it, I do. Thanks for apologizing." They lapsed back into silence until Valora spoke again. "I miss my parents, and my little brothers. I know they'll never hear me on that radio, not all the way in Sweden, but calling out on it...it still feels like trying to reach out to them. Like maybe there will be some miraculous alignment of everything that effects radio waves and my voice will make it all the way there, even for just a moment."

Conifer hummed.

"You're from here, though, right?" Valora asked. "Or at

least hearish. Could your family...could your family hear it?"

"My parents would be the only ones who *might* hear it, if they were alive," Conifer replied, though she doubted the signal would ever reach all the way to Denver. "The rest of my family is scattered all over the country."

"You don't think they're alive?" She asked.

Conifer shook her head. "They lived north of Denver, but probably not north enough." Far enough away the main blast probably wouldn't have killed them, but close enough they would've died a slow death over the next several days as radiation melted through their bodies. Or maybe not. It all depended on where the bomb dropped exactly. These were thoughts that she knew would upset most people more than they did her, but she'd always grieved differently. It was probably something to do with the autism, she suspected, but she didn't really care. It was what it was now. Her parents were gone. She loved them, but they were gone.

"I'm sorry," Valora said.

"I'm sorry you can't speak to yours."

"Do you have any siblings?" Valora asked.

Conifer shook her head again. "Not living ones. I was supposed to have a little brother, two years younger than me, but he was stillborn."

"I'm sorry," Valora whispered again.

Unable to sit still any longer, Conifer rolled to her feet and started back to Polar Bear's cabin. Valora followed at a slower pace.

"Conifer, wait. Jackalope...Jackalope asked me to talk to you," Valora said as Conifer reached for the door latch.

Conifer turned back to see the other woman looking apprehensive. "I'm not taking charge of this camp, no matter who Jack has ask me to do it."

"Well why not?" Valora asked, face open and earnest.

Conifer threw up my hands. "Because I don't know the first thing about running this place! And, despite what everyone seems to think, I do not, in fact, know how to keep this many people alive!" Her voice had gotten a little louder than she intended towards the end and she bit her lip to keep herself from continuing. "I'm fucking winging it, Valora."

Valora was quiet for a moment, staring intently at Conifer who squirmed under the steady gaze. "So that's it? You're afraid that some of us are going to die, and you're scared to have that on your conscience, so you'd rather Jackalope be the one to bare it?"

"What? No! That's.... No!" Conifer spluttered.

Valora, the prominent parts of her face highlighted by the weak moonlight, stared at Conifer. "You're already in charge, Conifer. Ignore it all you want, but you're in charge. You're calling the shots about what we do, and you have been since the beginning."

"I am *not in charge*," Conifer snapped.

She continued as if Conifer hadn't spoken. "You say you don't know how to keep all of us alive, well guess what, you already have. The food would have run out by now, we wouldn't have enough shelter, everyone may have even left camp. You've already saved everyone's life. And, for the record, the rest of us are winging it too, Jackalope included."

"Well I can't keep that shit up! I learned how to survive on my own, maybe with a small group of ten to fifteen people, not almost two-hundred!"

"Do you really think anyone expects you to keep it up?" Valora asked, voice softening. "We all know that death is coming at some point, for some of us sooner than others. But because of you it will hopefully be less of us, and not quite as soon. Why can't you be proud of that?"

Her softer tone stung more than when she'd called Conifer a bitch.

"Just think about it, that's all I'm asking. No one is asking you to be perfect, just to keep doing the best that you can."

"There's nothing to think about. It isn't happening," Conifer muttered, turning away before Valora could press the conversation any further.

CHAPTER 18
ATTACK

"Time to go," Conifer said, shaking Valora awake.

She groaned and looked around bleary eyed. "'S not ev'n light ou'," she muttered.

"Not for another hour and a half, no," Conifer said. "Up."

She groaned again and shimmied out of her bag on Polar Bear's floor. Polar Bear was snoring away up on the bed.

"Take off your clothes, wipe yourself down with these, and change into clean clothes," Conifer instructed, handing her a packet of descenting wipes and a bag containing a freshly washed—with unscented soap—brown jacket. A full shower would've been better, but they didn't have that option.

Valora complied in a way that made it obvious she was still somewhat asleep and not fully aware of what she was doing, but by the time she was changed she seemed to have woken up a bit more. They each ate a couple granola bars and some jerky before heading outside and tossing some blankets over Iroh and Rockheart's backs, leaving the saddles behind. Tension still hung between them, but Conifer knew it needed to be put aside for this hunt to go well, so she dug one of her tools out of a pocket in her jacket, holding it out to Valora.

"Alright, this is a range finder," Conifer told her as they rode. Valora took the palm sized device and peered through the lens. "Easy enough. Point at the target, whisper the number it says to me."

"Got it," she replied. "What else?"

"For now, just that. I can teach you to use my elk calls tonight if you want, but it takes practice to be any good at them. Today, just ride behind me and stay silent. We're going to a blind I set up last time, near a little pond they've been coming to drink at."

It didn't take long to get there, only about twenty minutes on the horses. They left them tied in a clearing away from the pond before making their way to the blind another ten minutes away. The blind was set up about twenty yards from the west edge of what would be more accurately called a mud hole. Conifer could have walked across it without getting her belt wet, and the creek that filled it had gone dry without recent rain. To the north and west, about fifteen yards from the edge, curved the line of the forest. To the south and east was an alpine field of clover and boulders. The blind itself was one Conifer taken from town, a simple one with just enough room for two people and a couple cheap stools for chairs. Valora settled in next to Conifer who indicated for her to keep her eyes on the treeline.

"Nudge me and point if you see something," Conifer whispered.

She nodded and Conifer pulled out a diaphragm elk call, popping it into her mouth and sealing it against the top. Resting her tongue against the latex, she breathed out slowly, moving her tongue to make the call chirp. Valora looked mildly alarmed at the noise, apparently having missed Conifer putting the call in her mouth. Conifer chuckled and popped the call back out, letting it rest on her tongue as she stuck it out at Valora. Settling the call back in place, Conifer called again with a longer, lower note.

The sun wasn't up yet, but the sky had begun to lighten. Conifer continued to call, keeping it varied and taking breaks. Her bow was ready, lying across her lap with an arrow nocked. A fox stopped at the pond for a drink, but Conifer didn't think it was worth shooting. She didn't want to risk startling away bigger game that might be lingering just out of sight.

Conifer was rewarded for waiting several minutes later when Valora nudged her and pointed to a spot between two trees. Nothing was quite visible yet, but something was moving through the low branches. Valora already had the range finder hovering near her chin and Conifer slipped off her stool to stand, clipping her release to the string and preparing to draw it back. Whatever was behind the branches was big, bigger than a deer. Conifer let out a short chirp with the call and waited. The movement paused at the sound, then a beautiful six by six bull elk strode out into the watery early morning sunlight.

"Forty-two," Valora whispered.

He walked towards the pond, presenting a perfect broadside shot. Conifer pulled back her arrow, finger hovering over the trigger as she tracked him to the edge of the water, her third sight-pin resting on his heart. Shifting her eyes a bit, she eyed the downy feathers she'd secured with thread to a nearby branch as a wind gage. They were still. When the bull stopped a few feet from the pond to look around Conifer let the arrow fly. He hardly flinched as it buried itself into his side, just behind his shoulder blade. For a moment everything was frozen, then he slowly fell face forward, thudding into the ground without another sound.

"Jävlar!" Valora muttered, and Conifer glanced over to see her eyes had gone wide. Conifer wasn't sure what she'd said, but it sounded astonished.

"What?"

"That was…quick," she said, eyes still wide.

"That tends to happen when you hit the heart and lungs," Conifer replied. "Come on, let's go get him."

Valora followed Conifer out of the blind and towards the elk until Conifer held a hand out to stop her. The antlers were facing them and the last thing they needed was for one of them to get gored if he wasn't as dead as he looked.

Conifer watched his chest carefully for a few moments, as well as his nostrils for any steam. Seeing none she walked to his butt and toed at his legs. He did not move. Being extra cautious, Conifer moved up his body and used the end of her bow to tap at his shiny, wide open eye. No matter how serious the injury, if there was any life left in him, tapping his eye would've triggered some sort of reflexive movement, but there was none.

"We're good," Conifer said, still keeping her voice low. "Go grab Rockheart from the clearing, and stay quiet. I'll get started gutting him."

Valora nodded and turned back the way they'd came. Going around to the elk's stomach, Conifer knelt down, setting her bow aside. Pulling some paracord out of her fanny pack she started knotting a length around each upper leg, laying the trailing ends out. Once each leg was tied she secured the trailing ends to stakes and tossed them over his back. The methods were so familiar her mind started to drift as she went through the motions. Stepping over the elk she picked up the stakes, holding them tightly and leaning back to pull the legs up and over, rolling the animal somewhat onto his back, exposing his chest and stomach. With a convenient rock she hammered the stakes into the ground, making sure they were secure and holding the legs up enough before going back around. Pulling out her gutting knife, she made a clean slice from his groin up to his neck. He was easily the biggest kill anyone had made so far, at least seven-hundred pounds. She was already parceling him out in her head, planning what bits could be used for what. Ground burger meat, steaks, jerky. If she had gotten him later in the week many of his organs could've been used as well, but as it was they didn't have a good way to preserve them for as long as needed before getting back to camp. The organs could be used as bait, though, to lure other animals in, so they wouldn't go totally to waste.

Once he was split open Conifer moved to saw through

his sternum, but before she could get the saw in position she froze, instinct drawing her eyes back to the trees. It had gone silent. Too silent. Conifer saw Valora stepping out from behind the blind, holding Rockheart's reins, and held up a hand to stop her, shooting her a meaningful look. She frowned but stopped, and Conifer turned her eyes back to the trees, hand still held up. Slowly she reached out her other hand towards her bow, dropping the saw in the dirt and gently lifting the bow from the ground. She brought it to her lap, not caring at the moment that she was smearing blood on it.

She could see Valora out of the corner of her eye, still about forty yards away. She was watching the trees as well, but Conifer couldn't tell if Valora actually sensed what Conifer did or if she was just looking because Conifer was. Conifer still hadn't seen anything, but *something* was there. Watching them. Eying her kill. Ordinarily Conifer would've stood up, started shouting, made herself big to scare it off. But now....

Conifer nocked an arrow and waited. A branch twitched and Conifer raised the bow to sight in on it, staying on her knees to keep her form obscured through the antlers of the bull that was between her and whatever was in the forest. A nose parted the branches first, which made it clear that it was a bear. Except there was only supposed to be one kind of bear in this area: black bears. And this was not a black bear nose. It was way too big, and way too high up, to be a black bear.

The nose was quickly followed by the massive, shaggy body of a grizzly. Conifer sucked in an involuntary breath, knowing at this point that her only good options were to either give up the bull or kill the bear. She had her pistol if it came to that, but she doubted the pistol had enough power to kill a bear, not without it being the luckiest shot she ever took. She wasn't sure her bow would do any better. Bears were difficult to kill under the best of circumstances due to their fat as well as their loose skin. It was easy to miss the vitals. Easy for that loose skin to slip over a wound and staunch the bleeding.

Conifer's options continued to dwindle as the bear took another step out of the trees, twitching nose held high and pointing toward Conifer and the bull. The thing was massive. All rippling muscle and sharp teeth. Conifer could see it well, but the tangle of antlers between her and it was blocking any attempt at a clean shot.

It took another step and in one swift movement Conifer stood up, took a stance, drew her arrow, and let it fly. It hit, but the shot was not as clean as the one she'd taken at the elk. The angle was wrong and it hadn't gone in as deep. Conifer suspected it hit some bone in the shoulder. The bear gave an ear-splitting roar, staggering, its huge head swinging side to side, searching out the threat. Conifer nocked and loosed a second arrow, this one burying in a couple inches from the first and going much deeper. The bear froze, coughing out a strangled roar as its eyes focused in on Conifer.

"Fuck," Conifer muttered, dropping her bow against the bull and drawing the pistol.

The bear loped towards her, gasping for breath, its left front leg dragging slightly. Conifer heard Valora shout, but ignored her as she raised the gun and squeezed off three shots aimed at the bear's neck. The damn thing didn't even flinch, so Conifer did the only thing she could think of. She dropped, shoving herself as close to the elk as she could. The bear vaulted over both the carcass and Conifer, skidding in the dirt as it turned around. Some part of Conifer was detached enough from the situation to hear Valora screaming, to feel the warm blood of the elk soaking into her clothes, her hair. There was fear there, but Conifer shoved it aside and aimed two more shots at the underside of the massive animal. It still didn't care, and now Conifer had nowhere to go.

And she was running out of bullets.

One of its huge paws swiped out at Conifer's boot, claws digging into the leather and tangling in the laces. There was too much adrenaline racing through Conifer's system for her to tell if she'd been hurt. She jammed her other foot against its nose as it began to drag her towards its dripping mouth. It let out a deafening roar of anger and she took the chance, yanking her foot away from its nose and firing several more shots straight down its throat.

This time, it cared, stumbling backwards. Its claws were still hooked into Conifer's boot, pulling her along with it as its eyes rolled back. With a whump that shook the ground, it collapsed, but its chest continued to rise and fall off rhythm. Tugging her boot until it was free, Conifer got up and staggered around to deliver her final bullet to its heart.

Valora arrived just as the sound from the shot faded. Conifer couldn't tell if it had taken Valora an absurdly long time to run the distance to where she was, or if the attack had really been that quick. Valora wrapped her arms around Conifer, pulling her away from the bear and lowering her to the ground a few feet away.

Conifer's heart was racing, and she was experiencing one of those rare moments where she realized how thin the air was up there. The now empty pistol was still gripped tightly in her hand and, empty or not, she didn't feel like putting it down.

"Do you have a fucking death wish?" Valora gasped, clutching her chest as it heaved with heavy breaths. Her eyes were stretched wide and pupils blown out enough to nearly swallow her irises entirely.

"I didn't ask the bear to attack me!" Conifer said, panting just as hard. "And no, no I do not! I quite like living, actually. Do you think I would have learned all this shit about surviving the end of the world if I had a death wish?"

"I have seen you do, like, a dozen life threatening things in just the two months I've known you, not counting the bear!"

"Yeah, but that doesn't mean I want to fucking die! It means I've got bad judgment about my own personal safety!"

They'd both been shouting, but now that the adrenaline

was leaving her system, Conifer was fighting not to laugh. What. The. Hell. She'd just killed a grizzly with a pistol. Too bad she'd likely never have a bar to tell that fish story in.

The laughs finally forced their way out and she slid to the ground, giggling and not caring about how much mud she was adding to the elk blood she was covered in. Valora looked at her like she'd lost her mind, but it didn't take long before she broke out laughing as well, plopping into the mud next to Conifer.

"It better not be like this every time I come hunting with you," Valora said, laughter still shaping the words.

"I make no promises," Conifer replied.

"Are you okay?" Valora asked once they'd calmed down, using a tone Conifer was sure she normally reserved for her work as a firefighter. It was clinical, but Conifer could hear the true concern in it as she leaned over and pulled apart Conifer's tattered boot to get at her foot.

"That was, ah…that was a bit more adventure than I had anticipated this morning," Conifer said between deep breaths.

"No kidding."

She pulled off the boot and Conifer's sock, both of them immediately releasing a deep breath. The skin wasn't broken, but some nasty bruises were beginning to form.

"Can you move it?" Valora asked.

Conifer carefully wiggled her toes. The foot felt sore, but she didn't feel any bones grinding and she told Valora as much. Valora helped her to stand, keeping an arm out for Conifer to hang onto as she tested her weight, glad to find she could take it without pain.

"I thought grizzlies were extinct here," Valora said.

"Technically they are," Conifer replied, slowly regaining the ability to breathe normally. "But they aren't in areas not that far north. This one could've easily made it here in the last two months, scared out of its territory by what's happening. It looks like it has been eating, but not as much as I'd expect for an animal about to go into hibernation."

"Well. Does grizzly at least taste good?" Valora asked.

This startled a short laugh out of Conifer. "Don't know. Never had one. Predators are hit or miss on how they taste."

"Guess we'll find out."

They were interrupted by Polar Bear galloping around the corner on Knight. She splashed through the edge of the pond, stopping right near the bear. Knight snorted and backed up a bit, eying the shaggy form warily.

"Shit damn, ladies, you okay?" She said, surveying the scene, eyes widening as she saw the blood Conifer was covered in. "I heard the roar and the shots. Knew you prefer your bow, so I figured I should come check on you."

"Yeah," Conifer told her. "We're good. I'm good, it's just elk blood. I think it smelled the bull when I started gutting it, maybe heard my calls too."

Polar Bear shook her head once and slid off Knight, going over to crouch next to the bear, then looking down at Conifer's bare foot and the mangled boot lying next to it.

"Saw a lot of these in the Northern Territories," she said. "Mean fuckers when you piss 'em off. Can't imagine the kind of mood they're in under these circumstances."

"Not a good one, apparently," Valora said.

"We need to get them both gutted," Conifer told them. Sliding her pistol back into its holster, she bent down and pulled her ripped boot back on, though the sock was beyond saving. The boot had a big gash down the inner side, and the laces were broken in a few places, but a bit of creative knot tying with some more paracord from her fanny pack held it on well enough for now. She was glad it had at least been her hiking boots, not her good winter boots. The hiking boots were a loss, but one that would be less important in the immediate future. "We'll get them back to the cabin and start butchering them there, then go back out this evening for a bit."

"You sure you're okay, Conifer?" Valora asked, eyebrows knotted and hand hovering near Conifer's elbow.

Conifer thought about it, staring at the bear. It had been a terrifying few minutes, but she was still standing. She'd survived a grizzly attack with only a bow and a pistol, and she'd come out of it with only a few bruises. "Yeah, I think I am."

They had to quarter the bear and bring it back in two trips for Knight and Iroh to manage it, but Rockheart was able to handle the whole bull once it was gutted—though Conifer did have to cut off the lower parts of all four of its legs so they didn't drag on the ground, and tie the antlers to its abdomen so they didn't flop around and snag on things. Once at Polar Bear's cabin they set to work on skinning the animals, hanging them from trees to make the work easier. Polar Bear had some practice at it, but not much, and Conifer had to show her how to do it more efficiently. Valora went inside to check the radio while they worked.

"You're quiet," Polar Bear observed.

Conifer shrugged. "I'm always quiet."

She shot Conifer a pointed look.

Conifer sighed. "Just thinking. Of all the ways I could die right now, a locally extinct animal didn't even break the top hundred possibilities before this morning."

"You handled it, though," she replied. The last of the skin dropped off the quarter of the bear she was working on and she picked it up, hanging it inside-out over a branch. Once they were done preparing the meat Conifer was going to show Polar Bear how to ready it for tanning.

"I did," Conifer admitted. In less than five minutes she'd gone from not knowing the bear existed, to having it dead at her feet despite multiple failed shots. If she hadn't killed it, it would've killed her. Easily. She suspected that scaring it off wouldn't have worked either, not with the condition it was in. It had showed up and the only thing to be done was to handle it. So she had.

As the afternoon stretched towards evening Conifer went down the hill to a creek to wash out her clothes and hair. She'd scrubbed the worst of the blood off her arms back at the pond, but she would need to get rid of the rest if she wanted to continue hunting effectively. She'd left Polar Bear and Valora to continue working on the bull and the bear.

She stripped off her clothes and set them in the bottom of the creek, weighted down with rocks. Using a cup, she bent forward and poured the glacially cold water over her hair, scrubbing a hand through it as she did but being careful she didn't go too fast. The cold shock, with her head hanging upside-down could make her pass out if she wasn't careful, something she'd learned the hard way when she was a kid.

"Want some help?" Valora asked, and Conifer stood to see her standing a few yards up the hill, hands in her pockets.

"You should warn people when you're going to walk up on them while they're nude," Conifer muttered. Honestly, she didn't care about Valora seeing her, she just wanted Valora to go away and leave her alone for a bit.

"You shouldn't be nude," she replied, walking over. "It's only forty-five degrees out."

"Positively balmy," Conifer returned, voice flat.

"Conifer—" Valora said, tone tentative.

"I can only handle one heart to heart per week," Conifer interrupted. "You used up my weekly quota last night talking about family. Also, the bear used up my emotional range for the next week, so you're doubly out of luck."

Valora huffed and went silent. After a few seconds she pulled one hand out of her pocket, holding something Conifer couldn't quite make out in the falling light. When she held it up Conifer realized it was a claw from the bear, with a bit of leather cording tied around it to turn it into a necklace. Valora closed the distance between them, then reached over and dropped the string over Conifer's head.

"Thanks for saving us this morning, Conifer."

"You would've been able to get away," Conifer pointed out. "It was interested in the bull and in me. It didn't even see you."

"Just take the compliment, would you?" She said, a hint of a smile on her face.

Conifer tangled her fingers in the cording around the claw, running her thumb up and down the softly curved top side. "Sure."

The weather held throughout the week and they continued with their routine of an early morning hunt, butchering and prep work during the day, and another hunt in the evening. When they came back from the evening hunts they'd get cleaned up and head into Polar Bear's cabin to call out on the radio. Valora had figured out that they could use a hair tie and a chunk of wood to hold the button down, which made the longer broadcasts easier. They still hadn't gotten any answer, but Valora was determined to keep trying. The routine was that they'd call out twice across at least ten frequencies, then they'd do Buckskin for an hour or so. Valora generally talked first, telling random stories, before handing it over to Conifer for what she'd started calling "survival hour." Valora had told the story of Conifer killing the bear four times now, somehow managing to make it sound more like a Hollywood film every time.

On the sixth day they decided it was time to head out. Hunting had been even more successful than Conifer had hoped, and they were close to the limit of what the horses could carry even with Valora and Conifer walking and carrying some of the meat themselves. Aside from the bear and the bull, Conifer had gotten four cow elk, three doe deer, and two buck deer. On the smaller side, she'd gotten half a dozen turkeys, several woodchucks, and a coyote.

Three of the deer had all been shot the day before, in the morning. They'd come across a big herd of them and Conifer managed to pick off stragglers around the edges without immediately spooking the others. All told, it was about 2,000 pounds of meat and hides. Her father would've been proud, calling up all his friends to brag about his daughter, the mighty hunter. It stung to think about.

Once the horses were packed up they bid Polar Bear goodbye and headed down. A storm had been visible to the west when they'd woken up that morning, but the sky had since taken on a layer of low, hazy gray clouds that made it hard to tell how big the storm was, or how fast it was moving.

"Do you think we'll be able to go up the cliffs again?" Valora asked. She had three of the horses and was walking a safe distance behind Conifer's group of three, so Conifer had to strain a bit to hear her. She had to focus on her steps more than usual as well, as her boot was still not in the best shape. She'd stabbed some holes in it to lace the gash together better, but it would need a more serious, and less irritating, repair back in camp, if it could even be repaired enough to matter at all.

Conifer glanced up at the sky and shrugged. "No idea."

"Will Polar Bear really be okay up there alone?"

Conifer shrugged again. "She's got the skills, as far as I know. We'll just have to trust that she knows what she's doing."

Turning around the last switchback, the lake campground came into view, and Conifer was surprised to see a group of campers sitting there. Cheyenne was with them, her hair loose and blowing in the wind. She waved and Conifer waved back, spotting Marauder with the group as well. Looking over them as they got closer, Conifer realized it was most of her and Marauder's original unit, along with Jack who was standing at the edge of the trees, a little aside from the group.

"Did you really get a bear?" Cheyenne called once Conifer and Valora were closer.

"How do you know about that?" Conifer shouted back.

"We heard you on the camp radio!" Cheyenne replied. "Jackalope heard you the first night and then the whole camp came to listen every night before bed!"

"Jackalope wouldn't let us answer you, though," Farrah said. "She said it was too risky."

"Jack was right," Conifer told them.

Valora and Conifer stopped the horses as they reached the knot of curious children at the lakeside, all of them peering hopefully at the horses.

"Already butchered, sorry," Conifer told them. "But yeah, I got a bear. Here, this is some of the pelt." Conifer pointed to the bundle of pelts on Iroh's back, holding up a piece of the long brown fur that was sticking out one end.

A chorus of awed "woah"s went around the group as the campers clustered around to stroke it.

"And you really are okay?" Marauder asked, eyes going up and down Conifer's body, stalling out when they reached her damaged boot.

"Just fine," Conifer assured. "My boot took the brunt of it."

"Buckskin radio," Jack said, speaking for the first time. Conifer stiffened a little, wondering if she and Valora were about to be told off for broadcasting like that. Jack smiled a bit, but it didn't quite reach her eyes, which looked exhausted like always. "I'm glad you reached out to help people like that."

Conifer nodded once. "Thanks, Jack."

She nodded back.

Conifer took a deep breath. "Jack, you and I need to have a talk."

Chapter 19
The First Storm

"Have a seat," Jack said, waving towards one of the chairs in front of her. Jack had been sleeping in her office on the couch in there, but aside from the blankets and pillow, nothing about the office had changed.

Conifer sat, but didn't settle into the chair.

"That was a very dramatic story, about the bear," Jack said, sitting in her chair on the other side.

"Valora oversold it," Conifer told her.

"The core of it was pretty clear, oversold or not. You got charged by a grizzly with maybe thirty yards between you and it and came out the other side with your boot as the only casualty. That's damn impressive," Jack said, crossing her arms on the desktop and leaning forward. Her sleeves pulled up slightly and Conifer saw the dark purple edge of a bruise around her right wrist.

"What's that?" Conifer asked, nodding towards the mottled skin.

She glanced down at it. "Oh, just knocked my arm against a log when I was helping with firewood yesterday. But you didn't come here to talk about a bruise on my arm."

"No, I..." Conifer sighed and straightened up. "You've been trying to get me to take control of this camp since we first went into town. If, *if*, I were to do that...what would it mean?"

"Just being the formal decision maker," Jack said. "Which,

let's be honest, you already are."

"I admit that's true, in some ways," Conifer told her. "But keeping this camp running, these people alive, it isn't just making decisions about shelter and when to go hunting and what to take from town. It's about breaking up fights between the kids, talking the other counselors out of leaving, organizing activities, organizing everything. I can make the survival decisions, but I don't know that I can do that *and* make the people decisions."

"What do you suggest, then?" Jack asked.

"You said in the beginning that our ability to survive came from all of us working together, from each person offering the things only they know, and you're right. So let's split it. We'll run this place together, fifty-fifty. You worry about the people, the day-to-day, I'll worry about the bigger picture of survival." Conifer held her breath, hoping she'd accept this compromise.

Jack contemplated for a long moment before giving a slow nod. "I can see the logic in that."

Conifer deflated, settling back into the chair. "Is that a yes, then?"

She nodded again, just as slow but a couple of times. "Yes, it is. For now, at least. We'll need to create a more formal division of who is in charge of what, and make sure it is clear to everyone else, and we'll need to continue to meet at least once a week."

"For now?" Conifer asked.

She shrugged, casting her eyes away. "Let's just get through winter."

⁂

"So how'd it gooooo?" Marauder asked as Conifer entered their cabin. She was alone in there, though it looked like she'd just been carrying wood inside and was about to head back out. There was sawdust all over her flannel. One of Conifer's flannel, she realized. She didn't mind. Marauder borrowed her flannels all the time, even though they were huge on her.

"We're splitting formal control of the camp," Conifer told her. Pushing aside the canvass that blocked off the bedroom, she strode over to her bed, Marauder following behind. The bunk was slightly larger than the others so that it would be long enough for Valora on the bottom and Conifer on the top. Conifer technically—technically—fit on the regular beds, but she didn't mind the few inches of extra legroom she now had. "I'll handle the survival side of things, she'll handle the day-to-day side. We're making the formal announcement at breakfast tomorrow."

"Well that sounds fair," Marauder said. She sat across from Conifer on her own bed, which was under Cheyenne's, as Conifer peeled off everything but her bra and underwear. There were showers in the lodge, a couple of them anyway, but they were in use.

"Could you grab me the water bucket and a washcloth?" Conifer asked.

Marauder nodded and slid out of the room, returning with the half full bucket and a cloth a moment later. Conifer wiped down her skin, getting off the top layer of sweat and dirt before tossing the cloth back in the water. It had been cold, but she was getting used to that.

"This will be good, Conifer," Marauder said.

"I know," Conifer admitted. "It just…feels strange. Taking control of this place, even partially. I grew up here, you know?"

She nodded sympathetically.

Conifer went to grab some clean jeans only for Marauder to snatch them away and offer up a pair of sweats instead.

"If anyone deserves to nap for the rest of the day, it's you," she said.

"There's work to do."

"You already did work," Marauder returned. "About 2,000 pounds of it. I'm not a hunter but even I know that is an insane amount of kills in a week."

"I got lucky," Conifer said, making a grab for the jeans.

She shook her head and leaned back to keep them out of reach. "Luck or not, work is work. Take. A. Nap."

"If I nap I'll be up all night," Conifer tried.

"Then read a book."

"Conifer!" Someone shouted from outside. The shout wasn't in the tone of someone just trying to find Conifer, it was in the tone of someone who was worried.

Both of them stilled before scrambling towards the door. Conifer yanked on the jeans as she went, not bothering with a shirt as she kicked her feet into her boots. They made it to the door at the same time and almost got stuck trying to exit together, but they didn't have to get outside to know what was wrong. Cheyenne, Orla, Aadila, and Farrah were all standing by a half-empty cart of firewood, looking up at the darkening gray sky. Fat, fluffy flakes of white were slowly falling on them, dusting their shoulders and hair. Even as Conifer and Marauder watched the flakes grew in number and speed.

"Marauder, call out to everyone, now. This is a real storm. The rest of you, get as much of the wood inside as you can," Conifer ordered.

Everyone nodded and leaped into action. Conifer went back inside, pulling on a shirt and gloves and grabbing extra shirts for the kids to wrap around their faces. Marauder was busy on the walkie as Conifer dashed out to help the kids. Within five minutes the rest of their cabin had joined them, rushing to get the wood inside. The other two cabins were doing their own preparations. Cabin two was better securing the canvass flap that covered the entrance to their outdoor wood storage, while cabin three was securing their rope line that would guide them to the lodge if they needed it. The lodge already had enough wood stored out of the way of the storm, but those staying in there were still busy checking all the windows and pulling the curtains. They also had to check the canvass that now enclosed the porch, Conifer knew. Enclosing the porch that way provided a large dry area for storing the wood, with the added benefit of blocking any light from the windows. Having so much wood stored so close to the lodge was a fire hazard, something Valora had immediately pointed out, but it had still been the best option. The lodge was already made of wood anyway. What was a little more?

Within twenty minutes everyone was inside, shucking off snow-damp clothes and standing there shivering in their underwear while Valora got the fire going. Conifer hoped all the meat she'd brought down had been properly secured. She'd have to remember to ask later, but for now she just wanted to get warmed up.

"There's already half an inch of snow," Farrah said, peering out the window.

"So much for Halloween," Lorelai said, inching closer to the stove as it started to roar.

"It's Halloween?" Cheyenne asked, voice taking on an odd tone.

"Tomorrow," Lorelai clarified.

Everyone in the group went quiet. Conifer had given up on keeping track of the date weeks ago and it seemed many of the others had as well, or they'd just lost track. Having such a distinct reminder of how much time had passed felt strange. It both felt like summer had only been a day or two before, but also years and years ago. How could it be Halloween? How could it *not* be Halloween?

"Should we celebrate?" Sammy-Jo said after a moment.

"Ask again once we're warm," Paloma told her.

⁂

Half-an-hour later everyone was changed into warm, comfortable clothes and the cabin was nearing an acceptable temperature. Arrow, having checked that each of her herd of children were alright after the panic, settled in on her blanket next to the fire. The wet clothes were divided into batches to be run through the peddle powered washing machine they'd made out of a small plastic barrel. Everyone would take turns running it and the clothes would be hung to dry from ropes attached to the rafters.

"How would we even celebrate Halloween?" Orla asked. She was sprawled out on the floor in front of the stove, as was everyone else. "I don't think we even have candy in camp."

"We can make candy next time we get to the lodge," Valora said.

"Yeah, but that might be awhile..." Farrah responded, glancing out the window. She was right. The wind was howling and it was impossible to see more than a foot through the driving snow despite the fact the sun had not yet set. They couldn't even see all the way to the ground to guess at how much accumulation there had been.

"I'm going to say no to scary stories right now," Sammy-Jo said.

"Agreed," Marauder said. "Nothing scary."

"Well, if we've tossed out scary and tossed out candy, that's about all there is to Halloween," Lorelai muttered, looking a bit annoyed.

"Just the modern parts," Marauder told them. "It started as a Celtic festival to mark the changing of the seasons and honor the dead. They'd build big bonfires and make sacrifices to the fire to ensure their survival through winter."

"That seems rather fitting," Conifer murmured.

"Can you tell our fortunes with your tarot cards, Marauder?" Lorelai asked.

Marauder and Conifer shared a glance. Conifer knew Marauder believed in the power of her cards and guessed she was worried about what they might tell the kids.

"How about she teaches y'all about the cards?" Conifer suggested. "It'll keep us occupied longer."

This was met with sounds of agreement so Marauder got up, coming back with her deck. It was in a lovely cherry stained wood box with a gold clasp. She slid the large, silky cards into her hand. They were a soft peach color, blocky, expressive brush strokes in pastel colors twisting together to form the images on the deck. Many of the kids scooted closer, listening intently as Marauder began to explain the cards one by one.

Cheyenne was busy working the washing machine, but once she handed it off to Sierra she didn't join the others around Marauder. Instead she vanished into the bedroom. When she didn't come back out Conifer got up and followed her. She was sitting in the middle of Marauder's bed under her own, arms wrapped around her legs and face buried in her knees. Conifer sat down on Valora's bed across from her, so Cheyenne wouldn't feel crowded.

"Hey," Conifer said softly.

"Hey," she sniffed. It was clear from her voice she'd been crying.

"Want to talk?" Conifer asked.

She shook her head.

"Want a hug?" Conifer tried.

She gave a little nod, so Conifer moved over and wrapped her arms around Cheyenne, tucking the girl's head under her own.

"It's my mom's birthday today," she hiccupped after a few minutes.

"Oh Cheyenne," Conifer said, hugging her a little tighter. "I'm sorry."

She uncurled slightly, rubbing at her eyes and continuing to hiccup as she spoke. "We'd always go—go out for break—breakfast, at one of those—those places with the pan—pancakes as big as the plate and—and an inch thick."

Conifer rubbed her back, letting her get it out.

"I—I want to go—home," she sobbed.

Conifer felt a few tears leaking down her face as well.

"I'm sorry Cheyenne, I'm so sorry."

Before Cheyenne managed to work up more words Farrah poked her head around the canvass wall, looking worried.

"Cheyenne?" Farrah asked, taking a tentative step inside. "What's wrong?"

Conifer glanced down at Cheyenne, who just started to cry harder.

"It's her mom's birthday," Conifer said softly.

"Oh," Farrah said, voice quiet and eyes wide.

She watched Cheyenne for another moment before turning back to the main room. The canvass was still pulled back, but not enough for Conifer to see what Farrah was doing. Conifer could hear what was going on, though. Everyone went quiet and then there was a shuffle of movement. A moment later everyone had followed Farrah into the bedroom and over to Cheyenne's bed. Cheyenne watched them all, still crying and hiccuping and curled up in Conifer's arms.

"Can we hug you too?" Farrah asked.

Cheyenne glanced around at everyone before she gave a shaky nod. After some awkward shuffling everyone had their arms around Cheyenne and Conifer. Half the group was standing, leaned awkwardly over one another. Arrow kept shoving her nose into the pile, trying to find a way to insert herself into the bunch.

"Okay, okay," Cheyenne said after a minute, wiggling everyone off. "Don't break the bed." She smiled out at everyone, wiping away a few last tears. "Thanks."

Arrow, taking advantage of the clear space, leaped onto Cheyenne's lap and started earnestly licking her chin. Cheyenne laughed, scrunching Arrow's ears in her hands and trying to lean away.

"Do you want to do something to honor your mom?" Marauder asked gently.

"Like what?" Cheyenne sniffed, patting Arrow's head.

"Well, it's not quite a Halloween thing, though I suppose it would be similar to the old bonfires. I was thinking you could carve her name into a stick, along with a simple message, and burn it while thinking about happy memories of her," Marauder said. "Think of it as a way to wrap up everything you're feeling right now, acknowledge it, and move forward from it."

Cheyenne contemplated a minute before giving a slow nod. She reached over and grabbed her pocket knife from where it sat next to her skinning knife on the shelf of her things. Quietly she padded back out to the main room, stopping to select a stick from the wood pile. Everyone followed, a few of the others bringing their own pocket knives and selecting sticks as well.

"Away from your bodies," Valora reminded them. "Go slow."

For the next hour the only sounds were the howling of the wind, and the quiet flicking of steel through wood. Cheyenne finished first and Conifer saw that her stick read "Miranda, Mom, Goodbye, I love you." She got up and carefully opened the stove, kneeling in front of it. Taking the poker, she nudged the burning logs around to create a good spot for the stick. With a quick flick of her wrist she slid it inside, sitting back on her heels to watch as it caught and burned. Once the words were no longer visible she shuffled out of the way and Lorelai moved to slide hers in.

Conifer couldn't help but be reminded of the balloon ceremony, and how similar this felt. They were probably always going to need to do little things like this, she realized. Little things to acknowledge the pain and let it go. Maybe she'd suggest the rest of the camp carve—or paint—their own sticks as well.

Cheyenne made her way over to Conifer where she was leaning against the front wall, coming to lean next to her.

"When your mom dropped you off, she told me how much you loved this place," Conifer said quietly. "How much it meant to you. I think she'd be happy that, if you couldn't be with her, at least you could be here."

"She went here too, once, when she was my age," Cheyenne said. "And her mom was a counselor here for a couple summers before she had my mom."

Conifer was a little surprised she hadn't mentioned any of that before.

"All the more reason for her to be glad you're here," Conifer said. "It's a place you have a legacy, like me."

⁂

Between everyone's nerves about the storm and the wailing of the storm itself they all struggled to settle once they went to bed. Conifer could hear everyone shifting around in their beds. Every now and then someone would get out of bed to put a few more logs on the fire or use the bathroom. Time slipped around in Conifer's mind and she knew she was dozing on and off, but even the mental and physical exhaustion of the previous week was not enough to keep her under for long. The wind never settled and by morning the snow was still going just as strong.

"Can't we open the door for a second and check?" Orla asked.

"We still won't be able to see enough to matter," Conifer told them. "Come eat breakfast."

The meal that morning was bread and jam, along with granola bars. They'd debated putting a fridge in the cabin and burying an electrical cord out to the lodge to power it, but they'd never gotten around to it. Now it was too late. All their food that couldn't go into the pantry would have to come from the lodge, which would mean crossing through the storm. It wasn't that far, at least, but they had enough in the pantry to last for roughly a week so they'd worry about it later.

"Happy Halloween," Lorelai said as they all ate.

"You really like Halloween," Aadila replied, amusement in her voice.

"Best holiday ever," Lorelai told her. "My family goes all out. We turn the backyard into a little carnival for the whole neighborhood."

They continued to chatter, cleaning up after themselves once they were done. The clothes from the day before were taken down from where they'd been hung from the rafters to dry and brought back to everyone's bunks, stored in the boxes underneath. Still the wind continued to howl. They checked in with the lodge and the other two cabins, as well as Horseshoe in the barn and Aloe in the nurse's shed, throughout the day. Everyone was fine, but it was clear their nerves were getting more and more frayed.

"What if the storm doesn't stop?" Tabatha asked around noon. She was attempting to see out the window, though they still couldn't see more than a foot.

"It will stop," Conifer assured.

"What if it buries the cabin?" Paloma asked, looking out the window with Tabatha.

"It is nowhere near to burying the cabin, I promise. We can still see it blowing, and we can see at least a foot out into it. That means, *at most*, it is up to a foot below the window." Conifer left out the very real possibility they could be buried by the end of winter. Plans had already been made for that, should it happen. They'd be digging out as much as possible after each storm to clear room for more snow. Should it get to the point they were buried anyway, the people staying in the lodge would come dig them out.

"Remember how I was looking forward to seeing snow for the first time?" Aadila said. "I would like to say that, after these first couple impressions, I've decided I hate it."

This sent a chuckle around the group, and echoed agreement.

As quickly as the storm came, it was gone. The wind died

off so fast just after midday it was almost startling. Everyone looked around at one another, not quite believing it. Once everyone realized it had truly gone silent there was a scramble for the two windows. It took a few moments for the last bits of snow to settle, revealing a landscape of white. There were huge drifts, but it looked like, overall, there was only about two-and-a-half feet of snow blanketing the ground, maybe a bit less.

"Yeah, I don't like it," Aadila muttered.

"We'll manage," Conifer assured the kids. Carefully, she cracked open the door, not wanting to let snow inside if there was a drift there. There was a bit of one, about five inches on the top step, but it remained in place, an imprint of the door panels in it.

"We have to shovel that, don't we?" Cheyenne asked from where she was peering out next to Conifer.

"Mmmhm," Conifer said, not quite focused on her. Two feet of snow this time of year wasn't unheard of, but it wasn't exactly common either. Colorado's snowiest months tended to be towards later winter, not late fall. There had been predictions all year that it was going to be a bad winter, and now it was looking like that might be true.

CHAPTER 20
SICKNESS

It took an hour, but with campers and counselors digging towards the cabins from the lodge as those in the cabins dug towards them, they eventually got a decent path dug to each cabin. Other teams were working on digging out to the barn and Aloe's shed, but that would take longer. With the paths dug, though, everyone quickly moved to widening them and removing as much snow as possible.

"You know, we're going to have to find a way to re-dye Marauder's hair pink or we're going to lose her in a drift," Valora said with a laugh.

Marauder stuck her tongue out at Valora but smiled. Conifer smiled at both of them, though it felt somewhat forced. As soon as the main paths were completely clear Conifer handed off her shovel and went into the lodge and up the back steps to the second floor. They'd left the largest room there open as a communal and activity space. Wildfire, who was outside helping with shoveling, had told her Elizabeth was up there with the campers too young to help dig out. Conifer found her leading them in a game of duck-duck-goose. Lia was dashing around the circle, tapping people's heads and laughing. Elizabeth looked more laid back than usual, clapping her hands along with the song coming over a bluetooth speaker sitting in a corner. She'd chopped off her curly brown hair shortly after pick up day, but it had already grown back enough to start curling around her ears.

"Elizabeth, can I talk to you in the hall for a second?" Conifer asked from the doorway.

Instantly her expression hardened and for a moment Conifer didn't think she was going to come. After a moment, though, Elizabeth gave a large sigh and waved at Robin to continue the game with the campers.

"What do you want?" Elizabeth asked after stepping out into the hall. Her arms were crossed and lips taught with dislike.

Conifer closed the door to the room before answering her. "When this started, you said you know more about nuclear weaponry than I do."

"I *know* I do," she spat.

Conifer resisted the urge to point out that she'd never disagreed with her on that fact.

"Look," Conifer said, "you don't like me, fine. Just tell me this: do you think we need to worry about a nuclear winter? Because what I know is that it is a major focus of a lot of survivalists, but I've also heard that the science is shaky."

She didn't answer for a long moment, and Conifer could see her thinking it over. "It's impossible to say for sure. You're right that the science is shaky. The concept has been blown up a lot by popular media, and a lot of people disagree on the accuracy of the models that have been made. Most of the models are based around the concept of big cities firestorming after they're hit by the initial bombs, sending debris into the atmosphere and blocking out the sun, but firestorms aren't guaranteed. Nagasaki didn't firestorm."

"Great, another unknown," Conifer muttered, pinching the bridge of her nose.

"Well excuse me for not being psychic," Elizabeth returned.

"Never asked you to be. The frustration wasn't directed at you, just at the circumstances," Conifer snapped back.

They stood there in silence, staring one another down. After a minute or so Conifer saw Elizabeth's eyes flick down to the bear claw she was still wearing.

Elizabeth huffed out a short breath through her nose. "I think we should assume that we'll get at least some climate effects. What they are, and how long they may last, we have no way to know. But if it does happen, if it does get as bad as the worst models, we're looking at global temperature drops of ten-degrees-Celsius *or more* for up to ten years *or more*. We *cannot* survive that, no matter what survival tricks you've got up your sleeve. We'll starve."

"I know," Conifer said, taking a shaky breath. "What about the not-so-worst-case models?"

She shrugged. "Could be anything. A nuclear winter freezing us to death, a nuclear summer from damage to the ozone layer burning us to death. Both would kill crops."

"How would you prepare, then?" Conifer asked.

She finally uncrossed her arms, throwing her hands up a bit. "The greenhouses, I guess? Some way for us to grow food whenever we want in a more controlled environment. They'd have to be heated, though, and we can't burn enough wood to keep ours heated year-round. They're too big. We could grow some food in the lodge too, I guess. Keep it heated with us, but we'd have to find a way to get the plants enough sun despite being inside. The greenhouses might need simulated sunlight as well, if this cloud cover sticks around."

"Okay, okay," Conifer said, thinking it through. They hadn't given much thought to the greenhouses as of yet, given how late it was in the year. If they needed too, though, there were a handful of crops they could try even through the winter if they could just figure out heat. "There are ways to passively heat greenhouses. Water barrels and angling everything right, for starters, though that would be more difficult with less sun. There's food that grows better in low light and cold-weather conditions too. Mushrooms, potatoes—"

A crash sounded down the hall from the direction of Jack's office. Elizabeth turned to face it, a frown on her face, as Conifer called out to Jack to check that she was alright. No answer came.

"Jack?" Conifer called again, already moving towards her office, Elizabeth following.

Stepping into the office, Conifer didn't see Jack at first. Not until she spotted her legs sprawling out from behind her desk.

"Fuck!" Conifer dashed over, dropping to the floor next to Jack. Elizabeth went around the other side of the desk and crouched next to Jack's head. Jack was sprawled out on her back, a little trickle of blood coming from her mouth and her skin a sickly pale, but she was breathing.

"Jackalope," Elizabeth said, gently squeezing her shoulder. "Jackalope, can you hear me?"

Conifer pulled Jack's wrist towards her and started counting her heartbeats, struggling to find the pulse. As she pressed harder her eyes caught again on the bruise she'd spotted before. A sinking feeling in her stomach, Conifer stopped trying to get her pulse and instead unbuttoned her sleeve, pushing it up to reveal more bruises.

Elizabeth was staring at Conifer when she looked up again. "Conifer—"

"I know," Conifer said. "Go get Aloe. Don't tell anyone else."

"Should we move her first? To the couch?" Elizabeth asked.

Conifer shook her head. "We don't know how she fell. Just get Aloe."

Elizabeth nodded and dashed out of the room.

Once she was gone Conifer reached out and gently stroked Jack's hair, wincing as a chunk of it came away. How was she this sick this quickly? She'd seemed worn down, but this was more than worn down. And if she was this sick, why was no one else? Or were they? Conifer's heart was racing but there was nothing she could do except wait for Aloe. Conifer's limited first aid knowledge was not enough for this.

"Jack, come on, you've got to come around," Conifer said, voice firm.

It took a bit more coaxing, but she eventually started to stir, blinking up at Conifer with a confused expression.

"Why am I on the floor?"

"You passed out," Conifer said, keeping her tone even. "How long have you been feeling sick?"

She pushed herself up into a sitting position and Conifer let her, glad to see that she seemed to be moving alright. "I'm just a little stressed out, and I didn't sleep well because of the storm, that's all."

Conifer could hear the lie in her voice.

"No, Jack, it isn't," Conifer told her.

She waved Conifer off, trying and failing to look unconcerned. "It's nothing."

Conifer took a deep breath, shaking her head and willing her voice to stay steady. "I'm going to make a few guesses here, and you can tell me if I'm right or wrong, fair?"

She hesitated but gave a short nod, looking wary.

"You first felt sick a few weeks ago. Your stomach hurt and maybe you figured that the food just didn't agree with you. You got some headaches, but you already have migraine issues so you didn't really notice. You got dizzy sometimes, but you wrote it off as pushing yourself too hard and forgetting to drink enough water, or just another thing connected to your migraines. Maybe you banged into things but didn't really feel it when you did, maybe didn't even notice until you saw the bruises. After a few days or so you started to feel better, and you've been relatively alright since then, until now. Any of that sound wrong?"

She didn't answer for a long moment before she slowly shook her head. "Not...exactly. This isn't radiation sickness, Conifer."

"Jack, all the symptoms match," Conifer said, feeling sick as the words left her mouth. This was it. They were doomed now.

Jack sighed, but it sounded wrong. Wheezy. "Help me to the couch, please."

Conifer hesitated but did as she asked, keeping an arm around her to prevent her falling as she swayed. Gently, Conifer settled her on the cushions, taking a step back and looking down at her.

"If it was radiation sickness," Jack said, "others would be sick too. You know that. I know you do."

"But your symptoms, Jack," Conifer pressed. "Maybe we just haven't spotted it in the othe—"

Jack cut her off. "My symptoms are of bone cancer, Conifer."

Every muscle in Conifer's body went tight, every thought dropped out of her mind.

Jack's voice was heavy as she continued. "I've been feeling off since early summer, and I tried to ignore it. I think it was because, deep down, I knew what was happening. It was too similar to my grandfather. I finally went in to get tested right before things went bad, but I never got the results back."

Conifer just stared at her without responding. The world had turned upside down and she was still stuck to it while all her words tumbled away into the sky. Before either of them broke the silence Aloe came in with Elizabeth behind her. Aloe had a medical bag in one hand and a harried look on her face. She was a short, plump woman in her late twenties and something in the shape of her wide eyes made her worry seem more pronounced.

Jack didn't wait for Aloe to speak. "This isn't radiation sickness. It is bone cancer. Stage four, I think, based on what happened to my grandfather."

Aloe's eyes managed to go even wider.

"Let me examine you," Aloe said, setting her bag down next to Jack and pulling up a chair.

Conifer retreated, standing next to Elizabeth as Aloe checked Jack over and questioned her about her symptoms over the last few months.

"Well?" Conifer asked as Aloe's questions trailed off.

Aloe glanced between Conifer and Jack before giving a

little nod. "I think...yes, I think she's right. I think this is bone cancer, and it seems to have spread, probably to her lungs and other areas. The bruising, the blood in her mouth, the fainting, the hair loss, it all fits."

Jack deflated with the conformation, sinking back into the couch and closing her eyes.

"What can we do?" Elizabeth asked. "Can we treat her?"

They couldn't lose Jack. Conifer couldn't lose Jack.

Aloe shook her head, a few tears escaping her eyes. "Not that we're capable of here. Even in a full hospital, at this stage—"

"Enough," Jack said, holding up a hand and taking a shaky breath. "For the moment, please do not tell anyone I am sick. I need time to make some decisions. Right now, I need a few minutes alone to speak with Conifer."

Aloe and Elizabeth nodded, shuffling out of the room looking dejected.

"Jack, I—" Conifer trailed off, no idea what to say.

Jack took a wheezy breath and dropped her head into her hands. "So much for splitting things fifty-fifty."

"Please don't," Conifer said, feeling tears gathering in her eyes. "Don't joke around right now."

"Why not? It's not often one gets a chance for literal gallows humor."

"*Jack*," Conifer begged. "I already lost one mom, okay? I'm not looking forward to losing another." Especially not when she would have to actually watch this one die. To know exactly what happened and then put her body in the ground.

This caused Jack to lift her head, her eyes searching Conifer's. "I'm sorry," she whispered.

Conifer shook her head, trying to chase away the reality of what was happening. "I don't...I'm not sure I can do this without you."

"Come here," Jack said, waving a hand at the chair Aloe left in front of her. Conifer came over and Jack wrapped her hands around hers, squeezing gently. "I grew up here just like you did. A camper, a counselor, and then the owner when the old owners decided to sell the place. I didn't think I could do it either. I was in my twenties, less than a thousand dollars to my name, no business experience, but I was determined not to lose it. To this day I'm still not entirely sure how I pulled it off. I applied for so many grants, so many loans, literally begged my rich uncle on my knees for help. And it *worked*. I saved this place, and I *grew* it too. Added three more units, started our greenhouse program, expanded what types of sessions we offered."

"But I—"

"Can do it too," she said, picking up from where she'd cut Conifer off. "I *know* you can. Trust yourself, Conifer. Trust what you know and trust the people around you to help."

"Taking over a camp is not the same as leading two-hundred people through the after-effects of a *nuclear war*, Jack," Conifer said, frustrated tears building in her eyes.

Jack smiled softly. "Maybe not, but I'm not the same person you are. I had the skills to take over this camp, you have the skills to help it survive." She reached out and lifted the bear claw from Conifer's chest. "Just take things as they come."

Elizabeth found Conifer a little later, tucked into a corner of a large storage closet. It had been the only empty place Conifer could find.

"Marauder is looking for you," Elizabeth said.

Conifer hummed, but didn't respond. She didn't want to be around anyone right now. Elizabeth stood there silhouetted in the door for several long moments while Conifer stayed on the floor with her arms around her knees.

"Where's Jackalope?" Elizabeth asked eventually.

"She wanted to be alone for a bit," Conifer replied.

"Oh. Did you two...did you talk about telling everyone?"

Conifer shook her head.

Elizabeth sighed and stepped fully into the closet, sitting down across from Conifer. "This sucks."

Conifer huffed out a mirthless laugh.

"I really like Jackalope," Elizabeth said. "And I only met her this summer. This place will be so...different without her."

Conifer nodded. "Since you already hate me, can I tell you something?"

"I guess."

"I think this will be so much worse, with her being the first to die. It would've been easier to take if it was someone, anyone else other than the person that is supposed to be leading us."

She stared at Conifer across the few feet between them, her mouth set in a grim line. "That's a shitty thing to say."

Conifer shrugged. "I agree."

The silence hung longer this time.

"We can't hide what's happening," Elizabeth said eventually.

"No, we can't."

"So?"

Conifer sighed, closing her eyes and letting her head fall back against the wall. So what? Jack had made it clear Conifer was going to be the one to take over the camp, and Conifer had agreed. She still didn't know if she could do it, but at this point it was Jack's dying wish.

"Jack wants me to be the one to take over the camp," Conifer said.

"Figures. She's been deferring to you since the start."

"How do you feel about that?" Conifer asked, eyes still closed.

She didn't answer for awhile, but Conifer didn't hear her leave either. When she spoke her voice was clipped. "I still don't like you. But you have gotten us this far. Everyone knows you well, has seen your skills. I guess...better you than any sort of fight over it."

"Such confidence in your tone."

"Whatever. Just make sure Jackalope gives a clear hand-off. Everyone knowing it's what she wants will be important."

Conifer nodded. "I'll talk to Jack. As long as she's up for it, we'll bring everyone together after dinner to...to let them know what's going on."

"And where are you going to make this announcement? There's no place in the lodge that can fit two-hundred people now, not with the beds in the dining room and every other spare bit of space."

"Are you enjoying needling at me?" Conifer said, opening her eyes finally to glare at her.

"Someone has to. A leader who thinks they know everything is dangerous."

Conifer rolled her eyes, unsurprised that even now she refused to try and get along. It was hardly like Elizabeth was the only one to call Conifer out; Valora had proven she was more than willing during their hunting trip. Despite what she said, it seemed more like Elizabeth just wanted an excuse to continue not liking her.

"We'll do it in groups, then," Conifer decided. "Honestly, that's probably better anyway. Do it by age. Counselors, then the oldest campers, that way they can help when the younger campers get upset."

"See you after dinner, then," Elizabeth said, getting up and dusting herself off. "Go find Marauder so she stops hounding everyone about where you are."

CHAPTER 21
HANDOFF

Marauder was on the roof of their cabin with Valora, clearing the snow there. Everyone else was still working on clearing the front of the cabin, and Conifer was surprised by how much they'd accomplished while she'd been gone. They'd laid scrap plywood across the top of the snow and were using wheelbarrows to transport the snow away from the cabins, dumping it as far away as they could get.

Conifer stopped at the foot of the ladder to the roof. "I need you two to come inside for a minute."

Valora and Marauder both looked down at her over the edge of the roof and frowned. Conifer had splashed cold water on her face before coming outside, but she doubted it had done much. They came down immediately, both looking worried. Without a word they came into the empty cabin with Conifer, looking wary. For a moment Conifer stood with her back to them, trying to work up the courage to tell them what was happening.

"Conifer?" Marauder said tentatively.

"Jack's dying," Conifer said without turning around.

Marauder gave a little gasp.

"Of what?" Valora asked.

"Stage four bone cancer, it looks like," Conifer said, finally turning around. Marauder's hands were clasped over her mouth, her eyes wide and filling with tears. Valora just looked grim. "She collapsed in her office a little over an hour ago. Jack said she's been feeling off all summer, and she got tested, but she never got the results. Bone cancer is what her grandfather died of, though, and she recognizes the symptoms."

They stood there, staring at one another. The sound of shoveling and chatter came in through the walls. Conifer caught snatches of some of the campers singing a happy little work song from the camp song book, one about all the things women could do. Flying airplanes, fighting fires, fixing engines, leading nations. Too bad they didn't have most of those things around anymore.

"What do we do?" Marauder asked, voice shaky.

"Tonight, after dinner, we're going to tell everyone in groups about Jack, starting with the counselors," Conifer told them. It was the only solid thing she knew right now.

"And what about you, Conifer?" Valora asked, frowning. "You seem…numb."

Numb was a good word for it. She shrugged. "I guess I'm taking full control of the camp after all."

Marauder stepped forward and wrapped her arms around Conifer, burying her face in Conifer's chest. Valora hesitated a moment before joining them, wrapping her arms around both. At first, Conifer felt the strong urge to wiggle away, but she resisted it and, after a moment, leaned into the comfort just slightly. She wasn't sure how long they stood like that before there was a knock on the door. They pulled apart to see Elizabeth stepping inside the cabin.

"Marauder, Valora," she said, nodding at each of them. "Jack wants you," Elizabeth said to Conifer. "She's still in her office."

"Want me to come?" Marauder asked softly.

Conifer shook her head. "I need to talk to her alone first."

She nodded and gave Conifer another quick hug before she left, trudging across the distance between their cabin and the lodge, avoiding eye contact with everyone as she went.

She found Jack sitting at her desk. She looked somewhat less pale, and there was steam rising from a thermos on the desktop. It smelled earthy and Conifer guessed it was some sort of tea. Conifer wondered if it was regular tea, or something Aloe had given her.

"Elizabeth told me about your plan for us to tell everyone tonight, for me to formally hand over control to you to make things go smoother. It's a good plan," Jack said, shuffling some papers around.

Conifer sighed and dropped into one of the chairs across from her, telling herself to just push through this. Minute by minute if she had to.

"Yeah," Conifer said.

"She still doesn't like you much," Jack added.

Conifer huffed. "No, she doesn't. Did she try to say she'd be a better person to put in charge or something?"

"No, she said you were the best of a lot of terrible options and she'd find a way to put up with you," Jack said, her lips curling minutely at the corners.

"How charitable."

Jack chuckled. "I wish you hadn't ended up the target of her ire, but at least we know you can handle it. If she'd directed it at someone else we might have had problems that were harder to solve."

Conifer sighed. "Fair."

"Anyway, I've been thinking a lot over the last hour. Trying to figure out what I should do. What I should tell you. And, well, I keep pulling things out and then realizing they don't matter," Jack said. "Half of what I think I should tell you, it's all things that don't matter anymore. You hardly need to know the passwords to the camp's bank accounts, or the phone number of our accountant."

"If the world puts itself back together in a way that still requires accountants, I think we'll have done it wrong," Conifer replied.

This got a real laugh out of her and it warmed Conifer's

heart a few degrees.

"I have to agree," she said, leaning back in her chair. Her eyes roved around the office, over all the pictures. She smiled at many of them. "I want you to take over my office too, Conifer. I know you'll take care of it. All the memories in here."

"I...yeah, I'll take it over," Conifers said, choking a little on the words.

Jack nodded and got up, keeping one hand on the desk for support, and pulled one photo down from the hundreds pinned to the walls. Sitting back down, she set it in front of Conifer. It was a little faded and featured three young women standing under the entrance gate of the camp. The sky behind them was a cloudless blue and they were wearing an old style of yellow counselor shirts. The girl in the middle had straight chestnut brown hair down to her waist, the front pinned back with two barrettes on either side. She had cut-off jean shorts, the edges frayed, and she was sticking her tongue out. Both her hands were held up to make bunny-ears behind her fellow counselors, both of whom looked younger. One had the white circle around her nametag that indicated she was a junior counselor.

"This is you," Conifer said, brushing her thumb across the face of the girl in the middle.

She nodded. "My last summer as a counselor, back in the nineties, before I bought the camp. I went by Moth back then."

Conifer looked up at her, raising an eyebrow. "Moth? As in Mothman? I'm sensing a cryptid theme here."

She grinned. "Couldn't resist. I signed the desk, too."

Leaning over, she tapped a spot on the edge of the desktop, near one of the corners. There was carved the name "Moth" in little letters, but the O had been replaced with a crude depiction of a moth. Just a few inches away was Conifer's own carving from her first summer as a counselor. It was fresher, clearer. She'd replaced the F with a little pine tree, a couple longer branches forming the bars of the letter.

Conifer ran her fingers over Jack's carving. "I'll miss you," Conifer whispered.

She smiled sadly. "But you'll remember me, that's what's important."

"Why didn't you say anything?" Conifer said, still focused on Jack's carving.

Conifer felt Jack's sigh drift over her before she spoke. "What you said, about me writing off my symptoms as stress and migraines and the shitty situation we're in, you were right about that part. I ignored it."

"Not completely," Conifer murmured. An idea had taken root in her mind, and she couldn't shake it. "That's why you were so insistent on me taking over ever since we went to town, why you said splitting control was only for now."

She finally looked up, confused to find that Jack was smiling, fondness in her eyes.

"You taking over was my plan from the moment I went to get tested, Conifer, before the bombs ever dropped."

"...What?" Conifer's world had turned over far too many times in one day, and she had not been prepared for it to happen again. She felt physically dizzy, gripping the edge of the desktop to steady herself.

Jack continued, "I have no living family, Conifer, and I knew what I was staring down the barrel of once I let myself admit it. Even if I got treatment, survived treatment, I wasn't going to be running this camp next year, maybe ever again. When the appointment ended I went straight to my lawyer and had you named as my beneficiary and inheritor of everything related to the camp, as a precaution. You're young, but I know how much you love this place, and I knew you'd fight for it the way I always have. Besides, I wasn't much older than you when I bought the place. I was going to tell you once I got the test results back, but, well," she trailed off with a shrug.

Valora had been wrong. Conifer wasn't numb before. She was numb now. Jack seemed to sense it, leaning over to take Conifer's hands.

"I'm so sorry, Conifer. I'm sorry I never told you, and that I tried to ignore it once things went wrong. I thought... I thought I had more time."

Conifer gripped her hands as tightly as she dared, taking a few steadying breaths before she spoke. "It's not your fault the world went to shit."

"But it is my fault I didn't tell you," Jack said. "I wouldn't blame you if you didn't accept the apology, but I am sorry. So sorry."

Conifer took a big breath, struggling to do it evenly and continuing to hold on to Jack's hands. She wanted to be angry, wanted to insist that if Jack had told someone they could've helped her, could have bought her more time. But the anger just wasn't there.

"What..." Conifer trailed off, trying to gather the strength to ask her next question. "We can't...bury you, Jack. The ground is frozen now. I don't know if you're religious, but... what do you want?"

She sighed, tilting her head back. "I don't want resources wasted on me. A pyre would require a lot of wood. I think...I think the best option is to just leave me in the woods, as far from camp as you can safely get. I kind of like that idea, honestly. Going back to nature. Or maybe the mineshafts, up by the lake. They're hardly a safety issue if I'm dead."

"They flood every spring, though," Conifer said. "We don't know where the water comes out, and we can't risk polluting our water supply."

She smiled sadly. "See, you do know what you're doing. Out in nature it is then."

"Okay," Conifer agreed. "But we're putting a marker up for you in camp. Do you want it to say Jackalope or...?"

She grinned. "You don't even know my real name, do you?"

Conifer shrugged, letting go of Jack's hands and turning hers up. "You've always been Jackalope to me. It's not like I've read your personnel file."

"It's Anya," she replied. "Anya Demarcus."

Conifer couldn't stop herself from making a face and Jack laughed.

"Doesn't fit me, does it?" She said, a bit of the laugh still caught in her voice.

"No, I can't say that it does."

"I never thought so either. I went through dozens of nicknames as a kid. Ann. Annie. Yaya. Moth. I've been Jackalope longer than I've been anyone else, though, so put that."

The knot that had been hanging in Conifer's chest since she'd found Jack on the floor was still wound tight, but it didn't feel quite so heavy anymore. Thinking about losing Jack still felt like choking, but laying it all out, piece by piece, grounded it in a way that lightened the load enough that Conifer could breathe again, just a little. They spent the time until dinner going over the important information Jack felt Conifer needed. The rationing schedules, the supply lists, the personnel and camper files. Marauder brought them dinner and said the groups had been divided. The first one would be waiting for them in the activity room at seven and would be a mix of counselors and older campers. Jack picked at her food, not eating much, until it was time to go.

Conifer held Jack's arm as they walked down the hall to the activity room, keeping her steady. Conifer couldn't help but wonder how no one, herself included, had noticed Jack going downhill so much. When she thought about it now, she did realize that Jack had been helping with outdoor activities less and less, but at the time Conifer had just figured it was because she was busy with other things.

When they entered the activity room they found it filled with about forty campers sitting in clusters on the floor with half the unit counselors ringed around the edge of the room, along with all the cooks and Horseshoe. Looking around, Conifer saw all of her and Marauder's original unit, except for Giselle. Everyone had been talking, but they went silent as Jack and Conifer entered. Conifer watched them all tracking Jack as Conifer helped her to a chair. There was no hiding that something was very, very wrong.

Jack spoke first, her voice carrying easily in the silent room. "Well, everyone, we've got some bad news. I suppose it's a bit obvious, but I am sick. I have a family history of bone cancer, and Aloe agrees that is likely what this is." She paused, taking a deep breath. "It is…not something I can recover from."

A nervous rustling went around the group. There was so little reaction from the counselors that Conifer guessed someone had spread the word to them already. Some were crying silently, others had their arms crossed tightly across their bodies, but none seemed surprised. The campers just looked shocked, and a little confused.

Conifer took up the conversation. "We're going to do everything we can to keep Jack comfortable—"

"So Jackalope is going to die?" A girl at the back interrupted.

"Yes," Jack said, voice soft. "And I know that is scary for all of you, especially because I promised to be here for you, but I want you to know that you will still be safe here even after I am gone. Conifer has officially taken control of the camp, and she will continue to do everything in her power to keep you safe and healthy, just as she has been helping me do since the beginning."

"But any of us could get sick next!" An older girl said, voice shaking. "I have a family history of cancer too!"

Silver went over to the girl, wrapping an arm around her and whispering softly as the girl panicked. Conifer hoped Silver knew her well enough to comfort her, because Conifer had nothing. The girl was right to be scared. Conifer was in charge now, though. Officially in charge. She had to say something. Anything.

"We'll be organizing more regular health checks," Conifer said, trying to make her tone soothing as she scrambled together a plan, wishing she'd had more time to prepare. "Aloe will work with the other medically certified people in camp to put something together. Right now you are not sick, which means if you do get sick we'll be able to catch it sooner and be able to help you more." Somehow. Maybe.

"You couldn't help Jackalope! You didn't catch it before she got sick!" A new girl shouted.

Conifer felt things spiraling out of control, saw the panic building in the group, and she didn't know how to fix it. This is exactly what she meant when she'd told Jack she sucked at the people part of leadership.

Jack held up a hand until the room quieted. "Firstly, no one catching it in me is my own fault. I wrote a lot of the symptoms off and just tried to ignore them. Conifer will be putting systems in place to make sure that can't happen again, to anyone. Secondly, you have every right to be scared. I'm scared too. But, please, don't let your fear consume you. We have accomplished so, so much already. Survived beyond what anyone could have expected. None of us know what will happen tomorrow, but we know what we can do today, and that is keep going. When you start to feel scared, look around. Look at the cabins we built. Look at the food we've stored. Look at the wood we've cut. Look at the beds we've made. Look at the things you have learned. All in just a couple of months. Remember that *you* did those things. Even though you were scared, even though you felt alone, you did those things. Be scared, it's okay that you are. But don't give up."

Conifer gently squeezed Jack's shoulder and nodded. None of the campers said anything back, but they all still looked wary.

"Let's make a promise," Jack said, holding out her hand in

the camp promise gesture. "Repeat after me: We are scared, and that is okay."

"We are scared, and that is okay."

"Even when we are scared, we won't give in to that fear."

"Even when we are scared, we won't give in to that fear."

"We promise to care for one another, and to stay strong."

"We promise to care for one another, and to stay strong."

Jack smiled and lowered her hand. She looked paler than when they entered the room.

"I love all of you so much," Jack said.

"We need to move on to the next group," Conifer said, already dreading doing this two more times.

Everyone got up, many stopping to hug Jack as they left the room. Cheyenne hugged her and hugged Conifer as well before leaving, putting an arm around Farrah who was crying. Marauder gave Conifer's hand a gentle squeeze as she went by.

The other two groups went much the same as the first, Jack ending each one with the same promise. It felt like the day they'd first told the campers about the bombs, but somehow so much worse. That had been external to the camp. Terrifying, but distant. This was close. So close.

"I'm going to get you something to eat, since you didn't have much dinner, and grab my bedroll from the cabin," Conifer told Jack as she helped her back to her office, leading her over to the couch. "I'll stay on your floor."

She waved Conifer off. "No, go sleep in your own bed, please. You'll be more comfortable there, and there's nothing you can do for me up here."

"Jack—"

"Please," she said again, finality in her tone.

Conifer gave in, reluctantly. Grabbing Jack's walkie from her desk, Conifer checked that it was charged before setting it on the floor next to the couch.

"I'll have mine on me," she said. "Radio if you need anything."

Jack nodded, grabbing Conifer's hand as she moved

to leave. Without a word she pulled Conifer down to her, wrapping her in a hug. Conifer hugged her back as tightly as she dared. It felt like she should be crying, but she was just too wrung out to muster the energy.

Chapter 21
The Letter

Exhaustion pulled Conifer under more than any willingness to actually sleep. She borrowed a watch from someone and set an alarm to make sure she woke up by five a.m. to check on Jack, keeping one hand wrapped around her walkie as she slept. When the alarm went off Conifer jolted awake, quickly silencing it. Marauder stirred down in her bunk, leaning out and blinking blearily up at Conifer.

"Want me to come?" She whispered.

Conifer hesitated a moment, then nodded, sliding out from under the blankets and climbing down the ladder at the end of the bed. Valora was awake as well and followed them out into the main room after Marauder and Conifer had dressed. Valora promised to look after the kids until Marauder and Conifer came back. They thanked her and set out into the dark, a little flashlight in Conifer's hand. It was snowing again, but not hard. Just a few flurries.

The lodge was silent as they went inside. Conifer avoided the spots on the steps that creaked the loudest, but Marauder hit a few of them, disrupting the quiet. Jack's office door was closed and Conifer stopped before opening it. If Jack was sleeping Conifer didn't want to wake her, and the door was almost impossible to open without it creaking. Resting her hand on the tarnished brass handle, Conifer turned it slowly, intending to only open it a few inches and peer inside. Just enough to ascertain that Jack was doing alright. It took a few moments for Conifer's eyes to adjust to the lack of light in Jack's office, and at first she wasn't sure why her heart started tripping over itself, fear sliding down her spine. It was just dark. She wasn't scared of the dark.

"Conifer..." Marauder said, her voice fearful. It was the only sound in the still air.

The only sound.

Conifer flung the door open and slammed her hand against the light switch, staring down at Jack in horror where she was sprawled out on the floor. She was still. Completely still. Her chest did not rise and fall. Her eyes didn't move behind their lids. The blankets were tangled around her legs, one still up on the couch, and one hand was raised to her throat, like she'd struggled. No color was left in her face, and all she was wearing was a bathrobe, her clothes folded neatly on top of her boots, which had been placed by her desk. The walkie had been shoved across the room, the battery separated from the body of the device. Foam flecked her lips and red lines trailed across her throat from her fingers.

Distantly Conifer was aware of Marauder sobbing, but she couldn't tear her eyes away from Jack. What was left of Jack. One day. One day from realizing she was sick to her dying.

One day.

Jack.

Dead.

"Con—Conifer," Marauder said, and Conifer felt her tugging at her sleeve. Conifer still didn't take her eyes off Jack. "Conifer, there's a note."

This was enough to get Conifer's attention. She forced herself to look at the folded piece of paper Marauder was holding out. It had Conifer's name on the outside, in Jack's precise, blocky hand. Shakily, Conifer took the paper and opened it.

Did you know I am, was, deathly allergic to macadamia nuts? Probably not. It was such a bad allergy I always kept them out of the camp. But that wasn't really important when we started raiding the town. I knew we had some in those cans of assorted nuts.

I could not in good conscience continue to take up resources that the rest of this camp needs to survive. Nor was I willing to suffer through a slow death over who knows how long. I needed this to be on my terms. I am aware that this does not quite mesh with the things I said to everyone last night. It may be better to tell them I passed away naturally, in my sleep. I will leave the decision up to you.

I'm sorry to leave you sooner than you may have expected, Conifer. Please know that I love you, and that it is a mark of how much I trust you that I knew I could make this decision for myself without worrying about what it would mean for the safety of this camp.

You are the daughter I never had. Stay strong. You will make it to tomorrow, and the tomorrow after that.

-Jackalope

Conifer fell to her knees, the letter shaking in her hands and tears sliding silently down her face. Marauder knelt down next to her, and this time Conifer did pull away from the hug Marauder tried to give. She didn't want it right now, so they ended up just kneeling there together, a few inches of space between them. The sound of something falling to the floor startled them some time later and Conifer looked up to see Aloe standing in the doorway. Her hands were over her mouth and her medical bag was on its side at her feet. Making an impulse decision, Conifer slid the note into her jacket, tucking it in an inner pocket, and stood to face her.

"She was gone when we got here," Conifer said, voice raw.

"I didn't—didn't realize she was that bad," Aloe sobbed. "I should've made her come stay with me for the night, or stayed here with her."

Conifer shook her head. "It isn't your fault, Aloe. I tried to get her to let me stay with her too, but she wanted to be alone. I think...she must have known, deep down, that it was coming. Sensed it."

Marauder was watching silently, still on the floor, but she didn't contradict Conifer. Conifer wasn't sure how much of the note she may have read over her shoulder, if any of it, but the presence of the note alone told the true story of what had happened, never mind the contents of it.

"I've never had a patient die," Aloe whispered. "Not—not one where I was the main carer. That's why I came to work at a camp instead of...instead of in a hospital." She seemed to be having a hard time looking at Jack. Part of Conifer thought that was a good thing. She suspected a trained nurse would recognize the signs of an allergic reaction.

Clenching and unclenching her fists, Conifer forced herself to put together a plan.

"Okay," Conifer said. "Okay. Marauder, I want you to go get me some canvass, and some rope, from storage. We're going to wrap her up. She...yesterday she told me she wanted to be left out in the woods. We'll take her out on horseback. Everyone will be waking up soon. We'll have a ceremony out in front of the lodge. Aloe, I need you to get me Horseshoe."

Marauder nodded, slowly getting up from the floor and wiping at her eyes. Aloe took a moment longer to respond, but nodded as well. Once both were gone Conifer let herself look at Jack again. Slowly, Conifer reached out and lifted Jack's hand off her throat, setting it on her stomach. She placed Jack's other hand next to it, then untangled the blanket from her legs, straightening them out. Gently, Conifer lifted her head and smoothed out her hair.

Marauder came back in with a bundle of canvass and rope. Together, they spread the canvass out on the floor next to Jack. Without speaking Marauder went to Jack's shoulders and Conifer went to Jack's feet. Together they lifted her onto the canvass. After a moment of hesitation Conifer removed Jack's robe, leaving her bare. She said she hadn't wanted to waste resources, and Conifer felt that must've been why she'd undressed in the first place. Marauder watched as she repositioned Jack's limbs, resmoothed her hair. Conifer heard her move to the office's closet and start rummaging around, but didn't pay her any mind until she was back and kneeling next to Jack. Conifer watched as she gently lifted one of Jack's hands, placing a folded bandanna with the camp logo under it.

Together, they wrapped the canvass around Jack, securing it in place with ropes. The room began to lighten with the coming dawn, light peeking in around the edges of the cardboard they'd taped over the window to keep the light from being seen. Through a small rip near one corner Conifer saw that the snow had stopped and the sky was blue, bluer than she had seen it in awhile. Horseshoe came in just as they finished securing the last knots. Aloe was behind her, and it was clear both had been crying.

"Thank you, Aloe," Conifer said. Her voice wasn't as raw anymore, but it still felt hollow. "I know you're struggling right now, but I need you to quietly alert the other adults. Marauder, please help her. Gather everyone out in front of the lodge. Those without good boots can stay on the porch and on the steps. We'll roll up the canvas so they can see out."

The two of them nodded and left.

"What do you need me to do?" Horseshoe sniffed.

"She wants…wanted to be left in the woods," Conifer said, still kneeling next to Jack's body. "Do you have a horse that can handle the snow and two people?"

"Whiskey," Horseshoe said. "She's strong and the most surefooted."

Conifer nodded. "We need to take her as far as possible. And leave her exposed."

"I'll do it," Horseshoe said, voice firm. Conifer looked up to see tears tracing down her cheeks.

"I can do it," Conifer said.

Horseshoe shook her head. "I want to. And you're in charge now. You should—should stay here. The camp needs you here."

Conifer couldn't argue with that, as much as she wanted to.

"Okay. Please get Whiskey ready and meet us in front of the lodge."

Horseshoe nodded and left, closing the door behind her.

Around her Conifer heard the building slowly coming to life. Feet shuffling, bathrooms being jockeyed for. She stayed sitting next to Jack, her mind empty until she was interrupted by a soft knock. She had no idea how much time had passed.

"It's Valora."

"Come in," Conifer told her.

She slid into the room without opening the door very far. Conifer could hear campers on the other side, caught the end of a question about why they had to go outside in the cold.

"Marauder asked me to come help you move Jackalope," Valora said once the door was shut.

"We need to wait until everyone is outside," Conifer said.

She nodded and after a moment came to sit a few feet

away, near Jack's feet.

"Do you want to talk?" She asked.

"Not at the moment."

She nodded again and they listened to the campers passing by on the main stairs just outside Jack's office. A few tears trailed down Valora's face and she wiped them away with the hem of her jacket sleeve. Once the noises outside the room faded Conifer's radio crackled to life at her hip where she'd clipped it to her waistband, Marauder's voice coming through.

"Everyone is outside," she said.

Conifer let Marauder know she'd heard her before turning to Valora. "Can you manage her on the stairs on your own?"

"Yes," Valora said.

Conifer watched as Valora carefully slid her arms under the canvass wrappings, stepping forward to make sure Jack's head was tucked safely against Valora's shoulder once Valora was on her feet.

"Just follow me," Conifer said. "Horseshoe is going to be waiting for us, and she'll take Jack away from camp."

Valora nodded and together they left the office. Conifer waited at the bottom of the stairs for Valora, who was coming down sideways and slowly. At the bottom of the stairs was a little alcove, with doors going off to the post-office—now a bedroom, on one side and a hallway leading to several offices—also bedrooms now, on the other. The third door led out to the porch and Conifer could hear everyone gathered on the other side. The thick wood wasn't enough to hide the tones of confusion and fear and worry in their conversations.

Conifer opened the door, feeling as much as hearing the silence that rippled out from the doorway. Everyone was watching her as she looked over all of them. Most of the snow in front of the lodge had drifted under and against the porch, leaving a large area with no more than a few inches, which was where most of the camp now stood. Horseshoe was at the back of the group on Whiskey. Silver was with her on Knight, as were two of the cooks on horses of their own. Valora was waiting just behind Conifer, mostly unseen in the shadowed space. Gently Conifer waved away the campers standing closest, indicating for them to clear a space. Some of them could see Valora behind her and had started to cry. When there was enough room Conifer stepped out, Valora coming as well. The silence was replaced with sobs. Conifer watched as campers and counselors alike clung to one another. Valora stopped next to Conifer, Jack in her arms.

"Jackalope passed away in her sleep last night," Conifer told everyone. "It was her wish that she be allowed to go back to nature, so Horseshoe and several others will be honoring that wish and taking her out into the woods. Remember the promise we made her last night, that we will care for one another and stay strong, even when we're scared."

Raising her hand again, Conifer indicated for everyone to clear a path down to the horses. As Valora and Conifer started to walk forward everyone laid out their hands in the gesture of the camp promise. Silver began to sing from her horse. It was a soft, slow song about a hero appearing when they were most needed, and inspiring others to go on in their name. Conifer had seen it in their camp song book before, but she'd never heard it sung.

Conifer felt tears pricking at her eyes again, and she didn't attempt to stop them, letting them fall as she and Valora walked. Valora was tall enough, and Whiskey short enough, that it didn't take much work to transfer Jack to Horseshoe's arms.

Another counselor, Conifer didn't turn around to see who, picked up the singing as Silver turned away to follow Horseshoe and the others. The songs shifted through other ones about remembrance and peace, everyone else joining in. Horseshoe led the way down from the lodge and south along the road out of camp. The singing continued until they were out of sight.

CHAPTER 23
MEMORIAL

Conifer found herself back in Jack's office several hours later. Everyone had moved back inside, breaking into different groups throughout the lodge. All activities had been canceled for the day. Marauder managed to turn the mood around somewhat, getting everyone to tell stories about Jack. Conifer tried to think of one to add, but she couldn't find it in her. She'd needed some space, so had retreated to Jack's office. Her office. Marauder promised to come get her when Horseshoe and the others were back.

The doorway was as far as Conifer got, closing it behind her and sliding down to sit with her back against it. Jack's clothes were still by her desk, her robe where Conifer placed it on the couch. The papers she'd been shuffling through yesterday were still spread on the desk, the photo of her as a counselor resting on top of them.

If Conifer separated herself from the situation, she could understand Jack's decision. She wouldn't want to slowly, painfully waste away either. Not only did Conifer not want that for herself, she wouldn't want to put those around her through it. But at the same time, she missed Jack so damn much. There were things she'd thought she still had time to ask her, stories she wished she could've heard Jack tell one more time.

Pulling herself up from the floor she went to the desk,

forcing herself around to Jack's side of it. Her side of it. She choked a little as she glanced at the floor behind it, remembering Jack sprawled out there. Had that really only been yesterday? The chair slid out with squeaking wheels and Conifer lowered herself into it. Inch by inch, she slid closer to the desk. The photo looked up at her, the figures upside down and facing the chair she'd sat in before. Conifer left it where it was, focusing instead on the papers Jack had been looking through, feeling an urge to know what they were, because they weren't the ones Jack had been showing her the day before.

The first few were just useless bits of paperwork about the finances of the camp. As Conifer moved them aside a glossy corner peeked out from underneath. Conifer slid it out and found herself staring at her own face. She was laughing, her freshly dyed hair flaming around her face in a breeze. Marauder was next to her, laughing as well. In the background but not far away was Cheyenne, hand clasped in her mother's as the two of them dragged Cheyenne's suitcase through the dirt towards the check-in tables.

A new round of sobs worked their way up her throat and Conifer pushed the photo away, not wanting to damage it before Cheyenne could see. Conifer remembered Jack walking around taking photos that day. She'd been doing it all summer, making plans to commission a new brochure over the winter. Conifer knew she needed to hunt down the camera, the memory card, to see what other photos she might find of the other campers' parents, but it didn't matter in that moment. All Conifer could focus on was her own face, how happy she'd been. Happy enough for Jack to decide the moment had been worth capturing and printing out on the camp's janky old photo printer.

"Why did you leave this here?" Conifer asked the empty room.

She hadn't really seen her own reflection in weeks, but she knew there was no way she looked that happy now. Her hair had faded, the dyed ends mostly turning to a mottled orange, and she'd even found the beginnings of a few grays. Her mouth didn't feel like it was capable of smiling that widely anymore, and she didn't remember what her own laugh sounded like when she was that happy.

Without meaning to she shoved her hands out across the papers, sending them flying along with the photo. She regretted it instantly and dashed around the desk to make sure she hadn't damaged it, or the other one of Jack as a young woman. The photo of herself had landed upside down and under several other papers. When Conifer lifted them away she froze. There were words scrawled on the back of the photo in Jack's hand, with a little bear claw drawn underneath.

"You're...cleaning?" Valora said.

Conifer turned to see her standing in the doorway of the office along with Marauder.

"I needed something to do with my hands," Conifer said. "I'm just straightening up, more than anything."

"We wanted to check on you," Marauder said. She looked a bit tentative, hands held behind her back.

"Horseshoe and the others are back," Valora added, closing the door behind her.

"Did they say where...?" Conifer asked.

"On the edge of a clearing, with a view of the mountains through the trees," Marauder told her. "Silver carved a cross into one of the aspens to mark it."

Conifer nodded, sniffing away a few tears.

"Everyone wants to know what we do now, Conifer," Valora

said. Her tone wasn't pushy, but it was clear she wouldn't leave without an answer.

Conifer took a deep breath and nodded, waving both of them to the chairs in front of the desk. Once again she had to force herself to go around the desk and sit in Jack's chair. Her chair. The papers had all been cleared off of the desktop, and she'd put the photo of Jack back in its place on the wall, but she'd left out the photo of Marauder and herself. Marauder picked it up and smiled sadly. Valora peered at it as well.

"When was this?" Valora asked.

"At drop off for the last session," Conifer told her. The chair felt even more uncomfortable with other people sitting across from her. She was in charge now. Really in charge.

"Just before the bombs..." Valora whispered.

Conifer nodded. Just after Jack had gotten tested, and gone to her lawyer to put the camp in Conifer's name if the treatments didn't go well. Conifer hadn't told anyone about that yet, and she found that she couldn't. Not right now.

"Do you remember what we were laughing about?" Marauder asked.

Conifer shook her head. "No."

She sighed and set the photo back down. "Well, anyway, Valora is right. People want to know what happens next."

Conifer tangled her fingers in the cord that held the bear claw, running her thumb up and down the side of the claw itself. What did happen next?

"I can't do this alone," Conifer said eventually. "There's too much for just one person. I need help."

"You've got it, always," Marauder said, voice earnest.

Conifer didn't like asking for help like this, she never had, but she still said, "I know I do."

"How do you want to divide it up?" Valora asked.

"Well, I was hoping to start with the two of you," Conifer told them. "Marauder, you're a wilderness EMT, and you've got a good knowledge of herbal medicine. I want you to take charge of keeping the medical side of things organized.

Regular checkups for everyone, finding ways to develop natural medicines. Let Aloe focus on the actual care, while you keep things organized."

Marauder nodded. "I can do that."

"And Valora," Conifer said, turning to her. "You've never hesitated to call me on my shit." Valora gave a wry smile. "And you always do it in a way that's productive. You've also shown that you're good with people, that you get them in ways I frequently don't. I was hoping…I was hoping you'd take the roles Jack originally planned to when she and I were going to split things fifty-fifty. The day-to-day things. That would leave me to focus on the survival side. The hunting, the greenhouses, the shelter."

"Well, it sounds like a decent plan to me," Valora said. "But it isn't just our decision. We need to let the rest of the camp decide as well. The adults, at least, if not the older campers as well."

"There you go, calling me on my shit already," Conifer said. "We'll hold a meeting tomorrow. Once everyone has had a chance to recover a little."

They both agreed.

"Now, how are the campers doing?" Conifer asked.

"Some good, some bad," Marauder said. "A lot of them didn't really know her, honestly. They saw her around, listened to her during the camp meetings, but most never interacted with her directly."

"They're scared because she died, but they didn't know her well enough to mourn, I think," Valora said. "It's like losing an aunt that they only saw on the holidays."

"And the other counselors?" Conifer asked.

"About the same," Marauder said. "To a lot of them she was just their boss, but the ones who have been working here for multiple summers, they're taking it harder."

Conifer nodded, leaning forward to press the heels of her hands into her eyes. There were more things they needed to figure out, more things they needed to say. Except she just couldn't keep pretending to care about any of that right now.

"Let everyone know I'll be calling a meeting of the counselors in the morning," Conifer said eventually. "The older campers can watch the younger ones while we meet in the activity room. I just...I need some time alone right now."

"Okay," Marauder said, voice soft. She and Valora both stood up and left.

Once Conifer heard the door close behind Marauder and Valora, she stood up and grabbed her heavy jacket off the coat tree in the corner. No one stopped her as she went down the stairs and across the yard, slogging down the uncleared path to the art shed. Inside was cold, but the light was at the right angle to illuminate the inside enough for her purposes.

Leaving the door open she began to dig through the myriad of cabinets and drawers. Much of it had been picked clean for various projects, but a little rooting around gave her the things she wanted. First was a clean, smooth piece of wood about one foot long, half a foot tall, and nearly an inch thick. It had decoratively beveled edges, a craft-store price tag still on the back. Another drawer produced a few carving tools and a jug of wood stain and another of lacquer. Conifer wasn't sure if the wood stain and lacquerer were still good—she knew the stuff wasn't meant to freeze—but if they had gone bad she'd find some other option.

Laying it all out on a workbench in front of the one window, Conifer grabbed a pencil and started to sketch out letters, using a ruler to make sure they were precise. With the letters laid out she grabbed a V shaped tool and set to work carving the letters out. Little by little wood shavings piled up around her as the letters sunk into the wood. It was a bit sloppy—she didn't have a ton of experience in wood carving—but she liked that. It made it feel more personal.

The light stayed with her long enough to finish the last of the letters, and she brushed away the remaining wood shavings and taking a moment to look at what she'd carved.

"What are you doing?" Cheyenne asked, watching her climb the steps.

"Memorial," Conifer replied, lifting the board a bit in her direction.

She nodded and got up to open the door to the stairs for Conifer. She followed her inside and Conifer turned back to raise an eyebrow at her.

"Can we talk?" She asked.

"Sure, come on," Conifer told her, leading the way to Jack's office. Her office. "I've got something to show you anyway."

Once inside Conifer deposited her project on the desk and shrugged off her jacket. She was already sitting behind the desk before she realized she hadn't hesitated this time.

"Here," Conifer said, handing Cheyenne a copy of the photo of her and her mother she'd made earlier, when she was straightening up. She'd cropped out herself and Marauder, zooming in on Cheyenne and her mom as much as possible without losing too much quality. "Jack took this on drop off day. I found it...after."

Cheyenne's eyes lit up and she cradled the piece of paper. For a moment Conifer thought she was going to cry, but in the end she just smiled, though a few tears hung in the corner of her eyes.

"Thanks," she said.

Conifer nodded. "What did you want to talk about?"

She shrugged, still looking down at the photo. "Nothing, I guess. I just wanted to talk."

"Well, pick a topic then," Conifer said, shaking the jar of wood stain. It sounded like it was, at least, not frozen.

"Do you think we're going to be here forever?" Cheyenne asked, her voice rushed.

"Sounds like you had a topic in mind after all," Conifer replied.

She gave a guilty little smile, raising her eyes to meet Conifer.

Conifer sighed, setting the wood stain back down. "Honestly? I think there's a chance of that, yeah. At least for some of us."

"So...we're all going to die here?"

Conifer looked at her, neither of their gazes wavering. There was a resilience in Cheyenne's eyes that had only been a flicker when she'd arrived at camp. It should've been years before it grew into the flame Conifer saw there now.

"Those of us who choose to stay...yes. But I think it's likely that, as time goes on, as people grow up, people will leave. I'm sure some parents will find their way here eventually as well, once winter passes, and take their kids away with them."

"I won't leave," Cheyenne said.

"Neither will I," Conifer replied.

Cheyenne nodded slowly. "Well...I want what Jackalope got. When I die. I want to be out in the woods like her."

Conifer flinched internally at how matter of fact she sounded. This poor girl had been staring death in the face her whole life. She'd said as much months ago, when she stood up in the dining room and talked about buckets of rocks in her classrooms at school. She'd already known she might die young long before any bombs had dropped. Those bombs had shattered her, but only because the cracks were already there. Now she sat in front of Conifer, cobbled back together but likely with some pieces still missing. The youth shaped pieces, at least, were unlikely to ever be found.

"Well, as far as I'm concerned you won't be dying for a damn long time, so don't start thinking you need to worry about that right now," Conifer told her.

Once Cheyenne left Conifer laid out her jacket on the desktop and put the memorial board on top of it. She didn't much care about getting the jacket dirty. It was already stained with blood from butchering, paint from the cabin, and plenty of dirt. Dipping a cloth into the wood stain, she swatched it along the back of the board to check that it was good. The lovely, dark walnut color spread out evenly so Conifer flipped the board back over and began working it along the grain, being careful to leave the letters a natural wood color. A few mistakes had to be sanded away, but soon it was done, the letters standing out nicely against the dark background. The lacquer came next, smoothed over the wood with a fine bristled brush.

Once the sign was dry, Conifer flipped it over and attached a wire to the back, then went and pounded a nail into the wall just outside the office door. She hung the sign from it and stepped back, hands on her hips and heart aching. Marauder found her standing there and came to stand at Conifer's side, examining the sign with her.

"That looks lovely," she said eventually. She had two plates of food with her, Conifer realized. It occurred to her that she hadn't eaten since the day before.

"Thanks," Conifer told her, taking a plate of food when Marauder offered it.

They stepped back into the office and both eyed the couch for a moment before electing to sit on the floor.

"I think I need to take that couch out of here," Conifer said.

"I wouldn't blame you," Marauder agreed.

They ate in companionable silence, each trailing their eyes around the room. Conifer wondered what Marauder thought about it, about the clutter and the history there, but didn't ask. She didn't have the energy for whatever the answer was right now.

"I did a reading with my cards a little while ago," Marauder said after a bit. "I asked them about you. About our future. The camp's future, I mean. Not you and I's specific future."

"Thought you weren't asking them questions like that anymore," Conifer said.

"I felt like I needed to," she replied. "I needed guidance after today."

"What did they tell you?"

She smiled wistfully. "To be patient, to take it slowly."

Conifer found herself smiling too. "One tomorrow at a time."

For now, they could do that.

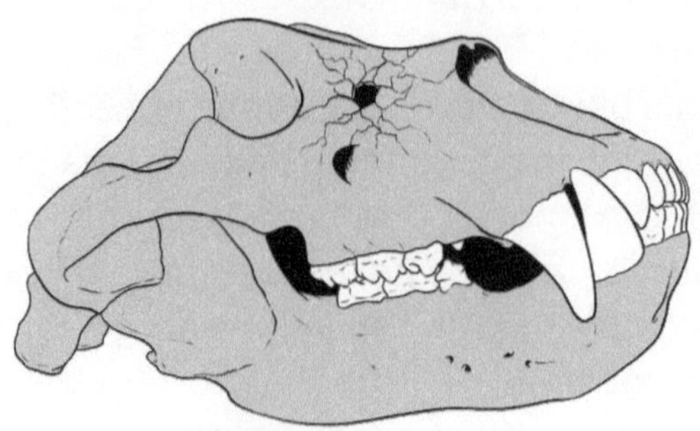

EPILOGUE
HELLO

ONE MONTH LATER

"What are you doing?" Cheyenne asked, about sending Conifer through the roof of their cabin, along with the kettle of coffee she'd been warming on the stove. She hadn't heard Cheyenne get out of bed.

Over the long, boring first half of winter her braiding skills had grown by leaps and bounds. Conifer had started jokingly calling her a little Viking. Her current style had one braid curving down the right side of her skull, following the line of her ear, and a handful of little ones spread through the rest, all of it pulled back in a ponytail with multiple bands going down the length.

"I'm going up the cliffs. Food is running low, and I need to hunt," Conifer told her. Her estimations on how much they could stretch the food they'd gathered just weren't holding up. Not all the households had been as stocked as they'd hoped. They'd need to find a way to address it, aside from just getting more meat, but more meat was the first priority as they had a limited window to get up the cliffs after a few weeks with no serious snow accumulation. "We just aren't getting enough down here. The elk have gone down lower, but I don't want to risk running into people. There won't be elk up top, but there will still be deer and other animals."

Cheyenne eyed Conifer suspiciously, eyes narrowed and arms crossed. "You said we can't get up the cliffs during the winter."

"Okay, let me rephrase: I'm taking Whiskey *around* the cliffs from the bottom because she's great in the snow, along with a few other horses for packing out. And then I am going to hunt. It'll take at least a week, but we're running out of options."

"I'm coming," Cheyenne said.

Conifer raised an eyebrow. "Want to try that again as a question?"

She pursed out her lips and shook her head. "Nope, because I'm coming. You've been teaching me to hunt for months, and you know how good of a shot I am. I can track now too, and use your calls. A single hunter can't get enough to feed this whole camp."

Conifer appraised her for a moment. Cheyenne had gone on a few hunts with Conifer so far, even killing two deer. Conifer herself had only been a touch older than Cheyenne was now when she'd first gone out alone on a big game hunt, though "alone" had just meant being stationed in a treestand while her dad and an uncle went out to scout the area. She supposed she could do the same with Cheyenne, setting her up in a blind.

"Okay," Conifer agreed eventually. "But if we're doing this, we may as well go all the way. Wake everyone else up, see who else wants to come. Those who don't hunt can stay with Polar Bear and help butcher."

Cheyenne's eyes lit up and she vanished behind the curtain. There was a lot of grumbling, but as soon as she told them we were going up the cliffs some of the grumbling turned to excitement and a mad scramble to get dressed. It was clear they found the idea of getting out of camp more exciting than the actual idea of going hunting, but Conifer didn't mind.

Conifer radioed down to Marauder and Valora, who she'd sent to the barn to get a few horses prepared, that they'd be needing more, likely all ten if possible. The kids would be walking, but if they had multiple hunters they'd need more horses to bring down any kills. Leaving took a lot longer than Conifer planned, with more food and packs to prepare. They ended up with seven people going; Conifer herself, Valora, Marauder, Cheyenne, Farrah, Aadila, and the older girl from Silver's unit who also knew how to hunt with a bow—her name was Shannon. None of the others wanted to brave the cold.

After camping out half way on the first night, they found Polar Bear waiting for them at the top of the cliffs. Conifer was relieved to see that she looked healthy. Communication had been spotty with her at times, but her warnings in advance of the worst storms saved them so many times she'd lost track.

"Look at this, all the social interaction I've missed in one go!" She laughed as everyone made their way to her.

"Wouldn't want you to think we forgot about you!" Marauder said, bounding forward for a hug, snow crunching under her boots.

They stopped to gather around Polar Bear and everyone turned to look at the view, awe in their expressions. Conifer knew Cheyenne had been up there once before, on a backpacking trip, but even she looked amazed. She'd only seen it in summer, as had Conifer, and it was quite a different thing in winter. The whole world was frosted in shades of white, tapering into grayed out greens and browns where the snow had melted away at lower elevations. There was no scent to the air aside from the crisp, cold scent of the snow. Above them the sky was the same hazy gray it had been for weeks, but that did nothing to ruin the view.

"I think I forgot how big the world is," Farrah said breathlessly. The other campers nodded.

"Where...where do you think other people are?" Aadila asked.

"Everywhere," Conifer told them. "There's probably other little enclaves throughout the mountains, and not all big cities were bombed."

"Will we ever see other people again?" Shannon asked.

"Someday, eventually," Conifer replied.

Everyone lapsed back into silence, still looking out at the view. It was winding towards sunset, the icy world around them shifting from grays and whites to having just a tinge of pink from the sunlight that fought its way through. Eventually they set out again for Polar Bear's cabin a little way down the slope. Conifer stopped dead when she caught sight of it. Hanging above the door was a gleaming white grizzly skull.

"Is that Conifer's bear?" Cheyenne asked, dashing over to stare up at it with the other campers.

"Sure is," Polar Bear said. "Figured it should be preserved."

Conifer stared at it, tangling her fingers around the claw Valora had given her. She'd forgotten how big the thing had been. Even stripped of flesh and fur, the skull was massive.

During lulls in the winter Polar Bear had felled trees to create a shed and a permanent paddock, so the group turned the horses out into it. As darkness fell the campers set up their tents, insulating the ground beneath them with pine boughs. A small fire was lit and they all gathered around it, warming their hands while a dinner of stew cooked. The potatoes in it had been grown from The Magnificent Spud, which continued to be magnificent and showed no signs of stopping its continued reproduction. Some of the potatoes did come out a little deformed, but they tasted fine. There was a general consensus not to focus too much on the reasons behind the deformities, and what they might mean. There was nothing to be done for it, so they'd keep pressing forward as they had since the beginning, focusing on what we could control.

"I just don't know what went wrong with it," Polar Bear said. "The battery is still good, but your radio won't turn on anymore."

Conifer shrugged. "Something in it probably burned out, or another wire came loose. I got the thing at a garage sale."

"Well, can you fix it?" Valora asked from across the fire.

Conifer shrugged again. "I could try, but I barely got it fixed last time, and I'm still not actually sure how I did it."

"Well, can you try?" Farrah asked.

Conifer glanced around the group, looked at their hopeful faces, and started to suspect many of them may have had a motive beyond hunting or a little break from camp for coming on this trip.

"I really don't know much," Conifer said, feeling a pang of guilt in her stomach. She should've studied that thing more, not just treated it as a fun toy to pass time on the road. Maybe they could dig through the town library once spring came, or try and find an old manual of some sort that could help figure it out.

"Can I try?" Shannon asked. "I was in the electronics club at my high school."

"Have at it," Conifer told her, waving her spork in the direction of the cabin.

Polar Bear got up and led the way inside, everyone else trailing in as she lit an oil lamp on the table. Everyone crowded in as Shannon pulled the chair up to the radio, clipped it into the battery, and started fiddling with switches and dials. Nothing happened. Flicking out the Phillips-head from her swiss-army knife, Shannon lifted off the top panel only to be met with an astonishing amount of wires, way more than Conifer would ever know what to do with. Last time, she'd just poked at them a lot until suddenly the radio started working again. Valora was at Conifer's elbow and wordlessly handed over her headlamp to Shannon who slid it on and set to work, disconnecting the battery before gently running her fingers along wires to trace their origins.

Just as Conifer was starting to think they were out of luck Shannon let out a triumphant, "Ah ha!"

Leaning closer, Conifer saw that three loose wires were

resting on the end of her finger. They hadn't appeared loose at first, close enough to their initial connection point that Conifer didn't notice they weren't attached until Shannon nudged them.

"Can you fix it?" Valora asked.

"Well, there's a bit of corrosion built up," Shannon said, chewing on her lip. "If I can clean it off I can maybe make a temporary fix. But if we want a permanent fix, I'll need a soldering iron."

"Do we have anything that can remove corrosion?" Marauder asked, eyes dancing around Polar Bear's cluttered cabin.

Polar Bear gave a dramatic sigh and went over to her bed, pulling a box out from under it. She came up with a single can of Coke.

"Was gonna save this for my birthday, but at least it'll go to a good cause," Polar Bear muttered. She cracked it open and the tantalizingly familiar, yet long unheard sound of escaping carbonation sizzled out into the room. She handed the can over to Shannon who took it and, dousing a scrap of cloth, began scrubbing at the damaged connection point. Polar Bear took the can back, took a swig, then passed it to Cheyenne. Cheyenne eyed her for a moment, then, upon an encouraging nod from Polar Bear, took a swig of her own before passing it on to Farrah. Conifer took it next and, even though it was lukewarm, the familiar bite of flavor sent a nostalgic pang through her. It was likely the last sip of Coke she'd ever have. The last sip of soda in general. Once the can made it around the room Polar Bear set the empty bit of aluminum on her mantle which also contained a flattened Kit-Kat wrapper, a picture of her partner, and a bunch of postcards.

Shannon leaned back and, without putting the top panel back on, reconnected the battery. She glanced up at Conifer, gesturing to the switch. Conifer took her place in front of the radio and, as her finger hovered over the same switch, she heard everyone in the room collectively hold their breath. Taking a deep breath of her own, she flipped it. Instantly the screen flickered to life and static crackled out of the speakers. The room broke into elated whoops but Valora shushed them as Conifer started scanning the frequencies. The emergency signal to shelter in place was no longer there, replaced with empty static. As Conifer worked through staticky frequency after staticky frequency the room became more and more subdued. When she reached the last one and still heard nothing she turned around to look at everyone. Several of them were crying.

"Could it be the radio? Maybe you didn't fix it right?" Valora asked, looking at Shannon. Valora looked as crestfallen as many of the kids.

"Maybe," Shannon offered. "I'm sorry."

"Don't apologize," Conifer said. "You did great, way more than any of the rest of us could have. We'll find a way to really fix it in spring, somehow."

"Spring is so far away, though," Cheyenne whispered. She wasn't crying, just eying the radio forlornly. Conifer saw the exact moment something flipped in her head and, after it did, she reached out a hand for the mic. "What frequency did you broadcast Buckskin radio on?"

Conifer hesitated a moment before handing the mic over, then turned back and adjusted the dial to the right spot.

Cheyenne took a deep breath, then pushed down the button on the mic. "Hello hello, can anyone hear me? This is someone reaching out."

Seconds ticked by, and she tried again, repeating the same words.

As soon as the words faded away a new voice sounded through the cabin.

"Hello?"

KICKSTARTER BACKERS

Thank you to everyone who backed
this book on Kickstarter to help bring it to life!

Lilith Blackthron
Kyle Yang
Anonymous
R.M. Finegold
Caitlyn Baker
Ash M.
Olivia Smith
Kassandra Topper
Katie Ashe
Mystery Weber
Kristen Altmann
Sage
Carrie Anderson
Jamil Candia
Elly S.
Lila Ellis
Genevieve Griffin
Jenn Christopher

And thank you to everyone else who backed as well!

Author's Note

This book had a very long, wandering path to publication. I started it in 2018, ran the whole thing through my critique group bit by bit, and decided this was one I wanted to pursue traditional publishing for. Problem was, it reached a query ready state in mid-2020. AKA The Dark Times. But I figured I'd query anyway, just a bit slower than I had with previous projects. Not like I had anything else to do at the time. To make a long story short, it got me my first agent! She sent it around to a lot of publishers, but we consistently got the feedback of, "This is great, but I just can't deal with a book about isolation right now."

Which is. Ya know. Fair.

So we decided to shelve it and move on to other projects. A lot has changed in the three years since then. I've gone back to college. I have a different agent now and I'm pursuing traditional publishing with other projects, but I've also self-published two other novels and an artbook. Plus the critique group that helped bring *Camp Daze* to life in its first version self-destructed due to disagreements started by the sequel. Whoops.

But despite all the changes, I really wanted to bring this book to life. It means a lot to me for a variety of reasons, not the least of which being how heavily Aspen Heart is based around my own childhood summer camp, Flying "G" Ranch. I lost that camp when I was 12 and the camp was sold, but I'll never forget my summers there and how much they shaped me.

I did a pretty extensive rewrite on *Camp Daze* before finally publishing this version, shifting it from first person to third and aging up the book to more of a New Adult than a Young Adult. I also took out a romance I just didn't feel like I enjoyed as much as when I'd originally written it, among other changes. Overall, I'm much happier with what the book is now, and what I've got planned for the rest of the series.

I also want to take a moment here to talk about Conifer's autism. When I first wrote the book, I was aware that I probably had ADHD, but I'd never gotten an official diagnosis nor explored anything beyond that. In the three years since, I've started to try and understand myself better and, as part of that, have come to also suspect I may have autism. When I went back to edit the book into the version you just read, I found many of the traits that had led me to consider myself probably autistic reflected in Conifer. I made the conscious decision to bring those traits to the forefront because I've never seen a character quite like myself in a novel, so I wanted to lean into it. This includes Conifer and I's asexuality, something I know many people may consider "problematic" to combine with autism, but it really is just a reflection of myself. Yes, making autistic characters nonsexual can be problematic, but sometimes that's just how it is. It's how I am.

Thank you, Reader, for picking up this little book of mine. It took a lot to get it into your hands, and I hope you enjoyed it.